"When I read Elías Miguel Muñoz, I always feel like I'm encountering a slice of my own life I haven't discovered yet. This sensation was even stronger reading *Diary of Fire*, a roman à clef that explores exile and alienation through the lens of gender, sexual orientation and ethnicity. Surprisingly, *Diary of Fire* also dares take on the possibility of—gulp—contentment, of coming to peace with our contradictions. So there's hope! *Diary of Fire* is delivered with Muñoz's usual brilliance, humor and passion, which means it's, as expected, utterly delightful."

—ACHY OBEJAS,
author of the novels *Memory Mambo*, *Days of Awe*, and *Ruins*

"This captivating novel is a tribute to the voice: the voice of memory and history, the voices of memorable songs, the voices of friends, lovers, family, mentors, other writers, critics and philosophers, all woven together like an elegiac and often hilarious symphony. The narrator states at one point, paraphrasing Mikhail Bakhtin that 'Truth, to be uttered, needs a multitude of voices.' It is this multitude of voices—from the novels of Manuel Puig to Roland Barthes to musical numbers in *Mame* and of the many characters—that yields an intimate epic of 'small yet significant lives, not great deeds.' These unheroic yet meaningful lives are poignantly rendered by Muñoz in a clean, poetic prose, laced with longing, desire, and good old Cuban *choteo*."

—ALAN WEST-DURÁN,
author of *Tropics of History*, *Finding Voices in the Rain*, and
Cuba: A Reference Guide

see overleaf...

"Quintessentially Caribbean in its rejection of a binary approach to identity formation, *Diary of Fire* proposes a kind of poetics of indeterminacy, an alchemistic vision in which the contrapuntal and paradoxical reside alongside the monophonic and homogeneous. The novel takes account of the complex, fluid aspects of human apprehension and the intersectional nature of experience in its exploration of the myriad ways in which one reconstitutes, translates and transforms the self in the context of movement and cultural dislocation. Striving to *erase himself from all maps* and *break those mirrors that reflect backwards*, Muñoz's protagonist embraces the ephemeral, and inhabits an interstitial Puigian space where past, present and future coalesce; gender, ethnicity, and sexuality are on a continuum; pleasure and desire are polyphonic; and art and lived reality interface."

—ANDREA O'REILLY HERRERA,
author of *Remembering Cuba: Legacy of a Diaspora, The Pearl of the Antilles*, and *Cuban Artists Across the Diaspora: Setting the Tent Against the House*

"*Diary of Fire* by Elías Miguel Muñoz is *the* compelling immigrant story that has not been told before. The novel opens with the protagonist Camilo attending grad school in Southern California where he cannot seem to meet anyone's expectations. Whether it is his bisexuality, his anti-Castro yet leftist political views, or being the only Cuban among other Latino immigrants, his mother and father, friends and academic colleagues are each pushing him to conform to their own image. When Camilo decides to reveal a secret that has haunted him since his childhood in Cuba, he enters a new path of his choosing through this strange American landscape. As Muñoz describes Camilo's journey, he treats the reader as an intimate, with knowing details and presence, as if he were describing your own friends or perhaps aspects of your own life. With the reestablishment of relations with Cuba, *Diary of Fire* is a must read to understand the complexities of Cuban life and culture."

—ALAN LESSIK,
author of *The Troubleseeker*

Diary of Fire

Diary of Fire

A Novel by

Elias Miguel Muñoz

Tincture
AN IMPRINT OF LETHE PRESS

Diary of Fire

Published in 2016 by Tincture, an imprint of Lethe Press, Inc.
118 Heritage Avenue • Maple Shade, NJ 08052-3018 USA
www.lethepressbooks.com • lethepress@aol.com
ISBN: 978-1-59021-580-7 / 1-59021-580-X

Some chapters in this book were previously published in slightly different form.
"The Unequivocal Moon" appeared in *Ambientes: New Queer Latino Writing*. Lázaro Lima and Felice Picano, eds. (Wisconsin: The University of Wisconsin Press, 2011.) And in *Best Gay Stories 2012*. Peter Dubé, ed. (New Jersey: Lethe Press, 2012.)
"Havana Ice Cream" appeared in *Caribe: Revista de Cultura y Literatura*, Vol. 13, No. 2 (Winter 2010-2011.)
"A Minor Movement" (excerpt) was published in the webzine *Cuba Counterpoints*. Ariana Hernández-Reguant, 30 Jun. 2015.

Set in Garvis, Sedona, and Missiva.
Interior design: Alex Jeffers.
Cover design: Inkspiral Design.

LIBRARY OF CONGRESS CATALOGING-IN-PUBLICATION DATA
Names: Muñoz, Elâias Miguel, author.
Title: Diary of fire : a novel / by Elías Miguel Muñoz.
Description: Maple Shade, NJ : Tincture, an imprint of Lethe Press, 2016. |
   Includes bibliographical references and index.
Identifiers: LCCN 2016018708 | ISBN 9781590215807 (pbk. : alk. paper)
Classification: LCC PS3563.U494 D53 2016 | DDC 813/.54--dc23
LC record available at https://lccn.loc.gov/2016018708

To Miguel Gallegos, dearest friend,
always remembered.

Contents

"I have it in me in being that I am resisting in being..."
Gertrude Stein, *The Making of Americans*

I

Away from Sanity

PARTY TIME

A hungry fire. I know I should start there, with the drama of an event that left me once again uprooted. But it's too soon. The embers still linger, glowing among the ruins as remnants of a world turned ghostly, a world whose material meaning went up in flames. Time needs to do its healing work; I count on its help to rebuild my life not out of fear and cruelty and ashes, but out of hope. And I must do my part, which for now means weaving a jumble of scattered writings into this story: a task that might reward me with the anchor of memory, sure as I am that somewhere in the past hides the key to this present. My fantasy of being a writer took shape in graduate school, where I met the people who would grow to be my closest friends. I read important books there, became a teacher and a critic. But I also spent too much energy trying to pass for a scholar. All in vain. I sought refuge in a fiction project—the tale of a boy in revolutionary Cuba—to escape the prison house of academia; worked on it by fits and starts, ridden with guilt, stealing scraps of time from my reading list. Oh, the mortal sin of wanting to be creative instead of analytical, of not taking my scholarly mission seriously! Off with his head!

Friday afternoons were reserved for "the project." I'd write in long-hand, on the floor in my apartment, tripping, flying away from the ivory tower to depict a childhood of terror and wonder in my native country; a realm where the sky unleashed storms of blinding rain, where vicious sirens would deceive the angels by appearing to them as birds; where a dead poet regained life through his words, and human blood could turn a pine branch into a beast. Where an island became a cayman...

No academic duties could keep me from telling that story, just as no intellectual pursuits would get in the way of partying hard. What else could we do in Alton but cut loose once in a while? We needed our festive acts of rebellion in that Orange County city that allowed nothing to grow outside its "ideal" strategic plan and had no downtown, hence no heart. In lieu of a lively center, you got car-infested boulevards and avenues without pedestrians, a couple of chain supermarkets, and several residential areas—some gated—where you never saw neighbors chatting or children playing. We also had Valley Park in South Alton, a perfectly mown and foliaged expanse with ubiquitous palm trees that had appeared overnight and a pond populated by rare aquatic turtles. And there was the Muir Corporation looming over the entire community, a central metal tower—informally known as the Bullet—that shone like silver, surrounded by three domes of dark green glass and fifteen acres of lawn.

How could a university sprout from such infertile soil? Alton University, reportedly designed for both practicality and image, had been built at the extreme opposite end of the Muir behemoth, in north Alton. You could glimpse the campus from the 405 Freeway as you approached the Campus Drive off-ramp, quite a sight from afar, a mirage devoid of human spirit. Its buildings were desolate giants, cement beehives. They seemed to emerge from a hardened, unwelcoming future.

That future had to be erased, if only temporarily, with booze, weed, and music in the dark and warm and very human niche of our parties. The climax of these gatherings usually came at the stroke of midnight, when Tano would streak through my place flaunting his bubble butt and wearing only a red sock on his left foot. He'd dangle his privates in people's faces, moving to the beat of some disco hymn, then hide behind the room divider and toss the sock at his audience as he laughed hysterically. This was his way of yanking us out of our reefer-induced comfort zones and making his statement about the "innocence of nudity." Tano was always trying to make some kind of declaration about sex, which was partly the reason I was drawn to him. Sex could've become both a burden and the absence of meaning for me, given my experiences as a child. But instead it unfolded as a quest, a means to find the truth of my nature. And Tano seemed bent on helping me find that truth. There was no time to waste! My diary from grad school is filled with entries about this feisty yet lovable queen from Argentina, self-described as a handsome Caucasian male of slight build, with strawberry-blond hair, a fine Italian nose, naturally curled eyelashes, dimples, and a mouth to fucking die for. Whenever we had a shindig, he'd show up early in his pink Volvo, bringing a baggie full of joints and a bottle of wine or a six-pack. He'd help me move things out of the way, fill bowls with chips and salsa, and select the song for his act. After his stellar performance he'd get an ovation, then we'd all move on to the jacuzzi. On nights when the neighbors bitched or the cops showed up, we'd head to the Big Bang Room in Laguna Beach—a fairly short drive down the Pacific Coast Highway. The music was great at the Big Bang, though not as varied as *chez* Camilo. At my parties you got the whole shebang: Donna Summer, Stevie Wonder, Van McCoy, Bette Midler, Michael Jackson; and mellower stuff as night moved into day, Cat Stevens, Janis Ian, Alberto Cortez, Charles Aznavour, Antonio Jobim. Songs that were a bridge to morning.

Amazing that I could pack so many people—ten to fifteen on average, including a few friends and classmates and a handful of my students—into the tiny pad I rented, one of forty identical units in the sunny Parkside complex on Michelson Avenue. Parkside was relatively close to the Alton University campus but not within walking distance, so I drove every day—just when my old Datsun was ready to kick back! I was thrilled to be able to afford my six-hundred-square-feet nook on a Teaching Assistant budget. A movable divider separated "living room" from "bedroom," if I chose to pull out the "wall." On the window side I'd placed my secondhand rolltop desk, a reading lamp, and my twin bed; on the other, two beanbag chairs, a battered table, a nineteen-inch TV set; and the sound system, the most valuable thing I owned, other than my LP collection—a Technics component set (amplifier, turntable, diamond needle, eight-inch speakers) that was off-limits to everyone with no exceptions.

The only neighbor I socialized with was Carl, an engineer who lived upstairs. Carl danced like a stick and put up with the academic bullshit at my parties. He was after my good friend Alina—an unlikely pair, the Puerto Rican princess and her white knight. Carl worked for the Muir Corporation, the eyesore that took up the entire corner of Alton Boulevard and Mason Avenue. Nobody knew what that company actually did, and Carl was very secretive about it. Alina didn't trust him, but I liked him. There was a centeredness to him I envied. While straight in every way, my neighbor didn't mind our gender-bending trips and the pot we consumed. I thought he actually dug our outré atmosphere, so unlike his barbecue get-togethers with people from work, whom he described as "stale white bread."

It was Carl who turned me on to running. He showed me the ropes and stuck with me for a while, but then he started to lose patience (I was too slow) and eventually stopped doing his daily four-mile run with me. I was glad he did: less pressure, better therapy. When I ran I'd rage against the world or dream up projects, research papers, poems, stories—stuff that kept my mind reeling, distracting me from the pain. I liked everything about jogging, the freedom, the goal of higher speeds, the high. Alton was ideal for this activity, as long as you could avoid getting stopped by the cops for vagrancy. I'd try to run in parks and empty lots, careful not to end up in someone's garden or desecrating the lawn of the Muir Corporation. Rumor had it that there was a force field around its tower (Carl confirmed it), and that the company's guards would shoot you just for looking at the ghastly structure. The latter was highly exaggerated, said Carl, though he advised me not to get too close just in case.

The Spanish and Portuguese Department at Alton University wasn't creepy like the Muir Corporation, but some days it seemed just as unwelcoming. It looked and felt like the reception room of a doctor's office, down to the detail of magazines—actually, literary journals—neatly set by the comfy couch. The department was housed in the second floor of the Humanities building, an edifice that could easily pass for a high-end clinic somewhere in the heart of Fashion Island: lots of picture windows and round, open spaces like portholes where you could peer out and stare off into the distance, taking in the vast yellowish-green fields surrounding the campus. The look of the office itself was minimalist, with off-white walls, a large coffee table set on an oblong-shaped gray rug, a black leather couch, some scattered chairs, and two poster-size photos on the back wall: Miguel de Cervantes and Gabriel García Márquez, stars of our academic firmament. This scant decor was the handiwork of Doña Magda, the department's secretary and gatekeeper, a fifty-something Mexican woman who'd been there from the start, having helped Dr. Mirabal kick-start the department in the late Sixties. Doña Magda was sweet to us graduate students, always ready with a smile, a hug, a kiss. But she was also a gossip, an overdressed and over-perfumed spinster whose life revolved around her nine-to-five, and who infamously spread rumors about everyone in her field of vision, including the faculty. You'd think that someone like her would've made the place look more festive in an Olvera Street sort of way. But we suspected she wanted to humor Mirabal, a man whose idea of dressing up was putting on a clip-on butterfly bow tie.

I liked Doña Magda, but I was also guarded around her, loath to provide any fuel for her blabbermouth fire. She had her favorites, both among the faculty and the student body. You could tell by the way she treated you, the length of a hug, the resonance or coldness in her voice. She claimed I was one of her faves, which surprised me, since I knew what she thought of my "decadent fiestas."

This omnipresent woman had the master key to all our offices, most of these adjacent to the department and surrounding the indoor patio—the spacious ones for our professors and the small, windowless boxes for us TAs, each box assigned to three to four students. I shared my workplace with Alina Sotovélez, a beautiful thirty-something student from Puerto Rico, and Isabel Rosas-Clark, a strait-laced Colombian woman. I didn't like either one at first. Alina seemed affected, too much the embodiment of what my father called an *hembra guitarra*: big breasts, small waist, shapely ass, pretty face, long hair. I didn't see how the mind of a scholar could thrive within such hyper-femininity. It took some time for me to see Alina as the funny, smart, well-read, creative intellectual that she was and not a stereotype. We were fated to be very close friends, always eager to share our dirty little secrets with each other and laugh at silly things. I'd hear about Alina's fiasco of a marriage to an alcoholic, her struggles as a single mother in Brooklyn after the divorce; and her affair with a prof of Economics at Alton City College, an Anglo man who didn't get her sense of humor but who was hot-hot-hot in bed.

Isabel was uptight and conservative, hence her reaction whenever I invited her to my parties. "I wouldn't fit in," she'd say. Alina heard the truth from her, that she disapproved of what went on at my place, the libertine goings-on, the depraved tone of it all. Alina would tell her that the only substances we consumed were beer and weed (purposely choosing not to mention the poppers Tano brought on occasion to make our hearts race.) No, there were no orgies and no nudity at my fiestas. (Alina would also opt not to disclose Tano's tradition of streaking because you couldn't call that adorable routine decadent, could you?) But there was dancing, chatting, sometimes a dip in the jacuzzi. Yet no amount of explaining could change Isabel's mind because her main issue with my parties—with *me*—was a deep-seated dislike and rejection of people who weren't just like her.

Lucky me, ending up in an office with those women, even with goody-two-shoes Isabel. Several of the other female students in the department would've been fine too; definitely Elena Medina, a Chicana much admired by Alina for taking our macho profs to task. It might've been interesting to share an office with the only other Cuban in our program, a woman who commuted from Tustin. But she wasn't a TA and never stuck around; would split as soon as her classes were over. I knew I would've hated being cooped up with any of the "boys." To name just a few, there was the Chilean clique, made up of three self-proclaimed intellectuals from Valparaíso who talked about nothing but overthrowing capitalism everywhere in the world and replacing it with a socialist utopia that sounded like Cuba's regime to me, not like Salvador Allende's democratic brand of socialism. We had a handsome womanizer from Colombia and an older family man from Paraguay who played the guitar at department parties. There were five students from Mexico, one mustachioed à la Emiliano Zapata who boasted (with no proof) that he could recite Juan Rulfo's *Pedro Páramo* by heart. Plus half a dozen Gringos who always seemed way over their heads. And last but certainly not least, Pablo "Tano" Ricci, a sassy Argentine working on his MA and the only one of the male students I befriended.

Ay, Pablo. I got a kick out of him but he could also piss me off bigtime. He liked to go by "Tano" (from *italiano*) to honor his ancestors, and he was fond of calling me *perroquet* and *mignon*, French endearments I didn't care for. Tano was frequently seen in jeans patched at the knees, a straw hat adorned with paper flowers, and with a macramé bag hanging from his shoulder. We became friends when he audited an undergraduate class I was student-teaching, a course on the Latin American novel that included all the sacred bulls (Rulfo, García Márquez, Cortázar, Fuentes, Vargas Llosa) and Argentine novelist Manuel Puig, not yet a bona fide member of the canon but more exciting than all those other dudes, I thought. Puig's enticing premise in his *Kiss of the Spider Woman*—his fourth novel and the one I snuck in—was deceivingly easy to summarize: A flaming queen, charged with corruption of a minor, is thrown into a prison cell with a Marxist political activist, then an amazing thing happens.

During a discussion of this book in class, Tano left my students in a daze after embarking on a heated defense of the novel's sexual utopia. "What Manuel Puig presents in this masterpiece," he pontificated, echoing my own thoughts and trying to cite Herbert Marcuse, "is an alternate world by way of Valentín, a straight man who has freed his inner woman. In this ideal and *brave* new world that the text proposes, there would be no traditional gender roles nor simplistic binaries like gay and straight. Sexuality would be *totally* total. It would be... polymorphous!" He paused for effect. "And now you must be thinking, Yeah, that's a nice fantasy. Too bad it would never come to be. But you see, *depicting* this utopia *is* the first step toward making it happen. So in a way it already exists!"

Later that day, over coffee, I thanked Tano for sharing his inspired thoughts on Puig's novel. And, winning me over, he said that he couldn't have come up with any of those ideas by himself, without sitting in on my class. I learned from him that he was the son of a *porteño* family, enlightened Buenos Aires folks who joyously accepted his gayness. He'd lived a life so full that he made me feel deprived, stagnant, as though I hadn't had the *cojones* to thrive on the edge, in that interstice between sanity and madness that Tano seemed to know first-hand. He'd worn so many hats! Had been a hippie in a socialist commune, a Gucci employee, a flight attendant for Aerolíneas Argentinas, a painter of surrealist canvases; and, in his most recent incarnation, a student of Latin American literature. Add his numerous lovers, his impersonation of Carlos Gardel in sleazy New York clubs, the times he nearly lost his life while driving a Vespa in Paris or procuring hard drugs, and Tano's portrait would seem to be almost complete. Yet there was much more to him...

Soon he was trying to turn me on to opera and serenading me with tangos and arias. The tangos I could get into; I actually loved many of them, "Uno," "A media luz," "Volver," "Madreselva." But I despised the operatic stuff. "Art doesn't move you!" Tano would gripe as my stereo played his scratchy LP of *La Traviata*, blasting the only piece I liked, "Libbiamo."

"But this isn't art," I'd react. "It's artifice." Not only did I refuse to let myself be moved by Verdi's musical beauty, I also took pleasure in mocking it. "Can you believe that bitch? Violetta is on her deathbed, barely breathing, and she's screeching at the top of her lungs!"

"Don't be so literal, mignon. Listen with your heart, not your fucking brain."

"Somebody please put her out of her misery!"

Pablo had Italian blood, but he professed to have a soul that was Argentine through and through. And he did fully embody his River Plate identity when it came to wandering, roaming, psychoanalyzing himself, looking in the mirror and asking his reflection, "*¿Y vos? ¿Quién sos vos? ¡Decime, loca!* Who the hell are you and where the fuck do you think you're headed?!"

He had snatched an apartment on campus that was furnished and came with a quiet pre-med roommate from China. A great deal. Affordable housing was a privilege reserved for AU grad students, and one I didn't take advantage of—just didn't want my place to be so close to all those classrooms. Tano liked living there but hated the "ominous cloud" that enveloped the campus complex. "Too much mental crap," he complained, "and not enough sex." Refusing to hang out with his neighbors, he'd show up at my apartment two or three times a week, announcing, "Violetta Valèry is here! Come to me, my fellow courtesans, and enjoy the Good Airs elixir I bring you!"

His pet peeve was the barrenness of Orange County. "Ay, perroquet," he'd cry out, "what a reality meltdown I'm having in this fucking wasteland!" And then he'd usually enact his favorite and "most divine" line from *La Traviata*, where Paris was described as a populated desert... "*Questa solitudine! Sóla, abbandonata, in questo popoloso desérto qu'appelanno Parigi!*"

"*Qu'appelanno Alton,*" I'd clarify. "That's what our populated desert is called, Alton!"

"Oh, yes, but what I'd give to be in Paris right now, with the muses of L'Opéra. I wouldn't bitch about feeling lonely and abandoned there, like Violetta, that's for sure!"

The sea soothed his nostalgia, so he turned Laguna Beach into his Locus Amoenus. "I always take my books there in case I feel like reading," he'd explain. "Which I normally do, though not for long 'cause *sempre posso girare*, play a little with the surfer boys. And I mean 'boys' in the most adult sense of the word, *comprendés*? 'Cause I'm not into chicken."

"I did psychoanalysis for fifteen years," he confessed to me once. "Ay, mignon, even the way I pooped was analyzed. I thought all that probing was going to help me. I had this idea that once you faced your most painful truths, traumas, and fears, you were left like a white wall, a blank screen; able to remake yourself, to create an ideal or at least better version of yourself. But not so, perroquet. Not at all. One day I realized I was stuck with my fucked-up self till the end, and no shrink could ever save me from being Pablo Ricci. And that's when I handed myself a clean bill of health. My analyst was all weirded out about it, 'You can't quit now! We still have work to do.' But I said *Ciao, amore, ciao...*"

It was thanks to Tano that I discovered our very own academic Tea Room on campus, though I never partook of its offerings—not my cup of tea? One day I ran into Ricci on the Humanities patio. (Some of us would hang out there on occasion to socialize or work. The patio had tables, plants, sunlight; better to be there than locked up in a crowded office.) But this time my friend seemed unusually edgy. He said hello and dashed into the restroom, which was by the stairs on our floor. I thought he might be sick so I followed him. Once inside I heard a peculiar noise, like a rubber band snapping repeatedly. "Tano?" I said, "Is anything wrong?" He peeked over the door of a stall. "What could possibly be wrong, perroquet? Go on, I'll be out in a minute. Wait for me at your desk... *Andá!*"

Tano showed up in my office twenty minutes later and shut the door. "Good! We're alone," he observed. "Let me have a *pucho*, please." I lit a cig for him and one for myself.

"Was it good for you?" I asked, laughing, after taking a drag.

He sat on my desk, legs crossed, right hand on left knee; said, "It was marvelous, d*aaaa*rling."

"Okay, now tell me about our restroom," I said.

"*Ay*, that Tea Room gets more action than the Bang's back hole!"

"Says the voice of experience..."

"You bet! It's just what the doctor ordered, the meds for my daily meltdowns, when I lose track of my academic obligations. It happens once a day at least; depends on the mood. You know I'm an Argentine lady who still observes certain traditions. The five-o'clock tea, which was taken at the Molino Café in Buenos Aires with gobs of Marxist sugar, is served here sans political gabble, in huge quantities and intoxicatingly strong. Tell me, Camilo, *decime*, doesn't it seem historically transcendent that the most frequented restroom at AU happens to be in the Humanities building?"

"Transcendent indeed. Any of our profs visit the pub?"

"Are you joking? Of course not! But our dean enjoys a hot cup now and then."

"No, not the dean."

"Yes, I've seen him, I swear! Just yesterday he was in there *fifando* with some young stud. And it was no surprise to me; I knew it all along. Just look at her strut."

"You think he saw you?"

"Hope not! I've been careful, you know. But just in case, I'll stop going to my five-o'clock for a while. It's so unfair, but I have no choice. What if I bumped into that queen in there? She'd freak out, wouldn't she? Or what if I'm cornered, forced to fuck her? No way. She's revolting!"

Revolting, the word Tano used to describe not just the dean but all our professors: Dr. McDougal, whose lectures on Latin American theater consisted of excerpts he read from his favorite plays—not all of them from Latin America. And Dr. Beym, a specialist in peninsular fiction who bragged about his application of literary theory to the novels he taught yet seemed to be familiar with only one concept, "intertextuality." An interesting concept, yes, but not when you had to pull apart every damn book in search of hidden texts within a text. Yet Dr. Beym's intertextual approach wasn't as bad as that of Dr. Jiménez, a Golden Age poetry specialist who sat with a box of index cards on his lap, leafing through them as he tried to remember which course he was teaching at the moment.

The most revolting professor of all (Tano and I agreed) was without a doubt the old-timer from Chile, Dr. Oropeza, not just because of the dye job he did on his hair, so black it shone blue; or the fact that he was an uninspired teacher. But also because he was a dirty old man and a bigot and a homophobe. Standing in front of his students like an aging rooster, all façade in his polyester suit and his overdone tan, bored with his own lectures, Oropeza would insist on placing all writers and historical events in one of two groups, *Cosmopolitismo* and *Criollismo*. "Borges and Cortázar are cosmopolitan authors, big city creatures, inhabitants of an alienating metropolis," he'd declare, raising his index finger like Fidel Castro. "On the other hand, Palma and Rulfo are *crio-*

llistas, genuine fruits of the earth, spokesmen for the peasants and the underdogs!"

Naturally there was more to those people than the "revolting" parodies they embodied for us grads. We got glimpses of their real selves at Department parties and academic functions. Sometimes the profs would let their hair down in their offices, when we sought clarification or advice. There they might express their true feelings toward their colleagues (they all hated each other), or talk about their families and travels. But it was too much info. We needed them to play only one role for us; and part of that role was to serve as target for the students' mockery, the butt of jokes. All of those professors would go through our grinder, even Dr. Varela, known simply as *Sofía* to us.

Ah, yes, Sofía, the only prof I admired. She was the workhorse of the department; taught two courses per quarter, did her share of advising and committee work, directed several dissertations, and she was also in charge of training those of us with an Assistantship. Her approach to teaching Spanish was fun yet effective, as it didn't rely on grammar lectures but on "communicated messages." She incorporated some cutting-edge research (Krashen, Terrell, Levine) about the way children acquired language. The idea was to have students listen to your "discourse in the target tongue" as if they were pre-verbal; and then, when they began to speak, you wouldn't correct their errors, only their messages. Although I had issues with the prospect of making people regress to childhood (no way!), I was sold on this method. It worked for my students; I wished I'd learned French, Italian, and Portuguese that way.

Rumor had it that Sofía's colleagues abhorred her "mayhem-in-the-classroom." Not rigorous, not academic, not demanding enough! But they wouldn't dare criticize her because she got students to be proficient by the end of their first year, trained us TAs to be good teachers, and those profs were neither willing nor able to do the job of training us. They wouldn't have had a clue!

How can Sofía spread herself so thin and not go schizoid, I wondered. But Alina used to ask a rather different question about Dr. Varela: How can she wear those clothes and think she's getting away with it? That's where Alina's feline fangs were the sharpest, in her assessment of our professors' attire, especially that of the only woman in the department. Alina's style was all about simplicity and comfort, always showcasing her curves, of course: breezy blouses, blue jeans, T-shirts, sandals, and all-natural fabrics. No outlandish garments or strident colors for her. Quite the opposite of Dr. Varela's wardrobe! Sadly, Alina was right about our professor. Not all of her outfits became her, not the satin dresses, polyester bolero jackets, and stiletto heels she'd put on for work; outfits that, in their glamorous pomposity, seemed better suited for a banquet or a wedding. Sofía's gowns tended to be excessively tight on her short and stout physique. She was a handsome woman, if perhaps not pretty in a traditional sense, but she tried too hard (this was obvious) to project herself as a classy *white* lady. Problem was, the makeup she wore did little to disguise her brown complexion and features that bore the genetic markings of her Quechua ancestors. (Sofía hailed from Jujuy province, an arid region in Argentina's northwest that contained the highest percentage of indigenous people in the country.)

So dare I say, as Alina claimed, that in spite of Sofía's progressive, feminist ideals, she was still colonized by the mainstream image of European beauty and class? After all, it was the fine-featured Italians and the strapping Germans that gave Argentina its predominant face and body type. The face and body that Sofía wanted to have, or thought she had? Who knows and who cares, I thought. Aren't we all trying to pass for something—someone—we're not? Maybe Alina was the exception; she seemed centered, at ease in her skin. Which didn't mean she was exempt from feminine vanity. "I have my womanly hang-ups," she'd admit, laughing at the overblown reaction she had upon her first visit to the Big Bang Room. Eager for a night of dancing and carousing, she couldn't get one single man in that place to deign to look at her, let alone ask her to dance. How rude and demeaning was that?!

My friend didn't worship Sofía, didn't seek her advice and try to emulate her like I did. There was a certain edge of prejudice in our professor, she said, that made Alina distrust her; a poorly masked rejection of her attractive and smart female students. Was it jealousy? No, I thought, Sofía was above that brand of cattiness. She wouldn't have denigrated anyone, let alone the very people with whom she was supposed to be in solidarity. Sofía wouldn't have given women lower grades or a harder time in her courses, nor would she have felt threatened by someone like Alina. And yet she did, according to my friend. "Look closely next time she talks to me in class," suggested Alina. "Read her body language. You'll see what I mean." But of course I would avoid

reading that language. Couldn't afford to feel disappointed in Dr. Varela.
Who else could I look up to in that wretched department?

SOMETIMES A ROSE

You haven't thrown a party in weeks!" Tano wailed one Saturday evening, seconds after showing up at my place. He said I was becoming a bore, a typical grad student like the ones in his complex. He offered me a toke, which I refused. "I need a clear head," I said. "Lots of work to do." Tano seemed genuinely concerned. *"Ma questo è orribile!"* he bawled. *"Quel horreur!* You've been needing a clear head every day for the last month, perroquet! Our profs have managed to kill your festive Cuban soul. They've turned you into a scholar who never gets laid and never has any fun. How about throwing a *fête* next weekend? I promise you I'll add a new and exciting detail to my usual performance."

I was curious about this detail he promised to include (a wig? a sexy garter à la Moulin Rouge?) but not enough to humor him. Tano was right, and it bugged the hell out of me to have to admit this to myself: I had indeed turned into a bore. Yet I was doing precisely what I was supposed to do in Alton, which was to train as a scholar so I could prepare other eager youngsters for the worthy job of scholar.

When Tano rang my doorbell that day I was deep in the process of analyzing Julio Cortázar's *Hopscotch* and writing a paper on the *homo ludens* in the novel, highlighting the book's ludic or game-like elements. Nothing strikingly new but Sofía said I must acquaint myself with the basics as I prepared for my comprehensive exams, hence my focus on the hopscotch motif in a work that was structured around that game. (This canonical novel was a mind-blowing trip, but in order to write about it I'd had to overcome my dislike of its protagonist and his intellectual friends, their self-indulgence and obliviousness: sitting around

shooting the bull while a baby cried himself to death in another room!)
Tano happened to find me up-to-here in Cortázar's existential trips and
narrative pyrotechnics, so I unloaded all my bad blood on him. Misery
loves company. I made us a mixed salad for a change (had been eating
too much junk food lately) and put on some of the synthesizer-driven
rock and pop we were into at the time, Eurhythmics, Soft Cell, Thomas
Dolby, Kim Carnes. "Discipline yourself, che!" I told him then. "Keep a
diary, write a memoir. How about a novel? What's the sense in all that
crazy living you've done if you can't put it into words? Document your
damn life!"

"Why, mignon? Why should I?" he asked in a tone much too serious
for Tano. "I don't want to turn my life into a book, me entendés? All I
need is a backpack and my freedom to fly and feed off poetry and arias.
I'm into living and loving and fucking, not writing. I'm not like you."

"Hey, I'm into living too!" I snapped, tellingly defensive. "I have my
escapades..."

"Okay, let's hear about one of them. I want details!"

"How about the dude I see sometimes at Valley Park, when I'm jogging?"

"One of your many tricks?"

"Drop the sarcasm or I won't tell you a thing."

"Go on. I'm all ears."

"He hangs out at the park with his golden retriever. One day I stop
and pet the dog, and the hunk likes that. 'My dog's name is Tipper,' he
says, 'and I'm Josh.' We shake hands. 'I'm Camilo,' I say as I hunker
down by the beast, looking up at the dude's crotch. Josh digs this canine
bonding. He squats beside me, nudges me with his knee... Minutes later
we're in the bushes, and things get thick after that. We jog together,
walk Tipper, get stoned. We become buddies. No one's talking about
the future, yet we know our thing might turn into something deeper,
some kind of happily-ever-after..."

"You know there's no happily-ever-after," said Tano, laughing. "And
you made up that story!"

"I did not!"

I tried to offer him more details about Josh, but he knew the truth:
Yes, I'd had a couple of encounters at the park, and on occasion I'd gotten it on with people I met at the club. But there hadn't been any type of
no-strings-attached kind of thing developing from my flings. All I ever

got after the sex with men was a fleeting "Catch you later," sometimes not even that. The impersonal nature of these "meetings" depressed me, to the point that I'd decided to put an end to them. Tano saw right through my fantasy of finding a "buddy" among those tricks, not just someone who gave me a blowjob and whom I serviced in return. But he was wrong about there being no happily-ever-after. Had to be! Maybe he'd been in love with someone who broke his heart, which might explain why he didn't believe in lasting relationships—the kind I secretly longed for. Tano never spoke of his former lovers. He indulged in plenty of one-night stands and tricks whose names didn't ever come up in our conversations. He drank huge quantities of intoxicatingly strong tea in the Humanities bathroom, met frequently with his surfer boys. Yet there was no one special in his life, that I knew of, no one who meant more to him than sex.

He finally talked me into sharing a joint and leaving my cave that Saturday night. "Enough fantasizing," he declared. "Let's go try to get laid!" We were mildly stoned when we got to the Big Bang. As always, the place was packed with tanned hard bodies and blond mustaches, with manes that were perfectly bleached out by the Laguna Beach sun. We got drinks. I hadn't taken a sip of my Seven&Seven yet and Tano was gone already, off to land one of the sun-bathed clones.

I soon heard a voice behind me, through the pounding disco music, "Why so serious, love?" I turned around; the question had come from a man in drag as Marilyn—the silver-blonde wig was a tip-off. He was wearing a tight, low-cut black evening gown. There was a tasteful layer of makeup on his face, which assured the Monroe illusion, and a faint scent of cheap perfume. But underneath it all he was young and eager, the only one who'd defied the numbing sameness of that crowd. The transvestite looked me over and once again asked, "Why so serious?"

I replied on impulse, "Because it's what my dick wants."

He offered me a batting of eyelashes, "How about a dance?"

I wanted to rip every garment off of him and leave him exposed, then fuck his brains out in the club's "back hole." I felt both disturbed and consumed by desire, not for the doomed star of *Some Like It Hot* but for the male youth behind the icon, whom I pushed aside with the standard line, "I'm with someone. So beat it!" No sooner had he split, making a dash for the dance floor, than Tano reappeared.

"I was listening to your chat with La Monroe," he said. "You didn't have to be that mean just to get rid of her. You macho bastard!"

"Let's get out of here, Tano. I'm not in the mood for this scene tonight."

"Not yet." He began touching my face, studying it. "Lovely cheek bones," he observed.

"What are you doing?" I asked him, knowing full well what he was up to.

"The cheeks are a tad puffy but workable," he went on. "The goatee has to go. Let the world enjoy your gorgeous complexion without the blemish of facial hair. I love that black mane you're blessed with, perroquet, but don't comb it back like some pitiful Thirties gangster! Let the natural curls fall loosely over your forehead and ears. Your eyes are a plus, large and almond-shaped, with thick, curved lashes that would need only a touch of mascara. We must find the perfect eye shadow to accentuate their hazel color, maybe a very subtle hue of..."

"Are you done?" I cut in, even though I was enjoying this imagined makeover.

"*Mais non!* I haven't gotten to the body yet. Let's take a look. Oh, yes, I'm sure it could project a fabulous female illusion. We'll highlight the buttocks, round and firm and quite inviting already. And you'll know what to do about the crotch, won't you? Challenging, I'm sure; the size might prove to be an issue, from what I can tell. Those broad shoulders are a bit of a problem, but we can disguise them with a classy shawl over a tightly fitted dress. It's good you don't have a Cuban paunch, or not much of one. Pull up your T-shirt, will you?"

"Get your hands off of me!"

"You're svelte enough but even so you'll need a girdle. And stockings as well but definitely not stiletto heels; you're too tall for those, and we don't want you to seem intimidating. What about the hips? Walk a little for me, please."

"Hey, no pushing!"

"Nice, with a rather small waist..."

"Will you shut up already?"

"Sure. But keep in mind that, with just a little effort, you'd be a doll."

"Lucky me!"

"It's fun to put on a show, Camilo."

"Makeup and perfume and dresses aren't my thing, okay?"

"You're such a liar! What about that boy in grade school, huh? What was his name? The kid who liked to dress in his mother's clothes. You had the hots for him, didn't you?"

"I told you about Roli? That was a lifetime ago. People change."

"Roli turned you on because he was fem and he loved to crossdress. Admit it."

"What's your point, Tano?"

"My point? I've got several! Let's start with that drag queen you treated like shit. That charming young Marilyn has the guts to be who she wants to be."

"The simulacrum of a woman."

"And she doesn't hide her trip. She dares to embody her dream. You, on the other hand..."

"I'm a repressed faggot. Right. You've told me already."

"You're the simulacrum of a man, a disguise that cries out, *I am the Real Thing!*"

"I don't claim to be a *real* anything, Tano. Get off your high horse."

"Okay, so there are trips—or should I say 'perversions'?—that you think you can't relate to. But aren't you supposed to be an expert on Herbert Marcuse?"

"I'm no expert..."

"Remind yourself of what good old Herbert says about perversions. Or perhaps you can't theorize when the subject is your asshole."

"Yes, yes. Sex with no utilitarian function. Got it."

"You don't sound very convinced."

"Convinced enough to footnote it."

"That doesn't count, not unless you've had the experience of screwing with every pore of your body, not just with your cock. *Fifar por entero*, that's what I'm talking about, mignon. All-encompassing, annihilating sex."

"You mean *exhilarating*. Unless you're quoting Bataille."

"You know what I mean. Most men never suffer any pain during sex. They live and die without ever breaking or being invaded."

"Anal sex. I'd hardly call that *every pore*."

"Nothing else can happen without it. It's the first step..."

"Thanks but no thanks."

"Tell me something, perroquet. What turns you on when you fuck a woman?"

"It's simple, really. You kiss her, lick her neck, her tits. You get hard. You touch her pussy and it's a living thing, a wet, warm, hungry creature. She's flooding. And now you realize that if you don't stick your boner in there you'll go crazy."

"See? For you it's all about the 'boner.' But there's more, mignon!"

"If you say so."

"Put yourself in the woman's place. Become that wet, hungry creature. Be the flood."

"That's not my trip."

"Unleash the Marilyn in you! I'll show you how. I'll be your guide..."

"It wouldn't work, Tano."

"Why not?"

"Because Marilyn wouldn't want to get fucked by another woman. She wouldn't dig sex with La Traviata, but with a real man like Brando or DiMaggio."

"So that's it! I'm not real enough for you!"

"Wrong. You're not *man* enough for me."

"I can be all the man you need. And then some..."

"Get your hands off my ass, Tanita."

"You're turning me down?! *Moi*?!"

"Yes, I know. The opportunity of a lifetime."

"How dare you? May you live to regret it, Camilo Macías!"

"I'm sure I will."

"May you fall in love with a ruthless macho and suffer!"

"How scary."

"*Ay*, you're hopeless."

"If you say so."

Me, falling in love with a macho? Fat chance, I thought. It was more likely that I'd fall for a beautiful young woman, someone like Laurie Silverman, and in fact I was convinced that such was the case: I almost asked Laurie to marry me! She'd been my student in a second-year course; turned me on from day one but I managed to keep my libido in check till the day I turned in the grades, when I called her. Not long thereafter she was addressing me as "Babe" and sending me love letters in Spanish—elaborate stuff, considering her level. Laurie had a knack for languages (she was also proficient in French), and that excited me. She was nineteen and had wavy brown hair, sensuous lips, dimples, boundless energy. She happened to be Jewish and thus described our religions (since I was supposed to be Catholic): "You people have Jesus, we're still waiting for our Messiah." As simple as that. Most importantly for hedonist *moi*, Laurie liked to get it on. I dug her big ass; her breasts, which were supple and solid. We went at it anywhere, on the floor, in the shower. I rode her, sailed her. She wrapped around me and became my skin. I didn't fantasize a lot about females but when I was with Laurie—with a woman—I couldn't imagine anything better. I loved the way her thighs felt against my hips, how she opened up, held me in, while my tongue and hers would melt together. Yes, it was all about melting.

My Jewish girlfriend became a fringe member of our partying clique. She was oblivious to the group's highfaluting airs and didn't get the academic jokes, yet she kept returning. Alina liked Laurie and deigned to talk to her. But Tano, oh that bitch actually pretended that my girlfriend wasn't in the room. I wanted to punch him sometimes! Laurie had no idea that Ricci was being a prick, that he saw her as a trophy girlfriend I liked to show off. To her he was just a typically obnoxious literature student.

Laurie assumed I was sleeping with Tano and seemed to find that relationship completely normal. "Gay people are cool," she'd say, hoping for a reaction in me, some sort of confirmation of her assumption. But I never took the bait. I didn't want to broach the subject or talk about my bisexuality (for lack of a better word) with Laurie, since whatever I was had no bearing on our relationship. We both knew there was no future for us as a couple, anyway. I'd be leaving town eventually, and she had no plans to relocate yet. She lived in Costa Mesa with her folks and planned to finish her BA at Alton U, then go on to get an MBA. Laurie was happy to live in the moment, a festive present where she dwelled with aplomb. What my friends didn't see was how mature she was for her age. More so than me.

Maturity was a gift that Castel Romero brought to my life, a maturity of soul that I admired and which was compounded with a brilliant intellect. Castel wasn't learned in the dull academic way many of us grads were but was rather of a deep, creative sensibility. He felt a passion for literature that was rare among my classmates, even among most of my professors. I loved his name; it sounded to me like that of a movie star from the silent era. Castel did have a certain 1920s male softness to him, as seen in the Valentino films; could probably play the leading man if

he made "just a little effort," as Tano would've said. Castel was gay, but
that was all he and Tano had in common. He was tall, poised, charming; had a fair complexion and slightly indigenous features. Identifying
himself as Mexican American, he rejected the *Chicano* label. "Sounds
too much like chicanery," said Castel, so you wouldn't see him wearing
Viva La Raza T-shirts or Chicano Power buttons. He had read Anaya
and Rivera, but for fun he preferred to indulge in Modernist U.S. and
British fiction. In fact he was majoring in English and took my conversation course to brush up on his Spanish; did surprisingly well, considering that he'd picked up the language at home and had never studied
it. "Spanish is the most important gift my *mamá* ever gave me," he said.
"I'm immensely grateful to her for that."

   At the time he took my class, Castel was living in Santa Ana with his
mother and two sisters (no father in the picture). But then he moved to
Hollywood, said he couldn't take any more of the Alton badlands. He
rented an apartment the size of a closet on Fountain Street and loved
living there by himself. The first night I spent with him in that rat hole
we got high, ate cheeseburgers at a funky diner, took a walk. "The scene
of the crime!" he blurted out as we passed Selma Street. "Some nights
I'd turn a bunch of tricks out here, depending on how broke I was." He
laughed. "But that was ages ago. Now I'm a virtuous student!" A huge
cowboy followed us for a while, offering himself. The idea of a threesome intrigued me, but not with Castel. There seemed to be an unspo-
ken agreement between us that sex wasn't going to happen: not what
we wanted from each other. That night we had literature and music
instead. Castel was into Gertrude Stein. His pipe dream was to move
to Mexico City and live there on his very own Rue de Fleurus, a street
like the one where Gertrude had lived in Paris, a gathering place for
the greatest artists of our time. Castel also admired the contemporary
American poet Ruth Martin; he read to me several poems from Martin's first collection, *The Glass Heart*. There was a line from the opening
piece that he'd framed and placed by his bed: *For you in the glass heart,
trapped and alone as an unborn child, imagined as fiction, for you the
world is a faraway dream.*

   "A beautiful yet disturbing image," I offered, and Castel confessed
that he felt that way sometimes, like a confined spirit, alone, not real
but imagined by some fiendish creator. I told him I could relate but decided not to delve just yet into other writers who'd featured that same

theme in their work, such as Jorge Luis Borges and Lewis Carroll and Calderón de la Barca. Instead I chose to listen to Castel as he sang the praises of Gertrude and Ruth, his beloved muses, and I tried to form an honest, educated opinion about them. Glad I did, since Castel was soon asking for my take.

"Ruth Martin I can get into," I said, and thanked him for introducing me to her poetry. "But Stein's writing...well, I admit it leaves me cold. I know all the reasons why I should appreciate, even enjoy her visionary work. But I just can't get excited about it."

"What?!" Castel was livid. "That's blasphemy!"

"Sorry, my friend. But what you call 'flowing' and 'minimalist' and 'circular' when describing Gertrude's style, I see as repetitious, unimaginative, and tedious."

"But repeating is in everyone!" he exclaimed, quoting one of Stein's proclaimed truths.

"Yes, and so is boredom!"

He seemed truly hurt. "I can't believe you just used that word..."

"I shouldn't have," I said. "Wrong choice. Anyway, I do agree that the best writing is unconscious, though not automatic," I added. "And to write is to write is to write. But, you know, Castel, sometimes a rose is a rose but also a thorn, and to write is to survive."

Castel was trying to recover from his shock. "You've just broken my heart," he confessed.

"I didn't mean to..."

"Let me finish!" he snapped. "Even though for some bizarre, unexplainable reason you don't appreciate my dear old Gertie as you should, I'd have to agree with what you just said—which, by the way, I'd like to add to my list of memorable quotes, if it's okay with you... *A rose is a rose but also a thorn, and to write is to survive.* I do like that. It rings true."

"Thank you."

"You're welcome. But I still hate you," he said, slapping me lightly.

"Yes, but you also love me just a little."

We listened to Castel's tapes, indulging his weakness for torch-song dames Judy Garland, Billie Holiday, and Edith Piaf. Two of his all-time favorite movies were *A Star Is Born* (with Garland, not Streisand) and *Lady Sings the Blues* (Diana Ross having done an okay job of embodying the great Holiday). He played half a dozen of his favorite songs repeatedly, among them Billie's "Strange Fruit," Judy's "The Man That Got Away," and Piaf's "Non, Je Ne Regrette Rien." Too much of a good thing...

Castel was curious about what he called my "bi trip," since he'd seen me hanging out with both Laurie and Tano and was sure I was bisexual. He liked Laurie but didn't care for Tano; found him conceited and phony. "Like other Argentines I've known," said Castel. "Except for Puig," he was quick to point out. "I'd bet he's down-to-earth. Manuel isn't from Buenos Aires, right? "

"No, he's not afflicted with the *porteño* virus."

"Good for him, having nothing in common with those egomaniacs from the capital!"

I told him that Pablo Ricci did share some essential traits with many other *porteños*. "Yet he's quite unique too, and fun. And he loves Puig's work."

Castel wasn't convinced. "Maybe I'll give him a chance," he said in jest. "He couldn't be all that bad if he's into Manuel. But don't hold your breath!"

"Tano and I are not an item," I clarified. "But I do go on a 'bi trip' now and then."

"What's it like?" he asked. "Bisexuality, I mean."

A challenge to answer that question late at night, stoned and stuffed as I was. "Okay, here's the scoop," I said, not sure how to broach it. "My bisexual nature thrives in the experience of desire, and it is most fully realized in the realm of fantasies."

Castel laughed and told me I sounded like a damn professor. Which I did. So instead of rephrasing I shared with him a memory having to do with *carnaval* in Cuba—an experience that would point to the answer he sought. "I remember being blown away by those festivities when I was a kid," I said. "There was a shortage of everything in our country, but during the week of *carnaval* we had it all, music, dancing, delicious and abundant food, magnificent costumes. Many of the men in drag were perfect replicas of voluptuous *jevas* and were considered artists, yet any other time they'd be condemned as deviants and perverts. The faces of people I knew were transformed, remade by pleasure and magic. Those who wore a disguise seemed to own the world. A disguise was freedom, the banishing of taboos. Cubans put such care into their costumes!"

"All right, so you took care of your setting," noted Castel, grinning.

"Yes, yes, I'll cut to the chase... It was late afternoon. A group of us kids decided to go frolicking around the neighborhood, all in costume, screaming, getting down. The members of my group were a ghost, a corsair, a Zorro; and Rosita Fornés, a popular Cuban singer and TV star. I was the righteously clad hero and loved my black cape, which my grandmother had made for me. Rosita was embodied by Roli, one of my classmates. Roli acted very nelly at times, and he took a lot of shit at school and at home for that. But that afternoon he was a daring and much admired *mascarita*. He wore a tight red dress he borrowed from his mother, black pumps, a white kerchief over his curly black hair, and a blue satin mask over his eyes; his lips were painted bright carmine..."

"An important character, no doubt. Please go on."

"We stop at a neighbor's porch, and the woman of the house welcomes us with *chibiricos*, a type of fritter. Then her husband looks at Roli and yells, '*Te conozco, mascarita!*' That was the game, you had to guess who the disguised person was. The woman says, 'Yes, I know who you are. You're Mayda, Cuca's granddaughter.' We burst out laughing, since the real Mayda was dressed as a corsair. The man tells Roli, 'You're a girl. You couldn't be a boy.' And his wife asks him, '*Oye, chico*, and just how do you figure that?' 'Look at the legs,' he replies. 'Those are the handsome legs of a little lady!' Then, on impulse, Roli shouts, 'I'm not a girl. I am Rosita Fornés!'

"We all teased him, but now he was laughing, too. How free he must've felt! I imagined myself dancing with Roli. I saw him undressing and baring his masculine body. I caressed him, desired him—I'm sure I did—because he was a boy but also a beautiful woman..."

Castel got the point of my story. He understood that for me transvestism was a site of desire, and that it entailed a sort of bisexual head trip. But he couldn't relate. Castel didn't feel attracted to "the representation of femaleness" in the least nor did he desire women. He'd had sex with a girl a couple of times when he was a teenager, out of mere curiosity, and the experience had left him feeling disgusted and sad. "To be honest," he told me, "the smells and textures of the female body turn my stomach." And he didn't care for women's garments either, especially not if they conveyed extreme femininity—whether this was superimposed as pastiche on a body that was anatomically male or on one that was female. Castel liked men, but only if they looked and felt like men, in private as well as in public. Not to say that he wasn't versatile. He'd adjust to the preferences of his mate (bottom or top), as long as that man remained masculine and showed no signs of womanliness in bed.

"I can't stand any type of transvestism," Castel admitted, "especially, oh especially not the grotesque kind like that of Divine in the movie *Pink Flamingos*. Edgy and counterculture and avant-garde, yes, but also vulgar, inelegant, over-the-top. Not my thing, no, no, no. Please!"

"Sorry. Never saw *Pink Flamingos*."

"Good. Don't! Not unless you want to be grossed out for the rest of your life."

"So I guess there's no chance you'll ever go see a drag show with me..."

"Not the slightest chance, no."

"There's a famous one right around the corner, you know."

"Yes, and I've heard that someone in that club does a superb Garland."

"What better reason to go?"

"Not my thing. Sorry."

Castel found female impersonators depressing. All that makeup, all that strained posing and their failed imitation of *real* great women. "Pathetic clowns," he called them, including drag queens who didn't claim to be anybody famous but who nevertheless lived to imitate and pose. "It's true they embody a fantasy," he acknowledged, "and fantasies are much needed nutrients for the human soul. I can surely connect with that part of their statement, with their need for spiritual nourishment. But let them keep their enameled claws as far away from me as possible!"

He suggested I find another friend to go see one of those "pitiful spectacles" with me. Maybe Tano. And I thought, No way. Not Ricci. I wouldn't give that bitch one more reason to allege that I was messed up, that I didn't know myself. *Didn't you tell me that makeup and perfume turn you off? And now you want to go see drag queens on stage?! Be honest with yourself and with me, perroquet!*

Tano would've had plenty of ammo to get on my case and with good reason: I wasn't being forthright with him, while to Castel I was an (almost) open book. I wanted to be the same Camilo to both, hence I concluded, naïvely, that they should become friends. If the three of us could hang out together, I wouldn't be able to act differently with each of them. Besides, we'd have such fun as a threesome, I thought. Yes, we all want our friends to be friends. But I should've known better!

Luck would have it that Tano and Castel would end up in my cramped galley kitchen the night of a party, and it didn't take long for them to become *perro y gato*, as my mother would say, a dog and a cat bent on ripping each other to shreds. That's how the scene appeared to me: two beasts in fierce battle to the death. Castel started the brawl, and Tano retaliated with a nasty verbal attack, making Castel feel hurt, belittled. And then Castel lashed back in a way I found completely out of character.

Turns out that Ricci was holding court, telling some of my guests the story of how he found himself living in Alton, embellishing his tale as he did for new listeners, when suddenly Castel had had enough of his monologue. He told Ricci he was being verbose like a typical *porteño* and would he please give us all a break from his unbearable voice. And now Tano, enraged, called Castel a *mexicano arrepentido*, a reluctant Mexican. "What does your father do for a living?" Ricci asked him. "Does he tend people's gardens or does he work in the fields? Wait, it's all about your mother, right? You're ashamed of the fact that she's a cleaning lady for the rich folks in Bel Air! That's why you try so hard to pass for a Gringo. Well, let me tell you, *Chicanito*, you ain't getting away with it!"

And that's when Castel's fist fell smack in the middle of Tano's face, giving him a bloody nose. Castel then stormed out saying he'd had enough of that Argentine fiend. And Tano went screaming through the place, plugging up his nostrils with napkins and threatening to call the cops. He didn't press charges, of course not, but the party ended quickly after the incident, all of us steeped in the darkest vibes. Fucking party poopers! How could they be so hurtful and petty and childish? Shame on them. Castel and Tano couldn't get past the debasing stereotypes they had imposed on each other: All *porteños* were intolerable megalomaniacs, and all Chicanos had an inferiority complex. I despised them both that night. It would take weeks before I'd want to talk to either one again.

HEARTBEAT IN THE ROCK

I tried to make time on weekends to rummage through the last four boxes I'd been keeping in my parents' garage. My father had given me an ultimatum: "Come get this stuff or it'll go in the trash!" Just in case he meant it, I brought it all to my apartment. There I was one Sunday afternoon, bending over memories like a hungry bag lady—a character you never saw in Alton—when suddenly I came across a long-forgotten treasure. Class notes, faded photographs, some drawings, an award certificate, a newspaper clipping, and a trophy came out of a box labeled *High School*. I grabbed the trophy, held it, touched it the way we tend to touch beloved objects, as if this physical connection could transmit to us the knowledge these objects contain, or transport us back in time, or simply make us feel more real and rooted. Indeed, that thing in my hand would gradually unravel the story of my family's early exile, the first chapter of a chronicle of loss that is now keeping me anchored in this present.

Harlequin Awards, Most Promising in Art, read the tiny plaque at the base of the gold-plated figurine of a man holding a torch. The poor guy was rusty, cracked, but he would now claim his rightful place among Camilo's other icons. Still today it saddens me that my folks, Elio and Mechy, weren't there when I received that award my senior year. Elio (or *Papi*, what I always called him) thought he and his wife would feel out of place at the school event, and she didn't stand up to him, as usual. I found myself alone, itchy in my polyester suit but pleased to be sitting next to the art teacher, noticing the sparkle in her eyes when, later, she called my name from the podium. "It makes me very happy to present this award to Camilo Macías," said Miss Albrecht before she handed me the trophy. "He's talented, hard-working, and he has an artist's vision. Camilo will go far." I didn't think I'd ever live up to those words, but I was comforted by them. "Thank you so much!" was all I could say.

I imagined then a portrait I'd paint and hang in my bedroom, the oil painting of a strapping, thirty-something woman with wavy blonde hair combed back at the temples. She'd be wearing a fitted skirt and one of her colorful blouses with lace ruffles that disguised her bosom, and holding her palette and brush. There would be a title: *Joan Albrecht, the first American woman Camilo ever loved.*

In class, Miss Albrecht would play music for us while she helped us create simple yet unique little things (papier-mâché figurines, awkward sketches of flowers) as well as more complex works like seascapes in pastel and landscapes in watercolor, and portraits of family members or friends in oil. She was fond of Herb Alpert, Burt Bacharach, Dionne Warwick, and Ray Conniff but truly loved only the Carpenters, their hits "Close to You" and "We've Only Just Begun" especially. She said their music was good for the world. "Our world is tired of fighting and suffering," Miss Albrecht would tell us, echoing another popular song. "It's weary of violence, in need of our love."

Gentle yet commanding, she'd teach us about primary and secondary colors, the spectrum, and things I didn't know existed, like color temperature and psychology. Blue, she said, was cool but red was warm; and this made sense to me. I also grasped the concept of a dominant color attracting because of its intensity; and the term *subordination*, which meant of less importance because of location, size, or tone. But how could there be a *psychology* of color? By this our teacher meant that colors had either a negative or a positive effect on our moods. Red, for example, might elicit passion and give us energy but it might also provoke aggression. How can a simple pigment hold such power over us, I wondered.

Most of her students were drawn to Miss Albrecht, inspired by her. Many fluttered around her like fawning groupies, carrying her bag of art supplies to her car, offering to do whatever chores she needed. They loved her, yes, but none of those kids would ever get as close to our teacher as I did, for she gave me a glimpse—brief yet revealing—inside her artist heart.

"We'll paint a mural right here, in this room," she told me excitedly one morning, after class. "We'll work on it together, Camilo. Are you up for it?" Without waiting for my reaction, she dashed off a sketch of our future project. "We'll call it *A Brief History of Art*, which should include Altamira, of course, but we'll do Michelangelo first, to set the mood and get us inspired." Then she sized up the back wall of her class-room, where she had her work station in a corner. "I've always found this wall too barren," she said. "Like a blank screen promising breath-taking vistas." She touched it, caressed it. "But I should warn you, Camilo, it'll be quite a time commitment. Several hours after school, some weekends, and then full time over the Christmas holidays. What do you say?"

"Yes!" I said, and my response was all the encouragement she sought.

"Let's get to work, then." She described our project in detail. Our "brief history" would unfold starting with God's hand from the Sistine Chapel in the center; this would be her task. We would have illustrative images encircling that hand, many of which were to be my job to create, from the earliest cave paintings to some of Picasso's Cubist masterpiec-es. "Michelangelo heard a heartbeat in the rock," she told me, "so he picked up his chisel to bring out something wondrous that was thriving inside, something he heard crying, asking to be set free." She paused, looked at me. "Well, then, Camilo, think of this wall as Michelangelo's rock, which awaits our hands and our passion."

But there's nothing pulsing inside, I thought. Rocks are dead, and you can't bring life out of death. Yet days later I started to believe in the power of art to conceive living things, when I saw Miss Albrecht con-juring up the likeness of Michelangelo in her precise, hyperrealist style, and the Italian artist's skin suddenly breathed. There was a glow in his sorrowful eyes, perspiration in his scraggly beard; his lips seemed moist yet thirsty. You could almost touch him!

Would I be able to do the same for *David*? My first task was to re-imagine the upper part of that statue, one of Michelangelo's greatest achievements, as a painting, giving it the "semblance of reality." Miss Albrecht believed that the young man who'd posed for the artist had been very handsome. So I tried to visualize David's tanned complexion and bluish-black curls, his olive green eyes, his nipples in a pale shade of rose. I drew several sketches that the teacher approved, and then I got to work, hesitantly at first but soon driven by joy and desire and anguish. Joy because I loved what I was doing. Desire because I felt pleasure in forging an image of beauty and perfection. Anguish because that image was mine yet I was giving it away; I'd never get to keep it. Anguish because, as hard as I tried to give that wall the texture of a human body, a beating heart, to the touch it was still a rigid, lifeless surface.

Predictably, some of the boys in our third-period class took to mocking the great Italian sculptor, calling him "that old faggot." *Faggot*, a word I learned then. Miss Albrecht was furious; I'd never seen her lose her temper. "It isn't fair," she pronounced. "Michelangelo isn't here to defend himself. If he were alive, he'd confront the malicious rumors and deny them all, I'm sure."

Deny them?—I wanted to ask her but didn't. What if he actually *was* a homosexual? He'd still need to stop the rumors, of course, since homosexuality—as I'd been taught—was an illness that you'd want to conceal, even if you were the most talented artist in history. Such was the prevailing belief that Miss Albrecht was confirming for all those budding machos, adding fuel to their homophobic fire. Yet Michelangelo would've found a caring friend in the art teacher, I thought, someone who'd keep his secret safe. I wondered if she was guarding a secret herself—something about her manners, her outfits, the hairdo. But this was a monstrous assumption. I wouldn't allow myself to think of Miss Albrecht as a *tortillera* (the demeaning Cuban word for lesbians). She was my idol. And I loved her.

Somehow I made time to work on the mural. "That damn teacher," my father ranted, "making you work for nothing!" He believed Miss Albrecht was taking advantage of me, and he demanded that I stop wasting my weekends in her classroom. Papi said I could be making some money instead. But I stood my ground; that mural meant too much to me. I threatened him, "Get off my case or I'll leave. I'll run away!" Papi knew I was bluffing, but eventually he let up, and I got to finish my work.

Toward the end of our project, a student came in to interview us for the school paper. The girl seemed eager with pad and pencil, a camera, and a list of questions. *Painting since September*—she'd end up writing—*but mostly during Christmas vacation, art teacher Miss Albrecht and junior Camilo Macías have created a bright mural which covers the entire east wall of Room 3, Building 4. "I hope this mural will be a good influ-*

ence on the students," says Miss Albrecht. "I hope it will inspire them."
And Camilo feels fortunate to have worked with the popular art teacher.
"I've learned a lot from Miss Albrecht," he says. The work features some of
the famous men Miss Albrecht wishes she had known, such as Beethoven,
Shakespeare, and Wagner, representing our history through the develop-
ment of the fine arts. The images range from busts to crumbling architec-
ture, from primitive cave drawings to portraits of Beethoven and Shake-
speare. Among the many depictions, Michelangelo's "David" stands out. It
is a vivid if imagined portrait of the young man who posed for the famous
Italian sculptor... Drop by Miss Albrecht's room. Don't miss this amazing
journey through time!

When the piece came out, the third-period students gave us an ovation and plastered the bulletin board with copies of the article, which
featured a photo of our teacher posing by the mural, next to David. The
caption read: *Miss Albrecht and her magnificent recreation of Michelan-*
gelo's famous subject. At the time it bothered me that she'd been given
credit for my work. But today, as I retrace this memory, it pleases me
to see that Miss Albrecht assumed authorship of my re-imagined adolescent; justifiably so, since she'd led me to him and helped me find the
key to his beauty.

Barely a week after we finished the mural, Miss Albrecht informed
me that Bay City was holding an art contest for local artists. "You must
participate," she insisted. "Show the best work you've done in class and
make sure to represent each medium." I felt honored yet pressured, as
the teacher had picked me out of all the students in our class to compete in the event. "I'm sure you'll do great," she said and then added,
laughing, "Oh, my dear Camilo, how I wish you could take your *David*
with you!"

The day of the contest, a Saturday, I arrived mid-morning at the City
Parks and Recreation Center, corner of Hawthorne and Artesia, and
found much of my competitors' work already on display. Some of the
pieces were spectacular! I took note of five portraits and three landscapes that had the hyperrealist look of my teacher's work, first-place
material. I didn't want to see the tags, for I was certain those projects
had been submitted by Miss Albrecht's *other* students at SHS. Obviously I wasn't the best, only fair competition. How could she have led me
to believe I stood a chance?! (I had no idea she was already planning to
nominate me for the Harlequin award.) Feeling discouraged, I set up my

work, taking up the little space left available. A piece in pastel, entitled *Libertad or Freedom*, depicted a light-green ocean and a sky of cotton-white clouds, with a blue bird taking flight in the foreground. There was a watercolor of a distant castle and a tower and a pier, my rendition of the Morro fortress in Havana, which I'd seen in pictures as a kid. And I also included an oil painting of my mother, her portrait (adapted from a photo) with luminous eyes and her hair in long, wavy strands of a reddish-brown color. I'd painted her wearing a beige silk gown with shoulders exposed, and with semi-transparent hands resting in her lap. I had given it the title *Mercedes Daydreams*.

A team of South Bay artists would be judging the participating projects that afternoon. I went home, anxious yet resigned to part with my mediocre stuff. When I returned hours later, the Center was packed. I approached my wall, psyched up for the bad news, and I couldn't believe my eyes... The Art Show judges had awarded me *First Place in Oils*. The portrait of Mechy—of my beloved *Mami*—had won first place! I was so excited to share the news with her! Sadly I didn't see my mother when I got home but Papi, who was washing his Rambler in the driveway. I knew he wouldn't be supportive, let alone happy for me. Yet I held out the certificate, my hand shaking as I pointed to its gold star. Elio glanced at me indifferently and said, "Put that away and grab the hose. I could use some help."

Help. *Ayuda.* I heard that word a lot from Papi in those early years. *Necesitamos ayuda.* Prompted by him, I took on several menial jobs as soon as I graduated from high school, losing sleep and study hours in order to "contribute to our household." Papi hoarded most of the money I made. He'd deposit my checks in his bank account and throw me a fistful of bucks, saying, "Here. And don't waste it on books or paint. Find yourself a Gringa with a big ass and spend it on her!" He wanted me to pursue a practical trade like carpentry or auto mechanics, or maybe go into business and plan on having my own grocery store. Elio's grand plans for his son! He didn't know I was taking Romance Languages, art, and breadth requirements at a four-year college in Torrance. Nothing "practical."

I had no idea what I'd do with a bachelor's degree in languages—teach? interpret? translate? All I knew was that I needed to get away from home, to escape the isolation Papi had imposed on our family. We lived in an immigrant cocoon where outsiders weren't welcome and those who ventured into our domestic prison (like Mami's friends from church) were treated to Elio's bad temper and awful manners. No one ever returned. Had we lived in Miami, like so many Cuban refugees, life might've been different for us. But in the vast Southland we had no community and no family. We'd ended up in California because Elio wanted to be far from that other Cuba nestled in Florida, from *el cubaneo*, the whole mess of a society of exiled Cubans. I suspect that for Elio his compatriots were a reminder of what he'd lost. He would become a hermit, his dislike of socializing exacerbated by his struggles to make ends meet. And he'd impose his seclusion on my mother, who was innately gregarious.

The immigration authorities had let my father choose, and he'd opted for Los Angeles. Then the welfare people gave us a hand—special refugees that we were! They helped Elio find a two-bedroom apartment in a quiet neighborhood of Bay City, on 138th Street, so I could attend South High School, which had a good reputation. The city and its reputable school were located in the sprawling South Bay area, ten miles inland from the Pacific Coast. Our neighbors were all decent American folks, according to Papi, but not very friendly. Only one of the families had kids my age; these teenagers showed no interest in me, and I was too insecure about my English to approach them. Hence I kept to myself.

In time our street would be peopled by other Cuban and Mexican families who gradually displaced most of the white Americans who lived there, yet we had the honor of being the first Latinos on 138th Street. That crowded suburb was to be my family's new *patria*, although it wouldn't feel like home to us for a long time. I know it never did to Elio.

One of the first "indispensable items" that Papi installed in our apartment was a color TV, a giant console of varnished pressed wood which also included a stereo system with a turntable and a radio. It was a luxury, considering that we could barely afford to pay for rent and groceries. But this object was of utmost importance to my parents, since they'd been told that watching television was the fastest way to learn a language. And sure enough, my knowledge of conversational English rocketed that summer thanks to my TV viewing. I liked the game shows, *Jeopardy, The Dating Game*, and most of the situation comedies now considered classics, *The Partridge Family, Bewitched, That Girl, The Brady Bunch, My Three Sons*. The sitcoms would play in the background as distant conversations, jokes and punch lines I didn't quite get. Those characters' concerns seemed childish to me. I just couldn't relate to the Partridges, though I liked their songs and had the hots for both Keith and Laurie. I loved Sam's power in *Bewitched* but hated her idiotic husband. The girl in *That Girl* had a wide-eyed face that verged on stupidity, I thought. And I wondered if the Bradys were a typical American family, always so cheery and sweet. Did the grandfather in *My Three Sons* really do all the cooking? No way!

I watched a lot of *I Love Lucy* reruns that first summer. I'd gulp down gallons of Coca-Cola while laughing my head off at Lucy's antics. My parents would watch the show with me sometimes, impressed with the fact that the main male character was Cuban and sounded like one, even in English. Imagine that, a famous *cubano* in this foreign North! Our compatriot seemed utterly real to me: loud, bossy, machista, too much like my father. And Lucy was hilarious, ingenious, but I felt angry at her the way I felt at Mami—for being submissive and letting her husband scold her, poke fun at her, oppress her, threaten to hit her, and confine her to the role of homemaker. Apparently there was no escaping domestic slavery if you were married to a Cuban male, whether you happened to be a gorgeous red-headed American woman or a Caribbean belle. I didn't know yet that Lucy and Ricky embodied widely accepted role models and weren't solely the handiwork of Cuban society in the 1950s.

The only show I truly loved was *Star Trek*, its haunting musical theme, its faraway stars, a ship that could travel at the speed of light! I'd fly through space with Captain Kirk and Mr. Spock, away from California and from the life I'd lived in Cuba. I felt strangely connected to the world of *Star Trek* in spite of its impenetrability, the language too complex for my basic English and its philosophies too profound for an immigrant teenager to grasp. It was reassuring for me to see my family, in a romantic sort of way, as a distant reflection of the show. We had no starship, no transporter, no ray guns. We hadn't even gone where no one had gone before. Yet we seemed to have a mission like that of the *Enterprise* crew, and the universe we were exploring was bizarre and novel, full of blinding lights. It was a planet called *Estados Unidos*, a world of larger-than-life aliens (though we were aliens too); a feast of new sounds and vistas and mind-boggling rules, not unlike the mirage of a color TV screen.

I enjoyed the commercials. Nothing had ever looked as alive to me as the people in the TV ads, especially ads promoting cereal. Wholesome blond girls and boys on the grass at a park, playing, waiting for their corn flakes and orange juice. Verdant hills, the soothing voice of an American mother calling them for breakfast, and those carefree children dressed in powerful blues, gentle pinks, dazzling oranges. I wanted to be like them, or at least dress like they did! The photos we'd brought from Cuba suddenly seemed old and faded, like ghosts that could no longer impress me.

Yet those photographs—certainly the ones Mami took once we got here—are invaluable to me now, as I try to flesh out my memories. Some of the images can still project a world that feels real, almost tangible. Here, for starters, is a candid Polaroid shot my mother snapped of me standing in front of our apartment. It was a smoggy June afternoon, one month after our arrival, and I was feeling aimless, lost. Since school didn't start till September, I was faced with a summer in limbo. I'd been watching too much TV, and smoking. I used to criticize Mami for her addiction, and there I was, stealing cigs from my parents' closet, where they stashed cartons of Elio's unfiltered Camels and Mechy's mentholated cigarettes. By now I was hooked on the latter; almost threw up the first time but endured the gagging sensation and forced myself to like it. Then one evening I lit up in the living room, and Mami cried out, "It's my fault, my fault! I should never have smoked around you!" And Papi just laughed. "It's okay," he said. "Men have the right to smoke. But buy your own!"

A photo of Elio in his khaki uniform by the entrance of South High School, where he started working as a janitor during my junior year. Another one from around the same time, Camilo packing his lunch of buttered toast, an apple, and a thermos brimming with chocolate milk. I was doing well in my classes and trying to avoid running into Elio. He didn't want anyone at school to know he was my father. Papi felt sorry for himself. "Who would've thought?" he pondered. "Who would've known that I'd come to the North to pick up young Gringos' garbage!" I had told him about the job opening, which was posted on a bulletin board at school. I went to the interview with him, helped him look good, rephrased his broken English, and the principal hired him on the spot. Mami was relieved—no more factory work for her husband. She'd quit the *factoría* herself and was earning a modest living as a seamstress. Elio would fare better at South High School: good pay and benefits, few coworkers, no major risks. Papi had started his job there partway through my next-to-last year, and by graduation I'd only run into him three times. Never did he look up from his trash bins.

Camilo photographed at home, working on the watercolor of a young man in profile, leaning against a tree—a thinly disguised self-portrait... *Naked torso, hair combed back, fine curls forced into waves.* "Who in his right mind would want to be an artist?!" Papi raged. "Only my crazy son!" *Blue skies, green hills, gray-black rocks, a lake, aspens reflected on the water.* Only I'd paint pictures of places I'd never been, and portraits of a young man who was too pale, too much like a corpse. *In a flowered shirt and white pants, he stands by the shore, arms crossed, facing us.* Surely Elio and Mechy suspected that those watercolors evoked their son's real, secret life, not just his adolescent fantasies. I'm sure Mami knew. But it was easier to chock it all up to Camilo's imagination, to his strange artistic needs. *Lying on the floor in a log cabin, wearing a white cotton shirt with a blue pattern of mermaids, about to take a drag from a filtered cigarette. Then by a window. The sun bathes his face, tracing his long eyelashes, casting a shadow under his eyes, turning his black hair a light shade of auburn.*

Those things I painted were all in my head, sure. They didn't depict my weekend escapades, when I was supposed to be working on the mural and was actually at Big Bear Lake, having sex and getting high on weed with a Gringo... *Logs in the water, two silhouettes. A lanky man in overalls and T-shirt reaches out to a young man who hesitates, who stops. Close-up of the tall man smiling, seated on the ground, baring his hairy chest. Then the other man captured in chiaroscuro, a wall of rustic pine behind him, the framed picture of a carnation on the wall. His face emerging, his glance fixed on some point beyond the door.* What was his name? Joe? John? No, it was Shawn, hard to pronounce. He was thin, tall, had long blond hair. He showed no obvious signs of homosexuality yet I knew Shawn was a "faggot." I met him one evening as he walked out of a beer joint on Rosecrans, while I made my way home from Room 3. I'd normally avoid that corner of Rosecrans Avenue and Hawthorne Boulevard, taking a shortcut across the school track so I wouldn't be tempted to peek in the bar as I had once, repulsed yet intrigued by the darkness of the place, its stench of booze, its pounding music. But that day I didn't want to go home yet; I hopped in Shawn's car after a nervous hello. Red as positive, cried a voice in the depths of my pleasure. Passion. Energy. I finally understood...

Shawn made plans. He hoped I wouldn't be just a trick. I didn't know the meaning of "trick" in this context, but I told him I liked him. "I really dug blowing you," he said, and his comment conjured up a comical if frightening image of my body as a balloon that this guy filled with hot air. I said I'd try to see him again some weekend... *Soft, early morning light on the porch, a table, a rainbow-colored umbrella. Young man under the umbrella, chin pressed against his knees. Same man standing by a fireplace in his briefs. Bedroom eyes, well-defined muscles, hairless nipples, a line of unruly hair traced with precision from the groin to the belly button. A shadow on the wall: the artist's shadow...*

There would be no trace of those watercolor "fantasies" if it weren't for Mami's photos, which captured them and saved them in an album. Did I give those works away or toss them? Or did Papi destroy them during one of his fits? Can't remember. But thankfully I get to see Camilo in cap and gown with his parents in this other picture. Mami's face beaming proudly. Papi looking disgruntled and spoiling my graduation. No wonder there's no smile on my face! Oh, but Elio was doing the right thing, *lo correcto*, by just being there. He was living up to his maxim: We must always do the right thing.

I did well at South High School, became fluent in English, learned about cell reproduction and the shoe-shaped paramecium, about the Founding Fathers. My work in Math was average but I excelled in Physical Education, much to Papi's surprise. I took the Driver's Ed class, which would soon allow me to get a permit and thus start driving a used Datsun we bought from a car dealer in Bay City. I didn't go to the Prom because I didn't work up the nerve to ask anyone. My best prospect was a buxom Costa Rican girl I made out with on occasion, never going all the way—virgin, she said, to the altar! But even if I'd had a partner, I would've had to get into a fight with Papi in order to go, since he refused to let me "waste money" on the tux rental. I guess I just didn't care that much.

I met a motley bunch of Latino students at SHS, just as I would later in college—Mexicans, Argentines, Colombians, Central Americans. I should've bonded with the five other Cuban kids on campus but didn't. Much as I hated to admit it, I was rejecting my compatriots in exile just like my father had. The mere sound of Cuban voices outside our home reminded me of a world I wanted to banish from my life. So I chose to hang out with the non-Cuban Latinos at South High. Ultimately, though, I made no lasting friends in high school. It seems I only went there to meet Miss Albrecht.

A critic had once accused my teacher of being a mere imitator of reality, not a true artist. She had me read the critic's brief review of one of her exhibits; said there was something important in it that she wanted me to learn... *Without concrete referents, Joan Albrecht wouldn't know what to do with her brushes. She is no better than a camera lens, but is in fact incapable of capturing reality with a camera's precision. What's the point of her so-called art, then? Give it up, Joan!* How could anyone describe Miss Albrecht that way?! An absolute of my universe had been crushed. I was shaking.

"It's fine, Camilo," said Miss Albrecht softly, holding my hand; we had never been this close. "You shouldn't feel bad for me." And she went on, "Critics are very useful to us artists. Not because they praise our work, but because they can challenge us."

I didn't understand. "What do you mean, challenge us?"

"By failing to see our worth," she explained, "critics dare us to show them who we are, how *good* we are. In a way, they help us refine and deepen our vision."

I wasn't sure what all that meant, or why I was supposed to learn this painful lesson. But I did know I'd never have the strength, the resolve to resist such attacks. I wouldn't "go far," not if I had to put up with such brutal criticism, humiliation, and utter disrespect. What was that vision I supposedly had, anyway? An artist, I thought, was someone with the ability and talent to produce a lifelike image, transposing reality to paper or canvas or a wall. Miss Albrecht could do that and more. She always knew what was required: subject, perspective, color scheme. And her version always improved on the original, be it a face, a landscape, or a fruit basket, bringing it all into vivid focus. Whereas all I could do was follow Miss Albrecht's suggestions. Oh, but what a fulfilling job that was! Nowhere else did I feel happier than there, by my teacher's side, basking in her talent and wisdom. I loved the smell of a fresh canvas, of mixed oils, and I loved watching her paint: likeness on likeness; erasure of an image with swift strokes, as a more truthful picture emerged, the one meant to be. How did she know that the outline of an eye or the skin tone was wrong? How could she see it all before it existed? I sure couldn't, not like she did, but I got glimpses of the process thanks to Miss Albrecht. Living within her universe, I had the freedom to forge the world out of nothing. It was a reality I was able to mold, a refuge—that classroom, my art work, that wall-turned-mural, and those Carpenters songs—where I discovered a private, comforting meaning; something that was mine alone and had nothing to do with my father.

"You have no ambition," Papi complained. "No urge to make a good living. What's wrong with you, *coño*?!" I had finished a BA in Romance Languages at a college in Torrance, had applied for graduate study at Alton University, and was welcomed into their doctoral program in Latin American literature. The Spanish and Portuguese Department also offered me a Teaching Assistantship to help me pay for tuition. Worthless degrees, thought Elio, and too much schooling for such an impractical career! There was no point in going to school if I wouldn't be making lots of money right away.

I paid a visit to South High the summer I moved to Alton. It was a weekend; the place was deserted. I snuck in through the track gate, the same unhinged iron gate where some kids used to sneak out to go for a smoke or a bite to eat at the corner diner. I headed to Building 4, Room 3, and peeked in through the windowpane. There was David on the wall, still young and perfect; and through the lens of my memory I saw Miss Albrecht posing proudly by our mural. When and how did we say goodbye? Was there a hug, a kiss, words of wisdom, promises? I wondered if she ever thought about me, about the dream Camilo was meant to fulfill. I ached to see her again but knew I shouldn't. How could I tell her that I'd given up art, that the work she saw me produce in her classroom was a fleeting whimsy? For if I'd truly felt a heartbeat in the rock, I would've given myself over to it with abandon, disregarding all the practical reasons that kept me from setting something wondrous free.

I lost track of time as I stood by the window, peering in. And then I started to hear a woman's sultry voice, a song about falling stars and new beginnings, as I kept looking at my painting of an Italian adolescent. I understood then, at last, that Michelangelo had only created an illusion. The real David had loved and cried and hurt. He'd felt hunger, joy. He exuded health yet was dying like all living bodies—had inevitably died one day. The David of rock, like the one on Miss Albrecht's wall, was also handsome and youthful, maybe even eternal. But his heart would never beat.

SPIDER WOMAN

"There'll come a time when homosexual literature will be a field of academic endeavor, with entire departments devoted to Gay Studies." It sounded amazing, implausible, but that's what Dr. Varela told me, what she saw happening in academia in the not too distant future. Sofía was totally into gayness but she wasn't gay, oh no, not even bisexual as far as I could tell. She was a gifted professor married to a nondescript American architect, a Marxist living the American Dream, a hetero Argentine lady. Not Evita by a long shot (too short and heavy), although she did love Mrs. Perón's chic look.

As my dissertation advisor, Sofía suggested I write about the work of Argentine novelist Manuel Puig. I was already familiar with *Kiss of the Spider Woman* and loved the book. In fact I'd liked all of Puig's titles—*Betrayed by Rita Hayworth, Heartbreak Tango, The Buenos Aires Affair*—before I ever read him. There was a profusion of scholarly articles about Puig's use of movies and tangos in his novels, so my mentor said I should focus on the "erotic discourse" articulated in his work instead.

Eroticism, yeah. There was plenty of it in Puig's books, some of the passages exciting enough to get me going. I did love to read and write about sex. But I was concerned that I'd also have to deal with the Hollywood films the writer was into. I couldn't stand that stuff, the stilted dialogue, the larger-than-life emotions, the ghastly faces in those interminable close-ups. In Puig's case, the obsession with those movies paid off big time: better to be a bestselling novelist than a mediocre script writer! (Having grown up in the pampas town of General Villegas and having watched a lot of Hollywood films, Puig wanted to make movies, so he ended up writing scripts for the Cinecittà film studios in Italy. But he was basically reworking Hollywood melodramas of the forties and fifties, which did not reflect the style of Italian cinema at the time, best represented by directors Visconti, De Sica, and Antonioni. Puig hated their Neorealist aesthetic and, feeling discouraged, started writing fiction. And the rest is literary history.) But it wasn't just classic Hollywood I had a problem with. Nearly all films were a waste of my time, although I'd enjoyed several, including most of Woody Allen's work. The movie theater felt oppressive to me. Too dark a place, it pulled you out of the world and offered you a momentary fix, transporting you, as promised, only to throw you back into the vastness of reality afterwards. The so-called movie experience left me feeling cheated and depressed. Why would I want to write about it? Fortunately, there was no mention of cinema in Sofía's grand plan for me.

It was impossible to say no to Dr. Varela. My mentor could be obstinate, definitely about literary theory. She was slightly interested in French historian Michel Foucault but primarily favored Marxist thought as developed by Georg Lukács and Lucien Goldmann. "As a social scientist," she said, quoting the Hungarian Lukács, "one must accept that dialectical materialism is the road to truth." She claimed that the epic poem was a precursor of the novel, and she defined the latter by citing Goldmann's story of a problematic hero who quests for authentic values in a degraded world. That story was best embodied by Don Quixote of La Mancha, a knight who wanted to save damsels in distress no longer in need of rescuing and whose only distress was not having enough to eat.

It was an interesting journey, that of a protagonist's search for ideals in a fucked-up world. Still, I didn't buy all that "hero" talk, didn't really believe there could be one single road to truth. I'd been making some discoveries of my own, the most exciting of which was Mikhail Bakhtin, a Russian theorist who'd fallen into disfavor with the Stalin regime (of course!) and was exiled to some godforsaken region in Russia. Yet that misfortune didn't stop him from producing some fascinating theoretical writing. Sofía dismissed Bakhtin—not sufficiently Marxist for her, I assumed—but I didn't care. I was planning to sneak several of his ideas into my dissertation (the concepts I loved, *carnival, laughter, dialogism, polyphony,* things I could wrap my mind around) whether she liked them or not.

Truth, to be uttered, needed a multitude of voices, said Bakhtin. And those voices could only flourish within the polyphonic context of a carnival, as embodied by a collectivity of costumes and masks. Yeah, I could relate to that! He asserted that the novel, as a nineteenth-century and post-industrial form, thrived on diversity. Yet it was diversity that the epic poem—a closed, self-contained genre—tried to eradicate from the world. Bakhtin didn't see the novel as a descendant of the epic poem but of satire. And I thought, Hey, I'd take *Satyricon* over *El Cid* anytime. Laughter instead of heroism. Individual utterances instead of patriotic proclamations. Small yet significant lives, not great deeds.

Take that, you epic Sofía! *Epic* Sofía. The immensity of the word fits her. She seemed larger than life sometimes, and she certainly spun a sticky web. Dr. Varela wreaked havoc in my subconscious some nights, when my sleeping mind turned her into a spider. I'd see a huge crawly creature, black and fat like a tarantula, with Sofía's face. She was deceivingly dormant at the center of her web, waiting for a clueless bystander to bump into it and get caught and eaten—an idiot like me! Sure enough, I'd fall in and get trapped. Sofía's long hairy legs would start moving slowly toward me. Any second now I'd be her lunch or dinner. But no, I always woke up before that happened. And I kept having this ridiculous dream with blatantly obvious symbolism; totally unoriginal, but it still scared the hell out of me.

No, Sofía wasn't the man-eating Spider Woman. (Oh but how she would love to have devoured all the men in our department, one by one, morsel by morsel. What a feast!) In spite of her bouts of intransigence and her Evita airs, Dr. Varela had her act together. Her scholarly articles were fiery, provocative, insightful. None of her male colleagues took her seriously, and—said Alina—that was a telltale sign. Alina didn't trust any of them. She knew that those stuffed shirts laughed behind Sofía's back about her women's literature and her "subversive feminist discourses." Because Jiménez, McDougal, Oropeza, Beym, and Mirabal couldn't think without their academic dicks. "Their maleness blinds them," said my friend, "and they're also dying of envy!" One of those men had come on to Alina. She wouldn't reveal the name but called him a *viejo verde,* a dirty old man. It had to be Oropeza, our resident chauvinist pig, I was certain. Could the Chilean old-timer still get it up? In his wet dreams!

The *viejo verde* called me to his office when he learned about my dissertation topic, wanting to offer me some "sound advice," as he put it. "Camilo, I know you've decided to write about Puig," he said in a faux tone of camaraderie. "He's a homosexual, you know. Very obvious and in terrible taste. Please reconsider. You wouldn't want to be associated with such an individual. Think about your future." This association—he implied—might ruin my career as I tried to enter the inner sanctum of hetero male academics, an old-boys network that required total adherence to the patriarchal code of honor. I was stunned, refusing to accept that all of academia was really *that* bad.

"I've written several chapters already," I said, lying (several chapters?!), instead of telling him exactly what he deserved: *Macho cabrón, how can you claim to be a professor?!*

"I think you should reassess your subject of inquiry," he insisted. "Weren't you planning to write about your compatriot, what's his name? The young Cuban writer you like so much..."

"Yovani López, yes, I did consider focusing on his work."

"What happened?"

"I changed my mind," I replied and left it at that.

No need to tell him that Sofía had shot down the idea because López wouldn't pull the weight of a García Márquez or a Cortázar, or even of the lesser known Puig. "You must be strategic," she'd said. It didn't matter that I loved Yovani's novel, *El rey del campo*, more than any other work on my reading list. This brief passage, for instance: *The boy's flights take him to the skies like a cenzontle, in search of cotton candy clouds. Through the tall sugar cane, he's a friendly majá snake. And he lights up the night like a cucuyo, with a family of giddy fireflies. He has the mind of a wise old guajiro but the heart of a child...* I had contacted Yovani through Casa de las Américas, his Cuban publisher, and we'd been corresponding. We'd shared thoughts about writing, careful to avoid any mention of politics. Our friendship and my strong connection with his fiction made complete sense: We were the same age and from the same region in Cuba (his native Najasa was in the province of Camagüey, like my native Las Tinajas.) And we both loved to write. Who cared if he was a communist and I was a *gusano*—a "maggot," what the Cuban government used to call those of us who were leaving the country. Who cared.

But no, I had to think about my future in academia and produce a marketable dissertation that I could publish as a book. Manuel Puig, according to Sofía, was already a stretch, since he wasn't listed yet among the *grandes*. But he was definitely more visible and widely popular than López. And now that Dr. Oropeza had belittled Puig, then all the more reason for me to write about him!

The Chilean prof chuckled and said, "I hope you won't regret it." And as I walked out of his office, I was sure I could hear his thoughts... *Camilo Macías has disgraced us all. He's writing his doctoral thesis on the filthy, unliterary novels of an Argentine faggot, which speaks to the fact that Macías must be a faggot himself. Let us show him no mercy. Off with his head!*

Alina thought I should've made Oropeza look like the ignorant fool he was and taught him a few facts he probably didn't know. Should've said something to him like: Okay, professor sir, so you don't want to read or teach Puig's novels because of the writer's homosexuality and the gay subtext in some of his books. That stuff offends your manhood, right, professor? But here's the thing, a scholar shouldn't discard a great writer because he disagrees with his politics or lifestyle. Or you wouldn't discuss Jung and Heidegger and teach Borges, I'm sure. Because Jung was an anti-Semite who invented his mythology of the subconscious so he wouldn't have to deal with empirical reality—the Jewish plight—and because he hated Freud. You wouldn't want to teach such a creep, would you, sir? No more discussions of archetypes in your very stimulating classes! And take Martin Heidegger, the notable philosopher of the "being-in-the-world," another one of your favorites. I bet you didn't know that Heidegger was a fascist and member of the Nazi Party, did you, sir? And what about good old Jorge Luis Borges, our *divino argentino*? His stories are brilliant, we all agree. He's the master of masters, the aleph, the book of all books. But he's also a racist who thinks and has expressed publicly that black people ruined Western civilization. Anyway, it's not my intention to throw Puig in the same bag with those dudes just because he happens to be gay. He's the author of four masterful novels, and I don't have to defend him or justify my interest in his fiction. But for the record, sir, his books turn me on!

True, there were passages in Manuel's books that aroused me, but his novels also made me question the ludicrous ideas instilled in me as a child, notions that forced me to engage the world as an oppressive male.

The thesis I'd come up with was informed by my rejection of those ideas and notions. But in order to develop it I was expected to "complicate" it and "problematize" it, quoting heavily from Sofía's theoretical bag, justifying every statement, footnoting it all. Puig's work had to be "analyzed" (hateful word, so clinical and nonliterary) with instructive concepts from the structuralist contingent: Barthes, Todorov, Genette, Althusser, among others; and the pillars of poststructuralist feminist thought. Puig was into Freud and Marcuse, hence I had to start there, throwing in a good dose of libido, a tablespoon of the subconscious, a teaspoon of sublimation, and gobs of polymorphous perverse sexualities. Those were the rules; gotta prove you know your stuff. Okay, fine, I'd give 'em psychobabble to support my thesis, which was too simple for that brainy bunch: *Patriarchy has fucked up everything!*

I found myself needing a dissertation committee, but only Sofía was on board initially; we couldn't get two other profs to sign on. They had the usual excuses, their research, committee work, and there was the "worth" issue. Our eminent scholars didn't regard Puig as a genuine writer like García Márquez et al. They alleged that his work was a bricolage that didn't amount to a true oeuvre, that it consisted of popular scraps unworthy of the great Latin American canon. But the real reason for their trashing of the Argentine novelist, said Sofía, was homophobia. *Surprise!* After some coaxing, Jiménez finally said yes, and Dr. Daniels from English would be the third member of my reluctant committee.

One day Sofía called me at home (there had to be an urgent reason!) to talk about the chapters I'd given her to read. The good news was that I had a "good grasp" of the material. The bad news: my introduction had to be completely redone. "It's too personal," she said. Doctoral dissertations were no place for "self-referential monologues" or allusions to the author's biography. Her demands came as a blow and a huge disappointment. I thought she'd welcome an intimate touch in what would be an otherwise dry and dull treatise. But Sofía did go by the book regarding criticism. She wanted me to succeed in the field and be regarded as a first-rate scholar (which I knew I'd never be); and only by writing a research-heavy, book-length scholarly piece could I aspire to such enviable status. I did want to find a job, thus it behooved me to heed Sofía's advice. Not that I had a choice about it, anyhow.

In my unacceptable intro, I had tried to convey a twofold idea: 1) that one couldn't read Puig's work without reading the man himself, his story, his thoughts and opinions expressed in interviews; 2) that Camilo couldn't "analyze" Puig without inserting himself—his life, his own story—into the text.

I intuitively knew that an author's life was rich in cues to the reading of his books, but I didn't know enough about Puig to mine that source for critical assumptions. Maybe some day, if I got to know him in person... In any case, what I proposed to do was a no-no; a scholarly work couldn't have such a heavy inclusion of both biographical and autobiographical elements—the latter in particular. I'd have to extricate from the written chapters all first-person assertions and all references to Puig's life. These changes, said Sofía, would ensure that my dissertation not be deemed unrigorous, impressionistic; that it be studied and quoted. Out with the passion and the intimacy and the creativity! I could be a voice but not a presence. I was to sound like a true scholar, objective, detached yet solemn and incisive.

No problem. I'd play the part of a critic to humor Sofía, and I'd have to get my creative kicks elsewhere—reading Puig's novels for fun, not as an academic; or writing *other* stuff; or watching Manuel on television. Yeah, Puig on TV! Sofía had alerted me about this program on one of the Mexican networks, and I made sure to watch it. What a trip, Puig chatting with the two actors who were portraying Molina and Valentín in the theatrical version of *Spider Woman*, written by the novelist himself. A scene from the Mexico City production was televised, where Molina declared that if women were so wonderful, well, then, that's what he wanted to be, a woman! An inspired performance. Then Puig appeared on the set with the director and congratulated the actors. He was thin, slightly hunched, balding, had dreamy eyes and long eyelashes. Clad in jeans, a shortsleeve shirt, and sandals, he said he was glad the audiences were laughing with Molina. "Their laughter is healthy," he offered and added that in *Kiss of the Spider Woman*, he wanted to explore profound themes that obsessed him, but in forms that were accessible and fun. "With *Kiss* I hoped to depict two minorities," he explained, "both of which reflect my personal history. And I tried to deal with the problem of intolerance."

Now the director expressed his joy, *"un inmenso regocijo,"* at seeing the creator in his imagined space, Puig within the spider's cell. "The artist enters his work," he stated, glancing at Manuel. "Like Velázquez in his *Meninas*." Big shoes for a humble bricoleur, I thought. Indeed, the famous Argentine writer smiled uneasily and didn't utter another word. The camera captured the actors embracing him, then it cut to a close-up of Manuel, which filled the screen.

Seeing Puig gave me a creative rush. Fortunately I had a novel-in-progress in which to take refuge. The project was hush-hush but word got out in the end, and most of my profs were alarmed—such a waste of precious scholarly time! None of your fucking business, I thought. I needed this sort of therapy and was going to get it: fleeting yet nourishing hours of writing in longhand (no PC for this), enjoying the feel of words on paper. The narrative was flowing out of me in English, and I wondered why. Maybe I sought a respite from Spanish because it was the language of my folks and my profs and the books I read and taught. Or perhaps I needed distance, the mediation of the Other's tongue to navigate the past and not drown in the memories. Spanish would've been too close to the pain. There was also the fact that English was at times the language of my thoughts, but not because I was being colonized by the dominant culture, as Alina believed. No. English was at my service. I commanded it.

Alina didn't like the title, *Cuba in Silence.* The word "silence" was too severe and negative, she said. Why not the opposite? *Cuba Screaming. Cuba Hollering.* That would grab you! But "silence" was what best represented my story, and what I wanted. Alina also thought it wasn't wise to use the name of the country, for readers might think the book was solely about Cuba. And once again I had to disagree. I was keeping the title, which I'd culled from "Dos patrias," a poem by José Martí, Cuba's apostle. Thus it began: *Dos patrias tengo yo: Cuba y la noche. / ¿O son una las dos? No bien retira / Su majestad el sol, con largos velos / Y un clavel en la mano, silenciosa / Cuba cual viuda triste me aparece...* Those first five lines would be the novel's epigraph, in my English translation: *I have two homelands: Cuba and the night. Or are they one and the same? No sooner does the sun withdraw its majesty than Cuba, wearing a long veil and holding a carnation, in silence, appears to me like a sad widow.*

Of course my novel could never live up to Martí's patriotism. I didn't suffer his nostalgia. I couldn't maintain, like the great Cuban apostle did in "Dos patrias," that... *ya no soy vivo... ¡me arrancaron de la tierra mía!* No, it was the opposite for me; I had been able to *live* because I'd been *torn away* from Cuba. My homeland wasn't a sad, loving widow. She was a fiend that haunted me, appearing in my dreams but never bearing a red carnation, the gift of comfort and meaning.

There were moments of joy in *Cuba in Silence*, thanks to the main character's mother—a happiness for which I'm grateful. But even Mami's love and care couldn't save the protagonist from his fate. Thus Cuba brought to me the memory of anguish, of the horrors I wasn't supposed to name, much less remember. The island was a shadow, a silent presence in my first novel.

CUBA IN SILENCE

ld bread for bread pudding. That's what Mami wanted this morning, so she sent me to El Kiosko to get some. But it was too early on a Saturday and I was still in bed. Hurry up, Lito, she said, before Eduardo runs out of it! And I hoped I wouldn't have to wait in line to get a stinking piece of bread that would probably have bugs in it. Mami says the pudding tastes better when the bread is old, and if it has bugs in it, she'll take them out with her long fingernails. So I don't have to worry.

We buy a lot of our food at El Kiosko, a *bodega* that's right around the corner from our house. Eduardo used to own that store but now he just works there 'cause Fidel took it from him. He sells us food under the counter. That means stuff that's not in our ration book, and we could all go to jail for buying it, even me though I'm just a little boy. But that'll never happen, says Papi, 'cause Eduardo is our friend and he's playing the communist game, whatever that means.

I told Mami I didn't want to wear shoes today, and she thought I was joking. She said that my feet weren't used to it but she let me go to the store barefoot anyway. Just watch where you step, she asked me. I stared at my feet for a while before I left, they looked so white I thought they weren't mine! Then I felt the damp grass and the pebbles when I walked, and I had to hop like a kangaroo. It was fun but it hurt a little. When I got to El Kiosko I saw Juan and Quique, those two mean boys standing outside, looking for trouble. They laughed at me and called me Big Foot but I just pretended they weren't there. I went in and saw some people but there was no line. Then Eduardo looked at me and said you forgot your shoes, Camilito! I told him I wanted to go barefoot like the other children, and he said in a loud voice that those kids didn't wear shoes 'cause they had none. Eduardo is nice, he always smiles and winks at me but this morning he was acting like an ogre, a big bad ogre 'cause he's bigger than Papi and has hair all over his arms and even on his neck. Like an ogre but not as ugly.

I used to walk to school with our neighbor Mayda sometimes. Mayda works downtown and has to pass by my school every day, so it's a good idea for me to go with her. That's what Mami said, and I thought it'd be exciting to walk with such a pretty girl. She had big tits! Not like the girls in my class, who have teeny ones. But Mayda turned out to be meaner than a witch, hitting me and yelling at me to hurry up. Then something happened the other day and that's when I asked Mami to please take me to school herself. We were passing by El Kiosko on the way home when suddenly Juan and Quique cornered me and started poking me and hitting me in the head real hard. And Mayda just stood there laughing, saying I deserved it all for being a sissy and a Little Mary. I hate her! Then Eduardo came out of his store yelling at the kids to let me go, and they did.

You owe me a favor, Camilito, for defending you from those boys, that's what Eduardo told me the next time I went to El Kiosko. I needed to get plantains for supper that time. Mami said there might not be any but I had to try, so I went and noticed that the big metal door that rolls up and down in front of the store was all the way down. I walked around the place and then Eduardo came out. He lives in the back where there's another door and a window, and I think he saw me through that window. He told me he'd been taking a short nap and asked me what I wanted. My mother needs ripe plantains, I said. Do you have any we could buy? Sure, follow me, he told me. I'll get you some, Camilito.

We went to the store through his house, a messy house that stank like a chicken coop. Then Eduardo started squeezing my arms. He said you're not skinny, not like the other kids in the neighborhood. He told me he liked them all, even Quique and Juan, but I was his favorite 'cause I had good manners. Then he pinched my butt and I didn't like that. He said he couldn't help himself 'cause I had a round little butt that begged to be pinched. Now I was confused 'cause Eduardo is my parents' friend, and grownup friends aren't supposed to do those things to children. I was nervous too, that's when you talk fast or ask stupid questions, so

I asked Eduardo why his store was called El Kiosko if it didn't have a sign with that name painted on it. That's just what people call it, he answered and then he said he knew I was a Little Mary when he saw my feet the day I went to his store barefoot. You have delicate feet, he told me, just like a girl. He took my tennis shoes off and started to touch my toes.

I asked him to stop 'cause it tickled and then he grabbed my hand and put it on his crotch, saying I have a big one, you want to see it? No, I said, let me go!

He cut three ripe plantains from a bunch on the floor and said here you are, tell your Mami it's a gift from me, tell her to have you come see me Sunday mornings for more stuff. You can leave now but make sure you come back next Sunday, when the store is closed. Just knock on the window, okay?

I told him no 'cause I go to Mass Sunday mornings. Then he asked me to drop by afterwards and said I shouldn't be going to church anyway 'cause Fidel doesn't believe in God. I told him that Mami would be sad if I didn't go with her, and he said she'd be even sadder if she knew I'd touched a man down there. Your father would kill you, he said, so you'd better keep quiet about this, Camilito. Not a word! I'll protect you, and I'll get you some chewing gum from the North but only if you come back.

Papi thinks Eduardo's a good man 'cause he lets us buy food under the counter. They smoke cigars on our porch sometimes, and Mami makes coffee for them. She says Eduardo needs a wife, he must be lonely, but Eduardo told me that he likes boys better than women, and boys can't get married so he'll spend his life alone. I don't care if he does 'cause he's not a good man at all. I hate him more than I hate Mayda and Quique and Juan, more than I hate darkness and bad dreams.

This whole mess happened 'cause Juan and Quique attacked me in front of Eduardo's store. It's really all their fault! They live in the huts by the hospital, I should feel bad for them but I don't. They're always hurting the other kids and causing trouble like they did one Sunday, when a bunch of religious people came to our barrio knocking on doors. The people were all dressed in white, and Juan and Quique started pulling at their clothes and calling them Freaks and kicking them. I felt sad for them. Mami said they were just spreading God's word, and even if we don't believe in their religion, 'cause it isn't Catholic, we should welcome them. But instead they were chased away by those two monsters!

Juan and Quique are jealous of me, says Mami, 'cause I live in a chalet and I have a room with a big bed, and the Three Kings bring me lots of toys each year in January. Oh and we take trips to Varadero Beach every summer. And those boys have nothing, they sleep on a dirt floor and eat yams every day. But that's no reason to do terrible things!

I don't have any homework this weekend. Thank you, Señor Raúl! That's my teacher, he's fat and bald and nicer than the teacher we had before, Señora Gil, who was ugly and had a loud, scary voice. I tried to look out the window whenever she talked, wishing I were outside, not cooped up in that classroom with the witch from *Snow White*. Sometimes I'd try to hide my head in my desk when she taught us her lessons, 'cause our desks open up so we can keep stuff inside, but I couldn't. There's no room in there for my big head! I guess Señora Gil just got tired of being a teacher so she retired. That's what people do when they get old, they retire and live a little while longer and then they die.

I like Señor Raúl but not when he gives us dictations about dates and science stuff, 'cause my hand starts to hurt. It's better when he tells us stories from history, like the one about the Cuban Indians called Tainos and about Hatuey, the brave Indian chief who fought the Spaniards. Those terrible Spanish people forced the Tainos to work like animals, and when the Indians complained, the Spaniards cut off their hands! One day they captured Hatuey, tied him to a stake, threw kindling at his feet, and made a fire with his flesh. I can't believe they did that to him just 'cause he wanted to be free!

Señor Raúl told us that now we enjoy freedom in Cuba, and we should think about how good we have it. But Papi says that my teacher's a liar, he should tell us the truth, that Fidel has robbed us of our freedom, and soon he'll take away our lives just like the Spaniards took Hatuey's. Papi says we have to get the hell out of Cuba before the revolution ties us to a stake and makes a fire with our flesh.

My teacher crosses his legs like a woman, that's what Papi thinks. He noticed it last weekend when we went to Señor Raúl's house 'cause his father had died. There was a wake, and all of us students were asked to pay our respects. That's what you do when someone dies, you pay your respects to the family, says Mami. So my parents took me there.

Señor Raúl's house is on Calle Libertad, the main street in our town. The house is small but full of nice stuff like pictures of palm trees and beaches on the walls and also a painting of a mermaid in the living room. I wonder if my teacher painted it, probably so 'cause he's a good artist, he always draws things on the board that look perfect to me. His mermaid had a pretty face with lips as red as Mami's and a long green tail. She was sitting on the sand at the beach combing her black hair with a sea shell. I wish I could paint like that.

Señor Raúl's father was in a big box in the bedroom. The corpse is what a dead person's called, and the box is a coffin. I didn't want to go near him but Papi forced me to 'cause all the other kids were doing it, even the girls. I just shut my eyes when I got close to the coffin and didn't see a thing. I was still scared the whole time, though, afraid not just of the corpse but of the crazy people in that house. All the women and Señor Raúl were crying real loud, and some of the women were screaming and asking God why He'd taken such a good man away from them. Oh, God, why why why?!! Señor Raúl's mother and his wife and a bunch of old ladies were making me feel like I'd gone to Hell or like I'd been thrown into a scary movie with monsters yelling and witches shrieking as they cooked up their evil brew in a huge cauldron. Why why why?! Oh, God, why?!

No one's ever died in my family, and I know I'd be very sad if someone did. I'd cry a lot for hours and wouldn't want to go to school or eat or take a shower or get out of bed in the morning. But I just hope that when a person I love dies, I won't start screaming, and that Mami won't act like a witch either or ask God questions He can't answer. No, in my house we will cry quietly!

When we were back at home, Papi made fun of my teacher for the way he blew his nose with those delicate hands, just like a Little Mary. But I didn't understand how Señor Raúl can be a Little Mary if he has a wife, and Papi said that having a wife doesn't mean shit. He told me about a man he knew who was married with three children but was sick just like Raúl, and one day his wife found him with a negro in their house and there was a big scandal about that. I wanted to know what the man and the negro were doing, and Papi said he wanted to punch me for being so stupid.

Now Papi wants to find another school for me, but there's no other school nearby. I'd better shape up, he says, and act like a man or he'll make me stay home all the time. Papi says he's noticed that I've started to copy Raúl's sick manners, moving my hands like a girl and crossing my legs when I sit at the dinner table. If I turn into a Little Mary it'll be my teacher's fault, Papi's sure, but he'll kill me before that happens. He's wrong, anyway. I'm not turning into a anything, I just act the way I do 'cause it feels good. And I'm not sick just 'cause I'm friends with Roli, the boy who sits in front of me in class. I like the way he laughs when I blow air on the back of his neck, and he says the air is hot like boiling bean soup. But I'm not copying him either, though Roli does sound like a girl sometimes.

Señor Raúl wants us to write a composition about anything we want. It's a free topic so I'll start by saying that I live with my parents in Las Tinajas, a city in the province of Camagüey, on an island called Cuba. The name Las Tinajas comes from our earthen jars. We have the most famous earthen jars in the whole country! There are two in our garden. Mami keeps water in them like you're supposed to, so the evil spirits stay away from our house. Señor Raúl hasn't told us where the name Cuba comes from, maybe he doesn't know but he says that our island is shaped like a cayman, and Camagüey lives in its belly, so we're in the guts of the beast. But living in there means you've been eaten up! Wouldn't that hurt a lot? I'd rather imagine myself on top of Pico Turquino, not in some cayman's belly!

Then I'll write about all my different names. I have lots. My mother calls me Lito, and my grandmother says I look more like a Milo so that's what she calls me, Milo. At school I'm Camilito, but my friend Roli makes it shorter and says Cami. And Señor Raúl uses our last names but when he calls me Señor Macías it sounds like he's calling my father. I wish he wouldn't do that!

My grandmother says she's glad that my parents named me Camilo, although they didn't know at the time that it was the name of a hero, Camilo Cienfuegos, a man who helped Fidel with his revolution and then died for our country. Abuela says I should honor that name and act like a revolutionary, and Papi gets mad when Abuela talks that way. He says he wants to punch that bitch and make her eat her Marxist shit. I don't like it when they fight 'cause Mami gets sad and sometimes she cries.

For my next topic I'll write about Christmas, about the yummy desserts like nougat and *buñuelos* that we eat at *Navidad*. The nougat comes from Spain but we buy it on the black market. The black market isn't a place painted black, no, it's just some people who sell food in secret, and if Fidel catches them he'll throw them in jail. Fidel doesn't want us to eat too much, and he hates parties.

In January after the day when the Three Kings visit us, we get our pig for the next Christmas. We feed it leftovers all year, then Eduardo kills it for us in December. Eduardo knows all about killing pigs and helps Mami cook the animal in a big pot. They make *masitas*, balls of pork that are crispy outside and soft inside and so hot they can burn your tongue. I love pork but I hate it when the pig gets stabbed and blood squirts out from its heart. The other kids drink that blood in big gulps 'cause they say it makes you strong like a macho man but I know if I did that, I'd throw up.

I told Señor Raúl I wanted to write a composition about my friend Roli and he said no, we can't write about our classmates. I guess I'll just think about my friend instead. A lot of the time Roli's sad. I wonder if that's 'cause his parents are peasants and very poor. But he also moves his hands in a funny way and sounds like a girl when he talks, and everyone at school makes fun of him for that. They make fun of me too 'cause Roli and I are friends. The other day a boy was pulling Roli's hair and saying he had duck shit on his head. The boy meant that my friend was a duck, that's what people call boys who act like girls. Ducks. I was so mad at that kid I punched him, then Señor Raúl had me sit in the corner with a donkey hat on my head. I hope Papi and Mami don't find out about that!

Later Roli thanked me for defending him, and I spoke to him like one of the heroes on the radio shows that Mami listens to. Like Zorro, who dresses all in black with a cape and helps the poor people. It was my duty to defend you, I said to Roli, and he started laughing. It felt good to see him laugh.

I'm glad that Señor Raúl is nice to my friend. He says that Roli has the best handwriting in our class. And it's true! Not just the best but also the prettiest. His a's are round like fat frogs, his e's are dancing girls and his t's look like umbrellas, and he can put his words in a straight line even if the paper has no lines. One morning Roli started to write the date in his notebook but he stopped to go sharpen his pencil. There were other kids at the pencil sharpener, which is hooked to the wall next to the blackboard, so he had to wait, and this gave me time to finish off the date for him. I tried to make the words round and pretty, day, month, year. I did it all fast but careful, and I felt proud of myself. But then when Roli saw what I'd done, he looked really mad. He gave me this look like I'd hurt him real bad, and he erased everything! I was sad and worried he wouldn't want to be my friend anymore. But when lunchtime came around, he pretended that nothing had happened.

We always have lunch together. I give Roli half of whatever I bring, like cheese sandwiches and *croquetas* and Serrano ham that Papi gets from Spain, lots of fruit like mango, guava, and my favorite, mamey. And for dessert I get *raspadura* bars which are made from sugar cane juice. But Roli always brings the same boring food, boiled yam and corn meal. After lunch we walk around the school patio telling each other stories. He talks a lot about what he wants to do when he grows up, like drive a car, and I tell him about my backyard which has trees and chickens and a fat pig and places to hide. No dogs though 'cause Papi says that dogs can get rabies which makes them go crazy wanting to bite everybody, even their owners. And if they bite you then you'll need a whole bunch of shots in your tummy.

I wish I could have Roli visit my house. He's curious about it, but I won't invite him over 'cause Papi would be mean to him for acting like a girl. Roli asked me today if the dirt in my backyard is red or black. I said we have both kinds and he said they must be tasty. I thought he was joking. What do you mean, tasty? I asked him, and Roli grabbed a handful of dirt from the ground and put it in his mouth. No, Roli, I said, dirt could make you sick! Then he told me not to worry, look, I'm spitting it all out. I wondered what it tasted like and he said just like chocolate. See for yourself, here, try some. No, I said, dirt is gross! And he finally stopped. But maybe Roli's hungry all the time 'cause food is getting hard to find lately, and his parents are too poor to buy stuff in the black market. That's why he digs into the ground and pretends he's dishing up a bowl of creamy pudding!

Papi says we're all poor now. That means you have to wait in line for your ration. I've waited in line a couple of times at El Kiosko and hated it 'cause people push you and sweat all over you, and you end up smelling like a wet dog. Women have to be magicians in the kitchen now, says Mami, they have to cook stuff that didn't exist before, like the rice she makes from soup noodles. She cuts the dry noodles into tiny pieces and puts cumin and cilantro in with them. Mami also makes meatballs from flour, pasty balls that look and taste like Play-Doh and give me heartburn. My mother isn't a good magician in the kitchen. Roli would hate her new food. I'm sure he'd rather eat dirt.

Sometimes I'd like to hug Roli but I won't. I gave him a hug at recess once and some of the boys started calling me Little Mary and saying that I'm just like him, that I like having a big red *chorizo* up my butt. That's the reason I won't hug Roli anymore. I'm afraid those boys might find out about Eduardo, so I'd better act like a normal boy, which I am anyway. Just 'cause Eduardo does things to me doesn't mean I'm not normal. I don't like it and if I did then I'd be a Little Mary, which I'm not!

There's lard in a big barrel at Eduardo's store. That's what he uses, then I have to wash myself many times so Mami doesn't smell it on me. I hate the smell of pork lard! Afterwards Eduardo gives me crackers from the jars on his counter and brings out some *cremita de leche*, a sweet I love, from the case on the shelf. I also like the glass of *guarapo* he serves me. He told me once that *guarapo* is just sugar cane juice, but I knew that! He says that sugar cane is good for a growing boy like me.

Eduardo keeps magazines on the rack by the door, many of them called *Vanidades*, and sometimes he lets me borrow them for Mami. She likes them a lot and doesn't care they're old copies. Those magazines are boring but they have pictures of women with nice dresses and blonde hair just like the ones in American movies. I've never seen perfect bodies like theirs in Las Tinajas. Eduardo looked at a magazine with me once. I asked him if he liked the pictures and that's when he told me he prefers boys. Women's bodies turn me off, he said, tits are gross. But I don't get that! Women's bodies are beautiful, especially the tits if they're big like Mami's.

There are cans up on the shelf that have labels with big letters and bright colors. Eduardo says those cans are empty, just for display, see? There's nothing in them. But the barrel in the corner by the scales where he weighs the vegetables and rice and flour, that barrel is full to the top. I wish the stuff in it tasted as good as it looks, white and creamy like flan, but it's just lard for frying and for doing nasty things. I hate the way it feels when it melts on my skin. Burning hot like a fever.

SWEET DREAMS

Some famous writers paraded through the department during my time there. They would stay for one quarter to teach a graduate seminar, in most cases an informal get-together where they'd talk about their accomplishments and barely touch on the subject to be taught. "It's an excellent way for our students to get exposed to a variety of voices and ideas," said our Chair, and for us grads this meant a welcome break from the regular faculty. Most of those writers deserved an anecdotal entry in my diary but only one visitor, the Spanish playwright Alonso Sánchez, got one. And that's because he seemed the most interesting to me, although there was another more compelling reason, of course.

It was hard to believe that Don Alonso could grace us with his wisdom, since he was an admirer of the Cuban Revolution (and one of Alina's idols) who was repeatedly incarcerated during Franco's regime for his leftist beliefs. Red alert! A communist in Alton! Sure, why not, this was academia. Yet except for Sofía, our profs were essentially a conservative bunch and must've been anxious about a living, breathing Marxist spreading the Soviet gospel in their midst. Indeed, all of us graduate students were briefed by Dr. Beym, our Peninsularist, who told us that Señor Sánchez had been invited to impart his knowledge about Spanish theater. But at the first symptom of Marxian flu, the playwright would be out the door. Such was the agreement, which the writer honored most of the time.

Alonso Sánchez had written skillfully layered dramas about social injustice, war crimes, oppressive institutions, and existential woes. His best—or at least best known—piece was *Soldados de humo* (*Smoke Soldiers*), a play about Republican soldiers in the Spanish Civil War who went on fighting the Fascists and waiting for a sure death, unaware that they'd already died. There was in-depth character development in this work, some relevant historical background, and an amazing revelation at the end. Good stuff. As the culmination of his visit, Don Alonso decided to put on a dramatic reading of his *Smoke Soldiers* for our department, a mise-en-scène directed by the playwright himself. And the small Humanities theater was the perfect venue for an inspired show, a feat when you considered that the actors, all men, had been recruited from Alonso's graduate seminar. A rather machista cast, they were the main reason I chose not to play a part. Endless hours rehearsing with those "boys"? Forget it! And poor Alina; she was disappointed that there were no roles for her.

I took Mami to see the play. (I'd try to give her a break from Papi on occasion, taking her to the movies or out to eat.) And she said she enjoyed the show, even the confusing scenes about life-in-death. Mechy looked hot in a tailored black dress with a bolero jacket and pumps, her hair in a chignon. Dr. Oropeza gave me a knowing macho glance, assuming she was my date. They all seemed to assume this, in fact, judging from their reaction when I revealed my date's identity during intermission, introducing this gorgeous woman by my side as my mother. *Oh! Wow!* Mechy felt like a star...

One day, as Alina and I walked with Don Alonso to his office after his seminar, she mentioned to him that I'd written a novel, and the bearded, stocky Señor Sánchez asked me for a copy. I was ecstatic; this would be the only feedback I'd have so far on *Cuba in Silence*, other than Alina's, and from an eminent writer! I told him that I had a first draft but hadn't polished it, and that I'd written the book in English. He said that surely the manuscript would be complete enough for him to assess its worth (why that word?!), even though he wasn't as proficient in English as he'd like to be. I rushed home and worked on *Cuba in Silence* the rest of that day and through the night. At the crack of dawn I forced myself to stop. I printed a copy and later that morning I put it in Don Alonso's department mailbox. I was blown away when two days later the playwright told me he was ready to discuss my novel. We talked in his office; actually he talked and I listened, my mind reeling with *italics*...

"You have some excellent ideas in your book," he said in thick Castilian Spanish. "I like the epigraph. What a great poet, José Martí! Regrettably there is too little of him in the novel. (*Here we go.*) If you're going to cite one of Martí's poems, then he needs to be featured more prominently throughout. (*But he is! See the last chapter!*) And the title, though I like it, could be read as an allusion to censorship. (*So?*) I'm sure many of your compatriots in Miami would interpret it that way, saying that Cuba is silent because its people are not allowed to speak their minds. (*But isn't that the case?*) The story is entertaining for the most part. It's important to entertain your readers, or the audience in my case. (*I know. You've told us ad nauseam in class.*) As Brecht said, without a good story there's no theatre. (*Got it!*) And you've captured the essence of a Cuban childhood convincingly; based on your own experiences, I assume? (*No, maybe, some. It's fiction!*) The voice of the child in the early chapters is endearing, if a bit monotonous. It is difficult to capture the language of childhood, a challenge to sustain that narration and render it believable through an entire book. Your compatriot Reinaldo Arenas does a great job of it in *Celestino Before Dawn*, I think. (*Sorry, I've only read Arenas' other book.*) I've never attempted it myself. You accomplish this rendering in a realist manner. Lamentably, when you delve into the boy's dreams toward the end, the images become much too surreal. (*Yeah, right, Don Alonso's into realism. Yet the characters in his best play are all dead! How realist is that?*) You seem to lose track of the story in those passages. (*But the boy's dreams are a major part of his story!*)

"By the way, it's unfortunate that you chose to write the book in English; all the richness of Cuban colloquial Spanish gets lost in translation. (*But I didn't "translate" anything!*) You might consider rewriting the novel in Spanish, and think about your readers. Who are you telling the story to? (*Good question. Myself?*) Absolutely not to Cubans in Cuba! Oh, I am very fond of your compatriots, Camilo. I've always supported your people (*"my" people?*), their struggle, their social ventures. (*I know. Now give me some dirt on Fidel, the inside scoop if you please.*) And I love their sense of humor!

"There is one last thought I'd like to articulate; two thoughts, in point of fact, both about your main character... (*Yes?*) First, I wonder if the novel would be diminished in any way if you omitted the boy's violation and all allusions to it. (*Why would I want to do that?*) I believe the book would gain from this deletion. (*Gain what?*) You see, Camilo, that passage takes the story to a place where many readers won't choose to go with you. (*Why should I care about those readers?*) And it makes a sad and problematic kind of statement—sending the wrong message, too—about revolutionary Cuba. (*Oh, yes, of course, this sort of thing didn't happen in revolutionary Cuba.*) Just think about it, my friend. As for my other comment, we assume that your character will come to the States with his family, correct? If you ever depict him as an adult in a follow-up novel, give him a bridge back to Cuba. (*Why would he want to go back?*) And give him praxis! (*How do I do that?!*) Finally, give the character a different name; unless you want your work to be read as an autobiography, which it isn't, right? (*Actually...*) Like I said, you have some fine writing in this book, Camilo. Thank you for letting me read it."

He seemed to be done, so I thanked him profusely and asked him, "Should I have it published, Don Alonso?" He glanced at me distractedly. "Oh, no," he said. "Don't rush into it. Write more and be selective, even ruthless with your writing. Pick the best of the best and never rush."

It was sound advice that I wish I'd always followed. There was no way I could rush that project, anyway. My fiction just wasn't a priority for me at the time. I'd have to put the novel and Don Alonso's comments on a back burner for now, since I was expected to finish my dissertation and defend it by the June deadline. I had taken a job in Overland City, Kansas, already, pressured by Sofía to get a jump-start on my career. It just so happened that Overland City University was a research institution, or it aspired to be. The Spanish division of the Foreign Languages Department had a couple of respected scholars. I'd be able to teach literature and some theory, although they had no PhD program and no teaching assistants. A big chunk of the workload was language. Sofía said I should be proud for succeeding that quickly in my search without having to go to the MLA "Meat Market" for a long, exhausting series of interviews. The job didn't pay great, not compared to what Alina made at her college. But it tripled the salary I got as a TA, more than I needed to live like a professor in Kansas.

What would I miss about Alton? Definitely not the Muir corporation, its force field and dystopian towers with all those aliens locked inside. But I'd miss the funky movie house on Balboa Island where I discovered Woody Allen, Carlos Saura, and Almodóvar; and where I had the pleasure of witnessing the *Rocky Horror Picture Show*, a fun musical with a gender-bending story that got the audience roaring—many of its members masterfully dressed up as characters in the movie.

I would miss Sofía. I was sure we'd stay in touch professionally (we did, for a while), run into each other at conferences (didn't happen) and maybe coauthor some article (never did). I'd miss my parties and the songs that told our story, "Breaking Away From Sanity," "I Feel Love," "Come In From the Rain," "Singing Cicada," "Antonio's Song," "A los amigos," "Hier Encore," "Tainted Love," "Sweet Dreams (Are Made of This)." I'd miss my Alton niche and its main dwellers, Alina, Castel, Tano, Carl, and Laurie. My girlfriend was handling the news of my departure like a sage. "I understand, Babe," she said when the topic first came up. "You have your career, and I still have some growing up to do." She kissed me and added, "I'll miss you," to which I replied, "Ditto." I fantasized about taking Laurie with me. In some implausible variation of this fantasy I'd even ask her to marry me, thinking that I'd be needing a little wife to soothe the stress of my new job. Fortunately, wisely, Laurie would answer No in this daydream, as surely she would have in reality. *Sorry, Babe. I'm too young for marriage.*

Tano wanted one last blast at the Big Bang. "We could cruise or just *ballare un po*," he said. But no, I was done with that place, ready to pack up and move. And so was Tano, for that matter. He had his MA finally and had become obsessed with the idea of splitting, of taking Miss Lite Rature to some other Tea Room, far from that populated desert called Alton. The flying colors of his academic stardom were whirling around him already, remaking him into Professor Ricci, an acclaimed specialist in early twentieth-century gay literature from Argentina. "I'm out of here, mignon!" he told me before our last goodbye. "I'm applying to ten doctoral programs at least, shooting for Harvard or Yale."

"You'll get into both places," I assured him.

"You really think so, perroquet?"

"Yes, I have no doubt."

"Thank you! That's encouraging. I'd better get going with my sex change ASAP."

"Your sex change?!"

"Yes, Camilo, it's the only way to achieve stardom in our profession. Haven't you noticed? Women are landing the best jobs and publication deals. It's time for the broads!"

"You're full of shit."

"Just look at Dr. Varela, how famous she's gotten."

"Deservedly so!"

"Oh, *per piacere*. Sofía Varela is such a hypocrite! I don't believe a word she says. She goes around making leftist proclamations about the 'indigenous plight' and the 'patriarchal episteme' and 'women's subversive discourses,' stuff that has nothing to do with her own bourgeois life."

"You're wrong about Sofía, totally wrong."

"She's a prima donna, Camilo. And she knows how to play the victim card to her advantage. If Sofía doesn't get what she wants, it's because she's a brilliant woman working with conniving bastards who don't want her to succeed. So there she goes crying, *Machismo! Chauvinismo!*"

"Listen here, you pitiful faggot..."

"*Moi*? Pitiful? Never pitiful, mignon!"

"Sofía is the life of our department. Without her that place would have no teacher-training program, no useful graduate advising, no literary theory, no nothing!"

"She is a good teacher, I'll grant you that."

"The best one. And she's a great model for us grads to emulate."

"Fine. But she's also an old-school Argentine lady with homophobic tendencies, a damsel disguised as a feminist, and with a face like melting putty because of all the surgery she's had."

"I hadn't noticed..."

"Of course not! We don't normally see the imperfections of our idols. But it's very obvious to me. Oh, yes, Dr. Varela has tried in vain—so in vain!—to alter her features and disguise the fact that she's an Indian from Jujuy. I'm quite familiar with her type, believe you me!"

"Wow. I didn't know you hated her that much. Did you get a 'B' in one of her classes?"

"As a matter of fact I did, in her Theory of the Novel seminar, which she talked me into taking. In my final paper I didn't include any of that crap she likes to throw around, you know, all that dialectical materialism and her problematic heroes. Bitch!"

"So that's it. You hate her guts because you didn't make an 'A' in her theory class."

"No, I hate her guts because she's an armchair Marxist who lives like a fucking queen and deep down scorns the proletariat."

"You don't know that!"

"Have her live in Cuba for a year and see what happens to her socialist delusions."

"And yet you want to be like her..."

"No, not like her. I'll be the real deal, my dear."

"Whatever that means."

"If you want to make it as a writer, turn yourself into a woman, Camilo. *Andá, che!*"

"Yeah, a new academic breed, the Transgender Opportunists. No, thanks."

"Wouldn't you be willing to give up your balls to gain immortality?"

"No, Tano, I wouldn't. Besides, academia is still ruled by the old boys."

"No, no, that was before! Now we have Affirmative Action. And since I can't qualify as a person of color—*ay*, look at my skin; it's whiter than sugar!—I'll have no other choice but to change my gender, or at least reinvent myself with a good drag."

"If anyone can pull it off..."

"Wait and see, perroquet. And don't be shocked if you open your door one day to find a stunning and transformed Pablo Ricci, not an ill-fated courtesan like Violetta but an empowered broad like Evita Perón. *Mais oui*, that divine dame richly clad in Dior will be a star of the academic firmament, quoted in prestigious journals, not *abbandonata* but adored by a multitude of students, envied and admired by her colleagues for her feminine beauty as much as for her intellect."

"Your destiny awaits you, Tano."

"And I shall meet it head on!"

"Without a hard-on."

"*Ay*, you and your boner obsession!"

"I wish you luck, Professor Ricci."

"Will you miss me, Camilo?" Suddenly he was all sweetness, Mademoiselle Dufour on her swing. "Will you miss your *caro amico*?"

"Let's not get sentimental, Pablito."

"Heaven forbid!"

By then we were already committing to memory our Grad Bohème. No more parties, no more Marcuse while we listened to Teresa Stratas in *La Traviata*. Califusa was our limbo, and the future lived elsewhere. When the day came to say *ciao, amore, ciao*, I wasn't honest enough to tell Ricci, "Yes, *caro amico*, I will miss you. And I'm grateful to you for busting the stupid ideas that clutter my heart in spite of all the brilliant stuff I've read and quoted." Instead I smiled and pretended that parting was such sweet sorrow. And I wrote a poem that I'd never get to show him...

When night returns wearing its wanderer's mask, you awaken. Your true, innate inversions are born then. And thus we hear your brothel tangos, your arias and fin-de-siècle torch songs. Music to our ears. When night falls the curtain goes up. Time for stardom! The Bella Porteña descends then, giving and willing. Nothing is said. Everything's felt. And Love appears.

There would be phone calls, letters, and one reunion at a conference. But in time we'd drift apart, as we both knew was meant to happen. Tano would make himself felt and heard in my life from a distance, as a voice, an unshakable memory. No doubt Professor Ricci would manage to find or found a cozy, well-stocked Tea Room in the Ivy League. And I'd always wonder what might've happened that one night at the Big Bang, had I accepted the offer he made me...

Castel's "offer," in contrast, was one I welcomed with no hesitation. What a great farewell present he gave me! Tickets to *La Cage Aux Folles*, the L.A. production of Jerry Herman's musical based on the popular French-Italian film, with book by Harvey Fierstein (who penned *Torch Song Trilogy*, a reportedly great show I hadn't seen). And if that weren't fantastic enough, *La Cage* was showing at an historic venue, the regal, art-deco Pantages Theater on Hollywood Boulevard.

"But why would you want to see a show about drag queens?" I asked Castel. "You hate them!"

"That's true, but..."

"You know, don't you, that the main character in *La Cage* is a faggot named Albin who makes a living dressed as a woman, all makeup and wig and feathers and a huge diva complex."

"Yes, but Albin-Zaza isn't your run-of-the-mill drag queen. Oh no no, we're talking about a Jerry Herman creation—or 'recreation,' if you will. Jerry can take the most pathetic stereotype and turn it into something beautiful, alluring, and inspired. I'm sure we're going to love his *folles!*"

We met at his place in Hollywood and hung there for a while. The plan was to walk to the Pantages (a long walk, as it turned out) and grab something to eat near the theater. To get psyched for *La Cage*, we listened to Castel's LP collection of Herman's music on his high-end compact stereo, the only "extravagance" he'd allowed himself. He played *Mame* first, both the Broadway play with Angela Lansbury and the Lucille Ball movie, then the shows Castel had never seen but which he'd staged in his mind and heart, *Hello, Dolly; Dear World; Mack and Mabel; The Grand Tour*.

After our Jerry feast we ended up dining Chinese at a surprisingly affordable joint on Cahuenga Blvd. There Castel brought me up to date. He was working at an employment agency, taking some literature classes at UCLA with no degree in mind, just to stay sane. He'd surrounded himself with Angeleno artistes, mostly struggling actors, hairdressers who dreamed of breaking into show biz, and papier-mâché sculptors who made floats for the Rose Parade. They all spent wild weekends in Tijuana, on Castel's imaginary Rue de Fleurus, where sometimes a rose was just a rose. He still wanted to move to Mexico City—soon, he hoped. That mega-city, also known as *el D.F.*, was larger than life and polluted, but Castel loved it. And that's where his mother was from, a compelling reason for the journey. I told him I'd visit him in Mexico, maybe attend a conference while there. He cracked a fortune cookie and had me read his fortune: *You will marry your present lover.*

"Would you ever..." he said shyly, "marry me, Camilo?"

"Sure, Castel. But I'm not your present lover."

"We could be very happy together, you know."

"Maybe. But lovers are supposed to have sex."

"We love each other, Camilo. That counts. Everything else should be secondary."

"Sex...secondary?"

"Okay," he laughed. "We'll break our own rules. Incest is best!"

"Gertrude and Alice were like sisters, right?"

"Yeah, and they got it on. Nothing platonic about those Jewish babes."

"Then let's do it, Castel. Let's get married today!" I was laughing too.

"I accept! We'll have our honeymoon in Tenochtitlán!"

I didn't show him the fortune in my cookie, implausibly on cue: *A new love awaits you...*

While we walked to the theater I told Castel again how grateful I was to him for getting us tickets to *La Cage*, but I was also honest in saying that I'd never been much into musicals, that I'd always found them silly—characters breaking into song in scenes that were presented as true to life.

"But you're into fantasies, aren't you?" he asked.

"Big time."

"You'd have to be, as a Puig scholar."

"Well...as someone who loves Puig's novels, yes."

"I've never read a book as steeped in fantasy as *Kiss of the Spider Woman*," he admitted. "Such a great novel! It turned me on and made me cry and gave me so much food for thought."

"In Manuel's name I thank you, Castel, even though it took you forever to read it."

"Then, think of the songs in a musical as fantasies, what the characters are feeling or dreaming about. Fantasies set to music..."

"Sure, I can dig that."

"It's all part of the magic, Camilo, when you surrender to the beauty of the melody, the story that the lyrics tell, the dancing, and forget quote-unquote reality. Suspension of disbelief, isn't that what it's called? Of course it isn't 'true to life.' It's a damn show! At any rate, who hasn't wanted to belt out a tune in the midst of some memorable situation?"

"I never have."

"Oh, you're such a bore!"

"Yeah, but you love me all the same."

They were both culture, said Castel, musical theater and literature. But they were also two kinds of text, one that knew itself as a popular construct and one that assumed itself as art. He favored both and found pleasure in each, depending on the mood, the place, and the form his angst might take at a given moment; depending on his need for a certain type of flight.

Eager to humor Castel, I told myself that tonight I needed the magic of the construct. I'd let myself be seduced by *La Cage Aux Folles* without problematizing it—something I wouldn't do with opera, which I hated and would never develop a taste for. (Sorry, Tano.) And seduced I was! We were elated after experiencing Herman's tour de force, gaily traipsing down the boulevard, pretending he was Albin and I was Georges after some negotiating...

"You be the drag queen, Camilo."

"No, Castel, I couldn't do her justice. You should be Albin. Keep in mind that you'd be performing as the fabulous Zaza, a character that Jerry loves."

"You're right, and that would be an honor. What the heck. Zaza I am!"

I had seen the *La Cage* movie and enjoyed it, but the theatrical version was so much more exciting—all those great songs! "In a way," I said to Castel, "this play is the realization of Molina's dream in *Kiss of the Spider Woman*, to have a normal family where he's a happily married wife."

"What?!" Castel reacted, cracking up. "Molina with a sexy stepson?"

"Well... maybe not."

"You know what," he said then, "I feel like singing."

"Go ahead. This situation definitely qualifies as memorable!"

And now Castel fully turned into Zaza in the limelight, as he belted out a hymn of self-affirmation beautifully, the best song from *La Cage*, in my opinion, "I Am What I Am." I'd never seen him so unchained, so much in character, turning a winning performance and yet wholeheartedly himself. Oblivious to the tourist onlookers, to the Hollywood crowds that ignored him, to the traffic and the neon and the hustlers, he sang his heart out.

"Bravo! You missed your calling," I said, giving him an ovation. "You're meant for Broadway!"

"Oh, no," he retorted. "I couldn't put up with all those theater bitches."

"How about if you just sing for me now and then?"

"You got it!"

Unlike Tano, Castel wasn't about to vanish from my life; whereas I'd never see any of my professors again, or Carl, or Laurie. Not even Sofía, though her web has always spread wide.

Alina and Isabel had completed all their graduate course work and were now ABDs: all but dissertation. They were both working at Alton City College by the time I got ready to leave for Kansas, Isabel as a full-time lecturer, Alina now promoted to tenure-track professor.

"Let's not call it a farewell, please," said Isabel when she invited Alina and me over for a "graduation lunch" at her house. She lived in Alton, in a tract home painstakingly decorated by Isabel herself. The living room décor looked motley yet seemed to work somehow: a trestle table, Mission-style chairs, a three-mirror room divider, a corner curio cabinet full of porcelain dolls; and a bonsai tree in a corner, below a Botero lithograph—the latter no doubt in honor of Isabel's Colombian roots. We sat in the breakfast nook with a view of the garden, an explosion of flowers like a bright watercolor. There we consumed the lunch of cold cuts, croissants, aged Manchego cheese, and fresh fruit that our hostess had prepared. Then Isabel unveiled a surprise for us, an article about her that had appeared in a local paper. The piece featured a glamour photo of Mrs. Rosas-Clark and described this superwoman who wrote poetry, raised three children, ran a home, got a PhD, and taught Spanish at Alton City College.

Alina and I were impressed; we wondered how the hell Isabel could do it all. Did she ever sleep?! Alina was barely able to get her act together most of the time, she admitted. And I had no dependents, no one to tend to but myself, yet I'd always struggled to do all the required reading and teach my classes. But of course Isabel hadn't idled away the hours partying, or writing a novel: one of the projects that ate up my hours that last year in Alton. I was determined to get *Cuba in Silence* ready for publication before I got to Kansas, and Alina was a big help—all those drafts I put her through, her insightful editing. I dedicated the novel to her, proud to use the nickname I'd given my friend, *To the Cicada, for her wings*, because that story was a place she'd often visited with me, sometimes leading me by the hand, others shoving me like a mischievous playmate. I couldn't have relived my childhood without her.

I was also fortunate to have Sofía on my side. She supported my creative writing when all the other profs accused me of neglecting my "academic duties." My mentor not only read the manuscript and gave me useful pointers, but she encouraged me to indulge my artistic impulse, as long as I could fulfill my scholarly obligations. "I don't see any reason why one can't be both a scholar and a novelist," she told me. "Both endeavors take research and writing and creativity. And it's all part of the same process." I asked her why she hadn't written any fiction, and she replied, grinning, "What makes you think I haven't?" We said *adiós* with a hug and some tears. She wished me luck, said she was sure that a brilliant career was in store for me. And I heard an artist's echo in her wishes, *Camilo will go far...*

II
Over the Rainbow

THE SCARECROWS OF OZ

It was the right decision to leave most of my junk behind when I moved to Kansas. I donated the greater part of it to Goodwill, shipped off my sound system and some of my books, and stored half of my five hundred-plus LPs in my parents' garage—not without Elio's protest. I stayed in a motel near the university while I scoured the city paper and the *Faculty Bulletin* for an apartment. The search took all of one day, at the end of which I found a two-story wood-frame in College Hill, an old Overland City neighborhood. I couldn't believe the rent was so low for such a large townhouse: two bedrooms, living room, dining room, breakfast nook, indoor garage, and a basement to hide from tornadoes. Had to do some serious shopping to furnish the place. The landlady was a bubbly widow in her late forties who tended to wear loose-fitting flowered dresses and wanted to be called Charlene, not Mrs. Torline. She worked part-time for the school district, she told me, and brought in a little extra cash with the shell necklaces and earrings she made. Though born and raised in Topeka, Charlene didn't fit the Bible Belt stereotype I was expecting to find in Kansas. She was liberal and forward-thinking (judging from her comments), and I felt grateful for that. But there were plenty of other stereotypical people in Overland City!

In time I learned that many Kansans were into tradition, wanting change yet seeming to be paralyzed by fear of it. They were ashamed of the shame they felt towards their provinciality, trapped as they were in their "heartland." Kansans could be cordial but also bigoted. There were things that bugged me living among them, like the stares I got everywhere I went. People assumed I didn't speak English after just one glance, and my slight accent always threw them off. *What was that? What did you say?* And driving in that city was a hassle; getting pulled over by the cops in my neighborhood got to be quite a routine! They never gave me a ticket; no way they could justify it. But I was harassed and kept waiting while they called in to make sure I was indeed a professor at Overland City University. To them I just didn't look the part of an academic or a College Hill resident. Scarecrows from Cuba (and even worse: partly made in California) weren't welcome in Oz.

The Foreign Languages Department at OCU was like most others in this country, from what I'd heard. Everybody hated everybody, and the profs didn't give a shit about their students, only about their earth-shattering research. The place was ruled by Dr. Carlos Andrade, a short, toupeed Peruvian; and Dr. Mary Scheckler, a fifty-something woman who bragged about being the only Kansas native in the department. Those two made all decisions and vetoed any attempts by their colleagues to implement new ideas. Andrade considered himself famous— a pervasive delusion among some academics. As a Latin American fiction specialist, he boasted about his Marxist approach to the analysis of literature but lived in the most exclusive area of Overland City. (Yet another charlatan, Tano would've proclaimed.) Although he was inept and disorganized, he'd been put in charge of several committees, none of which ever got their business done right or on time. At faculty meetings Andrade came across as the parody of a Latin American dictator, prefacing everything he said with the words, *"¡Atención, gente!"* A couple of years before I joined the department, the *peruano* had divorced his wife of thirty years, who helped him become a "star," to marry an ex-student half his age. Nothing typical about him, oh no, not at all!

Scheckler had been the chair for two decades, a powerful monarch more than a chairperson. She dressed like she was always ready for a close-up: business suits in strident pastels and with huge shoulder pads, lots of makeup and big hair, gargantuan earrings. The nickname she'd been given on campus was "Crystal-Alexis," which made reference to female characters in *Dynasty*, a TV show I'd never watched. From what I gathered, Dr. Scheckler was Crystal (the good wife) in her appearance but had the fangs of conniving Alexis (the ex-wife). Her pet project was a summer program in Oaxaca that she'd been directing for ten years. It was common knowledge in the department that during the program's orientation, she'd pick the male students she wanted to fuck, then make her move as soon as they were in Mexico. So much for men having all the power! Although I didn't like Mary, I secretly admired her guts. A man doing what she did would've been the norm, but a woman, wow, that was stereotype-busting; corrupt too, sure, but I doubted many of those guys minded their objectification.

Mary acted solicitous around me, slimily so. At first I flirted back, but eventually her passes became a nuisance, so I decided to play my gay card around her, and that did the trick. The last thing I wanted was a fling with my boss, let alone with a composite character from *Dynasty*. I avoided her but made sure to thank her frequently and profusely for giving me such a great office—spacious and with a pleasant view of a lush grove of cottonwoods. Those trees gave the campus, with all those brick buildings, its foresty atmosphere and only touch of beauty. They were everywhere in the city, their light green foliage providing ample shade in the spring, turning yellow before winter's arrival, then becoming gray fixtures of the icy white landscape that was all of Kansas in the winter.

Twice during my four years at Overland City University I got to teach a course in theory of the novel for students in the MA program; heady, stimulating stuff, a chance to mix my own theoretical salad and throw in some of Sofía's ingredients in her honor. A nice break from the many language classes I taught. The latter were courses I liked, but, hell, no one in that department had ever heard of communicative methodologies! They all freaked out at a faculty meeting when I said (channeling my mentor) that in introductory language courses, the goal should be communication of a message, regardless of the errors the message may contain, and these mustn't be corrected. Grammar is to be assigned as homework and not explained in class. My colleagues didn't get it and drilled me with the usual questions, "But how can you teach language without explaining the grammar rules and doing drills, without correcting mistakes and providing conjugation charts, practice sheets, exercises?!"

In spite of my heavy teaching load, I was managing to get some writing done, poetry and articles but no fiction. The poems were pouring out in Spanish, not as concerned with Cuba anymore but rather into Eros. And it figured, since I was in love. Well, definitely in lust. Her name was Susan Thompson. She was a native Kansan and a grad student in our department. Susan was beautiful; had piercing blue eyes, short blonde hair, a swimmer's build, and she wore mostly jeans and T-shirts, none of that shoulder-pad stuff that was in vogue. Yet I didn't really notice her at first. I couldn't have imagined hooking up with Susan when I saw her sitting in my theory class, one more nondescript Anglo student like the many who peopled that university. There was nothing distinct or special about her. But then she wrote a brilliant paper for me, a Bakhtinian reading of Puig's *Heartbreak Tango* that blew me away, and that was it: I fell in love with her mind. I wanted to pick her brain, to spend hours talking with Susan. She had an innately progressive outlook on things, which added to the allure. Soon I found myself desiring her strapping body, aching to kiss her. As I'd hoped, our kissing led to sex, an act that was strangely new to me. It wasn't just the physical pleasure itself, which engaged every pore of my skin, but a joy that sprang from deep within, that seemed to pour over every second we spent together. I had no point of reference and no words to describe the experience. Even today, language fails me as I try to convey what I felt with Susan. All I could say—then as now—is that I'd never made love before.

Susan told me that her parents were conservative like many folks in Kansas, but I hadn't dealt with people like the Thompsons before. I was in for a shock when I joined them for supper one night in their huge and dark and insanely stuffed house (stacks of magazines and old papers everywhere) on the outskirts of town. Not an experience I ever wanted to repeat. Mr. David Thompson ("Dave," he wanted to be called) was a burly man in his sixties. He informed me right off that he'd amassed a fortune in the moving business. "My trucks have relocated half the Midwest," he bragged. Dave asked me where in Mexico I was from. When I told him I was Cuban, not Mexican, he said he didn't understand why the United States hadn't gotten rid of Fidel Castro already. "We certainly have the power and the will!"

Susan's Canadian-born mother, Mrs. Elizabeth Thompson, was slightly younger than her husband. She was slender, had short hair and a jarring inflection to her voice. Mrs. Thompson, who liked to go by "Liz," was a picture-perfect homemaker with a perpetual smile and the stilted manners of a royal servant. She kept asking me if I knew the meaning of most everything she said, particularly the food she was serving. "We're having meatloaf and green beans. Do you know what meatloaf is...?"

Having said grace and swiftly devoured half his meal, Dave told me I must feel lucky to have come to *his* country. "And we're lucky too," he added. "We need smart immigrants like yourself."

"I didn't choose to come here," I clarified. "My parents did."

"Makes sense to me," Mr. Thompson reacted, "they wanted the best for their son, the freedom and opportunities we enjoy. Be grateful you live here, my friend, in this country blessed by God!"

"I am grateful, but...may I ask you a question, Mr. Thompson?"

"Call me Dave!"

"Okay, *Dave*, do you really believe that God favors the U.S. for some reason?"

"But of course!" he replied at once. "How else do you explain our prosperity? The whole world wants to be like us. We set the standards."

"Yes, we're the leaders for the time being," I said. Dave pretended he hadn't heard right, but I didn't let up. "The United States," I stated, "is going down the same path as all previous superpowers, Rome, Spain, England, Germany, imperialistic entities who defined themselves in conquest and eventually dug their own graves. History repeats itself, sometimes in lurid detail."

Mr. Thompson looked shocked. "How dare you describe America that way?!" he barked and stormed out of the room like a child having a tantrum, without finishing his meatloaf.

As if this were their daily routine, unfazed, Liz tried to lighten up the mood by asking Susan to play for us—they had a stunning grand piano. "Something sweet and melodious, dear," she told her daughter. And Susan surprised me with a Mozart sonata that she played masterfully—or so it sounded to me. I managed to relax and enjoy her effortless music, yet I couldn't help thinking about her parents' political views and ethnocentrism. A lot to take on. Worth tackling? My "thing" with Susan seemed promising, definitely the sex, but I hadn't opened up to her yet and wasn't sure I ever would. Regardless, my first obligation to her was to guide her academically. Susan was too smart for OCU. It was a good deal for her; she got a regent's grant and saved on rent by living at home. But I told her she needed to get the hell out of Kansas as soon as she got her MA—and out of that house too, I thought but didn't tell her. Susan agreed. She knew there was no place like home...to hold you back and hold you down.

Susan offered me a welcome distraction (and more than that) from the bewildering process of publishing my first novel. There was nothing truly aggravating about it, just some interesting surprises, starting with the publisher that ended up taking on *Cuba in Silence*. It was Sofía who'd put me in touch with this house, Pueblo Press, and its visionary founder, Sergio Viramontes. "Consider it my graduation present to you," she'd said right before I left Alton. Sergio was in his mid-forties; he was a talkative, code-switching Chicano with a PhD in Latin American Studies from UC Riverside, and a close friend of the gifted poet Alurista. He had started out on his "crazy venture" by publishing three books a year out of his parents' garage, against all odds and driven solely by a dream. And now his catalogue boasted a crowd of luminaries but, most importantly, could serve as a venue for up-and-coming young writers. There were years when Pueblo Press struggled, but the hurdles wouldn't keep Sergio from bringing out a list of exciting titles. He'd been looking to publish the work of someone like me, he said. Sergio saw me as a new ethnic voice, that of a Cuban-born American who wrote in English from a minority perspective. He said I needed to get in there and fight for a place in the American literary canon, just like the Chicanos had. But I wasn't sure what this "fight" might entail.

My writing was "problematic in the best sense of the word," according to Sofía. She hoped that *Cuba in Silence* would create a bit of trouble for the critics. Since I'd written the book in English, it couldn't be placed in the Cuban canon with the work of Arenas and López, much less with that of the Miami exiles who wrote in verbose Cubanish about their lost paradise and the bearded monster who stole it from them. But hey, most of my poetry had been published in Spain in *cubañol*, so I must be genuinely *cubano*, right? Who cared. Call me what they would, there was nothing I could do about it!

Sooner than expected there was a positive review of my novel in *LA Weekly*, thanks to the publisher's network, but nothing in New York, and the Miami folks had had little good to say about *Cuba in Silence*. Surprise! Most of their reviews appeared in small Spanish-language papers, but there was one in English by a University of Miami prof in the *Herald*. The critic said that my appropriation of our apostle José Martí was irresponsible, and he called my narrative style "infantile" and "muddled." My book, he said, was "a juvenile attempt at breaking away from the enduring tradition of Cuban exile literature." By tradition he meant all that vanity-press stuff that was published by rabid anti-Castro émigrés, the "real" writers of our community. When compared to the impressive literary body of Cuba's first wave of immigrants, alleged this critic, my work and that of other Cuban-American writers (who else he didn't say) seemed insignificant. It would all amount to a footnote in the history books.

Sergio believed that the ethnic thrust of my work was disconcerting to the Miami Cubans. There was also the fact that my book had been published by a Chicano house and not by Editorial Sagüesera, the leading exile press in Miami. Plus I didn't buy into Miami's angst, didn't glorify Cuba's past nor curse Fidel nor paint a Locus Amoenus picture of childhood. How dared I feature a sexually ambiguous character who was raped as a child; such horrid things never happened on our beloved island! Why, everyone in our diaspora was normal and respectful of our God-given gender roles! Whatever their reasons, in time it became blatantly obvious that the *Miamachos* were bent on making me disappear.

One day I came across an academic review of *The Guayaba Pack*, an English-language anthology of Cuban-American literature that had been published by Sagüesera and in which Camilo Macías *was not included*. This didn't surprise me but I felt disappointed. Anthologies are like history books for writers, our venue for authentication. And being part of history is what interests me, more than cranking out bestsellers. That's what I want most in exchange for my effort, inclusion, posterity. But it seemed I'd have to write my way into the Cuban-American niche with another book or not at all.

The *Guayaba Pack* editors depicted their contributors as bold and groundbreaking because "they have dared to write in English." Never mind their literary worth, questionable in several cases; those people were deserving of praise simply because they *espiqui di inglich*. Why the choice of language was seen as such a big deal I didn't quite get. Of course we couldn't write in Spanish like the old timers. For many members of our transitional generation, English had become the dominant tongue; many of us lived and breathed in it. How could it be otherwise? Moreover, the patriotic passions and exile concerns of our elders were becoming less and less a part of our lives. It was a natural, inevitable process. Yes, it was wise to underline our split from the émigré sensibility and our use of English as our mode of expression. But not if this break was highlighted as our main, unifying feature and most valuable contribution. In any case, hadn't I done just that with *Cuba in Silence*? Hadn't I broken away?

All but two of the ten anthologized writers were born in Cuba and came to the United States as children, and all had grown up in Miami. Because naturally there was nothing happening outside of Little Havana, right? Who ever heard of Cuban culture (other than Desi Arnaz) thriving in California? *Splain that to me, Lucy!* Only three of the writers had published before. One of them, Dina Pérez, had managed to get herself a juicy New York book deal—deservingly so, for she was a gifted storyteller. Hence Dina was being hailed as our mainstream Cubiche Goddess. The second member of the trio, Rafael Valdés Alfaro, was a poet but primarily known as a scholar of Golden Age Spanish poetry. And Francisco M. Rodríguez, the third Cubiche, had found his way to Pueblo Press after reading my novel, so he was now a member of the PP family. Why hadn't Francisco told me or Sergio about *The Guayaba Pack*? Benefit of the doubt: Maybe he thought I'd been contacted about it. Obviously the project had been kept under wraps, since not even my publisher knew about it.

This was flat-out censorship. But what were they censoring? The openly sexual thrust of my fiction, perhaps. Or my depiction of the paterfamilias as oppressive and dictatorial. Maybe word had gotten out—all the way to Miami!—that I'd been known to hang out with Marxist academics, or that I'd corresponded with Yovani López, writer of the Revolution. Bottom line was: the *Guayaba* editors had censored my work by denying its existence. And that sucked. Ironically, those exiles were exhibiting the same totalitarian ways they'd criticized in the Castro regime. Which made a certain sense. I had come to believe that a tendency toward extreme, authoritative positions thrived in the Cuban heart; that the *cubano* character was essentially repressive and censorial, regardless of class, education, or race.

Except in my mother's case. There seem to be no judgmental or authoritative tendencies in Mechy, and I'm grateful for that. The best part of publishing my first book was sharing it with her. Mami was overjoyed when I handed her a copy of *Cuba in Silence*. We celebrated the publication with ice-cold Materva and then dinner. Mechy didn't care that my novel had been published by a minor outfit in Riverside. She didn't note the humble monochromatic cover, the flimsy binding or the font, which was bulky and graceless. What she saw was a book writ-

ten by her son, a book that told a story she'd find too close for comfort
but wouldn't reproach me for it. Because Mami felt the joy I felt. The
high. She knew it was about creating something that would outlive you.
Mami knew.

I gave her a brief summary of what the critics were saying, including my exclusion from the Cuban-American anthology. I told her that
having people react to my stuff was great sometimes and other times
ego-crushing. But ultimately it was all about the work. "Regardless of
what anyone says," she told me then, "don't give up your writing, Lito."
As always, I found solace in Mami's words, at her table, pleased to heed
her advice and partake in the feast that she served me. Mechy was and
still is a chef who won't use recipes, who concocts sumptuous meals
(fricasé, ropa vieja, picadillo, congrí, tostones, platanitos, arroz con pollo)
in a flash. The ephemeral fruit of Mami's talent, of her art.

But then Elio spoiled a perfect experience. He'd been sick lately, and
grumpier than usual; had some kind of flu but refused to go to the doctor. Barely minutes after sitting down to eat, he started getting on his
wife's case about some grocery item she'd forgotten to get. I would've
been more understanding had I known what was going on in his body.
Or maybe not; maybe not even that knowledge would've made me stop
wanting to strike him. I decided to ignore him, pretending, as I often
did, that he wasn't at the table. Papi didn't want to hear about my travails as a writer, anyway, or about my job. It was all meaningless to him,
though not incomprehensible. He understood but didn't care.

Mami did. She cared, and I wished I'd been able to vent with her
about work. I didn't want to worry her, telling her how ready I was to
flee my Midwest dungeon; how willing to risk my life swimming the
moat so I could get away from it all—my megalomaniac colleagues, the
students with their personal problems, the fucking winter, down jackets and boots and snow. I hated snow! I couldn't do my daily run in that
weather; needed to find some other form of exercise but jogging was
my therapy. I was trapped in Overland City and feeling like a blob. I had
only one means of escape, my secret refuge from tornados: two hits of
killer weed (Castel's present), and a self-indulgent plunge into Cuba in
Silence, like a dragon eating its own tail. There was relief, a sort of confirmation in reading my published novel. It was about connecting with
someone out there, about feeling immortal somehow. And it also had

to do with learning—what not to do next time, what to improve, what to keep...

CUBA IN SILENCE

Poor Roli. He got into a fight with this older kid from another class 'cause the boy was saying bad things about peasants and black people, saying that this new government had let the hicks and the niggers into places like the Hunters Club. The mean boy used to go to that club on Sundays with his parents and brothers to swim in the pool and eat at the fancy restaurant. But not anymore, he said, because of people like Roli and the scummy black kids in our school.

I asked Papi and Mami once why so many people hate blacks, and Papi told me it's because they're black. I was confused and asked him another question, why is black so bad that it makes people hate you if your skin has that color? Papi just said, don't you dare be friends with any of them! Mami didn't say anything, but later, when we were alone, she gave me an answer I could understand. She told me that people hate other people who aren't like themselves, who are different. It's just the way humans beings are. And I said, but, Mami, I don't hate Roli or the black kids at school, and they're different from me! Mami then told me that I'm different myself, because I have a good heart. But I should try to stay away from black people to avoid having problems with Papi. Some day, she said, when I'm grown up and not living in the same house with him anymore, then I can have any friends I want, friends of any color. I asked her, even friends that are poor or girly hicks like Roli? And Mami answered me yes, even those, because then you'll be free to decide for yourself if they have a good heart.

I guess I'm lucky I got to visit the Hunters Club a couple of times, though I'm not a hick or black. That place is very far, out in the country, but we got there fast in Papi's car. The club has trees and a garden and a restaurant where they make the best *croqueta* sandwiches in town, said Papi, and so that's what we ate both times. There's also a big fountain and a wobbly bridge you cross to get to a forest but I didn't want to cross it and Papi was mad at me and said I was missing out on an adventure. I thought if Roli came along I'd sure go to the other side and have adventures in the forest with him. I'd wear my Zorro cape again and be brave for my friend. But that's not going to happen. Never ever.

The mean boy was saying that now the Hunters Club is full of trashy people, that he hates our new president and his stinking revolution. Roli told him he was wrong 'cause everyone has the right to enjoy the good things in Cuba and to get an education. Then the boy told Roli that this school is for decent and normal white students, not for niggers and nelly faggots like you! And that's when Roli told the boy to shut up and the boy punched my friend in the stomach and Roli couldn't breathe for a long time. When he started breathing again he was so mad that he kicked the boy real hard, over and over again till he made blood come out of his mouth. The whole time I was asking Roli to please stop, you'll kill him! But Roli wouldn't listen. I'd never seen my friend acting like that, like a brave hero.

Roli stopped when Señor Raúl and the principal and many other kids showed up, and the kids were screaming at Roli and saying he was a fucking monster. They were yelling, *¡Desgraciao! ¡Cabrón! Bestia 'e mierda! ¡Negro sucio! ¡Suéltalo, abusador!* I tried to tell them that the boy had started it, that it wasn't Roli's fault, but no one paid any attention to me. They had to pull Roli away from the boy who was just lying there looking dead and had to be taken to the hospital.

Because of that fight Roli was expelled, that's what Señor Raúl said, 'cause violence isn't something we want at our school, the revolution won't put up with that kind of behavior. But I wonder why they didn't kick the other boy out too, it was all his fault! Then Señor Raúl told us that the name of the boy was Leocadio, and that Leocadio was going to be fine. But now Roli won't be coming back. Never ever. Señor Raúl said that his family moved to Jicotea, which is far from our town. And Papi thinks that Roli will be rotting in jail for the rest of his life. I hope not, I hope he's wrong. I'm so sad 'cause my best friend is gone. I guess I could say that Mami is my best friend now.

I love the way Mami gets so pretty to go to the movies on Sundays. She wears a tight dress and paints her lips like a rose and makes her hair all curly. The theater we go to is called El Principal, it's big and has red curtains everywhere inside. Mami says those curtains are made of velvet, the fabric of kings. I like to touch them 'cause they feel like hair that's short and soft like mine. Some of the movies we get to see at El Principal are exciting and others are confusing. There are movies where people don't say what they mean but then you hear a voice explaining the whole thing for you, and that helps a little. I wish there was a voice like that in real life 'cause in real life no one helps you understand anything.

I like it when Mami takes me to the matinee. But I don't like it when the movie ends 'cause then we have to leave the theater and it's always hot and bright outside and I feel sad. The sadness goes away pretty soon, though, when we go strolling in the park and Mami buys me *guarapo* at El Kiosko.

Abuela went to the movies with us last Sunday but Papi didn't, and I was glad about that. He would've hated the movie they showed about the revolution, how the brave rebels hid in the Sierra Maestra and grew their beards and then attacked the evil Batista president and threw him out. I told Mami and Abuela that I wanted to see a real movie with adventures and magic, not that boring stuff about rebels, and then Abuela got mad, I'd never seen her like that. She said, Milo, that movie isn't boring, it's about the men who fought to free us from the enemy, from the horrible Yankees, you should respect them. I said fine, I'll respect them but I don't want to watch a movie about them!

It was better today 'cause they didn't show Fidel and his bearded men. Instead we got to watch a fantastic movie called *The Amphibian Boy* about a kid who lives in the ocean. He was born missing a lung so the doctors gave him gills from a shark, and now he can only breathe in the water. One day he meets a pretty girl by the shore and they fall in love. But she can't live in the sea, so their story ends sadly. They say goodbye with a kiss and cry 'cause they'll never see each other again. I didn't like that ending, I imagined my own where she gets gills too and now she can breathe under water. She and the amphibian boy get married on a gigantic silver shell in a church made of coral with a seahorse for a priest and all kinds of fishes around them. Time passes, they have babies, they are the first amphibian family in the whole world, a new race, the merpeople who build cities deep in the ocean. The end.

Next time I get a free topic for a composition I'll write about the new ending I came up with for *The Amphibian Boy*. I think my teacher would like it. And after that I'll write about the last pig we had. I loved my pig! I named him Filisberto, Fili for short, and I never let him know why he lived in our pig pen. I just gave him scraps from my meals and told him stories about me. The day when Fili was to die was a Sunday. Mami took me to El Principal so I wouldn't be sad, to see a movie about singing gnomes who lived in a beautiful forest. The whole time I was watching it I tried not to think about poor Fili.

My pig knew a lot about me. He knew I love to rub my eyes real hard 'cause that way I can see a bunch of bright dots that look like stars. Fili knew I loved our last summer vacation when we spent two whole weeks in Varadero, the most beautiful beach in the world. That's what Mami says, that there can be no other place as beautiful, and I believe her. I love Varadero!

Watching TV was a problem for Filisberto. My pig wouldn't sit still long enough and couldn't figure out what was going on, not even when I told him about the show like the voice that explains stuff in some movies. "What a stupid idea," Papi would say. "Who ever heard of a pig watching television?" But Mami laughed like it was a joke, and I laughed with her. It was easier for Fili to listen to music. He liked Mami's records as much as I do. My favorite's the one by a pretty black woman named Fara who sings songs called *boleros*. When I listen to her I pretend she's right here in my room singing my songs. I've invented a bunch, with words and music. Mami loves to hear me sing them. She's told me I have a knack for rhyming, and that means when a word sounds like the one before it. All songs are written that way. Mami is sure I'll be a songwriter or a poet when I grow up. I think I'd like that.

Papi says my songs talk about love but what does a twerp like me know about love? He also says that all I'm doing is copying the stuff on the radio, the hits of Aznavour and Luisa María and Los Memes. But I'd never want to copy Aznavour! His songs are too sad and his name is hard to spell 'cause he's from France, a country in Europe. Papi's right, though, about the other singers. I do try to invent songs like the ones Luisa María and Los Memes sing. I love listening to those people! If I could I'd buy all their records. Luisa María has a funny last name I can't remember. Mami doesn't like her 'cause she screams too much and her singing hurts your ears. But to me she sounds like her whole chest is bursting from the love she feels! And Los Memes are three men and one woman who are on the radio a lot 'cause they're the most popular group in Havana. Sometimes their voices blend like it's just one person singing, and the woman in the group sings by herself a lot. She's beautiful though Papi says she's just a nigger with a big smelly ass and how did she end up singing with three white men? Her voice is sweet and deep and when you listen to her it's like you're tasting some creamy *dulce de leche*. I wish I could sing with Los Memes to be near that woman and touch her and hear her voice all the time.

I sang my songs to Fili sometimes, he liked them and he liked Mami but he hated Papi. Whenever he heard Papi's voice he started running around in circles in his pigpen, afraid of my father like I am. Papi can't sing, his voice is hoarse like an ogre's. But he can yell real loud when he gets mad, especially when he talks about Fidel. He wants to kill that man with his bare hands, he says. But Papi won't tell anyone about that except me and Mami 'cause if you say anything bad about Fidel, even if it's just that you don't like his beard, they'll throw you in jail and call you names like dog and pig. Though being a pig isn't all that bad, except for the part when they kill you. Poor Fili.

There's one thing I told my pig that no one knows, not even Mami, and it's about this pain I get in my guts that makes it hard to breathe sometimes, like when you want to poop but can't. Mami would say it's indigestion from eating too many *croquetas* but then when I go to the bathroom blood comes out, and seeing the water all red scares me. I start crying quietly so Mami won't hear me. I should go to the doctor but I'm afraid to 'cause I know what gives me this pain, and if they find out about it I could be in big trouble. There's no cure for it anyway. I know what I have to do to make it stop but I can't, Eduardo won't let me. It's all his fault, I hate him! So the doctor wouldn't be able to help me. Better not say anything, that's why I only told Fili. I don't want to think about what Papi would do if he found out. First he'd be really mad and then... No! Better not think about it.

The last time Papi got really mad he said he had a good reason for it. And I thought, so there are bad reasons then, like when he blows up just 'cause he wants to and I have to hide from him. Papi was pissed this last time 'cause Fidel was sending teachers from Havana to the whole country so they could teach peasants to read and write. Papi said it was a waste of time 'cause peasants are too stupid to learn anything and besides they don't need to read to work the fields. He said this situation was a terrible thing for us. Fidel was forcing us to have one of those teachers, a goddam communist, stay at our home!

Our guest's name was Magaly but she wanted us to call her comrade. That word means devil in Russian, says Papi, but Abuela told me that it means brother or sister and we should use it 'cause now everyone is a brother or sister in Cuba. Comrade Magaly stayed with us for five days. She rode a jeep to visit the farms and teach the alphabet to a million peasants. I thought that was a good thing but I didn't tell Papi what I thought. He doesn't see how sad it is that some people can't sign their names and have to write an *X* instead. But all *X*'s look the same, how can that count?

Papi never spoke to Magaly when she was here. He'd stay in his room in the morning until she was gone or he'd leave really early, before she did. But Mami would have breakfast with her, and they'd talk about women stuff. Magaly was nice. She gave me a kiss on the head once and told me I was handsome and also lucky 'cause I'm getting an education. She told Mami and me about the peasants she was teaching, how they'd get all excited when they read the newspaper for the first time.

Before Magaly came, Papi said that she'd have to sleep with me 'cause we don't have an extra bed, only an old cot hidden away in the back shed. He didn't want Magaly sleeping on that cot 'cause if it broke or was uncomfortable then Magaly would complain to Fidel about it and Papi would end up in jail. I didn't like the idea of having to share my bed but Papi said it'd be good for me to sleep with a woman. And so that's what happened. I kept waking up and finding this woman next to me, her long hair all over her pillow, so beautiful in her blue pajamas! The pants went only to her knees, like Mami's bermudas, and you could see her nice brown legs. I imagined my hand slipping under her pajamas and squeezing her big tits. I don't think she noticed what I did the last night, while I looked at her butt. The next morning she smiled and thanked me for letting her use my bed. She told me she'd slept like a baby and hadn't seen or heard a thing...

I could write a composition about Magaly, but I don't know a lot about her so instead I'll write about the scar I have near my left eye. That topic would make Mami look bad, and I don't want that, but I do hate it when she tells people about my scar like she's proud of it. People always say that's fantastic and they want to touch it. Sometimes the kids at school call me Cayman Eye 'cause my scar looks like Cuba and our country has the shape of a cayman. They laugh and say I have one of those creepy lizards stuck on my face. Mami never says the truth, that she left me alone in the bathtub when I was little and that's when it happened. She just says that I fell and hit my face 'cause boys get in a lot of trouble, but it wasn't my fault! I wish Mami would stop showing people my scar. I hate that!

But the thing I hate even more about Mami is her smoking, 'cause it makes her hair and her clothes smell really bad. I'm just glad she doesn't smoke cigars like Papi. Those are big stinkers. Mami says the first thing she's going to buy in the North is a pack of cigarettes with menthol, the stuff they put in Vicks. She says that when the smoke fills your lungs it's like swallowing some nice cold air, the kind they have in the North, in cities like New York. I don't think she should be telling me these things. What if I tried those cold air cigarettes and liked them and started smoking too?

I think Mami likes to act like the women who smoke in American movies. There was this movie on TV about a blonde woman with a flat butt who drank water in tall glasses whenever her husband left the house. Mami said the woman was drinking something that helped her forget her troubles, not water. Poor thing, all alone in that big house, that's why she smoked all the time. But women aren't supposed to do that! Not Cuban women and not my mother anyway.

Mami and Eduardo were smoking in the living room when Papi got home today. He asked Eduardo what the fuck are you doing here with my wife and he answered just enjoying a little smoke. Mami said to Papi, look, Eduardo brought us a pack of American cigarettes, isn't that nice, he gets them from Miami. Then Papi grabbed Eduardo by the neck and shoved him out the door, and the whole time Mami kept saying how can you treat our friend that way, Elio! Eduardo rode off on his bike real fast. I hope he's gone forever. Mami thinks he's nice but she doesn't know, she could never guess!

When Eduardo started coming over at first I'd lock myself in the bathroom, but then I stuck around watching him in case he did something bad to Mami. I'd give him looks telling him with my eyes I hate you please leave us alone, and Eduardo would just smile and wink at me. He likes boys but maybe he likes married women too and wants to destroy our family like those villains on the radio shows. So I'll just be happy that Mami's safe from Eduardo. And I won't complain about her smoking, how it stinks up the whole house and makes it hard for me to breathe.

I wish I were safe too. I wish I didn't have to go see Eduardo on Sundays. He says if I don't, he'll tell everyone that my ass is ripe like a juicy papaya and that I love to have it cut open by men. But I don't 'cause it hurts! It's like I'm going to burst and then I see things, an ugly old woman with wings and no legs, only a fish tail, and I know she's not really there, it's what my pain makes me see but it's scary anyway. And afterwards I'm sore inside for a long time. It hurts like hell!

Poor Mami, that's why she cries at night when she's with Papi, at least she can cry and make loud noises. I sure can't. Eduardo shuts my mouth with his hand so I won't scream, and that's just what I want to do, scream and cry and call for help real loud... *¡Auxilio! ¡Socorro!*

Should I tell Papi? He talks a lot about how he'd like to kill somebody, especially Fidel, well then he'd have a good reason, he'd be doing it to save his son from an ogre. But I'm afraid to tell him 'cause I think he'd want to kill me too. He'd say it was my fault that Eduardo did all those things to me. He always blames me for all the bad stuff, and when I try to defend myself he just gets mad at me. So I call him names, *coño, cabrón,* shouting like he does. Then he hits me and locks me in the bathroom. Mami tries to get me out but he won't let her. She cries when he shoves her away. Sometimes she falls on the floor and gets hurt. I can hear her falling, my poor Mami.

Papi wants to make me strong like him, that's what he says, but if I turn out like him then I'll make my family suffer. I never want to be like Papi never ever! He says he has to punish me so I learn to act like a man. But men are mean! I wish Papi would just leave me alone. Why can't he be like Mami? She doesn't hurt me or scold me or treat me like I'm stupid. She says I'm her perfect boy.

A SHORT BUT HAPPY DREAM

Susan moved in at my suggestion. I wanted more time with her. Thus my empty house took on an aura of life, a sort of home life that was new to me. We cooked together, listened to piano music, went looking for fireflies—creatures we both loved—by the Arkansas riverbank on warm summer evenings. We read Martí and Neruda cuddled up in bed and talked about the books we cherished, those I hoped to write, those she hoped to read. Susan found *Cuba in Silence* "moving, funny, and heartbreaking in some places." The abuse Camilito was made to suffer disturbed her, more so when I told her it was partly based on my experience. "It's the first Cuban novel I've read," she admitted. She'd read poetry by Martí and Avellaneda but no Cuban fiction. How was that possible? No Lezama, Piñera, Arenas? I wanted to ask her why she'd assumed that my novel was *Cuban*. Was it because of the characters, the setting or themes, its author? But Susan had some reading to do before she could answer that question.

We rented a piano, badly in need of tuning but in good shape otherwise. "It'll do for now," said Susan. "Until we buy our own." She couldn't improvise well, and popular music wasn't her forte. Susan was trained in a classical repertoire and thrived on Mozart, Chopin, and Schubert. There was a piece she played that I loved, Chopin's *Valse in A Minor*. It had a cadence, a mood, an echo of Edith Piaf and Charles Aznavour, but also a purity of a sound that predated the popular song.

I met some of Susan's friends, childhood pals Laura and Jennifer. Laura was a high school English teacher in Kansas City (Susan didn't see her much), and Jenn worked as executive office manager—or glorified secretary, she said jokingly—for a law firm in Newton. There was also Calvin, a long-haired dude who lived off his cannabis sales. "Calvin is a reluctant pianist," said Susan, "talented but not committed." They'd met in a music class and had a fling, but his pot trips turned her off eventually. And there was Daniel, another buddy from the Music Department, a sexy queen with a diva complex. Always clad in black, he had auburn hair laboriously coiffed a la Duran Duran, and he worked at displaying a perpetual Liberace smile. "Danny can be insufferable," Susan told me. "He's an only child, used to getting what he wants, spoiled but also gifted and funny. He makes me laugh."

We started hanging out with Jennifer in Newton, where she lived in a two-story fixer-upper. Laura and Calvin joined us sometimes. At first I thought my gaydar could be off about Jenn, but then Susan confirmed that she did swing both ways—like Susan herself, I was pleased to find out. In fact they'd had sex numerous times. "We're close friends," Susan explained, "who enjoy each other's bodies." Those two women were hot in different ways, I thought, and they seemed to care for one another, so their thing made perfect sense to me. Jennifer was a looker, uncommonly chic for that part of the country. She did have the typical Kansas breeder butt and ample hips, the alabaster skin, the fine blond hair. But she managed to envelop it all in a cosmopolitan veneer, an East Coast look that clashed with everything around her and especially with the sleepy town of Newton.

Newton's heart was Bethel, a Mennonite college about thirty miles north of Overland City. I would've had no reason to visit that town if it hadn't been for Jenn, a gracious hostess who liked to cook her specialties for us: roast, buttery mashed potatoes, chicken pot pie. She and Susan and Laura did a lot of Kansas-bashing, which I dug. They also trashed their fathers as a sort of group therapy. Jenn: "that Creationist!" Laura: "the bigot!" Susan: "that ethnocentric fool!" I got into it but was guarded, content to let someone else indulge in patricidal fantasies for a change. I would definitely refrain from badmouthing Mr. Thompson, since I was feeling a bit guilty about luring Susan away from her parents. They must've thought she had fallen prey to the Cuban monster, the heathen!

The symphony on Sundays: one of the first routines Susan and I developed. What a trip, dressing up to go to the Hall, as the OC Music Center (a small-scale Dorothy Chandler Pavilion) was known. Susan

got a kick out of the blue-hair elderly ladies. "Why that color?! There
are no human beings with blue hair!" The average age of the audience
was seventy. I felt fucking young! My mind wandered off sometimes
during the performances, too many thoughts creeping in. But then, all
of a sudden the music grabbed me, propelled me, taking me somewhere
I didn't know, a place outside time.

We ran into Danny at the Hall most Sundays; he'd be there with an
entourage which included his parents and friends of the family. Daniel
Varley was well connected, said Susan. His parents were supporters of
the Hall, generous donors. They put up with their son's eccentric state-
ments, turned a blind eye to his homosexuality because they believed
in his talent and strove to showcase it. He was allowed to straddle the
margin (the gay underworld) and the mainstream (the Hall's upper
crust) because he had the chops. Danny was proud to know "Michael,"
the conductor, intimately (wink wink). A thin, fiery man, Michael was
obviously gifted, and he brought the crème de la crème to Kansas. One
of his guest artists I loved was Alicia de Larrocha, a great pianist and pe-
tite woman from Spain. Her tiny fingers were butterflies giving life to
Granados, Albéniz, and Bach. Again, what a trip, Lito at the symphony!
Next he'd be going to the opera. *If Tano could've seen me then!*

Poor Lito, so deprived of high culture when he was growing up. And
even later, when he became a scholar, he didn't much dig the classical
concert scene. Went to some amazing plays, *Angels in America*, *La Cage
Aux Folles*; to concerts by the likes of Neil Diamond and Pat McEvoy.
Fell in love with Mozart after watching the film *Amadeus*. But he wasn't
"cultured," just not born into that world. At home in Cuba the family
listened to lots of pop music but there were no books. His parents didn't
read, except for the newspaper and magazines. His father believed that
prolonged reading was a waste of time and bad for your health. He
criticized his son whenever he found him engrossed in some story he'd
brought from school. "You're gonna go blind," Elio would say, "from
reading so much crap!" Yet Lito persisted, devouring whatever text fell
into his hands. He had a creative impulse that led him to literature, and
now there he was, Professor Macías, alias Dr. Milo, a cultivated man after all and with a mission: prying his students away from cheap entertainment and guiding them to works of literary art...

Dr. Milo would admit to enjoying some television and film. He liked
Thirtysomething because that show was well written and had substance.

Milo also liked Woody Allen. He went on and on about *The Purple Rose of Cairo*, not just a movie but a cinematic masterpiece. He wished, oh how Milo wished he'd written it! When he showed that film in his literature classes, he'd stop the tape too many times and repeat ad nauseam, "Here, see? Woody borrowed this idea from so-and-so and he got that line from this or that novel." But it wasn't plagiarism, oh no, it was intertextuality. "Woody takes the original concept and rewrites it," he'd tell his students, "creating a fresh, wonderful work." Cecilia, the protagonist of *Purple Rose*, was much like the Molina character in *Kiss of the Spider Woman*, thought Milo. (He saw Puig everywhere!) There was one line in Allen's film that he loved to quote, something about Cecilia's lover being fictional but you can't have everything. "See what I mean?" he'd exclaim in class, much too excited for his listeners, "Fiction can save you. It saved her!"

But fiction didn't save Milo (didn't save *me*) from literature conferences, most of which I hated. Take the one in Las Vegas, for example. Whose idea was it to have a Latin American Studies meeting in the gambling capital of the world? Give the profs a chance to live it up a little, no? You betcha! Have them cite grim statistics about poverty in El Salvador, or address the plight of indigenous people in Guatemala, or discuss the Dirty War in Argentina, then let 'em indulge in a little gambling and a good show by the likes of Charo. All in a day's work! Yet a stay in LV was a small price to pay for spending some quality time with the Cicada. We would meet up at conferences several times a year just to hang out together, have a good laugh. In Vegas we didn't put a single penny in the machines and didn't catch the extravaganzas, not even Cuchi Cuchi. But we did have a couple of nice yet inexpensive dinners. Shame on us radicals! Made sense that food and alcohol would be cheap in Las Vegas. They stuffed you with chow and booze, all those free drinks at the casinos, so you could happily gamble your life and soul away. My paper on Puig was a rehashed bore (definitely for me), same old excerpts from my dissertation, as usual. But Alina whipped up an inspired piece on the stories of Ana Lydia Vega, her fellow Puerto Rican; a touch of humor in the midst of all that academic posturing.

Too bad Alina couldn't join me in Georgia. I asked her to submit a paper but she said not this time; she needed a break. Lucky Dr. Sotovélez was tenured already and could afford to kick back, whereas I was still paying my dues, having to fatten up my dossier in order to become a prof for life—which sounded like a death sentence! Alina would've liked Savannah much more than Vegas. She would've loved its mansions and plush gardens, its windows laden with wrought iron. My brilliant friend would've known some key facts about Savannah; for instance, that no other U.S. city has so many plazas and guns; that the machos there kill each other off for the stupidest reasons, because killing is the business of men. We would've had lunch at Palmer's, by the water. And then, finding ourselves with some extra time, we'd have been guided by an elderly lady with porcelain skin through a mansion that belonged to the Marquis de Lafayette. We'd have listened to this lady talk about Lafayette's life in a dense, somnolent voice that would lull us to sleep, and we wouldn't have remembered a word she said. But it was just as well that Alina couldn't be there with me, since the main reason I was attending that conference was to meet up with Tano, unbeknownst to him. *¡Sorpresa!*

I stayed at a bed and breakfast in Statesboro, another house of endless stairs, handrails of copper, chandeliers, lavish gardens. This one had rocking chairs on its porch; there the members of a larger-than-life family (father, mother, son) sat rocking themselves with a vigor that would seem better suited for horseback riding, as if announcing the family-oriented comfort of the premises inside. "Howdy!" they all said in unison when I greeted them. "Howdy to you!" I replied.

After a short cab ride I ended up in a crowded meeting hall at a three-star hotel. I registered, got my tag and looked for the room assigned to my panel. As I waited for the panel to get underway, not feeling up to hobnobbing, I dug into my critic's bag to find my paper on the Puiguian utopia: *a society where relationships are not based on gender hierarchies, where machismo is no longer a cultural obligation.* I thought maybe I'd do a more personal thing this time, for a change... *In Manuel Puig I found a world like the one I'd known in my Cuban hometown, and which I didn't think was worthy of literature. His novels urged me to question the ideas instilled in me as a child, notions that forced me to act and speak in a certain way, and to engage the world as a "real man."* Alina would've applauded my "personal intervention," but everybody else would've been appalled by it. Who does the Cuban Turd think he is, passing off personal anecdotes as research? The nerve! They'd have coughed and blown their noses, or stood up and left. Others would've looked at me in dismay, attributing my arrogant outburst to a painful review process, concluding that I hadn't gotten tenure, hence my derangement.

Tano appeared listed in the conference program as Dr. Pablo Ricci. I went to his panel and was surprised to see him in suit and tie—black leather suit and a pink tie, granted, but even so, no more torn jeans! It was obvious that the former flight attendant had found the right mentors, profitable Ivy League connections, after completing the course work for his PhD at Yale. I hadn't seen him since we parted ways in Alton, but there had been some info coming from him by way of brief letters and a few phone conversations. Ricci had written a brilliant dissertation on something *très* gay, of course: *Bellas locas porteñas, poesía del burdel bonaerense*, a hot, soon to be published thesis on the poetry of Buenos Aires male whores in the 1920s. My fate was an obscure Midwest university, whereas Pablo was reaching for the stars, a tenure-track position at Cornell. He'd had the campus visit, certain that he'd get the job. His muse would put in a good word for him, yes. Miss Lite Terature would make sure he triumphed, and Tano would have accomplished it all without having to become Evita or Violetta. But so much for his credo, *All I need is a backpack and my freedom to fly and feed off poetry and arias!*

While he read his paper, looking infrequently out at his audience, I thought about the poem I wrote the day we said goodbye in Alton, a portrait of my Argentine buddy. *The Bella Porteña descends then, giving and willing...* Was there any part of that *porteña* left in Dr. Ricci? I didn't see any signs of her in the subdued scholar who took the podium and was now expounding on the erotic sonnets of Argentine *locas*. What I saw was a transformed Pablo Ricci, not an empowered broad nor a stunning dame richly clad in designer garments, but just one more staid academic.

Done with the hugging and kissing, we headed to the hotel bar for a celebratory drink and some catching up. Our reunion might've gone better initially if I hadn't told him right off about Susan, but I didn't see any reason not to. In all truth, I was morbidly awaiting his reaction, which I foresaw. He mocked me, as always. "But that's pathetic, mignon!" he exclaimed, sounding more like his Alton self at last. "How can you be so utterly messed up, perroquet? Hey, everyone, look at him!" He was getting too loud. "This guy's a real man 'cause he's fucking a woman!" I told him to stop, to shut the fuck up or I'd split. He recoiled, said, "Okay, *va bene*. I shouldn't get so worked up. Sorry, darling."

It occurred to me just then that Tano didn't really believe in a sexual utopia à la *Spider Woman*. He was all for "totally total" sexuality as long as it didn't involve women. Like Manuel Puig, from what I'd heard. It was said that the writer wasn't aroused by females at all. In Puig's imagined, perfectly gendered society he was a full-fledged lady who had sex with straight men. But whether or not I was wrong about Tano, it was time for a long overdue conversation about this issue.

"What's your problem?" I asked him. "Why does it bug you so much that I'm with a woman?"

"You know the answer to that question."

"Why can't you accept me as I am, with all my flakiness and polymorphous confusion?"

"Because I know what's best for you, perroquet."

"If that were true, we wouldn't be having this conversation."

"We could talk about something else..."

"No. You've gotta stop wanting me to act and think and be just like you!"

"Okay, whatever!"

"I'm not Pablo Ricci. Nor Tano."

"*C'est dommage!*"

"I admire you, Pablo. And there was a time when I envied your life, your history..."

"I knew you envied the *loca* in me."

"Yes, but then I realized I could never be a *loca*. Or a real man or a *real* anything."

"You poor baby. *Ay*, you're still hopeless."

"There you go again!"

"Just don't tell me about your girlfriend, please. I've heard enough."

"Fine, I won't."

"We should see more of each other, you know."

"I'd like that."

"Let's have a toast for now, *d'accord*? To our brilliant careers!"

"And to our friendship, but only if you stop trying to change me."

"It's a deal. Cheers!"

"*¡Salud!*"

"Now let me tell you about the new project I've been working on. I'm having so much fun! You're going to love it, mignon. I'm trying to prove, through a postcolonial reading of Hernán Cortés' *Cartas de relación* and Columbus' *Diario de viaje*, that the great explorer was a closet faggot, and that Cortés had a reputation for upper-man fucking of Indian boys."

"You know they're going to rip you apart..."

"I know. Can't wait to get my findings published and ruffle some feathers."

"They'll burn you at the stake!"

"Yes, it's what happens to all of us plucky witches in academia. But not to worry, I've got my potions brewing already for those who dare cross me. Like I said, I can't wait!"

It was right after this reunion that my relationship with Susan started to go downhill. Did Tano (that "plucky witch") put a curse on us, triggering the beginning of the end? A silly thought, yet I began to wonder, because the end came so suddenly, so soon...

It happened during a trip to Mexico, our first getaway and a tax write-off for me, since I was going there reportedly to do research on the latest wave of Mexican fiction writers, such as Ángeles Mastretta. I'd buy some books, take a few notes—plenty of proof of my scholarly endeavors. Flying by way of L.A., wanting Susan to meet Mechy and Elio, we scheduled a weekend in Bay City. Susan and Mami hit it off; they talked about Cuban cuisine (Susan loved to cook, hence she was okay by Mami) and Kansas weather (yes, there was a tornado season!) And Papi was cordial—thrilled, I was sure, that his son was finally acting like a real Cuban man. "That's the ogre you've been telling me about?" said Susan jokingly about Elio. I explained that he was on good behavior because he wanted to impress her. "And why would he want to do that?" she asked, though she knew the answer: "So you'll stick around."

Susan loved Mexico the way Castel loved it, with unwavering passion. Puebla was our first stop, a discovery for me but not for Susan; she'd been there once before with her parents. "The trip from hell," she called it, and I could imagine why. Puebla was big and beautiful in spite of its patches of filth and its pollution. We stayed at the Hotel Colonial. I tried *mole poblano* (a local specialty) for the first time on the *portales* and liked its thick, sweet, spicy sauce poured over chicken. I also enjoyed our strolls through the town square or zócalo. Could've hung out there for hours.

Oaxaca was next. We were pleased by the sight of its balconies, many of them painted in rose and violet. And again we spent time at the zócalo, where a trio of guitar players in green guayaberas played Los Panchos songs for hours each day. There were places we visited that I wanted to remember: the Santo Domingo Cathedral, the Rufino Tamayo Museum; and especially Monte Albán, the ancient Zapotec city. But Oaxaca itself was a memory I didn't want to keep. It was there where I faced Susan's indifference for the first time. She seemed detached. She'd leave my side much too often, wanting to go exploring by herself and needing, she said, "space for my own thoughts." This need of hers should've been a clue, but I was in the clouds, unable to read her and unwilling to face the reason for her change, which had a lot to do with me. Whenever she left I'd try to write, but I felt haunted by Cortázar's novel. Like the character of La Maga in his *Hopscotch*, Susan wouldn't let herself be found...

The trip back to Overland City transpired in the most uncustomary silence, a silence that kept pouring like toxin over the life we'd lived together. But then Danny—of all people!—helped us break it, providing us with a pretext to interact and pretend there was no problem between us. He called to invite us to a concert he was giving at the Music Center, at its smaller, ninety-seat venue. Danny said he'd been practicing five hours a day for the last four months, doing the concert for the exposure and the pleasure. He offered us comp tickets, since we were part of his inner circle, and we promised we'd be there. Wouldn't have dared miss our famous friend as a featured artist at the Hall.

We saw a handful of old suits in the audience but no blue coifs, instead several purple punk heads. Danny's fan club? Rowdy and playful, that crowd, not what you'd expect to see at a classical piano concert in Kansas. They seemed to be into Daniel Varley's music as much as I was. He played Haydn and Mozart sonatas, a French suite by Bach, one of Chopin's preludes, all beautifully. I picked Susan's brain during intermission, "Is he as good as he sounds to me?"

"Yes," she said, "he has great technical ability but he's also passionate."

At the reception in the lobby after the performance, Danny was loving the attention, the fawning crowd around him. He looked glamorous in his tux, with a sensibly small pink carnation on his lapel, his hair tied back in a ponytail, and wearing only a tad of makeup.

"You made it!" he said, greeting us with a kiss. "Thank you for coming."

"You were great," Susan told him.

"I didn't disgrace the family?"

"Not this time!"

"I'm impressed," I admitted.

He smiled. "Really, Dr. Macías?" He grabbed the back of my neck and pulled me to him, whispering in my ear, "Impressed enough to let me give you a spectacular BJ?"

"Sorry. Can't," I replied, holding Susan's hand.

"Well, then," he reacted, walking away theatrically, "you're not getting my autograph!"

"What was that all about?" asked Susan once Danny was out of sight. I reported what he'd said, and she laughed, "Danny strikes again!"

Back in our silent home, Susan and I kept trying to salvage what had no salvation. She started talking in her sleep. "Who are you?" she'd ask, crying. "Why are you in my bed?" She wouldn't recognize me, and I couldn't console her. *Who are you?!* Now at least I knew what was troubling her. No, it had nothing to do with Danny or any of those students who wanted to get in my pants. She said she had to "get out from under my shadow." Obviously I'd been coming on too strong; unaware that, through all the loving and the sharing, I was still playing a mentoring role. I promised Susan I'd back off, give her all the space she needed, make things fair and equal. Stop being her professor.

We made a promise to each other, *We won't let it happen. We won't give this up.* But we knew it was a promise to be broken. Our love couldn't save us from the end, which came to us one cool spring afternoon, as we strolled by the Arkansas River. "If only the fireflies were out," I said, wishing to see Susan enraptured by them, as she always was. "It's not warm enough yet," she observed and said she loved what Cubans called those magical creatures. "*Cucuyos...* I just love that word."

"Let's start over, Susan," I pleaded.

"I can't. There's something I've lost, Camilo."

"I'll help you find it, whatever it is."

"No, I need to do this alone...because it's something within me."

She told me she'd be moving out in a couple of days and would leave the key in my mailbox. We said *adiós* with a tenuous kiss, and I sat on a bench on the riverbank, crying my heart out. Didn't want to go home, where I'd feel dead and buried now, huddled inside my mind like an imploding star. The river wasn't an option. No drowning scene for me! Normally I would've enjoyed running along the very popular and scenic River Trail. But today, just looking at those muddy waters turned my stomach.

At this point the happiness I'd known with Susan was making me feel miserable, as I became aware that our relationship had been an ephemeral fantasy, a short dream not unlike that of Molina and Valentín in *Kiss of the Spider Woman*. I hadn't seen it coming yet our breakup was my fault. For being so much into myself. Still I wondered, what was it that she'd lost? Her love for me? Her own strength?

I did make it home eventually and went for a long run, all the way to Southeast Overland City, the city's ghetto. Ended up twisting my ankle and provoking an ingrown nail to fester. Both required medical attention; I had to use crutches for a while and couldn't bear the looks of pity and words of concern from my students. *¡¿Qué le pasó, profesor?! ¡¿Qué tiene?!* Too much running, at times in bitter cold weather, was too much of a good thing. But I had no other way of coping. That and sleep.

Danny heard about my breakup with Susan and called to offer his support. (How kind of him.) We went out for a drink and had one too many; found ourselves on the couch later that night—the bed was off limits. He went gaily forward and gave me the blowjob of my life, the first of many during the following months. That was all there could be. Not love but his lips and his deep throat and a tongue like a snake that tightened, licked, and stung. (Yes, Tano, sometimes it was all about the boner.)

There was a gay bar Danny frequented, typically dark and smoke-filled, with lots of head-splitting music and lots of cruising. I agreed to go there with him once in a while but nowhere else, not to dinner, to the theater or the movies. I had no desire to be a part of his entourage. Danny was a looker, a unique character with his flashy style and androgynous beauty in that land of sameness, and he knew lots of people. I was used to folks staring at me in Kansas for looking "Hispanic" and having a goatee, for wearing pastel-colored shirts with thin black leather ties and for speaking English with a slight Cuban accent. But Danny got more than stares. He was famous. No, I preferred to just have him over...

I tried to indulge him the way he liked it, screwing him frequently enough to make it seem like a routine. "My reward for being a good little boy," he'd say. But I wished I hadn't let it happen. I wished I wouldn't get so turned on when I plunged into him. I didn't even care if I hurt him; in fact, the pain I inflicted on Danny was part of the pleasure, both mine and his. It was liberating not to be concerned with the other, to be driven only by the need to take and use. But it was also disturbing. A role I didn't want to play. I didn't want to be Eduardo raping Lito—an image that crept up as I indulged myself. There was one major difference, of course: Lito hadn't been a willing partner; he couldn't understand why he was being subjected to the pain and didn't derive much pleasure from it. But even so...

Daniel started moving into my life, giving me presents—bottles of wine, a gold bracelet, a Rolex watch, LPs, things he could afford because his parents were loaded. I only took some of the records, those of his favorite composers, which I loved. He drank too much and seemed almost proud of his alcoholism. Said we were in the same boat: He was a drunk, and I was a pothead. Maybe. But I didn't do weed several times every day, like he ingested booze.

Danny played for me often but hated my rented piano, wanted to show off his grand at home. His parents were okay with the prospect of my visit but no way. No family scene for me. I wondered if Danny would ever make it big as a musician. He could have if he'd gotten the hell out of that city and that state, but Kansas was a vortex. Stories abounded there about artists who had promise but never made it. Few Kansans ever left their wheatfields, and those who did, came back eventually. Like Jenn, who bitched about "this political wasteland, this cultural void" yet had no plans for splitting. Even Susan seemed destined to grow roots in the Midwest, to marry a man who looked like her and have children who looked like their parents and who'd never question their privileged lives.

I needed to do some serious thinking about my thing with Danny, so I had a little talk with myself... *Do you admire Daniel?* Yes, his talent blows me away. *Do you enjoy his music?* Sure, though it feels wrong to me somehow, like a reality that's not supposed to exist, where Susan—her presence in my house, her Chopin—has been erased. *Do you dig sex with Daniel?* Hell yeah. Better than beating off. *Do you like him?* Sometimes. *Love him?* Not at all. *You know what you must do, then.* I do know. *You miss Susan, don't you?* Painfully so. *What about the episode at Valley Park, back in Alton? You and Josh in the bushes.* Oh, that fantasy. Well, Josh is still at the park, waiting for me. I fantasize about other men too, but I'm in love with Susan. She's both real and ideal. *Oh, boy, are you in trouble!*

SEND IN THE CLOWN

He greeted us at the door of his trailer home in Southeast Overland City, not quite the poor side of town but getting there. James must've dressed in haste; he was wearing a slept-in undershirt and wrinkled army pants. His eyes were bloodshot. He hugged me, too excited to note that Lois was with me.

"Welcome to my home, professor!" he exclaimed and showed us inside.

"We've missed you in class, Señor Jaime," I reassured him. "You must come back."

Lois suggested we have coffee; she'd make it. "Strong, for a change," she announced.

James was stumbling as he looked for his smokes. "I lost my lighter at the VA hospital," he announced. "And it was a present from my wife. Did you know I've been working with the veterans, professor? Pushing paper mostly, but I'm quitting. Forget that place! I'm always losing something there. At least I haven't lost anything big, like my *cabeza*!"

James didn't resemble the cheerful clown he played in Spanish 101, good old Señor Jaime who laughed at my jokes and celebrated every word he managed to understand or utter correctly. When nothing else worked—activities, exercises, readings—I knew I could count on James' guffaw, on his hilarious self-mocking and enthusiasm to get us back on track and save the day. But the somber man I hugged in that mobile home had none of Señor Jaime's vitality. He'd lost weight and seemed wilted, worn out. That man was barely forty years old but suddenly looked sixty.

"Please, sit down." He offered me a chair. "And forgive the mess. It's been a long time since this house was cleaned up for real. Since Bev passed away. Two years, I think. Lost the battle with cancer, as they say. She'd never let me do any housework, said it was a wife's job, and now look at this pigpen!" I saw piles of junk mail on the dining room table; the sink was full of dirty dishes. "There they are!" He'd found his cigarettes by the sink and lit one with a match. "Would you like a smoke, professor? Hope you don't mind they're unfiltered. Help yourself."

I was used to filtered Lights but took one of his cigs as a courtesy. "*Gracias*, Jaime."

Lois opened the refrigerator. The milk had gone sour—she noted after a whiff—and the bread was moldy, but there were some eggs and okay bacon. She'd fix breakfast for James. "He needs a hot meal," she declared. Lois was a widow in her late forties who'd gone back to school. She had an ample German face, an honest smile. She was enjoying the break she could finally take from a lifetime of household chores and routines. Lois loved her classes (Spanish, Anthropology, Art History) and the ideas she was exposed to, the challenges, as well as the field trips and the parties. But she was also looking for projects, people to save or at least help. "I've been feeling selfish lately," she'd told me that morning, after class, "too involved with myself. And Jim needs me. He's not doing well; that's why he hasn't been in class. Poor Jim, he's drinking again. I think he's been reliving the war. A visit from you would cheer him up, professor. I'll be stopping by his place this afternoon..."

I meant to say no because I didn't want to care. I was tired of having to deal with my students' personal problems. I'd found myself playing counselor too many times, fending off lonely divorcees who burst into tears in my office, horny farm boys fresh out of the closet, randy housewives who saw me as some sort of Latin lover. At first it was rewarding to be needed, exciting to provoke such lust and adulation. But eventually the neediness got old, my job began to feel like a burden, and I came to dread my office hours. Yet I said yes to Lois because I, too, had been self-absorbed lately, pitying Dr. Milo and obsessing on Susan. It would do me good to think of someone other than her. Other than me.

James fetched a bottle of cheap burgundy from the fridge and brought out three glasses. "Care for a little *vino*?" he asked, and both Lois and I declined. He gulped down half a glass, seemingly put off by our refusal to join him. "I don't feel too good," he said and sat at the table. "It hurts all over, everywhere inside, you know." I wanted to tell him I could relate. Yes, *all over*, I know exactly what you mean, Señor Jaime. But that wouldn't have been true. I didn't know the pain a soldier felt.

"You shouldn't drink so much, Jim," chided Lois, busy in the kitchen.

"Yeah, I've been doing too much boozing. It helps me forget the awful stuff..."

"I hope you're hungry," she said. "When was the last time you ate a hot meal, Jim?"

"I don't remember," he muttered, sniffing the bacon like a hungry kid. "Smells great."

Lois cleared some space on the table for the plate of food she placed before him. The meal looked humble yet caringly presented. "Try the eggs. And let me know if you need salt."

"Thank you, Lois," he said, staring at his friend.

"*¡Buen provecho!*" I told him.

"*Gracias,*" he replied, smiling. "I know what that means, *buen provecho*. But there's nothing like it in English, right?"

"No, not really," answered Lois. "We just say something boring like, Enjoy!"

"I'm glad I was in class for the food chapter," said James, digging in with gusto.

"*La comida* is my favorite topic to teach," I admitted.

"I enjoy learning Spanish from you, professor. Never thought it could be so much fun."

"*Gracias,* Señor Jaime."

"I feel like a fool sometimes in your class, but you know what? It's a good way to feel. A blast! I love the way you teach new words by having us listen to them in context and use them..."

"Without having to memorize them," added Lois. "That's the best part. And you're so patient with us, professor. I mean, you seem interested in what we're trying to say! And when you speak to us it's like you're inside our heads, like you know exactly which words to use to get the idea across to us."

"What students need to hear is lots of language," I elaborated, "just like children. That's what I try to give you all, without stopping you to correct you. Parents don't stop a child to say, Sweetie, you just used the incorrect form of the past subjunctive! Or, Dear, what you just said calls for the indirect object pronoun, not the direct! Unless the parents are bizarre grammarians..."

"*Muy cómico*, professor!" Jaime called out.

"I like the idea," said Lois, "of acting like kids to learn a language."

"Me too!" Jaime chimed in, seeming more like a kid than he ever had in class.

And on that note I excused myself, stopping in the crammed living room on my way to the bathroom. The dusty coffee table was laden with books on astronomy and framed photographs of old and young faces, all smiling, all blond. Several plaques hung on the wall: *James Bailey, The First American Platoon... Brave Commander... A grateful nation hereby recognizes James Bailey...*

In the tiny bathroom, I tried not to look at the stains, an alcoholic's filth. While I peed, I let myself imagine a happy ending for that brave commander, one where he married Lois, and she saved him from his past; one where he was no longer helpless and tortured by his memories. But I resisted the comfort of this ending. I knew that James and Lois would fade into the background of my years in Kansas, characters in a story that I was bound to forget. Until I dug up an idea from a box of yellowing notes, *Alcoholic student, soldier—in Nam? My visit to his trailer home,* and that scribble would bring Jaime back instantly. Not his sobering up and his happy life with Lois, but his regrets.

Back in the kitchen, I found James looking out the window. "You know," he said to me, "I like taking pictures of the stars." He was suddenly excited. "You've got to see my pictures!" He rummaged in a manila folder buried somewhere on the table and brought out a photograph. "That's a burning nebula," he offered, eagerly, showing me an exploding sky, a formation of white fire that seemed to glow as it expanded. "Isn't it beautiful, professor?"

"Yes, it's quite beautiful, Señor Jaime. You're a good photographer."

He handed me the photo. "Here, you can have it."

"Are you sure? Thank you!"

"I'll take more. Will you come some day, professor, to take pictures of the stars with me?"

"Sure. Sounds like fun."

"Lois can come, too. You'll both enjoy yourselves, I just know it." He studied the picture. "There are no people killing people up there," he observed. "The stars are bright and peaceful."

I chose not to remind him—for surely he knew—that the stars were far from peaceful, that the cosmos was a ruthless entity never at peace with itself, never settled nor pure. Over the luminous, deceitful rainbow, life devoured itself in eternal darkness.

"Some nights," he told me, "I drive out to the wheatfields with my telescope and my camera and my Beethoven tape, and I spend hours out there. The cows don't like my music; they think I'm crazy but I don't care. What do cows know about beauty, anyway?"

Lois and I described our favorite *Far Side* comic strips featuring cows. James was laughing again. He told us about the time he rode a bull into camp...

"That was in 1969," he recalled. "I fought five battles that year."

"The year I left Cuba with my parents," I mused, "such a long time ago."

James was pensive. "That must've been hard for you, having to leave your country..."

"Yes, but it was harder for my folks."

"Why did you come to the U.S., professor?" A question from Lois I didn't expect.

The usual answer: "My parents brought me over. We were fleeing communism."

"Do you consider the United States your home?"

"I do." Surely this was the response she wanted; it happened to be the truth.

"This country can be a good home," James cut in. "But we've hurt a lot of people. Those guys in high places, I know how they think. They don't give a shit about anybody. Killing is their business." He was trembling. "But it wasn't mine!"

"We know, Jim," said Lois. "It's all right. Try to calm down now, please."

"I didn't want to kill anybody! You must believe me!"

"We believe you, Señor Jaime," I assured him. "*Te creemos.*"

"But they thought they were safe from the slaughter," he went on. "They slept like babies, with none of those visions creeping up on them, those things I still can't shake out of my head."

Lois held his hand. "It must be horrible, Jim..."

"I was the one who carried out the missions, their fucking orders. And I saw it all!" He pushed her away. "I was young and naïve, and I did what they told me. Those bastards!"

"Enough of that already!" Lois, finally in charge.

Silence ensued. Long, awkward minutes later James looked up at me. "There's something I've been meaning to tell you about your class, professor."

"Yes? What is it, Jaime?"

"I don't mean to be disrespectful or critical, but..."

"Go ahead, tell me."

"Well, you talk a lot of politics in class. And there's always some negative stuff about the U.S. and our... What do you call it? Our imperialist agenda, right? To be honest, it bothered me at first. I wondered why you were discussing our government in Spanish 101."

"I can tell you why, Señor Jaime."

"No, that's okay. It threw me off at first, that's all. Not just 'cause of the topic, but... when you talk politics you're so serious all of a sudden, and you speak to us in English."

"You know, professor," said Lois timidly, like a reproaching mother, "this country has done a lot of good in the world. You must keep that in mind."

"I do keep it in mind, Lois."

"Yes, a lot of good," James jumped in, "but there are too many things we should be ashamed of and we're not. The way we mess in other countries' business, to begin with. Like we have the right or something. It's a fucked-up way of dealing with the rest of the world."

"So, we have some growing up to do," Lois conceded.

"Anyway, I understand now, professor."

"I'm glad you do, Jaime."

James was right. I had no business discussing U.S. foreign policy in a language class. But those were the Reagan-North years, and it wouldn't have taken much for anyone to detect my leanings... Dr. Macías is out to change the world, or at the very least some of his students! He cites too many cases of right-wing abuse and ruthless military intervention by the United States. Isn't he a Cuban refugee? Why would he do such a commie thing? Maybe Professor Macías is a Castro spy!

Poor James, he enrolled in a language course just for the fun of it and ended up feeling judged, accused. His nightmares had been brewing for years, yet I had to take some of the blame for pushing him over the edge, for taking off my jolly-prof hat now and then and bringing the dark world into our haven of *Buenos días* greetings; a place that should always be relaxing and welcoming, where the biggest challenge should be describing your weekend activities... *Comí mucho, escuché música, bailé...*

"Hey, I've been reading our textbook!" James, eager again. "It takes my mind off things." He retrieved the book from a pile on the floor, handed it to me. "Write something in there, will you? Maybe one of your jokes. You're very funny, professor."

I humored him. On the title page I wrote: *Tú también eres cómico, Señor Jaime. Y tomas fotos fantásticas. ¡Regresa a clase!* He read the message, pleased with himself for understanding it. *"¡Sí, yo regreso pronto!"* he said, promising to come back to class soon. I hoped he meant it.

I thought about the many invitations from James that I'd turned down... "A group of us, we meet at the Student Center every morning and study for your class. We like to practice mucho español. Please join us some time, professor. We'll get you a nice breakfast, biscuits and gravy, which you've never tried, right?" But I was too busy reading impenetrable books, publishing unreadable articles, skimming memos for some irrelevant committee, attending conferences. It was a wonder that James would have good memories of my class at all; he didn't know how little I'd given of myself.

I had been working at Overland City University for four years. Gone was my initial passion, my drive to make changes. I was certain the faculty consensus about me wouldn't be kind after my departure... Dr. Macías only cared about advancing his career. His literature courses weren't about literature at all, but about trendy literary theories. Worse, about his left-leaning politics. And the language courses he taught were an appalling failure. Why, his students couldn't even conjugate their verbs! Unfortunate kids, they were the victims of Professor Macías' pedagogical wrongs, of his infantile teaching method. Students can't learn a language by just having someone talk to them in the target language. And how can you monitor students' speech when they work in groups?!

James had no idea what I was up against. None of my colleagues at OCU believed I was on the right track, not even the Frenchie dude with an Ivy League degree who thought he was so cutting edge. *"Non,*

non," he told me, irately. "*Pas du tout!* Our students must intellectual-
ize the learning process and exercise their memory muscles. They can't
be made to simply go through a listening stage and then mimic speech.
We must correct their errors or fossilization will occur!" So much for
his edge.

Señor Jaime didn't know that I was sick of defending my teaching
method, sick of faculty meetings; that I didn't give a shit about who'd
won the football game; that I couldn't have cared less if Engineering got
a juicy donation from a millionaire, if the language lab would be adding more hours and the department would now have access to several
computers. Didn't care at all. James had no idea.

The roar of a car engine jolted the thin walls. James shut his eyes,
pulled at the scant hair on his arms. "If you could see all those bodies,"
he mumbled. "There were so many..."

"Jim!" Lois snapped. "You've gotta stop tormenting yourself!"

"If you...if you could see them as I do."

What did he see? I wished I had the courage to ask him, to help him
exorcise those demons. Had he bombed entire villages? Had he shot
children? What was it like to carry the burden of so many casualties,
when you were once an agent of death yourself?

"It's been almost twenty years, Jim," said Lois.

"For me..." he cried, "it seems like yesterday."

"It happened a long time ago," Lois insisted.

"I should've refused those orders."

"But you couldn't. You had a job to do, Jim. And you were young."

"I was stupid!"

"We've all been young and stupid," noted Lois, as if facing her own
demons.

"See that medal there, at the top?" James was pointing to his uniform
coat, which was draped over the couch. "I'm proud of that one. I got it
for humanitarian work."

"What did you do to earn that medal?" I asked him, but he wouldn't
answer; he was elsewhere.

"He helped others, no doubt," answered Lois. "That's what Jim was
meant to do."

"I'm proud," he repeated, seeming exhausted all of a sudden. "I'm
proud...of that one."

"Looks like you need a nap, Jim. We'll leave you now, okay?"

"See you in class," I told him. "Tomorrow. Bright and early."

"Maybe," James nodded. "Thank you both...for the visit. *Muchas gracias.*"

As I hugged him goodbye, I realized I didn't really want the facts about his medals or his battles or his rank. Captain, lieutenant, army, navy, Viet Nam, Nicaragua, Chile. Did it matter which or where? The plaques were there in full view, but I didn't read them. No need to, since I'd already seen the horror in James' eyes; since I could now attest to a soldier's truth, which hurt everywhere.

SINGING CICADA

H er first sip of coffee, too strong for her own good, but she wants to indulge. Alina glances down the hill and sees a row of manicured patios just like hers, the California desert turned garden. No trace here of the mosquitoes and coquí frogs of Puerto Rico, of the gossip and small-town living in Quebradillas. Her youth seems distant this Sunday morning. Far away, too, are the New York winters of her first marriage, the teaching job in Queens. And her divorce. She'd rather think of the present: her life with William Pratt. How did a radical *portorra* hook up with a pragmatic, number-crunching Gringo? A cliché comes to her, unavoidably... Opposites attract. Yes, she fell in love with alterity. But there's more to it. There's the sex they have, which is furious and powerful. She hadn't known this kind of pleasure before Bill, and she'd never longed to have another child until she married him.

She used to fantasize about having a boy. A new experience for her, raising a nene. She'd name him Guillermo and call him "Guille," and he would inherit his mother's sense of humor, while taking his know-it-all airs from his father. But that's an experience she'll have to do without, unless they adopt—a prospect Bill won't embrace entirely, not yet. He can't have children; she knew about his infertility when they got married but still hasn't come to terms with it. The love she feels for him has helped, keeping her grounded, giving her strength to cope with her dream of a son who might never exist.

Curled up by the window, she'll choose to think of Leah instead, her adolescent daughter who has silky black hair, radiant eyes, *café con leche* skin just like her papá. Alina sees herself in this girl of sixteen who's going out in the evening, all dolled up and ready for the feast of her boyfriend's kisses. Barely emerging from her thoughts—like now, like this instant—Alina will tell her, "*Hija*, please don't come home late." As if that made any difference! Leah takes after her father in character, too; she's a nihilist and an atheist. Like him and unlike her mother, the girl is unconsoled by faith. Not that Alina is religious, not if that means accepting the God of Catholics, whom she was taught to fear and obey when she was child. Or the Christian fundamentalists' God, a misogynist, war-waging deity. No, if God exists, he wouldn't be as flawed as the human beings who've imagined him. Organized religion has brought more suffering than joy to humankind; Alina is convinced of this. But there's a spiritual core in her, an impulse to draw strength from creation, a deep-seated belief in the first spark of life and its inherent goodness. All of which is lacking in her daughter.

Leah might change still. She's so young! Alina isn't giving up on her, because she knows that a life without faith is bound to end in emptiness. Leah's nihilism—she hopes—will turn out to be only a stance, an outburst of adolescent rebellion. Some day the girl will realize that to be an atheist, one must deny the existence of mystery, the power of magic. Atheism bears no fruit.

Alina needs music this hazy morning, lyrics and melodies for times of reflection. She puts on the usual tape and readily awaits the first song, "Singing Cicada," written and performed by a folksy American singer from the early seventies, a woman with a sultry voice whose name Alina can never remember. The name, the person, doesn't matter anyhow. It's the song that lives on...

You have wings but you won't fly. You're afraid what you might find. You could swim in a river of light yet darkness rules your life. But I know you'll sing your song before nightfall, cicada. I know some day you will take flight. Sing your song for us, cicada. And leave the night behind...

"Singing Cicada" was blaring when she and Camilo first smoked pot together, too loud for his upstairs neighbor, Carl, who showed up at the door, asking, "Are you having a party without me?" He was a lanky engineer who'd been trying to get her to sleep with him—"go out" was his euphemism. But he didn't arouse her, physically or emotionally. And now, in Camilo's bedroom and stoned out of her mind, all she wanted to do was escape through a hole in the ceiling, a hole that would lead to the Gringo's room, so no way! Paranoid yet doubled over with laughter, she listened to Camilo while he talked to the neighbor, using sensible words he pulled out of a bag overflowing with language. How did he do it? Wasn't he high like a kite? Yes, like a gliding, carefree *chiringa* soaring in the sky. She heard their chatter, desperately needing to pee. But to get to the bathroom you had to go through the hallway, and the neighbor would see her, and she'd have to say hello, chit-chat, borrow a handful of pleasantries from Camilo's bag so the damn engineer wouldn't notice that she, that Camilo, that the two friends were merrily adrift on a windy day. A hole in the wall was what she needed!

The song resounds, as fresh as it did that summer. She had completed one term of graduate work, excited about her courses and encouraged by her well-paying Assistantship. She'd been renting a room from an older Anglo couple who suddenly decided not to house her and Leah anymore. The girl's noise was too disruptive, they said, so mother and daughter found themselves with no place to live. They were on the waiting list for a grad-student apartment and were assured a vacancy when classes started in five weeks. Leah would join Alina then, after spending those weeks with her grandparents in Quebradillas. And that's when Camilo came into the picture, bright and vivid and welcoming. He was a fellow student, from Cuba, a *caribeño* with whom she could indulge in existential trips and gut-splitting laughter. He offered her his apartment with no strings attached, and their brief stint as roommates set the tone for their friendship: a story she liked to conjure up sometimes, on sunny mornings.

It was Camilo who introduced her to "Singing Cicada," and who played many other indelible tunes for her: boleros by Lucecita, Puerto Rico's supreme vocalist; heartrending ballads by Luisa María Güell, a singer from Havana; *canciones del filin* by the Cuban quartet Los Memes; big love themes by French crooner Charles Aznavour. Whatever the mood needed, Camilo could provide it. She'd hum and sing along in her melancholy voice, and as a show of gratitude she'd serenade her friend with the songs she had loved since childhood, many by the great Daniel Santos.

"This song is about you," Camilo told her before he put on "Singing Cicada" that summer day. He said she'd like it. And, yes, she was transfixed by this melodic, poetic composition, although she couldn't relate to some of the lyrics. She empathized with the cicada's fear of flying, but it was light that ruled Alina's life, not darkness. The song became their secret theme, and Camilo seldom called her Alina again after that day, but *Cicada*. Someone once asked her if the nickname was in honor of her long brown legs, and she said, "No, it's because of my wings."

Another cup of coffee, for she hasn't yet resolved this issue called "Camilo." Alert and caffeinated, Alina draws up the memory of their first heart-to-heart. They were in the department's seminar room; a class on the Modernist poetry of Rubén Darío had just ended. She took his hand as though he were the brother she didn't have and said to him, "*Hermanito*, please talk to me. I'd like to help you. I know what you're going through." But did she really know? So typical of her, this need to straighten out people's lives, to decipher their conflicts and soothe their despairs. He opened up to her while they walked to Alina's apartment, admitting right off that he hadn't liked her initially. She was too much of a traditional female, he said, the type his father went for, *una hembra guitarra*. "I didn't know you," he confessed. "All I could see was your mask of extreme femininity." And there was a mask indeed; everyone wore them. But Alina didn't use this *hembra* façade to hide her "true" self. Why couldn't a woman be attractive—all modesty aside—and also empowered? Why couldn't a feminine woman have the soul of an intellectual, of a revolutionary? Appearances can be deceitful. Camilo was unable to see beyond the breasts, the Caribbean behind, the lipstick. At first.

Once he got to know her, there was yet another barrier for him to overcome: Alina's political beliefs. Camilo was a Cuban émigré who'd been fed *anticastrismo* his entire life, a young man with no credo and no ideology. But how could he aspire to be a writer (his most fervent wish) if he didn't question the fallacies and contradictions of all human projects? He needed to believe in something! Or at least to want to seek the truth. How would Camilo manage to write about someone like her, for instance, if he didn't care to know about the U.S. interventionist agenda, about its imperialist hold on Puerto Rico? Alina takes pride in having complicated Camilo's worldview, in humanizing his heart.

He used to insist that he hadn't felt anything deeply since childhood. That's why he sought in his memories the power to feel alive, or just to *feel*. Memories brought anguish; they made him confront the horror of what was done to him. Yet he kept reliving them, writing about them.

"I write because I remember the pain," he said. "And it's still with me."

"Most of us write when we hurt," she noted.

"Yes, but that act—writing out of pain—is an escape, Alina. It's a ruse your mind plays on your heart. A quick fix. A way of avoiding reality."

"Writing *is* reality, Camilo."

"I know. But it shouldn't be all of it."

"It isn't. Or you wouldn't be here with me."

"Oh, but I'm only here because I want to write about you."

"Go ahead, tell my story. See if I care!"

"Truth is, I became a writer by default."

"What do you mean?"

"I had this great art teacher in high school. She said I had 'the vision,' which I didn't, as it turned out. But I did love drawing and painting. I even got a prize for one of my works, a trophy. Then, one day, my father proclaimed that art was no good. 'That stuff is worthless,' he said, 'and it's a waste of time and money.' He couldn't afford my 'hobby,' anyway. No more supplies..."

"So you started writing."

"I only needed pencil and paper for this other 'hobby,' and I could use words instead of paint to escape my father and my life at home. I took to writing poems, trite and heartfelt little poems whenever the urge hit me. Whenever I hurt. And it's been that way ever since."

"Do you ever write when you're happy?"

"I've tried it. But only shit comes out."

"Well...at least it's *happy* shit!"

He knows she finds him obnoxious when he puts on his scholarly airs and tries to get "theoretical," yet Alina always tries to indulge him. Everyone is using literary theory these days, outdoing each other with grandiloquent jargon, even her colleagues at Alton City College who only teach introductory courses. So, when her friend gets *teórico*, Alina brings him down to earth.

"There is an *other*," he said to her recently, sounding like an essay on Borges. "There is an intangible other who reads me and defines himself in the act of reading."

"Yes. And who defines you in the process."

"But who the hell is that person, Alina?"

"Doesn't matter. What's important is that you need her or him."

"Right. I need the authority of others to define, or author, my self."

"You got it."

"But I don't want to have to *need* anyone, Cicada!"

"There's no way out of it, if you want to be writer."

"You know I do love writing, but what I really want is...to build a home with someone."

"And you will, *hermanito*."

"I'm not so sure, Cicada... It seems I'm incapable of having that kind of relationship."

"But you had it with Susan."

"Not really. I didn't give it my whole heart and time and energy. I didn't listen to her."

"Then learn from the experience."

"What choice do I have?"

Another sip, and she's almost ready to let go of Camilo for now. He hasn't quite accepted her bond with Bill, their marriage. "Why did you have to take a part-time job at Alton City College, damn it?!" Camilo used to ask, claiming, not convincingly, to be asking the question in jest. It was at ACC where Alina met her future spouse, having started working there the year after moving to Alton to supplement her income. It wasn't easy, adding two more classes to the one she taught at the university, while completing her own course work. But she had no choice. Too many expenses, plus the college fund for Leah and the monthly check she sent her parents. Bill was a tenured professor at Alton City College, and although she didn't want to have an affair with one of her colleagues, they ended up in bed. He was endearingly romantic, the kind of man she would never have gone for in her youth. It didn't take long for him to propose on his knees with flowers, fudgy bonbons, and a ring. She'll always wonder if her getting a job at that college was fateful, if she went there to meet the love of her life. Not her *soulmate*, however, for that word could only describe her Cuban friend.

One morning like this morning, over coffee and arepas and seated next to Camilo on her patio, Alina asked him to take her voice and run with it. "Make me a character," she urged him. "You have my permission. And write about us, from your first impression of Alina Sotovélez, so negative and wrong, to the day you had me listen to a song that would become our theme. Have your protagonist, who will have lived my life, expose the truths and contradictions she guards fiercely. Write about my first marriage to a New York school teacher who drank his life away, about my ensuing struggles as a single mother in Brooklyn, after my divorce. Write about my second life as the wife of Bill Pratt, an Economics professor whose main area of study is the Caribbean, a scholar who's devoted years to analyzing and denouncing Puerto Rico's bizarre status vis-à-vis the U.S., and who expressed his lust for me crudely as 'having the hots for a *portorra*.' Describe my efforts to guide him through the maze of my laughter, his frustrations when he just can't get my sense of humor. And you might also mention the discomfort he feels toward my friendship with you. Bill hasn't known the kind of relationship you and I have. He can't put us in a box like an equation. In his universe, love and passion can't exist between a man and a woman without sex. It's a mathematical impossibility, an aberration.

"You wonder how I can be married to Bill. Can't wrap your mind around it, no? But I've told you what he means to me. You know that raw masculinity arouses me, and Bill embodies the energy, the unbridled force of a man's sexuality. He can't fathom the role of pleasurable submission, since he'll never surrender. There's no gender ambivalence in him. Bill knows himself as a heterosexual male and feels centered as such. He can't grasp my love for you—for another man!—but, to his credit, he's never made a scene about it. Bill finds you too ambiguous, hard to pin down; and you see him as unbearably straight. Which he is. But that doesn't mean that he can't be sensitive and giving in his own alpha-male way. To you he's white-bread and dull. To me he's a brilliant scholar, a passionate lover...

"Sure, Bill and I clash about some of our cultural differences. But clashing in bed is something we want because it makes our physical union all the more exciting. We complement each other. I am a fantasy incarnate for Bill too, the voluptuous *portorra* he devours and who thrives on his debauchery. But please understand that I'd never let myself become a victim, or be the servant of a man if that's the price I must pay for the pleasure he gives me. I won't let sex be used as a weapon against me. Never. Sex should be a thrilling game, but not one that takes away one's dignity or defines us exclusively.

"Not all straight men are out to get us, Camilo. I know that's what you think, that no typical heterosexual male can be any good. But you're wrong. A man doesn't have to be gay or bisexual or sexually ambiguous to be kind and honest. A man doesn't have to think or feel like a woman to be gentle, sweet, even maternal. Not all human beings are stereotypes, my friend. I'm sure there are plenty of gay men who'd make Bill look like a passive little lamb. No, I'm not lecturing you, *hermanito*. Sorry if it seems that way. I just don't want you to become the thing you hate most."

Camilo listened, seeming enthralled and receptive. It all made sense to him, he said, and he thanked her for the insights and the "material," the latter very much in quotes. But he didn't want her story, or anyone else's, and definitely not his own. "There will be no more writing," he announced. He wanted to stop living for the sake of a text, ever trying to capture his experiences in words—experiences that shouldn't be captured, that should have no other purpose than to be lived. "*No más,*" he vowed. "Not even letters to you." Yet Alina is convinced that he'd wilt away if he stopped writing. Somewhere in his mind Camilo would still be seeking possible connections between what he sees and what he feels, between the poem he wants to forge and the one he ends up creating. Inevitably.

Sure, Camilo has written obsessively about the Cuba he strives to forget, but none of that work has quenched his creative thirst. And she knows why. She knows that, as a writer, her friend needs to venture away from himself, to see the world through the lens of other lives.

She glances at her manicured yard and notices her daughter on the grass, sunbathing. It's so seldom that Leah seems that tranquil. The girl is sensually endowed like her mother, but they differ in some essential ways. Alina can't relate to her daughter's pessimism, can't stand her doomsday diatribes. Alas, such is the lesson every parent must learn: At some level, our children will always be strangers to us. But Leah will manage to elude her father's self-destructiveness. She has a mother who loves her, who'll protect her and never leave her. Doesn't she know that? She must!

Camilo has managed to reach Leah in a way that her stepfather never could. They're much alike, those two. Both are ruled by distrust, marked by an early loss of innocence. He's learned to live with that loss, but she's still in its throes, angry at her father for abandoning her on her seventh birthday, unable to forgive him yet wanting to be part of his life. Leah thinks that if God existed, He wouldn't have let her papá leave. Just as Camilo used to think that a benevolent deity wouldn't have let him be abused as a child. But God—Alina realized somewhere along the way—isn't about protecting people from each other. God is about faith, about giving us strength to save ourselves from ourselves.

Leah will find a way out of her funk, Camilo is certain, just like he did. But has he? Hardly, for he's still struggling with his resentment toward the rapists of his childhood, toward a society that won't give him the freedom to be sexually fluid. Alina wants to believe his comforting words when he says that Leah will come around. "She hasn't realized how lucky she is," he says, "to have your love and your support. She rejects you for all the typical reasons, and also because you couldn't keep her father by your side. But eventually she'll be able to laugh like you do, for the sheer pleasure it gives you. Until that happens, give her some space. Stop forcing her to be the daughter you were. Lay off, *chica!*"

But what if Leah never comes around? Alina must be prepared for that possibility, her most challenging project. Maybe that's part of the problem, her tendency to turn people into projects, her need to play mother and sister and shrink. Camilo is right: Leah isn't the carefree adolescent Alina was. She has her own issues, and Alina has been coming on too strong, wanting her to take flight yet tying down her wings. She'll heed Camilo's advice, wait for Leah to swim her way out of darkness.

If only her friend were here this morning, sharing a big pot of coffee with her—Alina savoring her cup sip by dainty sip; Camilo in big, noisy gulps. "How's Leah these days?" he'd ask her, genuinely interested. "Still raging against God and expecting the End of Days? I hope she knows I plan to help her build the ark!" They would be laughing at the fakeness of Alina's desert-turned-garden. Like the last time, when, once the laughter subsided, she exhorted him to come out of himself, to weed out the history of things around him. "If you stop writing," she asked, "who, then, would listen to the cicadas?" And his reply didn't surprise her. "You and I would," he said. "We'll always listen together."

WAITING

The chemo was helping, said Alina, yet the face that greeted us at the door was too pale. Isabel's hair used to be dense, black, and now it looked patchy and gray. Her movements were measured, her body felt frail in my arms when I hugged her. We sat in the living room, which had the same motley décor I remembered from my previous visit. The trestle table, three-mirror room divider, porcelain dolls, and bonsai tree were all still there. But now the place looked lived-in; a futon had replaced the leather couch, and there were numerous throw pillows in bright colors. We followed our friend to the breakfast nook to have lunch—prepared for us by her caregiver, Isabel informed us. We were having sun-dried tomato pasta with sautéed vegetables, a spinach salad, vanilla frozen yogurt, and decaf espresso.

"She does a lot around the house," said Isabel about her helper, "more than she's supposed to, the stuff I used to do myself, from cooking to tending to my regimen of medications. I don't know what we'd do without her. Poor thing, I gave her a couple of days off so she can look after her own life."

Isabel's husband joined us for about fifteen minutes; Douglas was a busy financial consultant with no time to waste on his wife's pals. And their kids, too, visited with us briefly. The oldest ones, Paul, twenty-two, and Jan, twenty, were blond and lanky like their father. But Lionel, eighteen, was the spitting image of Isabel, if much more robust; he had a light brown complexion and the solid features of a Nasa Indian. Handsome people, all three, though Lionel was the best-looking one, I thought.

We had dessert outside, in Isabel's sunny, overflowing garden where pink azaleas and a variety of roses flourished. There, with champagne (which Isabel refrained from drinking), we made a toast to our friend's remission and to her new book. But Isabel looked fatigued all of a sudden. She dragged herself back to the kitchen and fetched a bottle of pills, took one with water.

"The medication makes me feel dopey," she told us, "but I'd rather not be in pain today."

"Will you read some of your poems?" Alina asked her, since we were there to celebrate the publication of *Joyas de sangre/Blood Jewels*, a bilingual edition of Isabel's poetry (with her own translations, too literal at times) that had been brought out by a small house in her native Medellín.

"Not yet," said Isabel. "First I'd like to share some wonderful news with the two of you."

"You've started working on another book?" ventured Alina.

"As a matter of fact I have. But what I want to tell you is more exciting than that... Are you ready? Paul is getting married!"

"That's wonderful!" Alina's immediate reaction.

"*¡Enhorabuena!*" I said. "When is the wedding?"

"In August. And he's marrying a very nice girl. With a college education, thank goodness."

"It's fun to plan a wedding, isn't it?" Alina mused.

"It is fun," said Isabel. "But I don't have the energy for it. There are so many details..."

"Just let someone else take care of things for a change, Isabel."

"I have, Alina. The problem is, well, it's just that...I'm running out of time."

"You will attend that wedding. I'm sure of it."

"There's nothing I want more," our friend pleaded.

"You will. August is right around the corner."

"No, Alina. It's eight months away. Eight *long* months."

"You'll make it. I promise you."

"Oh well, enough of that!" our hostess demanded. "See? This is what happens nowadays when I have company; we always end up talking about my *suplicio*." *Suplicio*: her torment, what she called the liver cancer that had spread through her body like wildfire.

Alina glanced at me, searching for a topic that would make us laugh, hoping I'd pitch in. We could always rely on the usual professor-bashing that characterized our reunions. The past we knew collectively was lodged in a period of seven years when we were graduate students. But this time the transition would be painful, the mood strained, going from Isabel's *suplicio* to our academic histrionics. Hard to inject comedy into a somber mood. We'd let the occasion be a tragicomedy, then, with laughter enveloping us like a balm, the pain forgotten for a while thanks to Isabel's magic pills.

"I'd rather talk about El Señor Escritor," said Isabel, sizing me up.

"Do we have to?" I protested, though they knew I was game.

"What are you working on these days, Camilo?"

"In my future work," I pronounced, in press-conference mode, "there'll be no autobiographical material. I'll be giving life to fresh characters, all born from moments of creative ecstasy."

"Ecstasy?" said Alina. "Sounds a bit heavy-handed, *hermanito*. But I applaud your decision to write about something—someone—other than yourself. It's about time!"

"Thank you, and yes, I'm finally venturing away from my own story."

"Tell us about some of the writers you know," asked Isabel. "But nothing obscene, please."

"Yes, *hermanito*, give us some new dirt."

Of course I would try to comply. "Let's see. How about a story about Cuban exile writer Diego Méndez Galván, author of the very dense and highly experimental novel *Five Feeble Fowl*, a man whose image was indelibly engraved in my mind at the Austin Book Fair, where I made his acquaintance. Surprisingly, I was invited to participate in the Fair having to my credit only a short first novel. There I was in the back room where all the book fair participants went to psyche themselves up—most of them stars of the literary firmament, people like the taciturn José Donoso and the loud but *très* chic Rita Mae Brown. The goateed Galván is pacing the room, his eyes scanning the floor. What did he lose down there? He shakes his gray mane as if trying to rid himself of some inner clatter. He looks anxious, cornered, trapped in that brightly lit coop like the fowl in his book. The ingenuous Camilo approaches the great Galván, tells the exiled writer how fascinating he found his novel about the nightclub scene in Havana on the eve of the 1959 Revolution. 'Wow, that book was an amazing trip!' I say. 'I read it in one sitting, totally blown away!' But Señor Galván won't react. I insist, 'You're my idol, my Cuban hero!' And Diego Méndez Galván finally acknowledges my annoying presence. 'Go away,' he says to me. *¡Fuera de mi vista, cubanito!* Can't you see I'm preparing for my entrance?!' How could I have been so insensitive? The great Cuban writer was about to face his fans!"

I took a bow. Applause.

"And by the way," Alina intimated to Isabel, "I think he's actually talking about Guillermo Cabrera Infante, who wrote *Three Trapped Tigers.*"

"Really? Why do you do that, Camilo? Why do you change people's names?"

"Please, Isabel." Alina, spilling her delicious sarcasm, her erudition. "He doesn't just change their names. He *reworks* people. He captures their essence in order to render them literary."

"Aha!" I cried out. "So I *am* able to do it, Professor Sotovélez! I can see the world through the lens of other lives, can weed out the history of things around me..."

"It's what most writers do, *hermanito*. They turn the people they know into fiction."

Isabel looked puzzled. "So," she said, "you change Infante's name to Méndez Galván and use his words and describe him just the way he is and quote him, and that's it? A new character?"

"You make it sound so easy, Isabel," I complained.

"It's not just names that get changed," Alina clarified. "Also places and titles of books and lines in poems and lyrics. Everything and everybody gets baptized anew in Camilo's universe. And there's also the language issue... He makes his Spanish-speaking characters carry on in English as if they were chatting in their native language. Thus he deprives them of their own, real voices."

"What does that accomplish, Alina?"

"Supposedly you get a certain distance, space for analysis. Isn't that right, Camilo?"

"You got it."

"But it's all kind of funny too," mused Isabel.

"Right on, Isabel!" I called out. "Can you picture anything as comical, as absurd as the three of us speaking English with each other? That's what would happen if I wrote a story about this visit."

"Same dog with a different collar," observed Isabel.

"Same dog, Isabel?" Alina, cracking up. "You're comparing Camilo's well rounded, re-imagined entities and biting parodies to a slobbering canine?! We know it's just a colloquial expression, but you must watch your tongue, *señora*! Artists are very sensitive."

"Has he ever...renamed you in one of his stories?"

"Not that I know of, but I hope he calls me Lucecita if he ever writes about me."

"But what about 'Cicada'?"

"That name hasn't made it into the books...yet."

"It suits you."

"Thank you, Isabel. I happen to like it. Anyway, it's all about poetic license, this renaming thing. Though when Camilo depicts himself and his family, the names don't change."

"Interesting. Well, then," Isabel turned to me, "I have a request for you, Mr. Nomenclator."

Another bow. "Your wish is my command."

"If you ever write about Isabel Rosas-Clark, I'd like you to call me Jazmín, okay? It's a name I love. Jazmín is what I wanted to call my daughter but Douglas didn't like it."

"Consider it done."

Isabel had a story herself, something she wanted to share, related to her illness. When she'd visited Colombia recently, a radio show host in Bogotá had presented her book by stating first that the author was recently deceased, thus her poetry collection had been published posthumously. An understandable error, given the author's condition. But since the program took calls, and Isabel *was* listening, she phoned in. "I'm still alive!" she declared, to everyone's surprise.

It had been an emotional journey, this trip to her homeland, she told us. Many people bought her book, commiserated with her, gave her home remedies for her "malignant growth." When the tour was over, Isabel was elated but exhausted. She knew this would be her last visit.

Our friend was ready to read from her book now. "But only one poem," she said, as she picked up her dog-eared copy of *Blood Jewels*. "I entitled it 'Waiting.'" Isabel stood, poised, holding on to the back of a chair with her left hand, for support; her right hand trembling as she gripped *Joyas de sangre*... "*Light here, when it comes at dawn, is limpid. You can almost drink it. That's what I've been doing lately, drinking light*

everywhere yet dying of thirst. As I wait for you. Just as the Buendías
waited for rain in Macondo. Or Gogo and Didi for Godot. Just as I waited
for the pain to pass this morning, eager like a baby bird, still refusing to
turn my nest into a graveyard. Your silence, no matter how brief, is always
a burden. Make yourself known to me again. Please come see me. I'm wait-
ing."

Alina and I praised the poem because it was honest and real and
maybe even beautiful. A challenge to define beauty just then. Easier to
believe that the shadow of death could bear lasting things. We knew
what Isabel was saying; we had both suffered the burden of someone's
silence. Or was it God that Isabel was waiting for? If so, I hoped He was
listening.

Minutes later, Alina was caressing Isabel's hand, offering support as
only she could do it, given over to friendship, driven by an immense
generosity. The next day, Isabel would be going back to the hospital for
her last, decisive treatment. A needle would be inserted in one of her
bones, thus her remaining red blood cells and platelets would be count-
ed. She'd have to endure more transfusions, more chemotherapy treat-
ments. As she'd rest and cope with the toxin inside her, Isabel would
try to take mental notes for her next book. She'd imagine her verses as
gems of a pale rose color. She'd envision her children making a necklace
with those poems and leaving it to their descendants, her poetry passing from hand to hand for generations.

We said *adiós* for now. Outside, away from Isabel's *suplicio*, I reproached myself for knowing so little about her, for not having cared
more. I admitted this to Alina: "She hasn't been a close friend, not like
you." Alina understood. "But close enough to feel for her," she said, and
I agreed.

I did know that Isabel had been born in Medellín to a repressive
Catholic family, the kind that abounds in pious Colombia. Which partly explained her refusal to attend my parties in Alton, her rejection of
what she assumed to be my lifestyle, my "polymorphous thing," as she
called it. Isabel just couldn't figure me out. And she couldn't bring herself to see Tano, whom she despised, without the filter of her mores, the
fear of sin that was pounded into her by an oppressive and homophobic religion. I tried to overlook her snide remarks whenever I'd show
up in the office with Ricci in tow, or when she'd find me chatting with
Castel; her disapproving looks when she'd notice I was eyeing a certain

sexy male student being tutored by her in our office; and her comments, which betrayed her disgust, when the young man would leave. "You liked him, right? It was very obvious!" I'd react with a shrug, ignoring her judgmental stance, which had a pungent stench of convent life and orthodox nunnery.

Isabel rejected what she didn't understand. How could I be attracted to both women and men? What was she to make of my "torrid affair" (her words, according to Alina) with "that poor young woman" (she meant Laurie) who followed me around like a lost puppy, if in her mind Isabel had already identified me as homosexual? Wasn't that dishonest? Wasn't I being disloyal and unfair to the unfortunate girl, leading her on, using her just to keep a straight front? Isabel felt more at home with her classmates who purported to be "real" men; definitely with the Don Juan of the department, her compatriot who flirted with her as he did with most women and made Isabel feel attractive, desirable— sinful, too, for she claimed to be a happily married Catholic woman. Heaven forbid!

Isabel had met Douglas Clark while on vacation in Los Angeles and married him one year later. She was in love, said Alina, but she was also naïve and romantic. Maybe she hoped that by marrying this Angeleno she'd be free at last from a culture that enslaved her, and she'd get some action, finally! Once they had children, Douglas became an absent, workaholic father and Isabel an overburdened mother. Alina and I remembered countless times when our friend had to skip class or a study group so she could take her kids to the doctor, or pick them up from school; when she had to tend to family needs like grocery shopping or a car tune-up. Yet Isabel was always prepared for our grad seminars, excited to be challenged and engaged, anxious to learn. What drove her? A hunger for knowledge? A vision of disciples whom she'd inspire? Like most of us, she must've been lured by the prospect of a job at a prestigious university. Or maybe it was fame that she awaited, willing to make huge sacrifices so that some day Dr. Rosas-Clark would be described as a great poet and a distinguished critic. The lecturer job she'd secured at Alton City College was far from ideal, but at least she didn't have to drive for hours in L.A. traffic to get to work, and she was able to be there for her children.

Douglas thought she spent too much time on her poetry, and all for naught. We didn't have to hear it straight from Isabel to know he couldn't care less about her creative work. His gestures, the looks he gave us all betrayed his disdain for what he called our "artistic efforts." He talked about his wife's "writer fantasy," which—he insinuated—she could indulge thanks to the money he made. "Isabel's poems are downers," he told us once. "Written for other poets like yourselves." Douglas just couldn't understand Isabel's dream, which wasn't about fame or wealth but about doing something you loved.

Near the end, Isabel could feel proud to have published a beautifully crafted collection of poetry and a handful of articles, essays on the lyrical voice in the works of Gabriela Mistral and Alfonsina Storni, on the feminist imagery in young women poets from Colombia. She could be content to have left a small yet indelible mark on the literary world. And, near the end, one August day, our friend would celebrate her biggest triumph, which had nothing to do with academic glory.

CHILL OUT!

I kept having allergies in Kansas. Didn't know you could run a high fever from allergies. It was exhausting. Fortunately I had a good doctor, caring and not out to make a buck. One of those bouts of allergies turned into a bronchial infection, no doubt exacerbated by my smoking. I was bound to bed for a week, barely aware of the passage of time. I kept seeing Susan in my room through a misty veil, like a ghost. And I saw her in a dream walking down the aisle on the arm of her future husband—who wasn't me. Only it wasn't just a dream; I'd actually heard that she was engaged to marry a lawyer from Newton, a Mennonite. I thought I'd die when I got the news. Slept away the hours, couldn't fathom the idea of Susan married to another man. Was that the freedom she sought? What about her need to learn and grow? She'd hooked up with a Mennonite to find herself?! I wished I could go back in time and never take a job in Kansas, never meet Susan Thompson, never fall in love with her...

Then I ran into her in the Department; she was there to sign graduation forms. We did the usual chit-chatting. I told her about some of my projects, and Susan listened while she searched in her bag for flyers, calls for papers, news she'd been saving to show me, a world she still wanted to share with me. Thankfully there was no mention of her "good news." Can't believe I managed to disguise my grief—perhaps I didn't. Can't believe I didn't carry her off in my arms into the horizon... *Camilo, my hero!*

I knew we'd never be together again, yet hope was driving my fingers as I wrote to Susan that same day... *I wanted to be there in the future you're embarking on, Susan, to help you build your world and learn to see mine through your eyes. You said you had to seek your own answers, and I could relate. Just keep in mind that only you can ask the needed questions. No one can do it for you, definitely not a man who won't burn with the fire thriving in your soul. The same fire that burns in mine. This passion I feel for you, which still overflows in everything I do, must begin to wane, Susan. Because it's meant to be, perhaps? Yet there will come a moment each day, for the rest of my life, when I must conjure you up, just like I need to breathe. And I must fight this urge to hold you, must banish you so I can keep from dying. It's time to live, Susan, time to stop loving you. But you know I always will.*

How old was Dr. Milo turning that year? Old enough to be a professor and young enough to still need his mother's embrace. Milo lived in a world of words, but when all the words were said or taught, he went back to his tower to dream of fame and glory. Deep down, or maybe not so deep, he knew he'd never make it big. He just wasn't capable of concocting a page-turner, a tale having nothing to do with his exile. Nor was he willing to sprinkle his stories with a bit of action, mystery, or adventure. Dr. Milo didn't know how to spin a good tale, one with an actual plot. Hence he was forever stuck in the Midwest, teaching Spanish at some out-in-the-boondocks university. What happened to the promising artist who was destined to go far? Well...he became a scholar who published cryptic little essays in journals that nobody read, a part-time novelist who'd revealed too many family secrets in his "literary" novels that didn't sell, an armchair Marxist who tried too hard to believe in all that class-struggle jive.

What Milo truly believed in were mythical monsters. Myth is something you take for granted, he'd tell his students, a truth you're not allowed to question, an idea that gets inside your head and makes you act a certain way. He'd go into this diatribe about the mind-numbing media and how they turned you into a stereotype and didn't give you a chance to think for yourself. But some day, if he quit academia, Dr. Milo wouldn't have a captive audience. There would be no one around to listen to his lectures. What was to happen to him then? Oh, he'd just have to get a cat or a dog or both...

I see him spouting truth in class, explaining the concept of "social conditioning" to a group of Republican farm boys and girls, then chain smoking and indulging in a fantasy set to music. I see him in front of

the mirror in suit and tie, looking victimized as he wonders what the
hell his life means. Or is he admiring his visage? Yes, he thinks he's Don
Johnson or that Hamlin guy in *L.A. Law*. Or Rocky Echevarría from *Qué
pasa, USA?* (one of Mechy's favorite sitcoms), whose career seemed to
have taken a dive when he tried to remake himself as "Steven Bauer."
Maybe Milo's a closet actor—happens to be the case with a lot of people
in the Ivory Tower. He's so full of it sometimes. Chill out, dude!

Turns out that he wasn't admiring his handsome face but looking
again at his scar, which he's prone to define as "patriotic." It's clearly
visible if you know what to look for: near the left eye and shaped like
Cuba, only it's the island in reverse, as if seen in a mirror. The cayman's
head is pushing inward toward the continent, making its way into the
Gulf of Mexico. Sounds literary, could make for interesting symbology
in a poem or a novel. Problem is, Milo didn't invent it and thus can't
take credit for it. Besides, his mother was the one who claimed he had
"proof" of his Cubanity. "Look, my Lito can prove he's Cuban," she'd
brag. "He has the island drawn on his face!"

Mechy would always blame herself for the fall that caused her son's
scar... She was giving him a bath. Lito was only three but he remem-
bers the lukewarm water, his mother's touch, and feeling frightened
when she left him alone. She'd gone to fetch a towel and hadn't gotten
far when she heard his cries. Lito had slipped, hitting his head on the
edge of the bathtub. Mechy rushed back in and saw blood on her son's
face, coloring the soap suds. She screamed. Then Matilde, Lito's grandmother, who had been making *empanadillas* in the kitchen, showed up
in the bathroom with her hands flour-coated. She groped to find the
source of the bleeding and tried to stop it by placing tiny dough balls
in the wound. And Mechy thought she was seeing pieces of flesh in the
bloody mess! She fainted. But Matilde knew what to do; she carried the
boy to the hospital, running down the street. It was a miracle that he
didn't lose his eye, said the doctor. But Elio never thanked his mother-
in-law for doing this, on the contrary... *Papi says Abuela is a witch, that
she made me fall in the bathtub and hurt myself and so now I have a headache that won't go away. Then she turned my scar into a cayman with her
communist voodoo so I'd be trapped on this island forever. But I know
that's a lie 'cause Abuela loves me.*

Anyway, there's Dr. Milo rediscovering a scar that he tends not to
see anymore when he looks in the mirror. Faded by time, disguised by

his wrinkles, the mark reappears whenever Mechy needs to revisit his babyhood. "There it is! You can still see the island!" Cuba's claim to his skin. To his soul?

"Your father is fighting for his life," Mami told me on the phone one night in June of that year, crying. "*Pobrecito.* He's in pain all the time now, and confused. Sometimes he forgets who I am and where he is. The medication is strong but it doesn't seem help; all it does is make him groggy and forgetful. I don't know what else to do for him, *mijo.* God help him!"

I had been enduring the boiling cauldron which was Kansas in early summer, pushing myself out of my funk to get some work done. But that job, my home, none of it felt real anymore without Susan. Reality had a different name now, all of a sudden, and it was *Elio.* I flew to L.A. before the end of my semester, claiming a family emergency. I was planning to be in Bay City anyway, till mid August at least, maybe longer. Normally it would depend on how long I could bear staying there without going nuts, but now it all depended on Papi. He was hanging on, his body undoing itself as he rebelled against it, unresigned. He was barely able to walk anymore but was still the same old grumpy Elio, though now he had rare moments of tenderness when he thanked Mechy for all she was doing. It seemed he needed the imminence of death to turn human...

Mami greeted me with a surprise: a handful of photos of Las Tinajas that Abuela had sent, the first recent images of our hometown I'd seen. It was unsettling to realize that a place I had learned to imagine *did exist*, that it'd been there all along, waiting. There was only one picture of Abuela, none of my grandfather. She looked heavier than I remembered; they must've been getting enough to eat somehow. Abuela was standing by a bench at the park, an iconic palm tree behind her. I wondered why she hadn't posed at home, in the house where she'd spent a lifetime. Not pretty enough, perhaps? What would that be like, looking at the same crumbling walls for sixty years? Would your home eventually feel like a tomb? One of the photos was of the church across from the park (still standing!), and there was a snapshot of my house, the red tile roof, the whitewashed façade, the front garden. I saw children peeking through a window. Who were they? Who'd been sleeping in my bed, playing with my toys?!

I took Mami to Redondo Beach one morning, while Papi slept; he never woke up before noon. I had given her no choice, "You need fresh air, some sun." And she acceded reluctantly, "But only for an hour, okay?" We were sleepwalkers pretending to enjoy the sight of brightly painted houses, balconies overlooking the surf, potted plants and flowers, seashells. I suggested we go somewhere for brunch, to a bistro on the pier maybe, but Mami wasn't hungry. And she was worried about Elio, so we went home, afraid we might find him awake. As soon as we walked in he started yelling, "Where the fuck were you two?!" In a fit of anger, he threw one of his slippers at Mami, then an empty glass, shouting, "Damn you!" He hit himself, hard blows to his head, thighs, knees, stomach.

Watching my father fall apart I thought about time, not the time measured by clocks, divided into years, days, hours, minutes. But human time, which lives within our bodies. That's the place we're all bound to, inevitably, and where my sick father was housed against his will. A dying body.

He needed medical attention around the clock, which we weren't trained to give him. We had no choice but to move him to a clinic. His room was spacious, with a view of a flower garden. The doctors seemed competent; they treated him with no less respect and no more condescension than their other patients; and the nurses were cheerful, caring. Mami kept Elio company as much as she could, spending the night with him on occasion. I wanted to help Mami look after Papi full-time. But she said no, she didn't want me to quit working, wouldn't hear of it. *"De eso nada,"* she insisted. Regardless, I had already decided to leave Oz for good, whether I had another job lined up or not.

My pickings were slim: possible interviews in Pittsburgh, Michigan, Alabama, but nothing good in California, where I needed to be. The market on the sunny West Coast was saturated. I just couldn't compete; had published only half a dozen articles and no book-length scholarly work. My best prospect was Lawson University in Jackson, Alabama. A solid PhD program, four grad courses a year, tenure-track. Why they wanted me, I wasn't sure. But I had a hunch and was curious. So there I went, interviewing for a job in a Southern town, home of the KKK... *Help!*

I met the usual assortment of profs in Lawson, did some shop talk about language teaching and answered questions about "the best Latin American novels of this century." Nothing I couldn't handle. The only problem there—ironically, the main reason I got an interview— was Professor Rubén Gaviña, a fellow Cuban. My compatriot wanted to bring *cubanos* to the department to fatten up his army and strengthen his reign. Fortyish, pot-bellied, Gaviña showed me around campus clad in a navy blue sweatsuit (sporty and hip!) and wearing white-framed sunglasses that matched his car interior. He gave me a ride through the picturesque town in his red Porsche. "*Negro 'e mierda!*" he cursed when he was forced to stop for a black pedestrian. Then he got confidential, "I've got it made, *compatriota*. One class per term, a top-of-the-scale salary, and a hot Gringa to fuck whenever I'm horny."

We drove to his home, a large log house among pine trees. There he introduced me to his Cuban wife, who looked older than him, and his teenage daughter. He wanted me to feel *en casa*. "If you take this job," he told me, "you'll be able to eat with us whenever you want to. My wife's a great cook!"

There seemed to be no conflict in him. His rampant infidelity had no bearing on his role as family man, devoted husband and father. What amazed me about Rubén was that he didn't see me, not for real; he couldn't imagine the existence of a Cuban male who wasn't like him. But this shouldn't have surprised me. Maleness tends to be that way, so sure of itself that you can fool it easily. Its assumed superiority renders it naïve. Because maleness considers itself absolute, it is unable to detect dissidents and spies. Maleness sees itself everywhere but is blind to alterity.

Rubén didn't chair the department but ran the show. The nominal chairperson was an Anglo woman whom he disparaged because, according to him, she was a disgusting dyke, a *tortillera*. He laughed about her flat butt, about her research on *lesbianas perversas*. But he'd let her "reign" in order to comply with the latest university mandates, a "stupid political trend" he couldn't grasp. "Gotta hire women, niggers, dykes, and faggots! These Gringos are crazy, man!"

He was sure I'd take the job. "You have to accept our offer, Camilo," he told me and threatened me playfully, "I know a lot of people, and if you piss me off I could hurt you!" What exactly would he do, I wondered. Badmouth me perhaps; call in favors with his buddies and pull strings so I'd be faced with closed doors everywhere, unable to get articles published or papers accepted, or to get interviews for prospective jobs. I'd heard of such cases in academic circles, people who got on somebody's black list and consequently suffered their vindictive wrath. But I just wasn't concerned about Gaviña's threat. If I took the job, it wouldn't be due to my fear of what he might do to hurt me if I didn't. And if I did join the Lawson faculty, I knew I'd have to find a way to repress the disgust Rubén provoked in me.

Gaviña didn't publish, and I suspected he didn't read much. The shelves in his office were bare, except for some scattered language textbooks and several modest Sagüesera-edition copies of José Martí's *Versos sencillos*. "It's my favorite book," Rubén told me when he saw me glancing at the copies. "Not just of the ones Martí wrote but of all the poetry collections I've ever read. I keep a whole bunch of copies here in my office to give to my best students as presents."

How sad, I thought. Martí appropriated both by Cubans like Gaviña and also by the so-called revolutionaries in Cuba. *Like a flag that calls to battle, the candle's red flame flutters...* Such seems to be the fate of our apostle, to be remade into whatever image and ideology is needed by both the current Cuban *caudillo* and the exile community. Dictators Machado and Batista quoted Martí to justify their brutal mandates, then Fidel turned him into a Marxist! This after the Cuban Communist Party, prior to the Revolution, had derided Martí for being an ally of the rich and an opportunist. How easily a man's words can be stolen, uttered out of context, and distorted!

The official story in the Cuban exile community, namely Miami, is that the U.S. stands for freedom, humanism, and prosperity. This great country can do no wrong; well, except for its apparent inability to kick some communist butt. Therefore exiles have had to overlook Martí's position vis-à-vis the United States, his denouncement of this country's ruthless imperialistic ways, in order to claim him, too, as their own. Good old Joe Marty was simply mistaken in his views of America!

Back in my musty hotel room in Jackson, Alabama, I read the copy of *Versos sencillos* that I'd received from Rubén as a token of his appreciation for the "right answer" he was sure I'd be giving him. I did love that book, but it was a line from a poem in another of Martí's works that I was remembering now... *Night is a good time to say farewell...* Couldn't this act of remembrance also be seen as one of appropriation, not unlike that of so many other Cubans? Indeed. Yet I've always felt as though it was José Martí who seized me, who gripped Lito both as guide and warden, as a source of inspiration as well as imprisonment. Our great apostle: an inescapable voice, the Poet of poets, the sine qua non of Cuban literature. But didn't Martí—with his ideals, his talent, his passion for justice and freedom and poetry—also try to save me? Or so I imagined when I had to write an ending for *Cuba in Silence*. He couldn't rescue the novel's protagonist from his fate (too late for that) but he did set Camilo free.

I had three days to decide about Lawson, but I'd made up my mind already. I would let Rubén's committee know my decision in a letter when I was back in Kansas. I wasn't accepting their offer—or taking any other job. No more teaching for now. First things first: my parents needed me. Giving them a hand would be a good transition for me, a passage to whatever awaited our family. Awaited me.

Here was the end of my academic dream, such as it was. I wanted to live with Camilo for a while, teach myself things, write, be happy. "You can't be happy unless you're willing to be," said Alina on the phone. "But I *am* willing, Cicada, and eager and ready!" She said if I quit academia I'd have to be more disciplined than ever, create my own schedule, new daily routines. Quite a challenge. She suggested I approach each day as a *proyecto de existencia*. It was what she did, and she believed it should also work for me. Another great idea from Alina... Live each day as a project of existence.

III
Into My Life

LIKE FATHER LIKE SON NO MORE

Papi is waking up, slowly turning into same old Elio. He did janitorial work for fifteen years, nothing like his sales job in Cuba yet an ideal occupation for someone who likes to be alone. But Papi won't be alone during the days he has left, while he withers away in this upscale Torrance clinic, and the only obligation (his defining word) left to him is bearing the ravenous course of his stomach cancer.

The nurse for the morning shift is a Filipina named Connie whom Papi likes. She greets him warmly, "You're looking good today, Mr. Macías!" She then checks his vitals, his IV and oxygen, refreshes his bedding and tells me he's stable. When she leaves, I grab the chart by his bed and study it. There's no new information on it since yesterday, no facts conveying any hope, but reading it gives me a sense of purpose. I helped Connie bathe Papi yesterday; he had peed all over my feet while I guided him to the bathroom. He must've thought there was time, but the short walk seemed tortuous to him, interminable. I pulled him close and held him after his bath, and he relaxed. He sat on the bed, inert, his pride wounded. I rubbed a perfumed lotion over his neck and arms and over the sores on his back. He cried out, "¡Coño, qué alivio!" Then he collapsed and fell asleep.

It seems I've learned a valuable lesson from my father after all. We must always do the right thing, *lo correcto*. That's why I'm here, having left behind the life I've forged on my own. Because it is my duty, and because my scholarly pursuits feel pointless to me now, as I face Elio's departure. Nothing I've ever read or written has prepared me for this day when I sit by his side with a photo album in my lap, this day when

I still ponder the same old questions. The bitter truths of my childhood would only crush my father, cutting to the core of who he is. Too cruel, unnecessary. No. Elio Macías must die believing that his mission in life was accomplished. He protected his family. He took care of me.

"Look, that's you and Mami," I tell him, pointing to a snapshot from the album. "What a handsome couple, like movie stars." I hand him his glasses, he inspects the photograph. "People said you were the spitting image of Clark Gable. Same mustache and haircut, no? And Mami was as pretty as Liz Taylor. Look. She was so beautiful." He smiles and points to his wife's ample hips in the picture. "Right," I tell him. "Liz with a Cuban butt!" He seems amused. "You were wearing a guayabera. Mami liked the way those shirts looked on you. But you never wore them again after we left Cuba..."

"Jevita..." he whispers.

"Yes, Papi, that's Jevita, your wife." He never called her Mercedes or Mechy, always *Jevita*. And she complained about it, didn't like the name because it meant "chick," or "young broad," and she saw herself as a dignified *señora*. Which she was!

He smiles faintly. "And here we all are, you, Mami, and me. That's our house, see? A beautiful chalet." He touches a spot on the print, the faded image of two earthen jars in the garden. "Our town was famous for its *tinajas*," I help him recall. "The best earthen jars in the country."

A photo of his Chevrolet Bel Air. "And this is your car."

"My Chevy," he says, finally tuned in. "It was green and...silver."

"Yes, with a black leather interior. You loved your '58 Chevy, Papi."

"They...they took it away."

"Yes, it was appropriated by the state."

"Communists," he says, his voice barely audible, "they steal your life."

"Here, look at these." Our vacation shots, the three of us riding in a horse-drawn carriage at a park in Camagüey, swimming at Varadero Beach, and Camilito standing by the mouth of a cave at the Bella Mar Cavern in Matanzas. "Remember the story they told us there, in Bella Mar? It was about a boy who'd been turned into rock and lived in a cavern wall..." But of course he has no memory of that story, and he can't remember our trip there, either. Has dementia set in? No, he's just too drugged up to recall much of anything. But he's "comfortable," the doctors claim.

I pull out a photo of Elio in burlap pants, khaki shirt, soiled boots. He laughs, says, "Elio the peasant!" True, he's dressed as a *guajiro*, home from the sugar cane fields for a weekend visit. February 1969, ten years since the triumph of the Revolution.

"You had to do farm labor," I tell him, "or they wouldn't let us leave the country."

"*¡Ay, coño!*" Papi cries out, suddenly anxious. "*Coño coño,*" he keeps saying, now as a murmur.

"Take it easy, Papi. What do you need? Some water?"

"Yes, a little. " He's trying to relax.

"Here. And I'll call the nurse."

"No, don't," he pleads, taking a couple of sips. "I'll be fine... Show me more."

"Not a good idea. The photos are upsetting you."

"Please, Camilo." His tone is sad yet endearing, so out of character.

"Okay," I humor him. "But just a few more pictures. Then it's nap time for you."

I show him a photo of our family at the Rancho Boyeros airport in Havana, May 22, 1969. We're about to board a United flight bound for Miami, Florida, on our way to Los Angeles.

"My...mother," he struggles, "Mamá wasn't...at the airport that morning."

"You're right, Papi, she wasn't."

"Poor Mamá," he says. "I have...I have forgotten her face."

He might've also forgotten that Eulalia, a widow, stayed in Cuba for the sake of Ester, her daughter. Elio's only sibling was married to a *miliciano* who hardly ever spent time at home and was rumored to have another wife in Camagüey. Ester had four sons to look after, and Elio resented Eulalia's decision to stay behind to help bring up those children. He cursed his sister for marrying a creep and for not asking Eulalia to leave for the North with him. Papi might've chosen to forget that his mother died three years after we parted, that the news of her death devastated him. It was all Castro's fault, he said. That bastard was responsible for the circumstances that caused Eulalia's heart attack. And he'd made it impossible for Elio to attend his mother's funeral.

"Jevita..." he mutters, deep in thought. "Jevita says I'll see Mamá in Heaven."

"Do you think you will?"

"No, that won't happen. Nothing happens after you die. You just... rot."

"How can you be so sure, Papi?"

"More photos, Camilo," he demands.

Fine, but here's one I'll skip, of Matilde and Mariano, his in-laws, the big Castro supporters. He hated their guts. Matilde reproached him for taking me to the States, "Milo belongs in his country! With his people!" Elio's reaction: "Shut up, you commie bitch! My son belongs where he can have a future and be free! Not in this fucking Soviet hell!" One day he almost slapped her in front of me. He stopped when he saw me burst into tears; and when she tried to console me, he pushed her away and dragged me to my room, shouting, "Stop crying, *coño*! Men don't cry!"

Another image I won't show him: Mechy with her parents, her mother donning a *miliciana* uniform. Why did Mami include this photo in the album, knowing how Elio would react if he saw it? Maybe it reminded her of all the good in the Cuban Revolution. I've often wondered if Mami was a revolutionary at heart. "Elio thinks Fidel is all bad," she said to me once, not long ago. "But Fidel did some great things. He tried to help the poor people like my parents; no one had cared about us before. It's sad that all the power went to his head later. But what could you expect? Castro is a typical Cuban man, stubborn and controlling. Full of himself, as you would say..." Whatever it was Mami felt about Castro, she had to make a painful decision. I know she was torn. If she left the country, there was a chance she'd never see her parents again. But being separated from her son—for surely Elio would've taken me with him—just wasn't an option. For consolation, Mechy told herself that Mariano and Matilde could count on the support of their comrades. The Party would now be their family, since they had no other children. Mami learned to let go of her parents over time, but she's never lost hope of bringing them to California, if only for a visit. And that could only happen after Elio is gone.

"Hey, here's the first color shot of our family in Bay City." Papi seems interested. "And here I am, stuffing my face with waffles and bacon and scrambled eggs. What a pig!" I point to a photo of Mami dressed in a sky-blue satin robe and wearing a cheap blond wig. "Check her out, Papi! She must've thought she was Marilyn Monroe! And this is our first apartment. Remember that green couch we had, upholstered in plastic? Your skin would stick to the plastic if you were wearing shorts, and it hurt like hell when you stood up. We all hated it! But the apartment was nice, wasn't it?"

Papi looks tired. "That's it," I tell him, putting the album away. "Time for a siesta."

"I did it for you," he declares. "I left my country for you, Camilo."

"I know, Papi, and I'll always be grateful..."

"I did it for Mechy too."

"You should relax now, okay? I'll be right here."

I tuck him in, thinking that he also "did it" for himself. His hatred of Fidel motivated him to wait in countless lines in Havana, requesting papers, filling out forms, being treated like shit. Not only to save me, but to save Elio Macías. For what is a salesman to do when his job has been declared a crime against the Nation? Working for the benefit of all your fellow Cubans (in reality, for the state) was the only option, the socialist way. But what did Elio know about socialism? He worked his butt off to support his family. Having just turned fifteen when he hit the road, he'd had no formal education; learned his trade from his father and succeeded at his job because he was charming and persuasive when pushing his merchandise. And then, out of the blue, the government was denouncing him as an enemy of the people, a vestige of the past, a maggot. How could he not be pissed at Fidel? Killing the "bearded bastard" became Elio's obsession, his *raison d'être*. Understandably so.

But we made it, Papi, thanks to you. We arrived in paradise, and Eden turned out to be a desolate planet of never-ending freeways, of strip malls and factories and billboards and smog. You couldn't walk down the street and see crowds or parks. The ocean was too cold, its waves dark and fierce. You began to seem wilted, Papi. You'd get home bedraggled and greasy from the *factoría*. Exile was hard work and loneliness and humiliation. English was so hard to learn. But now you could provide plenty for us. Such blissful abundance! Honey-baked ham, steaks, glazed donuts, soda pop, burgers, fries, milk shakes. The food Americans ate. We lived in a modern two-bedroom apartment, and you had a car again. Here it is, a photo of Elio in the driver's seat, proud owner of a freshly-waxed 1962 Rambler. Things were working out; your son was learning English at school, soon to start working, and both you and Mami had jobs. Yet the great North would never feel like home. You were still holding onto the hope of returning to Cuba. One day you realized we were never going back, and this realization was compounded by my apathy and my lack of respect for your nostalgia. I'd be able to slip into this alien culture with little effort, but you'd remain outside, resentful, uprooted, unleashing your wrath against me, *"¡Somos cubanos, coño!* Don't you dare forget where we come from!"

You hadn't changed, Papi. You were the same as always, violent, abusive. And Mami feared you, moving aside whenever your fists fell on my face. But I was in my late teens by then and felt stronger, ready to fight back. I started wearing makeup, donning necklaces of beads and seashells, tinting my hair. And you were outraged, ashamed, because your son was a hippie, or worse, a Little Mary. A *maricón*. I knew I was hitting you where it hurt you most...

It's mid-afternoon, and I haven't eaten since breakfast. I'm not really hungry, just needing some fresh air, a break. And my smokes. I leave Papi asleep and pick up a chicken sandwich at a drive-thru, then I stroll through a park near the clinic. The span of grass before me is dry, but there are tables and some trees. The freeway isn't visible from here, thankfully. I sit and eat and smoke, watching the old folks who amble by, the Mexican nannies looking after blond toddlers, the studs on skates.

I leaf through this photo album (just had to bring it along) that Mami put together for me. "So you can show your children some day," she said. The album itself is not exceptional: store-bought, cardboard dressed in cream-colored plastic simulating leather, a three-ring binder for the pages. Oh but the wealth it holds! Compelling proof of the life we've lived. I look for photos of my mother and find one I took, of Mechy at her sewing machine. She made dresses for weddings and *quinceañeras* and some outfits for herself. A welcome source of income, said Papi. But for me it was the stuff of dreams: supermodels wearing Mechy's haute couture designs down the catwalk and retailers vying for her "signature" creations. I think of my portrait of Mami, how little it captured of the creative seamstress, chef extraordinaire, photographer, devoted wife, and exemplary mother that she is. Mercedes, the only child of a domineering woman, wasn't allowed to go to parties or date until she turned twenty, and then only in the presence of a chaperone. She married late by Cuban standards, probably afraid by then of becoming a spinster, left behind to "dress the saints." In Elio Macías she saw a handsome man who courted her gallantly and who might provide a way out of her smothering home. If Mechy suspected that he'd become a tyrant, she simply chose to hope for the best. And maybe she was in love...

A photo of Mami watching a *telenovela*. Sometimes I'd catch the latest Mexican soap with her, always amazed at the triteness of it all. With those shows Mechy could put her life on hold; they told a story that was far removed from her own yet strangely familiar, easy to cry to. Sitting with her in front of the tube, both of us smoking (she never quit), I'd put up with her harangues about Elio. "He's such a penny-pincher!" she'd complain. "Don't buy this, don't buy that, that's too expensive. One has to save for the future, yes, Lito. But you also need some luxuries now, before you die!" Then it'd be Papi's turn, while I helped him wash his car or clean out the garage. He'd bemoan his wife's shopping sprees, her disdain for financial matters, her stupid comments about everything. Couldn't Elio and Mechy see that I didn't care? Poor Camilito, so burdened with his parents' petty grievances!

Lito is everywhere in this album, dressed as Zorro for Carnaval, posing by a cave wall in Bella Mar Cavern, feeding a pig in his backyard and eating like a pig himself, meals that Mami concocted magically. These images of the boy I used to be are here thanks to Mechy, who was always driven to photograph my life and thus paved the way for my writing. Photos can help us flesh out the world we're bringing to the page— a fruitful technique I've probably used in excess in my work. But I don't regret having depended on Mami's images. I couldn't have revisited my childhood without them.

Mechy scoffed at my suggestion that she take a photography class at a local college. "It would be a waste of time," she said, laughing at herself. "I already know how to press the button!" She thought I was being a "nice son" whenever I told her that she intuitively knew about color and contrast, about composition; that she had a keen eye for capturing scenes of daily life. Hoping to inspire her, I gave her several matted prints by Ansel Adams, whose work I'd discovered in my high school art class. The beautiful black-and-white photos of the American West (rivers, rocky mountains, lakes) would end up on Mami's bedroom wall, next to her own framed images of household plants and flowers. "Poor Mister Adams," she joked. "His work deserves better company!"

I cherish her photos from Cuba. The camera she had there was a birthday gift from Papi, so, in a sadly ironic way, it was Elio who incited his wife's passion for photography. He got her the latest model from Nikon, circa 1965. I doubt there were many of those in Cuba; surely he got it on the black market. I remember what an ordeal it was to get its pictures developed; Mami complained about it frequently. She nicknamed that camera *La chula Nikkor*, grateful to Elio for giving her such a unique present. Mechy loved her "cute" Nikkormat, though not as much as she would come to love her first Polaroid, which she bought at a garage sale shortly after our arrival in Los Angeles. It was a model 320 Land camera, still in good shape. It looked professional, we thought, and seemed musical with that middle part that contracted and stretched like an accordion. Mechy was very protective of it, wouldn't let my clumsy young hands near her gadget. Which was fine with me, as long as I got to have some of her amazing pictures. Mami's Nikkormat is long gone (she couldn't bring it with her when she left Cuba), but that Polaroid lives in a closet, packed in with hundreds of prints stashed away in padded mailers and some of those flash bulbs (kept as mementos) that were used in the Sixties, which left an acrid, fetid smell after going off. The Polaroid is the only camera Mami has held on to, of the many she's owned. For memory's sake, says Mercedes, as one of her *recuerdos*.

I'm missing the job I no longer have in Kansas. Who would've thought? Kansas as a welcome oasis: vast, golden fields and endless horizons; my spacious home office with a view of towering cottonwoods and irises and violets in the spring. It all seems ideal from this room, like a good dream from which you don't want to wake up and that, once you open your eyes, becomes the memory of a nightmare. To be fair, not all of my life in Kansas was nightmarish; I did meet Susan there. The main reason I went to the Midwest was to find and lose the love of my life. *Better to have loved and lost...* Bullshit! It's better to love and never lose. But this is not the time to be lamenting my bad breaks. What I miss isn't really a place, anyway, but a distance, a separateness from my role as Elio's son.

I just realized I've been chain-smoking; on autopilot, Susan would say. One last drag for the road, but I can't bring myself to leave this park and rejoin Papi's dying universe just yet. I puff away, ashamed to be one more suicidal Marlboro man, the *Lights* type. Milder dosages of poison—that delicious tar!—aren't as bad for you, right? I wonder how Papi managed to evade lung cancer, considering he was a heavy smoker for most of his life—his Camel sticks have only been off limits the last two years. It seems that for Elio it was going to be either the lungs or the stomach, although the pork lard he's consumed would've clogged up his arteries, not trigger his cancer. Miraculously, his lungs are in great shape, whereas mine... I find blood stains on my pillow some mornings, and some nights I cough too much. Been ingesting tar and nicotine (half a pack a day) for twenty-five years because cigs fill the void; they're an excuse to pull away and watch. But no more, unless I want to end up hooked to a machine like my father, awaiting an agonizing death. I'll always crave the burning in my throat, the hot trenches of smoke in my lungs. I'll miss the very act of bringing out the stick, holding it gently, giving it fire, bringing it to my lips and sucking in the venom. Must give up that pleasure. Can I be that strong? Can I cheat death at least in some small way? Okay, but just one more for the road...

Papi mutters something when I walk in the door. I think he wants to know where I was. I tell him I was having lunch. He shuts his eyes and says he's hungry for some real food. I sit closer to him and ask him, "If you could have real food, what would you have, Papi?"

"Black beans, rice...and a big chunk of pork. *Lechón*...like we ate for Christmas."

"Christmas was exciting in Cuba, wasn't it? Eduardo used to kill the pig for us, remember? He knew where to aim, which spot to jab. Straight to the heart! And it didn't take him long."

"I paid him well."

"Yes, because he was good at it."

I remember the bloody sight of it all, the smell, the sounds. Eduardo's knife would plunge straight to the pig's heart, then a river of blood would flow onto the mud. The gray-white beast was poked through from mouth to anus and placed over a fire, sparks bursting out and burning you ever so slightly. Everyone loved the swine's sizzling crisp skin smeared with *mojo*, turned into *chicharrón*. I did too, though I was tearful and anguished about the poor animal.

"Pork... Pork is the best meat," Papi says longingly. "Can't have *Navidad* without it."

"Sometimes I dream about those days. Do you, Papi?"

"Those...days?"

"Yes. Do you ever dream about Cuba?"

"No, never. I don't...I don't have dreams."

"Everybody has dreams, Papi, but some people can't recall them."

"I must be... I am one of those people. When I wake up..."

"Yes? Go on. When you wake up you can't remember anything, right?"

"Right. And all I can think about...are the real things in my life."

"Of course. Your obligations." Elio's key word, indeed: *obligaciones.*

"I feel...sleepy," he admits.

"Get some rest, then."

Christmas in Bay City. Ho ho ho. The food is great thanks to Mami; she serves *pernil, yuca, congrí,* and *casquitos de guayaba.* Easy to find presents for her; she's happy with a gift card to one of her favorite stores. But I never get anything for Elio anymore, not since the Christmas of the Briefcase. How long ago was it? The briefcase was encased in light brown leather and monogrammed. "For your papers," I told him, "all those things stashed away in your night table." He said it was too fancy. "Please, Elio," Mami intervened, "it'll be perfect for your documents and our checks and receipts." But no, Papi wouldn't accept it. Maybe he didn't think himself deserving of such a present, or it bugged him that it had come from me, or he just wanted to make me feel like shit. Ho ho ho to hell!

For one of his recent birthdays I gave him a card; it was a simple, no-frills kind of card. In it I wrote a message I felt he needed to hear... *I know you lost everything to forge a life of freedom for me, Papi. You left your country so I could have a future. Gracias...* And his reaction took me by surprise. "You're welcome, *mijo,*" he said, and he gave me a hug, weeping like a child.

The latest doctor who's been tending to him comes in and examines his patient, who barely opens his eyes. Dr. Morrow is young and not much for bedside manner. "I'll get to the point," he tells me. "All we can do for him now is keep him comfortable. The sad fact is..."

"Yes, I know the facts, doctor," I cut in. "Thank you." And save it! Keep him *comfortable,* he says. Such a stupid word. He means relatively free of pain, since there can be no comfort—ease, well-being, contentment—in any of this, not for Papi or anyone in his situation.

I phone Mami. She's ready for the next shift, but I'm staying. "Yes, Mami, I got a bite to eat. Yes, Papi's doing fine." A calming lie. She knows that Elio has a tube piercing his stomach, another in his urethra; that his mouth is sunken and his arms thin and bruised.

He's pulling at the IV. I take both his hands and hold them; gradually he desists. Minutes later he's babbling about his trashy Mexican neighbors with their loud mariachi music, about the drug-dealing negros who moved into the new building on the corner. Living in L.A. is a hassle these days, he says, because of "all those lowlife people." He means Blacks and Mexicans, since according to him Anglos and Cubans are not prone to be lowlife. If this city is a mess, blame it on those "inferior groups." He's still a bigot, to the very end. But he doesn't enrage me anymore, not like he used to when I was in grad school and had my head spinning with visions of a multicultural utopia. "You're a racist," I'd tell him, "a fucking Republican who stands in the way of social justice and change. At least you can't vote because you're not a citizen. One less vote for the enemy!" But he never took me seriously. "There goes Camilo again," he'd say, laughing, "pretending to be a commie professor!" It was all talk on my part, he alleged, because I hadn't had to put up with any crap from "those people." I didn't really know "them" whereas he did, of course. Elio was the expert on race issues in the United States.

"Camilo gets it from your side," he told Mami once in my presence, blaming her for my left-leaning ideas. "From all those hicks in your family who couldn't even read and all of a sudden were discussing Marxism! It must be something you inherit, this communist thing. And it's in Camilo's blood, coño. Because he got it from you!" Since Mami wouldn't fight back, as usual, it was up to me to contest him. "You know what, Papi," I said, "you're right. There's definitely a communist gene in Mami's family, especially on Matilde's side. 'Cause I sure got it good."

Papi is moaning in his sleep again. I wish I could get inside his head and give him a voice, a story that's truly his. Not that I feel ready to look into that mind, into that heart. Afraid, yes. Terrified. But not ready at all. If he believed in God I'd ask him to pray, and I'd pray with him for a peaceful transition, for relief, for death without regrets. But there's no point. The world exists for my father only when he can touch it and, even better, impact it. Meanings could never be found in the spirit; there's nothing real for Papi in that intangible place. Elio is an atheist but has never admitted it because—I suspect—it's one major thing he has in common with Fidel Castro.

It was Mami who insisted that I have my first communion—the only time she stood up to her husband, as far as I know. But going to church was risky. "They'll bring up your religion when it's our turn to leave," Papi warned. "They'll say you conspired against Fidel with all those priests." Yet the priests were far from conspiratorial; they never mentioned our leaders in their homilies nor lamented the fact that Catholics were being considered fringe, relics of the past. For the Marxist-Leninists who now ruled our country, there was no god to be worshipped and no devil to be fought. The only evil one should fight was capitalism. Paradise was a free society forged with the sweat of your brow, and for which you must be willing to die. Instead of Heaven, we had the glory of History. Instead of Hell, the joy of Equality. But Marxist ideology made little sense to me at the time. What did it mean to be remnants of a decadent system, the bourgeoisie? And why would I want to die for my country?

The only dogma I understood was found in my Catholic faith. Catholicism gave me comfort, hope; it didn't ask for major sacrifices. It offered me a church I loved—its tall arched windows, its impeccable altar, and the Savior's crucified body. I was drawn to the soft contour of his arms, to his praying lips. Mysteriously, Christ looked beautiful in the throes of death. I firmly believed in his power to heal me. I knew by heart the sacred words from first communion. *Concédenos, Señor, que Camilo Macías se encamine al banquete de tu Reino.* God's Kingdom promised salvation, and I wanted to be saved; wanted to have the Holy Spirit, an ethereal white dove, hovering around me at all times, keeping me from sin and possibly damnation. Each time I took communion, I imagined Jesus' body cleansing me inside. I envisioned him within me healthy, strong, alive. Not crucified. Not dying.

What Eduardo was doing to me wouldn't be held against me in Heaven, I thought. It wouldn't be fair, since it wasn't my idea, and I didn't want it. He was the one committing a mortal sin, not me. And yet I never confessed any of it to the priests; didn't have the courage, the will to put my horrible experience into words. I spoke directly to God. "Please, *Dios mío,*" I pleaded, "make Eduardo stop. Make him stop!" But my pleas fell on deaf ears. Nothing ever changed. Either God wasn't powerful enough to help me or He was heartless, and too busy to watch over a little boy who was being tortured.

Papi turns to me, slowly coming out of his slumber, says, "*Hola, mijo.*" I offer him a sip of water that he welcomes. A while later he asks, "Camilo, are you glad that we...left Cuba?" What he really wants

to know is if I'm glad *he* got me out. Elio needs to hear that the good
he's done is solid and lasting, that all his sacrifices are accounted for.
Yes, what Papi did for us took guts, faith. He must hear me say this
again: "I'm grateful to you for bringing me to freedom, Papi."

"*Qué bueno,*" he reacts.

"Life in Cuba was hell for me," I confess. "I couldn't wait to leave."

"It was hell for all of us, Camilo."

"You hated me, Papi. There was nothing I could do to please you."

"I didn't...hate you." He looks surprised.

I insist, "You must've, or you wouldn't have punished me so much."

"I punished you," he says, recoiling, "only when it was necessary, like
any other father."

"I see. So you did what you had to do."

"Yes. I did *lo correcto.* "

He claims—and has told me repeatedly—that I had a foul mouth,
that I didn't obey him. I was rebellious and moody and made things
difficult for my mother and him. But why didn't he ever try to find out
what was causing my mood swings, triggering my "disobedience"? I
suppose he didn't care. For him, it was all about suppressing the rebellion and making things normal, acceptable, convenient. But how could
he and Mami not know or suspect what was going on at El Kiosko on
Sundays? How could they be that oblivious?! Maybe it's time Elio knew,
though telling him would accomplish nothing. What did I expect from
him, a deathbed confession, some trite movie scene? Perhaps just the
truth, no matter how painful: that he wanted a healthy boy, but the
child he'd engendered was an oddity he couldn't recognize as his own. I
didn't play ball with the other kids, and I spent my afternoons drawing,
writing songs, daydreaming. Boys aren't supposed to act that way! Yes,
I was unreachable to him. I wouldn't celebrate his daily triumphs nor
commiserate with him about his burdens. My conduct didn't fit within
the mold Papi had envisioned for me. We were strangers to each other.
Yet my acts of mischief, such as they were, did not deserve the punish-
ments he gave me.

  You might as well admit it, Papi. You took a bizarre kind of pleasure
in bending my will, in crushing me. Or maybe the pleasure lay in the
fantasy of unmaking Lito and molding him like clay, bleeding clay, into
the likeness of Elio, thus forging an ideal new son with your own hands.
Just as you were forged by your father, a Spaniard who ran his house

like a despot, who believed that men were superior and women were weak. You were a victim, too. You suffered beatings, humiliation. You were punished unjustly. So there we are, from such a stick, such a splinter—as the saying goes. *De tal palo tal astilla.* Until the splinter crushed the stick, tore it to pieces, and it was like father like son no more.

He's restless again, asking, "Where is Jevita? I want to see my wife!" I assure him she'll be here soon, and he calms down. I show him one last snapshot for now; Papi glances at it indifferently. It's a photo of Elio and Mechy on their porch, a summer day five years ago. By now they owned a modest home here in Torrance, a place for which I co-signed and forked over one third of the down payment (a big chunk of my savings). Papi had agreed to this arrangement reluctantly, unwilling, as usual, to accept any gifts from anyone, especially not his son. He'd gotten plenty of handouts already in this generous country, he said. But no more, *coño*! In the end Mami persevered. Elio wasn't going to crush her dream of owning a splendid house finally. He wasn't getting his way this time! The property was a great deal considering the neighborhood. Built in 1974 on quiet Walnut Street, it offered three bedrooms, two bathrooms, a walk-in closet, a laundry room, and a remodeled kitchen with custom maple cabinets and granite countertops. Mechy felt in love with that immaculate kitchen, enticed by the cooking comfort it promised. She couldn't wait to tend the flower garden, to set up shop in one of the bedrooms where she'd sew, do crossword puzzles, and enjoy a respite from Elio's demands and crabby moods. The porch boasted a yellow-pine veranda, so picturesque that it begged to be in magazines, said Mechy. She and Elio would make a tradition of relaxing on that porch after supper, seated in cushioned wicker chairs. They'd hold hands, in love like they might've been once. I'd like to remember them that way.

Time for closure. Time to conjure up a yellow brick road and the wizard I never encountered in Kansas; beyond the rainbow, an emerald-green castle inhabited by Munchkins. I'll ask the wizard to give Elio the courage to admit his mistakes, and to give me the solace of oblivion. And if I can't forget it all, then please grant me the wisdom of forgiveness. I must forgive Papi and care for him. I must pretend that he suffers no remorse because he was an exemplary parent. We are at last who we want to be, not an ignorant macho and an abused little boy, but a father and a son who love each other. So what if this love feels like an obligation? Without it, there's no place called home.

"I'm tired," says Papi, dozing off. And I note how much he's shrunk; one of his thighs could fit within the circle I make with my hands. He used to be tall, heavyset; had his hair parted on the left and a thin mustache à la Clark Gable. That handsome, abusive young father still haunts me. But now he stands next to an old janitor on his deathbed. This other Papi is fragile but also real. He's a parent who won't bruise me; a man who left the world he knew so that I'd be free, so that one day I'd have the freedom to escape Elio's history. I will no longer hate you, Papi. Only in a two-dimensional world can Elio Macías be my enemy, and only there can a son avenge himself.

CUBA IN SILENCE

W e're riding the bus after Papi worked hard in Ciego and Morón and Jatibonico. He was selling his stuff, merchandise, that's what Papi calls the shirts and pants he sells. His clients bought everything from him, even those ugly pants made from burlap that give you an itch and you have to scratch all the time like there are ants running all over your skin. Papi told his customers that the pants were made from a fantastic new fabric the Soviets had invented, better than cotton. And everyone believed him! Papi says his work is risky but he has to fool Fidel and go on making money to support his family, that's what a good father and husband must do, it's *lo correcto*, and I should be like him some day.

I can't believe Papi brought me along on this trip, the first time we travel together, just Papi and me. I've told him many times, thank you Papi thank you! I wonder if maybe he's starting to love me like Mami does. But maybe not 'cause this has happened before, he treats me nice and I get all happy but then he goes back to being mean. Anyway, while Papi talked to his clients I ran around like crazy. But then after a while he told me I had to watch him work and learn from him in case I wanted to be a salesman some day. He said it was my duty to watch him, and I said that he sounded like a communist 'cause communists are always talking about duty. It's true, you hear that word all the time everywhere, as much as the word *revolutionary*. They always go together. It is our revolutionary duty!

Papi got mad, said he didn't like being compared to those bearded bastards and I should never ever compare him to them again. I promised him I wouldn't. To show me that he wasn't mad anymore, Papi bought me a burger at the Chino's dive with a guanábana shake for lunch. And before we got on the bus to go home we had *guarapo* at the park made from sugar cane that they crushed right in front of us! The juice was so sweet and I was so thirty I ended up having two glasses of it, not glasses really, not like the fancy ones of crystal that Mami keeps in a cupboard at home but cups made of thick paper.

Papi says he already went to Havana and got our passports ready to get us out of this hell. He's sure that in the North we'll never have to ride the bus again. But I don't mind riding the bus, even if it's packed and it smells bad and some people are snoring. It's a good thing we found two seats together so we can be comfortable during the trip, says Papi. It'd be terrible if we had to be standing the whole way back to Las Tinajas. Papi says I'd get really tired after a while and I'd fall from being on my feet for so long. That hasn't happened to any of the passengers who couldn't find seats in this bus and have to stand, and that's 'cause they're holding on to the metal bars on the sides of the bus, right above the seats. But maybe some of them fell down when I was asleep.

Besides that problem you also have to watch out for the perverts who ride the bus just for kicks, says Papi. It's a bigger problem when you take the bus in town 'cause the rides are short and a lot of different sickos get on all the time. I asked Papi why we have to watch out for those perverts, what can they do to us in here? He told me that they rub themselves against people, especially women and children 'cause they know better than to mess with grown men. They'd get the shit beaten out of them! So it's a good thing we're sitting, that way no one can rub against me like Eduardo does and hurt me like he does after all that rubbing and touching and pinching. Lucky me I never have to ride the bus in town 'cause I walk everywhere, this is my first time, and I'm so happy that Papi brought me along!

Too bad Papi can't drive his Chevy anymore. Fidel stole it from him and that's why he takes the bus, which is also terrible for business 'cause it's full of communists watching you like hawks. That's why we had to rent a car when we went on vacation last month to Matanzas, to visit the Bella Mar caverns. Mami told me that Bella Mar wasn't too far from Varadero, that it was a fantastic place. You go deep into the caves in a boat, and you get to see incredible things inside, rocks in the shape of people and water the color of silver. And she was right! Mami also said that it felt like you were in the Earth's tummy, and I wondered how she knew that 'cause no one's ever been inside our planet. But that's just the way Mami talks, with beautiful words like she knows everything, and I always believe her.

When we went down into the caves I felt like I'd been eaten up just like Pinocchio in the whale's belly, all in one piece but trapped and having no way to escape. It was hot and dark, and I was having a hard time breathing but I didn't mind 'cause a big surprise was waiting for me inside the Earth.

To go to Bella Mar, Papi had to find a driver who was willing to take us and pay him a ton of money 'cause the man could go to jail for doing his own business. Doing your own business is a crime now, as bad as having long hair like the Beatles and Los Memes or going to Mass or saying anything bad about Fidel. But Papi said we'd be safe, he knew the right people, and no fucking dirty communist was going to ruin our vacation. And this time he was right about everything.

I loved Bella Mar! The caverns were like an ogre's mouth 'cause an ogre's mouth would be dark like those caves, I think. We went down in a small boat with our guide. His name was Tony, and he looked a little like Papi but was shorter and darker. Mami was holding me by the shoulders. She said Lito please be careful, don't fall in the water, and I told her not to worry, I can swim 'cause you taught me in Varadero, remember? But Papi said maybe he'd push me so he could have a good laugh and I could practice my swimming. He was being mean to me again!

Tony knew a lot of words to talk about that place. He shone the flashlight on places he wanted us to see, and his words flew everywhere. It's the echo, he said, try it, talk, so I yelled *Buenos días* and my voice flew and bounced off the walls. *¡Bueeeenooos díaaaaas!* He told us about the shapes on the cavern walls that looked like human faces and animals. Then I noticed some pointy things that were sticking up from the ground and others hanging from the ceiling. I asked Tony if they were made of ice and he said no, those aren't icicles, it's hot in here and the ice would melt. They're made of sand.

We'll go deep into the cavern now, said Tony, to the bowels of the earth through narrow tunnels and slippery portals, so hold on tight! I sure liked the way he talked. And then suddenly there was color everywhere, green ponds, blue pools, and we got to see all kinds of shapes that looked like furniture, chairs, beds, tables, all of it made by nature! Tony pointed to a pond that had water the color of gold. There's a story about that pond, he said and asked us if we wanted to hear it. Mami said of course. And so he told us about this little boy who lost his way when he was swimming at the beach and found this cavern, and when he reached the pond, the Merman of the Depths came out of the water. He was part man part fish and had wings. The Merman said that he'd welcome some company, and if the boy stayed with him he'd give him the kingdom of eternity, that means living forever, but the boy said no. So the Merman, feeling rejected, turned the boy's flesh into rock and carved out a bed for him in the cavern wall. The boy's tears became pebbles. Now he would never see the sun again.

Tony flashed his light on one of the walls, the left corner up above and said there he is, can you see him? I saw a boy sitting inside the rock, yes! I saw his face, his big sad eyes, a tiny mouth, lots of curls. Papi complained 'cause he couldn't see anything, just a bunch of rock. Mami held my hand and said look Lito, the little boy is crying, oh the poor child. She could see him like I did!

Then there was a trickle of light far away, soft like the light when it's early in the morning. Tony said it was the cavern's mouth. We'll be out of Bella Mar soon, he told us, we're almost there! But I didn't want to leave yet and besides now the boy was calling me, his voice flying to me like an echo. He told me his name was Roli, just like the friend I used to have in school! What's it like to have a body made of rock, I asked him. It's good, he said, 'cause no one can hurt you or threaten you or make you do things you don't want to do. But it's also bad 'cause you feel lonely all the time.

Now it was really bright, like when you look up at the sun and it burns your eyes and it seems you'll never see anything but that light for the rest of your life. It was time to say goodbye to that unbelievable place and to Roli. If only I could've taken him with me! But I couldn't. Instead I told him I wanted to be his friend. I'll come back to this pond and visit you, I said. I wouldn't want to live inside a rock with you, though it'd be great not to have to see Eduardo anymore. But then I wouldn't be able to run and play and swim or hug and kiss my Mami. So I'd rather just stay the way I am, okay?

I'm sorry this terrible thing happened to you, I said, and I thought I saw him crying pebble tears. I hope the Merman will set you free some day. Maybe he will if I wish it with all my heart. Were you scared when you first saw him? The Merman must've been afraid to show his ugly face to us 'cause he knew my father would beat the crap out of him, right? Please think about me, Roli, and when you do, I promise you I'll hear your thoughts. I'll say to you in my head, *¡Bueeeenooos díaaaaas, Roliiiii!*

IT'S TODAY

We had to order flowers for Elio, one wreath from each family member. The flower shop clerk sounded surprised. *Only two?* Yes, and that would be too many. Mechy was the one into flowers, not Elio. He didn't appreciate her garden and complained about having to look at her photos of roses and lilies that crowded their bedroom walls. "How about one more wreath," said Mami, "three altogether, a meaningful number." Fine, why not. Then we were off to the funeral home in Torrance. Its owner was pallid, bald, the master vampire in a B-horror flick. He guided us to the "office," lime-green wall paper with a motif of tiny pink butterflies. His wife was there waiting for us, as pale as her husband, plump, and wearing a dress two sizes too small. She smiled profusely. They were both telling us about plaque types and prices, and then Lady Caretaker started blabbering about her work. "My husband picks them up," she said, "then I scrub them and dress them and make up their faces so they're clean and presentable..." Mr. Dracula: "Sign here. Will it be a check or plastic?"

The wake, *el velorio*. My visit with Papi's waxy, sunken face, with his hardened hands. He was in a dark blue formal suit and beige silk tie, an outfit Mami picked out for the occasion. I'd never seen him dressed so formally. He did look "presentable," if not peaceful or restful, nor like himself. I heard restrained crying, murmurs as I walked through the mortuary's halls and rooms, a clean but dark labyrinth. I wished Susan had been there. Missed her, needed her, should've called her. Alina would've come but she was in Puerto Rico, tending to her parents. She sent flowers and her love.

Mami held my hand while we greeted friends of the family I'd forgotten. She burst into tears whenever people expressed their condolences, as the rosary was read, while the priest offered his blessings. My mother wasn't putting on a show; she was truly hurting. Although when it comes to rituals Mercedes does go by the book. Case in point: that service, a chapel, a priest, the rosary. None of it would've meant anything to Papi. At least Mechy hadn't gone off the deep Cuban end, calling out her husband's name, asking *Why?! Why did you take him from me, Lord?! My beloved husband, gone!*

In a limousine, our caravan protected from the traffic, we crossed Lennox on our way to the cemetery in Inglewood. We drove by adult video stores, billboards, topless bars, clubs advertising Nude Girls. When we reached the graveyard, Mami was surprised to find it barren of crosses and trees. "American cemeteries are such grim places," she said. The coffin had to be carried by six pallbearers, and I was one of them; Mr. Dracula would provide the other five. He told me where to place my gloved hands exactly; it was a strict ritual. Then the Mexican priest talked about eternity in Heaven, about sin and God's merciful love... "*Te pedimos, Señor, que tu siervo Elio, muerto ya para este mundo, viva para ti, y que tu amor misericordioso borre los pecados que cometió por la fragilidad humana...*"

My father was buried that smoggy morning in a desolate, lawn-covered graveyard, while Mami and I wept. "We should've had him wear a guayabera," she said. "He looked so handsome in those shirts." Poor Mami, I thought, but also lucky Mechy. She was now a widow, not unlike the one in José Martí's poem. Sad and alone, yes, but also free, unburdened.

On our way home, I thought about the truths I'd never wanted to face till now, though I knew they existed. The truth of life, which was death. The truth of love among those too familiar people. The truth of silence like a balm in the world of words. The truth of faith summoned with prayer, pouring into the pit of hours, annihilating time, postponing the end illusively. The truth of wordless pain.

Hoping to find warmth again in Castel's friendship, I phoned him a couple of days later. He asked me to come over, and we spent a couple of hours together (didn't want to leave Mami alone for long yet). Castel would be moving to Mexico City at the end of the year and was excited. An existential pilgrimage, he called this move, a quest for his Rue de

Fleurus where he'd find his mother's roots at last. Castel needed to save
money. He had sold his car but not his stereo, "not till the last minute,"
and he rode the bus everywhere. It took forever to get places that way
but he welcomed the time to read, and he got a kick out of the passengers, liked to imagine stories about them, secret lives and dreams.

He asked me how my father was doing. I told him I didn't feel like
talking about Papi just now. Which was true; I needed a respite from
grief. But I did share some exciting news with him: I had quit my job!
Had left my academic dream hanging in a closet at the Oz Ivory Tower.
Tenure would've meant putting down roots in those flat wheatfields.
No way. "You were wise not to have been tempted by grad school," I
said to him. "I was concerned when you told me you wouldn't be applying. But now I know better, Castelín. I know that the literary life we
both crave can't be found in academia."

My friend was on a Jerry Herman kick again, needing his usual "Jerry fix." We were listening to the *Mame* movie soundtrack, to the title character and her nephew singing "My Best Girl" when suddenly
Castel became somber, pensive. "Poor Angela Lansbury, " he said minutes later. "She wanted so badly to play Mame in the film, after having
portrayed the character myriad times on Broadway. One thousand five
hundred and eight performances, to be exact! But the movie producers
didn't want her; they were looking for a box-office draw, someone with
a huge following. Enter Lucille Ball. And enter *moi*. I never got to see
the Broadway show, but I saw the Lucy movie; I was part of a mob of
faggots waving Lucy-Mame flags on Wilshire, or was it Sunset? Can't
remember the theater where the movie opened, which doesn't surprise
me. I was stoned most of the time in those days! I do know the movie premiered on a weekend in 1974... Oh, and I loved *Mame*, all of my
friends did. We couldn't believe what the critics were saying about the
film. They hated Lucille Ball, said that her acting was uninspired, that
she looked too old and wrinkled, that she sounded like Linda Blair's demon in *The Exorcist*. How vicious! I was a big fan of *I Love Lucy*, and I
adored Lucy's Mame, her gorgeous wardrobe and her comic timing and
her fading beauty; even that deep, growling, sorrowful voice of hers I
loved. I was transfixed by the songs, the lavish sets... Damn it, I was
fifteen and going through hell and that movie made me happy; it gave
me hope. I must've seen it twenty times at least. My friends and I had

a regular date to catch it twice a week during the film's run at...which theater was it? Shit, I can't remember!

"Anyhow, there was a scene where Lucy's blue-eyed visage filled the screen, when she and Patrick sang 'My Best Girl,' and I'd always cry during that number. Not just because of what the song meant to the characters. You see, I wanted an Auntie Mame too, someone who'd love me and protect me. In a way, I was an orphan like Patrick. I had run away from home and was living on the street, selling myself to men who used me and passed me around. I was hanging out with other homeless kids. Some of them hustled more than I did; they were in it for the money and the drugs, while I just wanted to survive. Around the time *Mame* came out I was wild, addicted, promiscuous. Then one day I was beaten and raped and nearly killed—I'll spare you the details—and something snapped in me. I headed for home, and Mamá welcomed me back without any questions. Things changed gradually after that, for the better... She stopped bringing men to the house, and I stopped cursing her for giving me life."

Castel paused. We were now listening to "If He Walked Into My Life." He closed his eyes and sang along, and I thought about the story he'd just told me. There was much in it I could relate to: being used and abused as a child, hating a parent who was cruel, oblivious. Unlike Castel, however, I'd had a caring mother. She wasn't strong enough to save me from my father, nor mature enough to note why I was hurting. But I knew she loved me. And I loved her.

The movie's finale was next, a medley of three songs, "Open A New Window," "Mame," and "It's Today." A tribute to Mame Dennis Picket Burnside, who coaxed the blues right out of the horn, but also to Miss Ball. We danced to it, camped it up. And it occurred to me that the *Mame* film was all about Castel, about his memories of being fifteen and also about this very moment.

"You know what?" I said to him. "I love this soundtrack."

"Really?!" Castel was beaming, barely able to contain his excitement.

I went on, "Yes, the songs tell a great story, with beautiful, memorable tunes. And Lucy's singing moves me. It's the voice of a lifetime, of survival."

"Yes yes yes!" Castel kissed me. "Lucy was a fucking fabulous Mame!"

And then I couldn't hold back the tears anymore. It was my chance to unburden.

"I'm tired of my own story, Castel," I confessed, sobbing.

"What do you mean? What's the matter?"

"And I'm scared of the last chapter. For even if I don't go as my father did—in excruciating pain and angry, feeling trapped—I'm certain now that death, in whatever guise, will happen to me."

"Your father died," Castel said and hugged me. "Why didn't you tell me? I'm so sorry."

"Elio is not in agony anymore, and I should be glad for that. Life, during the last ten months, was like a punishment for him. *Punishment*. A loaded word, isn't it? I'll admit the thought has crossed my mind, that he was paying for all the suffering he inflicted on my mother and me."

"Poetic justice, right?"

"Yes. But I know there's no divine plan involved here, no god examining Elio's deeds and making him accountable for them. There was just an explosion of ravenous cells that ate his stomach lining, then his pancreas, his liver, the rest of him."

"I'm sorry, my dear friend. *Cuánto lo siento*."

"I've realized that my father was a part of me, Castel. It feels as though Elio had been lodged in my heart since I was born, and now there's this corpse inside Camilo. Didn't know he was living in there all along. Can't accept that he's died in there, too."

"But there must be some trace of him, a memory you want to keep alive..."

"I suppose there is."

"Hold on to that memory, then."

"Is that what you've done?"

"Oh, no, I have nothing of my father to cling to, not even a picture."

"Well...chances are you were better off without a dad."

"For sure if he was one of my mother's loser boyfriends."

"I wonder what my life would've been like without Elio, who I'd be today..."

"Someone happier, possibly?"

"Possibly."

"You and I have something else in common now, Camilo."

"And what's that?"

"We're both fatherless."

"Like Patrick," I added, reaching for his hand. "But where's *our* Auntie Mame?"

"She's right here," he said, "sitting with us." And he consoled me with a smile.

We corresponded a lot after Castel's move to Mexico. He wrote frequently but my letters, though sporadic, were longer and packed with details. He'd always try to phone me to share his big news, such as the job he landed translating fiction for a U.S. gay press. "It seems I'll be making enough dough to live a comfortable life in *el D.F.*," he told me, laughing. "Quite a change for me!"

Alina and I also corresponded often once I settled back in California, even though we were living forty-five freeway miles away from each other and got together at least once a month. (I could always lure Alina to my lair with the promise of old songs to serenade us, a little wine, and the cicadas' open wings.) But of course writing to both of those friends was like entering my thoughts and dreams into a diary: not just a way of staying in touch but of taking stock of my life. A sort of chronicle.

It's obvious from the following letter (one of the few miraculously saved in a computer file) that I'd been aching to talk to Castel about some recent changes I'd experienced, first and foremost my move to the city of Colina in Orange County. It's been easy to adjust to living in Califusa again—I wrote. This is, after all, one of my *patrias*, perhaps my only homeland. I rented a light-filled condo on a hill where fools dare not go. The complex, as much of Colina, is largely populated by single people who commute to work in San Clemente, San Diego, Irvine, and Alton. Just what I needed, a fairly young SoCal town, one freeway hour north of S.D. and sixty miles south of L.A., with my mother close enough for me to keep an eye on her. Also, my dear Alina is in the area (a member of the Grad Bohème who never left the Alton galaxy.) Typically, Colina has no downtown. Most of its traffic runs along La Costa Avenue, which is flanked by palm trees and festooned with bougainvillea. Pretty as a picture! The city offers its residents a public pool, two movie theaters, a couple of chain restaurants, and one strip mall with a café where I sometimes grab a latte. What Colina doesn't have is good doctors, not like the ones I had in Kansas, and in that sense it is a lot like many other towns in Orange County.

You're wondering why I chose this Stepford community that sounds suspiciously like Alton, with none of the university life; why Orange County, one of the most conservative enclaves in California and home to the Muir Corporation, the Alton Business Center, Fascist Island, Newport Beach, the John Wayne airport, and Disneyland. (Yeah, the great OC has come a long way since Junipero Serra settled it in 1769. Betcha he's turning over in his grave!) So, why not Santa Monica or Hollywood or West L.A. to make my nest, a place where one can make things happen? Two main reasons: 1) I don't want to be distracted; I need my daily life to be uneventful so I can write; 2) rent is slightly cheaper here than in L.A. Gotta cut corners, now that I'm officially unemployed.

I love the empty look of my place for a change, the whiteness and lightness of it all. That's why I haven't installed shelves to turn my home into a library, like I did in Kansas. No, most of my books are going to the garage (indoor and adjacent to the kitchen, how convenient!); and my old, cranky Datsun will just have to enjoy the sunny outdoors. I've displayed Dr. Milo's degrees on a wall by my desk, evidence of the fact that I'm a recovering academic, and above the stereo I hung a portrait of my mother. It's an oil painting I did in high school, and which had lived in my parents' garage forever. Got a prize for it, can you believe it? Modesty aside, I love the way Mami looks in this painting, with a timid smile, her hair in glowing curls. You'll just have to see it. And feel free to read my fixation on this painting any way you like. Freud, Jung, Lacan. Take your pick.

You could say I'm having my mid-thirties crisis, melting goldfish to build golden sea monsters. But I'm holding onto my projects of existence. And I do love my new life, Castel. I write every day—a textbook, my second novel, letters, stories, poems; and entries in my diary, the source and dead-end for so many ideas. I abandon my cave to get groceries, for a plunge in the pool or a jog at the beach. Lately I've been hanging out with a Chicano named Ray who lives around the corner. You'd like him, butch yet sensitive and absurdly good-looking. But also married, so I won't go there. I do have my rules!

The Writer's Loft tightens its existential grip sometimes. I surprise myself at least once a day thinking about my students, the best ones I had. But then the tug of nostalgia passes, the *Dead Poets Society* moment, and I realize how much happier I am now. Not that my ex-profs understand this "happiness" thing, no, not at all. The fucking letters they've sent me! Oropeza says I have potential as a scholar but no talent as a creative writer: *Como novelista te falta madera.* And McDougal is certain I'm making a big mistake. "You became a scholar at Alton University," he tells me. "We gave you the tools to succeed in academia, and now you're throwing all that work and effort away."

The only prof who's behind me is Sofía, my mentor. She understands what I'm trying to do. Sofía says I should get an agent if I'm serious about writing, otherwise I'll only have access to small presses without a mainstream niche. She assumes that I want a mass audience and that I'm capable of cranking out a page-turner. But I'm not sure. Just to humor Sofía I contacted a dozen literary agents (from a list I got at the library) who sounded like they might be interested in my type of work, most of them based in New York. I sent them an excerpt from *Cuba in Silence* and a handful of poems, and the responses have been rather discouraging. Some of the lines I'm getting: "We like it but don't love it," "Your work does not evoke in us the kind of enthusiasm we need to feel to take it on," "I am not the right agent for your work," "The sample did not grab me."

I'm trying not to take all this as a true assessment of my talent, but some days the rejections eat away at my confidence. I wonder if it's my work those agents don't like or the fact that I'm Latino. The latter wouldn't surprise me but who knows. Luckily I get promotional help from Pueblo Press, and I have a textbook publisher with an army of reps to push the texts I'm contracted to write for them. The latter is part of a story I have yet to tell you... It has to do with the textbook I'm developing, which is actually a work of fiction for the university market, what they call a "reader." I've signed a contract with McAdam&Soulek, a publisher based in Washington, D.C., for a series appropriately titled the *Spanish Fiction Reader Series*: three more books, with a decent advance. If these texts do well, I won't have to teach again. Consequently, my second "real" novel will have to take a back seat, though Pueblo Press wants it by March for their fall list, and I can't let Sergio down. So we'll just see.

Signing up with McAdam&Soulek was a trip. This publisher, commonly known as M&S (probably S&M to their enslaved editors) contacted me by way of a sales representative. Textbook companies send their reps out to harass professors, trying to place their new titles but also looking for the next bestselling author. One day during my last

year at OCU, this power-suited woman came by my office and asked me
if I wanted to write for her company, which she described as "the leading publisher of foreign-language materials in the U.S." I said maybe, if
they were interested in a series of fiction books for language students.
She took notes, gave me her card, and told me to submit a proposal.

Yeah, I thought, don't call us we'll call you. But just in case, I wrote
down what I envisioned for the series, having Barthes's *Le plaisir du
texte* on the back burner ("writerly" vs. "readerly" texts; writerly texts
being my model, since they engage the reader); throwing in a dash of
Julio Cortázar's *lector macho* for effect (though I think his male reader/
female reader dichotomy is full of it); and quoting heavily from Michael
Levine's research. Do you know about his work? He's the renowned
linguist who chairs the Linguistics Department at Alton University.
Levine wrote the classic *Reading as Diversion* and continues to publish
about the benefits of reading in the first-year classroom. His ideas are
totally common-sense: 1) reading must be fun, should pique your interest, make you forget you're reading in a foreign language; 2) the text
should be accessible but slightly beyond your current level of proficien-
cy; 3) reading is the most effective way to acquire language, etc.

(It was Sofía who introduced me to Levine's work; she learned from
him to incorporate glossed short fiction in introductory courses. My
students seemed to enjoy the stories and acquired lots of vocab from
them. I recall that Sofía hated Levine—as she did most male profs at
AU. "Love his ideas but can't stand the man," she said. Supposedly he
was conceited and rude. "It's a wonder," she told me, "that he's had an
impact on the role of reading in language courses, considering that he
loathes students and, from what I hear, is a lousy teacher." Gee, not a
dude I'd ever want to meet—I thought then.)

Cut to the chase: I sent off the proposal, certain I wouldn't hear back
from McAdam&Soulek . But they did contact me months later, when I
was already living here. And they liked my pitch! A development editor
mailed me a contract and the production schedule with my deadlines,
then I had a conference call with the project manager. And that was it.
This is all very encouraging, isn't it, that young people are still into reading, that there's a market for the kind of pedagogical fiction I want to
write. As for the writing, I'm having fun with it but feel confined by the
limited vocab of my target audience. I pitched two outlines to the M&S
editors which were both approved. The first book is a novella entitled

Fuego taíno (*Taino Fire*). It tells the story of a present-day Cuban exile historian who travels to Cuba from L.A. to see his relatives and, having fallen asleep during his flight, wakes up to find himself on a deserted island that bears little resemblance to the one where he was born. In due course he learns that he's not alone; there are indigenous people, the long-gone Tainos, living there! In disbelief, the historian realizes he's traveled back in time to sixteenth-century Cuba. He must also face the inexplicable fact that he now embodies Hatuey, the Indian who fought the Spaniards and was burned alive by Velásquez in 1512. Living within Hatuey's body, the historian concludes that his mission must be to prevent the Indian's murder—his own murder!—and run the Spaniards out of Cuba. Thus, as speculative historical fiction, the story explores what might've happened if Hatuey had defeated the Spanish invaders, and if the island's Taino population hadn't been savagely exterminated.

There is a sad episode that's often quoted with regard to Hatuey, and which I'm planning to work into the story—but with a twist. It is told that, before the fire that would consume Hatuey was lit, a priest showed him the cross and asked him to take the Lord and his son Jesus Christ into his heart so he could go to Heaven. The brave Indian reacted with a question, "Are there Spaniards in Heaven?" The priest responded that of course, many *españoles* had gone there to be with *Dios Nuestro Señor*. "I would rather go to Hell, then," said Hatuey. "You people have brought nothing but pain and bloodshed to my brothers and sisters. I don't wish to spend eternity with any of you!"

I want to condemn those stinking colonizers for imposing their religion, for assuming they were superior, and for destroying everything they touched. But I'll have to tone down the anti-Spanish sentiment, or we'd have a troop of enraged Peninsularists writing nasty letters to M&S and threatening to burn my book! So here's my twist and my fantasy... Just as Velázquez' men are about to light Hatuey's fire, the Indian is rescued by his people and brought to safety. The Spaniards are vanquished and kicked out of Cuba. And the rest is... a new history.

Questions I have yet to answer: Does the historian fall in love with a Taino woman? (*Yes! And this love gives him the strength he needs to fight the invaders!*) How was the voyage through time possible? (*Better left unexplained?*) How did this new turn of events shape the future? (*It changed everything!*) What became of the historian? Did he remain entrapped in Hatuey's body? (*Perhaps. And happily married to an indig-*

enous beauty!) If he returned to himself and to his own time, what is his life like now, since he changed the course of history? (*Better leave him stuck in the past...*) You know I'll welcome your suggestions, Castelín. Alina has offered to read the first draft and mark it up in red, as always. I'd love your feedback too but please don't feel pressured.

I'm sure I'll have to do some workshops to promote the series and the activities I plan to include. Like, for example, discussing time travel and its recurrence in popular culture, ways to travel in time that don't require gadgets or wormholes, where you'd go if you could undergo such a journey and why, who you'd like to meet, etc. I'll be back on the road eventually, but for now I'm buckling down. And no, I won't listen to anyone who says I can't call myself a writer because I'm working on "pedagogical stuff." It's an understandable and justified viewpoint, since, for the most part, this type of educational material doesn't feature a lot of engaging, imaginary writing. Or didn't until now.

Hey, Castel, it just dawned on me that today is Halloween, and tonight this condo complex will be invaded by young witches and warlocks. But I won't be opening the door... except to Ray, if he wants to taste my "brew." The whirling spirits will just have to get their lollipops elsewhere. What about you, Castel? Who will you be this All Hallows Eve? As if I needed to ask! Príncipe Romero will incarnate La Garland, waiting with handfuls of kisses for the man that got away...

Almost forgot, and quite intentionally, ha! Guess who's living in lovely Alton now? Susan! She called me from her campus apartment, said she'd heard I was back in this area and wanted to touch bases. *Yeah, sure.* She dumped the lawyer and came here to develop her mind. Susan sought a well regarded Latin American literature program, and Alton University turned out to have one of the best. *Since when?!* She was hoping to work with Sofía, whose praises I've sung ad nauseam. But I wonder (*big ego trip coming*) if she might've been swayed by the fact that Yours Truly graduated from AU. No, her reasons must be practical: She was offered a generous fellowship and won't have to teach at all the first year. Long story short, my ex is now ten freeway miles from where I live. She wants us to hang out once in a while, do the L.A. thing, talk shop. I said sure, why not. But I won't go through that falling-in-love mess again, I swear! I'll postpone our "reunion" indefinitely. Maybe forever, if I can manage...

THE UNEQUIVOCAL MOON

Y ou're still working on that?" he asked. "Still," I replied, as I sipped the second margarita he'd made for me. His wife knew that Ray was getting drunk at my place. As usual, I'd scratch whatever plans I'd made before his call, and he'd give up an hour or two of sleep. Our occasional tête-à-tête (my word) was always a blast (his word), a place created by and for the *hombres amigos* that we were. He brought plenty of booze, I provided the entertainment: food, music, and a late-night rerun of *Star Trek: The Next Generation*. Ray had gotten me hooked on this great reincarnation of the series. Predictably, he liked the ships and gadgets and above all the ray guns, called phasers; while I went for the mind trips and the time traveling. We both liked some of the action scenes, loved all the space travel and sci-fi jargon—warp speed and black holes and aliens. But I couldn't wrap my mind around the premise of the program and the future that Gene Roddenberry, its creator, had imagined. Couldn't envision human beings ever evolving into galactic peacekeepers, or eliminating money altogether. It was yet another nice fantasy.

And speaking of fantasies, "There'll be a full moon in two weeks, on the fifteenth," Ray announced. "We should make plans, don't you think? Like the last time..."

"Oh, Ray," I said. "The moon is such a hackneyed symbol."

"Hackneyed?" he mispronounced. "What do you mean?"

"Trite, overused, meaningless."

"It's not meaningless."

"The moon is a parasite," I decreed, feeling playful. "It depends on the sun for its light."

"Bullshit!"

"The moon belongs in the Land of the Dead, *amigo mío*."

"You don't know what you're talking about."

"Oh, but I do."

"You don't know everything."

"*La Luna* is a treacherous monster, both a loving mother and a demon."

"Maybe. But you sure loved it the last time, up there, with me. Didn't you?" His eyes were retelling the story of one recent night, when up on the roof of my condo we got high on weed and Dos Equis, and we almost kissed. "It was a full moon," he recalled.

"Yes, quite beautiful," I said. "We toasted to its light."

He was laughing. "And you wanted my body!"

"No, I didn't," I lied.

"You kept touching me, holding me."

"I was cold!"

"Yeah, you wanted some heat, that's for sure." He lifted the coffee table with his legs, as we both lounged on the futon, his favorite spot. "*Ándale*, sit on it. I can take you."

"That's okay," I said, unwilling to comply. "I know you could take me."

He let go of the table and touched my thighs. A timid caress.

"Other men," I told him, "are afraid of this kind of intimacy."

He smiled. "But we're not like those other men."

"You know what makes us different, Ray?"

I imagined he'd say something like...the fact that we worship the moon when it's full. But he replied, "The size of our dicks," and his response didn't surprise me.

I seized the opportunity. "Let's compare."

Ray stuck his hand in his Bermuda shorts and fondled himself. "Like the baseball players," he said. "You know how they shift their dicks around all the time...?"

I made an effort to stay unmoved, not to let my *ganas* (longing, hunger) show. So I said, "Their pants are too tight." And I went on, nonchalant, "Mine is seven point five."

"What kind of a size is that?"

"Seven and a half inches. How about yourself?"

"I've got a big *verga*, nine at least. And I don't need no comparison to prove it."

"Who cares, anyway."

Ray wasn't deterred by my indifference. "Last weekend," he related, "Luisa sucked me off while we drove to Big Bear Lake. For two whole hours! She gets wet just looking at my dick."

He looked at me, between my legs where my hand was moving back and forth. Ray stared, asked, "Is that your boner, what I'm seeing?"

I had to disappoint him, "No. It's my thumb."

"Big thumb."

"You're drunk."

"Is your *verga* bigger than your thumb?"

"No more margaritas for you. How about some quesadillas?"

"Come here." He grabbed my wrist, pulled me to him. I tripped and fell on his lap. He was fondling himself again. "You can help," he said. "I know you want to. *¡Vamos!*"

It was my turn for some teasing. "What do you mean I can help, Ray? You mean grab your big brown dick and suck on it? Suck on it hard and hungry for two hours?"

He gave me a mischievous smile, said, "Yeah, but maybe just one hour, 'cause it's getting late."

"Sorry, *querido*. I'm not your Luisa."

I pulled away, walked to the kitchen. He followed me and touched my ass, rubbed himself against me. "You like the fact that I'm strong, don't you?" he said. "You dig my muscles."

I should've told him that I found his strength—or, rather, his fixation with it—boring. But I let him impress me instead. "Yeah, I'd say you're buff."

"Hit my arm," he demanded. "You'll see that it's like hitting a wall."

I hit him. He reacted with a wrestling maneuver, swiftly, pulling my right arm behind my body, twisting it, and placing his right leg between my legs. I couldn't move; my left hand was free, though, and I used it. I touched his left thigh and his buns.

"What do you think?" he asked.

"Yeah, you're right. You've got muscles of steel, Ray."

"Do they turn you on?"

"Yes. Now let go of me."

He did as I said, freeing me. But I didn't want him to let go, not really. I was envisioning a perfect fantasy, a story without a happy ending for Ray, because it would obliterate his wife and his domestic bliss. It was meant to happen at the stroke of twelve, under the moonlight... *He takes me. I fight back, but he's stronger. I am, after all, a delicate lady, the fragile Caribbean queen of his Aztlán kingdom. As he invades me—ay, his thrusts!—I realize that the fantasy has gone beyond its truest form, that a man who feels this pain would never fear the moon.*

Midnight found us sprawled on the futon, having just watched a first-season episode of *The Next Generation*. Ray seemed satisfied, relaxed, filled with booze and quesadillas.

"I always feel like a king here," he admitted, turning to me.

"Indeed, Your Highness," I reacted, again on cue, "under this humble roof you're wanted and beloved and well-fed by your faithful servant."

We both knew I wasn't his servant nor his queen. His royal spouse waited for him elsewhere. I was something else. His courtier? The court's buffoon? I had let myself be pushed, had played weak. My strength—*he* had decided it—lay in the mind. Mine was the power of words. I was the scribe.

The king brought out a binder that he carried with him everywhere. This multilayered notebook organized his life. *Work*: He was a land surveyor for the Colina Company. *Build shelves in garage*: He owned a brand new tract house. *Fix truck*: He was a part-time mechanic. *Dinner out*: at Denny's or Chili's. *Movie*: on cable. *Mass*: He was true to his Catholic roots.

Every five or six pages there was a short vocabulary list, many of its entries culled from our encounters. That night Ray entered *unequivocal*, a word Captain Picard had used in the episode we'd just watched, about desertion and the threat of intergalactic war. The captain, Ray's hero, had pronounced it in his usual way, male essence and wisdom teleported to us from a distant future.

"What does it mean?" Ray asked. "Do you know?"

"Yes, I do. When something—a word, a thought, an idea—is unequivocal, it has only one possible meaning or interpretation. It is clear and unambiguous, to the point. Absolute."

He tried to use the word but failed. Too drunk. I provided an example, "Your masculinity is unequivocal," and he nodded in agreement. Now I should've challenged him, wrestled with him and immobilized him, asked, What is the absolute meaning of your masculinity, Ray? What is so clear, so unambiguous, about your desire? How does your manliness fit into our moon ritual?

Hard questions. Not a fair match. "It's getting late," I told him.

He scrambled to his feet, headed for the door. *"Buenas noches,"* he mumbled.

In minutes he'd be gone, and I'd beat off imagining the sex we could've had, our long hour... Then I'd tell myself that this, whatever it was, had to end. Because I was supposed to be older and wiser, and because eventually I'd be leaving town for good. I knew I could never grow roots in Colina, a mirage of a city where Ray stood out because of his dark Mexican face, and where I sort of fit in, being a white Cuban American. He had helped build many areas of that Orange County community and was tempted by its beauty, its safety. So he left his native Santa Ana and poured his savings into a down payment. Ray could barely afford the mortgage, but he wanted to belong there. In his impeccable home on a verdant hill, he had a full-time housewife. He liked being the breadwinner, the ship's captain. Ray was fated to stay in Colina and have three children, enjoy barbecues on Sundays, picnics at Costa Lake, soccer games at Verde Hill Park. And I would renounce our friendship because it had to be done.

"There'll be a *luna llena* on the fifteenth," he reminded me.

"I'm sick of the moon, Ray."

"Yeah. But you'll be here all the same, waiting for me."

"Ray," I said as I hugged him. "What you have with Luisa...is it important to you?"

"The most important thing in my life."

"You'd never want to hurt her, right?"

"What are you telling me, Camilo?"

"I think you know."

"We haven't done anything bad," he whispered like a *niño* caught redhanded.

"Not yet," observed the old sage who could see the future.

"I always feel great when I'm with you," said Ray as he walked out the door. "There's nothing wrong with wanting to feel great."

"I agree."

"So you don't want me to come back?"

"No, I don't. Not until the next full moon..."

BELOVED MOUNDS

When friends and lovers part they leave us mounds, a scarf, a blanket, empty cigarette packs, a certain scent, a minor illness, or a poem. In Julie's case it was the condoms she'd always bring with her, tested for maximum protection and satisfaction. "Let's try them," she said the first time. "Let's play." And the name of her game (Julie's youth, her sexual hunger and multiple orgasms) could only be pleasure. Yet suddenly last weekend, Camilo looked at her and saw a stranger. Had he met her at the beach? Was she in the audience at his latest reading? Did he invite her to drive up or fly in for a few days? He might've picked her up at the store or the mall. He couldn't recall, so he dared to ask her, "Hey, where did we meet?" She laughed at his question, "You silly man!" Then she began to open up eagerly, proud of her feminine prowess. Camilo was seduced by this woman's knowledge of herself; by the all-giving, all-taking power of her sexuality. Julie's nature was realized in the ravenous depth of her vagina, how deftly it engulfed him, its ability to contract and grip, the way her labia performed as famished lips, licking and caressing. It made no difference where she'd come from. He'd been waiting for her...

There was another mound on the sofa, a bundle of sweaty sheets and illegible verses. Poetry infused with booze can't survive the sunlight. Camilo knew this but didn't care, because those poems cried out his friend's beautiful name, *Castel Romero*. The prince had left this morning after a weekend visit. But for Camilo it was still last night, and he could see Castel's lithe, light-brown hands trembling; and he could hear his friend's voice smothered by tears... "I heard my mother moan as she fucked her boyfriends. Clients, some of them. I heard it a lot when I was a child, that noise, that sound from hell. She brought them to the house, got drunk with them. Sometimes I'd get in the way, and the men hit me. Sometimes they hit *on* me..." It was midnight, and Castel was reading from his notebook, a letter to Camilo that he'd never sent... *I have tried to forgive my mother but I'm not certain I know how. Maybe I don't need to forgive her, particularly since I don't know what "forgiving" means in this case. The idea is vaguely lodged in my mind, and it remains just that, a vague idea. It is a vaporous image of some abstract notion. There are so many things I've had to learn in order to write about my mother, about who she is, who she has been to me. In particular how little we human beings are "natural," and how we nevertheless expect the world to behave in accordance to what is believed to be natural. How very surprised we are when someone we love does not do what we believe to be true to nature...*

Camilo placed his friend's poems in a desk drawer for now. Next weekend the prince would get high with someone else. His eyes foggy yet alert, he might remember Camilo as he listened to La Piaf, while rewriting Sexton's "Snow White" in his velvety calligraphy, as he read Ruth Martin's chilling *Glass Heart* for the tenth time, or indulged in Sylvia's suicidal imagery. Or when he found the note Camilo snuck into his notebook... *Don't let that pain define you.*

On the subject of definitions, there was Evan, a sales rep for McAdam&Soulek in San Francisco. Evan was sweet and loving at first, but soon he turned into the other side of love, a wicked mound. His modus operandi: assume the power, demand gratification. Be a man, a taker, never a queen. Because queens couldn't be trusted, only dominated like women and kept in their places. Evan scorned them yet without them he wouldn't have had a harem of slaves. He said he wanted a man but wasn't willing to accept a man entirely, dick and balls included. *I'm required to go down on him*—Camilo wrote in his diary—*and to let him penetrate me. Sometimes he'll jack me off so we come together, or he'll deep-throat me. I love his blowjobs but not so much our screwing. Evan is big; intercourse hurts. He says it'll stop hurting eventually, that it'll become natural and easy for me. But he has to do the penetrating. Those are the rules.* What Evan craved was a mate with a hungry ass and a meek cock. Therefore Camilo didn't meet his requirements, not by a long shot.

He was forced to become a helpless boy for his lover, a child at the mercy of an ogre, someone he'd exorcized in his first novel and who was now being rewritten with his flesh... *Nowhere to turn. If my father finds out he'll kill me, so I might as well enjoy it, learn from this man, become the object of a pederast's fantasy, his servant...* Fight the anguish—Camilo told himself. Stop thinking like a victim. Seize what you want, as Evan does. But he couldn't. "I'm just hanging out with friends," Evan would say on the phone from the city. He meant hot queens who writhed at his feet, not friends—he didn't have any. It was disturbing to imagine him with someone else, to picture Evan in a bathtub, the pungent smell of his genitals seeping through the water while a captive lover took in the musky fragrance, which wasn't the odor of decay but an overpowering aroma of dense tissue and flowing blood and hardness. It felt like a betrayal. Because Camilo was left behind with all the postponements of his pleasure, his head exploding, his heart seething like a beast that's been trapped. A raging voice would speak from within him then, *Destroy him!* And again he was driven by the passion he'd felt ages ago, when he fantasized about killing his father. He'd evoke the excitement derived from imagining Elio's surprise, sure that in this memory Camilo would find the strength to execute his plan. Nothing could stop him now. Nothing could halt the Cubiche Avenger. *Eliminate him!* The enemy would regard him with bemused yet condescending eyes. *Kill him!* And, seconds later, Camilo would stab the fucking monster to death.

Shortly after meeting Evan, he started having a disturbing dream. He was in bed, feeling the same old fear of dark rooms he felt as a child, when he'd cover his face so he wouldn't see the mouth of darkness. In the dream, he got up and dared to look out the window. There was someone in the bushes, leaping over puddles. Then he saw him: Evan smiling, arms extended, inviting him. Camilo would run to him as if moving through mist, unable to reach him. And at this point he'd always wake up.

Walking on the beach one day, he saw his body as a playful little boat being rocked by the surf, Rimbaud's "Bateau Ivre" plunging into the waves, unaware of the depths under its sails. *Comme je descendais des Fleuves impassibles.* He then saw his body in pieces that Evan buried in the sand with his feet. *Est-ce en ces nuits sans fonds que tu dors et t'exiles.* That night he thought of someone he still loved, someone he heard now, telling him to be strong and break away. *He has no power over you.* That person's voice in his head, urging him to break free, giving him the strength he needed to run and never turn back. *Don't let him consume you,* the voice would tell him. *Don't let him enslave you...*

Time to gather up Evan's mound (porno flicks, an assortment of lubricants, his business card) and burn it. Had there been love at all? No, Evan was simply feeding off Camilo's heart and consuming him. But Camilo fought for his sanity and won. He entered the depths of the Self, burning with a knowledge that both crushed him and saved him. And he survived.

There was yet another mound having to do with survival, and it belonged to Susan. But she was more than a mound; she was a mountain that rose each day, a mantle that covered everything. Susan showed him the beauty of wheatfields at dawn, the vast Kansas horizon. And in return he rescued her from a life of stagnation. Camilo—she thought, and told him so—was strong yet sensitive, an immigrant who waved no flags and claimed no roots, a man who could bare his soul yet still be empowered. What Camilo couldn't foresee was how much Susan would teach him. He, too, was in need of rescuing.

Living with her was easy. He loved her piano music, their dinners by the light of fireflies, their traveling, the sex they had. He'd lured Susan away from her home: one of his biggest victories, he thought. He had no way of knowing the pain he was causing her family. All he could see was the wrongness of her father's bigotry, her mother's cardboard niceness. Susan seemed to have so little in common with her parents! She was vibrant, real; and her folks, though cordial, came across as one-dimensional characters in an uninspired play. How could they have raised a woman like Susan? Mr. and Mrs. Thompson would end up regarding the Cuban professor as the man who corrupted their daughter. But Camilo hadn't set out to change Susan; she was just ripe for change. He saw himself as a bridge for her to cross...to freedom, to knowledge, maybe to happiness. And he saw the two of them as a team.

When they made love, they were two places at once, moving to the beat of an erection but also receiving it in a moist part of their bodies. They'd see themselves from the outside. Somehow they'd manage to both watch and incarnate the characters on stage, entities seeking pleasure, partners in games of arousal, in erotic masquerades. The two of them freed yet contained by their love scene. And then, seconds before the awaited climax, she and he would stop traveling between him and her, between *él* and *ella*. Because now they had arrived where they belonged, where they were one and the same.

Then a chasm opened up between them. There were no arguments, just Susan's silence, her emotional distance. One evening, a year after she moved in, she told him that no matter what happened between them, they would remain good friends. And Camilo knew what she meant: not lovers, not partners. No more commitment. And that's what he'd wanted most, commitment, for the first time in his life. Then Susan left not long thereafter. She took all that he'd taught her, all they had learned together, and she walked away from him. Soon his house became a tomb where he felt buried, gone insane.

He thought he knew how to cope with his psychoses. He exorcised them all through language, using words to bestow his fears and nightmares and desires on his characters. Psychotherapy would inevitably kill his demons, promising the comfort of self-knowledge in exchange for the death of the voices he heard inside him. The entities he wrote about—masks he wore through his fiction—would perish in the hands of a shrink, crushed by the obligatory meds, and he didn't want that. So he chose to live with the psychic pain, bearing the occasional plunge into madness in order to keep writing.

But the hurt after Susan's departure was greater than he'd ever known. This was a demon he just couldn't conquer. He lost his creative energy, would sit around for hours just "being," not reading or listening to music or concocting lavish scenarios for stories and novels he hoped to write some day. Nothing moved him. And then things got even darker. He plunged into self-examination, compelled, self-destructively, to invalidate his accomplishments in order to pursue a higher goal. Not God precisely but something bigger than humanity, something he could believe in. He saw himself stark naked and having to start from scratch. A terrifying prospect. What if he could never return to who he was?

His landlady in Kansas tried to rescue him then. "I can relate to what you're going through," said Charlene like a wise, middle-aged flower child. "I've been there, my friend." She brought him a scratchy record album, *MacArthur Park*. "This music brings me up when I'm down. Let it help you be reborn, Camilo!" she exclaimed and encouraged him to write about his plight. "You're lucky," she told him. "You don't need a shrink to guide you out of your despair. You have your writing." The landlady had one last piece of advice; she asked him to forget Susan. "Cut the cord and fly!"

Time might render flight possible, but at that instant Camilo couldn't imagine his rebirth. He knew that through a lifetime of lovers and projects and travels—the exciting world he was now beginning to inhabit—Susan would still be there, nestled somewhere warm and safe within him. And in that secret place he'd still be confessing his love to her. He'd see the two of them laughing at their carnal guises, pretending to be neither male nor female—even when their bodies would scream otherwise.

In his diary he'd describe Susan as a welcoming sea where he floated and bathed and fed, a bridge to a benign sort of insanity, a voyage to the center. Camilo was always thirsty for her, literally dying of thirst. And when he drank her, at that instant he thought—though he'd try not to think—that he wasn't missing out on anything. He knew, at that moment, that Susan would save him from all his empty words. And from his memories. He'd write in his diary that he was in love with her. *Love!* He filled page after page with that word next to her name. There were few people he hadn't had to leave behind, but he didn't want to leave Susan; didn't want to build her mound with a scarf containing her scent, with an LP of Chopin pieces that she gave him, *For my lover and friend, this music that binds us.*

Camilo would burn that bundle too, thus Susan's blue eyes would become the darkest night. So the next time she called from her campus apartment, he'd tell her what he'd told her before: "Sorry. I can't see you. I'm too busy." Or he'd tell her the truth, that he didn't want to die all over again.

If only he could face his memories of love without resorting to the already-said. But if he placed himself outside this confessional story, beyond the words *passion, absence, hurt*; if he rid himself of Castel's poems, of Julie's game, of Susan's scarf, what would be left of those people? What would be left of him? Only the language of convention could speak for all his beloved mounds.

Thus he succumbed to the love rhetoric, bought into its momentary comfort, its promise of healing. A form of therapy, that song, or was it self-inflicted pain? No, he sang of a mythical park, of a cake out in the rain because he wanted to stop hurting. He had to do as his landlady said. Cut the cord. He'd hide his face in his arms, as he did whenever people left him. But he wouldn't fall asleep.

WHAT GROWS IN DARKNESS

---

ear Castelín—thus I started most of my letters to Castel. The diminutive form of his name gave me the warm illusion that he was near me. I'd phone him occasionally after he moved to Mexico, and one of those times I found him in bed... He sounded awful, sick with the flu and hardly able to utter a sound or understand what I was saying. We said a hasty goodbye, but I had so much to talk to him about! I sat down to write him a letter jam-packed with thoughts, anecdotes, and news of my creative work, trusting that Auntie Mame would answer my prayers and take good care of my friend.

I just bought a gorgeous wicker chair—I wrote in my letter. It's the kind you'd see in a clove-scented harem, surrounded by tulips. I bought it for you, Castelín, so you have your own special place under the skylight to veg out when you return from Tenochtitlán—soon, I hope, even if just for a short visit! I picture you sitting in it like a monarch of the desert, commanding your male subjects with the wave of a hand. Príncipe Romero in his throne, where he reads and writes poetry; where his voice soars, flies, carries, and then lulls me softly to dream. Come sit in your chair, Your Majesty...

And let's talk literature, shall we? There's something—someone—I've been meaning to write to you about, and that's Gabriel García Márquez, alias Gabo. I know you dislike his work as much as you love Puig's. All that magic in *One Hundred Years of Solitude* seems contrived and silly to you. Flying carpets, pig tails, aging ghosts, a levitating priest, traveling blood, a storm of yellow flowers, a rain that lasts four years... *Oh, please!* And what about that gypsy named Melquíades who's written the story we've just read? An interesting twist but ultimately not very original, in your opinion. And why so many men with the same name? That's a total lack of imagination, right? But, more significantly, you're put off by Gabo's cardboard characters, his macho men and home-bound females. About the latter, well, chances are that García Márquez is a lot like Valentín in *Kiss of the Spider Woman*, a homophobic Latin male in spite of all his leftist ideals. Though I doubt he'd ever come around the way Puig's hetero character does in his novel. But, hey, I could be wrong! After all, Gabo and Fidel are buddies. Hint hint...

In the academic circles I used to frequent, Gabo is a sacred bull, the icon of all-things-Latin-American. Few scholars dare to question his thinly disguised misogyny, his male-centered universe, the pedophilia that permeates some of his tales, like *Erendira* and *Love in the Time of Cholera*. The latter tells a captivating love story, sure, but what about the fact that elderly Florentino ends up seducing a fourteen-year-old girl? A child entrusted to him and for whom he was supposed to provide as a father!

I'll admit I'm apprehensive about desecrating Gabo's oeuvre. I'm sure I'm going to Literary Hell for it. Fact is, I still think that he's a gifted writer and that you're missing out on a great storyteller. You need to delve a little deeper into his work, Castel, if only to rip him apart. Just coast along with Gabo's words, indulge in the craftsmanship of his writing. Focus on the way he tells a story, not on the story itself. I know that's no easy task, since the world depicted is intrinsic to the words that describe it, and the narrative reinforces oppressive archetypes. But there are outbursts of sheer brilliance (*Gabosophy*, I call it) in García Márquez' writing, and those should be your goal, the reward. Remember what you told me about musical theater? *Surrender to the beauty of the melody, the lyrics, and forget so-called reality.* I still find this type of theatrical form a tad silly, but now I can enjoy it thanks to you. And you must heed your own advice with regard to Gabo... *Surrender to the beauty of the words, the images, the poetry...*

In any case, I thought of you the other day when I was reading Gabo's latest, *The General in His Labyrinth* (about Simón Bolivar, yet another patriarch). I was conversing with you as I read, and it saddened me that we would never be having that conversation for real, because you won't read the novel. I was particularly struck by this bit of Gabosophy in *The General*: "There is nothing more dangerous than a written memory." I believe it should be the other way around: Nothing is more dangerous than an *un*written memory. Because those can grow inside you and destroy you eventually. That's why I must write it all down and never stop remembering...

But enough of all that serious literary stuff. How about some juicy gossip? You won't believe who slept here last night! None other than Dr. Michael Levine, the *Reading as Diversion* guru who used to chair Linguistics at Alton University. And talk about a trip!

Backstory: I wrote to Levine about the Reader Series, asking him for any pointers he might have and for his scholarly blessing. I didn't expect a reply, not from this reportedly egotistical scholar. But he wrote back—just two sentences scribbled on a postcard, *I'm intrigued by your Series concept. Let's discuss it in person.* So I sent him an effusive thank-you and expressed my availability for a meeting, anytime anywhere. In his next message, again on a card, he informed me that on such a date he'd be driving by Colina on his way to a conference in San Diego, where, as usual, he was the featured Big Name... *We could chat over coffee then. Let me know if that would work.* About a week later Levine (short, timid, typically unkempt and wearing horn-rimmed glasses) shows up at my door, greets me like he's known me for years, tells me he loves the Reader Series concept and would I like for him to write a preface. He'd welcome the exposure, this commercial venue to get his ideas out there. I said yes, of course I'd love a prologue by him, and offered him a beverage. He asked for water and then talked nonstop about the paper he was presenting in S.D., which sounded like a rehashing of his *Reading as Diversion* ideas. I was ready for him to split, tired of being lectured at, when he stopped and inquired if I had any cannabis. I thought he was joking—*cannabis*?!—but soon realized he was dead serious.

"My wife thinks I should loosen up," he confessed. "Married thirty years and now she tells me! I've read about cannabis, and I think it could do the trick. But only if I can try it with someone who knows the ropes and can take care of me. In case I have a bad 'trip,' you know. I thought that maybe you, being an artist—and I admire artists a great deal, particularly those whose medium is language—I thought you might happen to find yourself in possession of some marijuana and be willing to share a little with me. I don't know you that well, Camilo, don't know you at all! But I feel in my gut I can trust you. What do you say? Want to help me take a walk on the wild side?"

"Sure," I said, "I'll load you a pipe. But I'd hardly call reefer a walk on the wild side."

"It certainly would be for me!"

"I suppose you're right, especially with the stuff I've got, which is dynamite. A friend of mine sent it to me from Mexico as a birthday present. You'll only need a couple of hits..."

"Have you done other things?" he asked timidly. "Drugs, I mean."

"Snorted some coke and smoked a bit of crack, yes. But that stuff makes me feel too hyper, out of sorts. And it's risky and expensive. I'd rather stick to pot, which fuels my creativity."

"Well. I've never done anything. Not even alcohol. And no tobacco, either."

"Wow," I laughed. "Are you sure you want to ruin such a perfect track record?"

"I am sure, Camilo," he said, smiling. "It's time."

I sat him on the couch, served him a tall glass of OJ and got him going. It all brought back memories... Do you remember your first time, Castel? Mine was in high school, with a dude who picked me up near the school on a weekend. I was working on a mural for my art class and would spend part of my Saturdays and Sundays painting with the teacher, so I had the perfect alibi at home. We did it in his car. An unforgettable trip! There were two of me; someone else was speaking my words, thinking my thoughts, moving my hands and feet. In time I learned to use that doppelgänger feeling to zoom in on my writing. Yeah yeah, screwing while stoned ain't bad either!

I hoped Levine wouldn't freak out or have the kind of adverse reaction Susan told me she had her first time. Fortunately she was with friends (not me), because she became paranoid; and she developed a colossal hunger—not just the usual munchies—that prompted her to stuff herself till she got sick. Then a splitting headache struck and lingered for days. Her friends told her that her trips would get easier to handle, even enjoyable; that she owed it to herself to keep trying. But after a couple of more times Susan said no more. She never asked me to stop smoking cannabis, but my dependence on it bothered her. I eased up on my daily consumption when we lived together, would wait till she left the house to take a hit. But she always knew when I was "self-medicated" and tried to put up with it, which was not the case with tobacco: She hated cigarette smoke and begged me to quit; since I wouldn't, she told me to "poison" myself outside. Hard to do on cold Kansas days but I complied.

I suppose Susan's concern about pot was that I might move on to harder drugs. Fat chance. As you well know, I smoked crack with Tano a few times and snorted some coke with you twice. I admit I liked it, but the cost, the dependence, and the risks in trying to obtain the stuff were all too much for me to handle. There was also the fact that both coke and crack gave me an instant shot of well-being, of optimism, but neither drug prompted me to feel creative and write. So what would be the point?

Back to Levine. I asked him to go with the flow, think happy thoughts. Showed him how to inhale and sat by his side while he tried it. After his second hit, he took my hand and wouldn't let go of it for the next ten minutes. Any second now he'd be getting the munchies, so I brought out Ritz crackers and apples and Havarti cheese, most of which he devoured. I asked him if he wanted music, and he said no. He wasn't talking; this worried me. About an hour into the trip he took a couple more drags. "You wanna know the truth about reading?!" he blurted out then. "Do you? Okay! I'll tell you the fucking truth... There's too much reading to be done in this world! Too many books and magazines and newspapers and dissertations. Too many stories!" A certain anger pent up for years was bursting out of him, it seemed. "Stop reading, people! Get a goddamn life! Do something!" I had him drink some juice and told him to relax. "Too much to read," he kept saying. "Too much, damn it!"

As you must've guessed, Dr. Levine never made it to San Diego; he crashed on my futon. Right before he fell asleep he said to me, "Artist, please don't tell anyone..."

I promised him I wouldn't. "No one would believe me, anyway," I said, thinking of his true opinion of reading and not his first weed trip.

"You're right," he mumbled. "Nerds like me don't get stoned."

It seems Levine had a humbling experience, just what he needed. That's probably what his wife was after, a little humility for her conceited hubby. The famous linguist left this morning, having downed a gallon of coffee, looking a happy mess and thanking me profusely for taking care of him. "I'll get started on that preface right away," he said. "Would twelve pages suffice?" Twelve pages?! Hell, just a promotional blurb would've made me drool.

"Yes, of course," I replied, "and I'm sure the publisher will give you a flat fee for it, if that's okay with you." He nodded, but I'm not counting on him, though Levine owes me one. By the way, thanks for the Mexican dynamite, Castelín. You're a generous friend. Mua mua! (two kisses in Cuban.)

My mother is doing fine; thanks for asking. Elio had substantial savings; all his penny-pinching paid off, so Mechy has been financially secure. We sold their house and bought Mami a condo near Del Amo Mall, in Torrance. She still can't believe her shopping haven is within walking distance. And with the leftover money she bought herself the car of her dreams, a VW bug or *Cucaracha*, as she calls it, her little roach. Mami drives more these days, to the store, to Mass, to meet for lunch with her church friends—several of whom are black, heaven forbid! My mother isn't a racist like Papi was, but she never dared to confront him about his rampant bigotry (and about so many other things). I never did either, not directly. And I wonder if it's because of him that I can't count any African-American people among my friends today. In that regard Mami has done much better than me. I suppose (as the Spanish saying goes) that you can't ask pears of the elm tree. Black culture just wasn't part of my upbringing, though that's not a good excuse. Could it be that there's a racist part of me that I inherited from Elio? Nah, doubtful. In fact it would thrill me to discover that there's an Afro-Cuban streak in my family, most likely from my maternal side. It wouldn't surprise me, although if that were the case, my grandparents (yes, my Marxist grandparents!) sure did a good job of hiding it, like so many "white" Cubans do...

Mechy has taken up photography again and has her own darkroom now. I'm thrilled about that! I know she misses her husband, but she hasn't let widowhood get the best of her. She's had so very few choices in her life, never been able to speak her mind, never been truly *free*. But now...well, a lot has happened since Elio died. Mechy is more in touch with her parents. She was never a rabid *anticastrista* like Papi. I think she would've stayed in Cuba if she hadn't been the wife of Elio and the mother of Camilo. But I just can't picture Mercedes dressed as a *miliciana*, singing the "Himno Nacional," marching, and calling her parents *camaradas*. She believes that blood is thicker than any ideology, and that love is all that makes sense. So there's a good chance that my communist grandparents might be coming to the U.S. for a visit. And of course that could never have happened when Elio was alive.

Hey, your last letter was a trip—literally! You lucky dog! Can't believe you got to see *Kiss of the Spider Woman: The Musical* in New York City. A wild weekend with a Mexican sugar daddy who paid for everything, including a stay at a four-star hotel in Manhattan! How did you manage that? I want details about this mysterious Señor Azúcar, please. I love the way you describe the experience...

Book by Terrence McNally. Songs by John Kander and Fred Ebb, an amazing team who wrote great stuff for Liza Minnelli. I loved it, Camilo! Kiss is tuneful, impassioned; it captures the poetry of Puig's language. I adored the hot dancing; Chita Rivera's deep, raspy voice; the scenery, a cage-like prison house. I imagined Puig in the front row, quietly singing "Anything for Him," "Only in the Movies," "She's a Woman." Manuel sitting next to a sexy GQ type in a tux, having found his utopia at last...on Broadway! The finale was a celebration of Molina's gay soul. When the stardust rained on an empty stage I thought of you, Camilo. You, who guided me to the beauty of Puig's writing.

And you, Castel, you showed me the beauty of the American musical, so we're even! Thanks to you I know that the British duo Gilbert & Sullivan paved the way in the late 1800s for the great composers of the genre, such as the Irish-born American Victor Herbert. Without the famous duo we wouldn't have Irving Berlin, Jerome Kern, George Gershwin, Rodgers and Hammerstein. There would be no Sondheim, no Kander and Ebb; and (perish the thought!) no Jerry Herman, hence no *Mame* and no *La Cage Aux Folles*, the latter being the only drag show you've totally adored!

I'm sure I'll think of you when I get to see *Kiss, the Musical.* Because I must see it even if I have to spend my entire savings on a round-trip ticket to New York. I wonder if there's any chance they'll bring it here. After all, the L.A. Music Center has been known for showcasing the best and the latest. Like *Angels in America.* You and I were fortunate to have been there for its premiere at the Taper, to witness the birth of this monumental work by Tony Kushner. *Angels in America* will make history. I am still trying to absorb its themes, its message, its tragic arc. As you know, I don't much care for angels, find them as scary as demons. But Kushner's angel is magnificent. What a way to rewrite the archetype! The play blew us away to the point that we couldn't talk for a long time after the show. Later, as we savored a cappuccino at a café in West L.A., all I could say to you was, "Make sure you stay safe." To which you reacted with a smile and one word: "Always." Is that a promise, Castelín?

Anyhoo, I'm finally getting around to the main reason for this letter, which is to thank you for sending me *What Grows in Darkness*, your first book of poems. *¡GRACIAS!* The manuscript was a wonderful gift, Castel. Your collection is profound, deeply lyrical. I'm touched that you chose to bring me along as a fellow traveler on your voyage, this crossing through Tenochtitlán on dragonflies. Where you heard the voice of an ancient lake and learned to swim in the Sea of Olden Memory. As you drew an image that was time—cycles of life, death, and rebirth—but also timelessness. When you came to realize that very little grew in darkness and certainly not a flower. Where you met a boy whose laden shoulders offered you a bridge to your soul. Where you sang of two *amigos*...

Thank you for that song, my friend. Your poems have been both a respite from my own work and a boundless source of motivation. They've given me the companionship I've been needing, like having you near me as I delved into a story about madness, not the damaging kind but the kind that moves you to seek answers: my latest project. I believe, like you do, that one can only write about madness from within it. And I've been inside, thrust with no warning into the void, wondering who the hell speaks for me and commands this body that sometimes feels alien, who thinks these thoughts that propel me, who feels this paralyzing fear that Camilo will cease to be.

Is there really a productive, edifying type of madness, Castel? What do you think? Part of me wants to say hell no, there's nothing intrinsically good about insanity, even if it triggers your quest or your creative outpour, nothing romantic about the nightmares of derangement. I wonder if any artist who's ended up dead because he or she went nuts would've gladly given up the gift of their talent—and fame and glory in some cases—just to live a longer life; or one devoid of psychic pain. If only Woolf and Plath and van Gogh and so many others would've had a choice!

It seems that I do, Castel. I have a choice. I can snap out of these lapses and return to my "normal" life. I can have a glimpse of insanity, of the horrors of non-being, then out of the darkest of nights I begin to see dots of light, minuscule stars like when I used to rub my eyes as a kid, thus gradually the sense of reality returns. When I look at the computer screen after one of those episodes, I discover that I've written about my "trance" while in the throes of it, that I've managed to convey in words the absence of meaning, the desperation. What follows then is a conscious process that I undergo as I listen to music, always jazz or classical. This part of the job is fun—editing, polishing, filling in the details, providing descriptions. Susan would say that my trances are pot-induced, or, more to the point, that I simply get high and then attribute all sorts of crazy stuff to my trips. "You've been doing too much dope," she'd allege. "Give your brain a break!" To which I'd reply in all truthfulness that I haven't been getting high. "Not even one daily hit. My flights are wild and all-consuming enough already!"

Through my on-and-off process of derangement (if that's indeed the right word for this experience), I've managed to dream up a twisted little tale... Two Cuban men are sharing a room in a Miami psychiatric clinic. They don't know who they are, don't know that they hail from mutually exclusive segments of society. One is a thirty-something architect, the other a janitor in his mid-fifties. These characters are married and have children but can't recognize their family members nor remember that they've always defined themselves as heterosexual men. Having suffered great memory loss (due to a malignant brain tumor in the janitor's case and to a yet-to-be-determined psychotic disorder in the architect), the patients find great comfort (love?) in each other's company. To pass the time, they play at guessing who they are in the "real" world. Thus they find themselves in a funhouse of language where dreams and fantasies abound, where truth is elusive and desire is as real as the truth. Light comes in through the window, yet madness—an invasive shadow—seems to be the only end in sight. Or is it?

ARCHITECT: What are you thinking about? JANITOR: How weird it is. ARCHITECT: What's weird? JANITOR: When all those people barge in here claiming I'm someone's husband or father. Who are they?! ARCHITECT: I don't know any of them either, I mean the ones who are supposed to be my family. JANITOR: They look at us with those gushy eyes. ARCHITECT: Lying eyes! JANITOR: They're like vultures, birds of prey. ARCHITECT: But why are they putting on a show for us? JANITOR: You think it's all an act? ARCHITECT: Could be. If they really were who they claim to be, wouldn't you and I know it? JANITOR:

Yeah, we're not *that* crazy! ARCHITECT: Wouldn't there be some trace of our love for them in our hearts? JANITOR: Maybe they're all in cahoots with the doctors. ARCHITECT: Plotting against us? JANITOR: Yes, so they can have a reason to lock us up and take all our money. 'Cause I have an inkling that I'm filthy rich. ARCHITECT: We both are, I think. How else could we afford this upscale nuthouse? JANITOR: We might have some hefty health-insurance policy for this sort of thing. ARCHITECT: True, but even so. JANITOR: Forget all those damn people! ARCHITECT: Let's not play their game. JANITOR: You're shivering. Are you okay? ARCHITECT: I'm cold. And a little depressed. JANITOR: Come here, let's lie together for a while. I'll keep you warm. ARCHITECT: Is there enough room in your bed? JANITOR: We'll make room. ARCHITECT: Thank you. And could you also...? JANITOR: What? ARCHITECT: Could you hold me? JANITOR: Like this? ARCHITECT: Yes, that's perfect. JANITOR: Imagine that! Two *machos cubanos* cuddled up in bed. ARCHITECT: Speak for yourself. I never said I was a macho. JANITOR: You sure act and look like one. ARCHITECT: So do you. JANITOR: That's who we are, then. Anyway, tell me what you think your life was like before this place. ARCHITECT: You and I were good friends out there, I'm sure of it. JANITOR: Yeah, we partied together! ARCHITECT: What's so funny? JANITOR: I was picturing our wives' faces if they walked in on us. ARCHITECT: They'd have a *patatún*! Except I don't remember having a wife, so I wouldn't care how they'd react. JANITOR: Me either. ARCHITECT: To be honest, at this moment I don't want to remember. JANITOR: Well, I can't, whether I want to or not. ARCHITECT: Do you think you ever did anything with a man? JANITOR: You mean sex? Doubt it. ARCHITECT: Sometimes I wonder what it'd be like. Do you? JANITOR: No, I don't. And I'm not planning to find out. I won't be turning into a fucking *maricón* just because I'm nuts. ARCHITECT: But letting me touch you like this wouldn't mean you're a *maricón*. JANITOR: I guess not. Suit yourself, then. ARCHITECT: Not if it upsets you. JANITOR: It doesn't. I'll close my eyes and think about that nurse who brings the morning meds. ARCHITECT: The one from Nicaragua? JANITOR: Yes, that one. I get hard just thinking about her tits. ARCHITECT: Big tits. JANITOR: I wouldn't mind fucking her. You think she'd be game? ARCHITECT: Probably. She flirts with you all the time. JANITOR: *Oye,* what are you doing? ARCHITECT: I'm sorry. You said I could touch you. Should I stop? JANI-

TOR: No, go for it. ARCHITECT: I like being this close to you. JANI-TOR: It sure feels good. ARCHITECT: It's like we've known each other our whole lives. JANITOR: Maybe we have. ARCHITECT: You think so? JANITOR: Sure. And if not, we'll make it be. ARCHITECT: How? JANITOR: We call the shots in here, right? So if we say we were friends, then that's the fucking truth! ARCHITECT: I like that truth. JANITOR: Let's talk about the things we used to do together, okay? ARCHITECT: We had a blast! JANITOR: Do you remember that time when...?

Sadly, everyone tries to tear the friends apart. Their relationship—say the doctors—is not consistent with the men's personal histories and may very well be induced by illness, isolation, and their cohabitation in a clinic room. Their love is surely a byproduct of madness! The women who allege to be their wives tell the men that what they're feeling and presumably doing is sick and perverse, that it must stop. Thus the patients are separated, never to see each other again...

I don't know yet what happens to the men once they're discharged from the clinic. Do they resume their "normal" lives? Do they fight for their relationship? The janitor might die soon from the growth in his brain (not sure); whereas the architect might begin to accept or at least explore his gay nature. Has he been bisexual (or a closeted gay?) all along? Does he still love and desire his wife?

It occurs to me that there could be a cultural gap between the characters, not just a class difference. The architect could be U.S.-born, hence his strong identification with mainstream American values. (But then would he know the word *patatún*? Sure, Cuban Americans tend to be fluent in Cubanish.) While the janitor could be a Marielito, one of the *cubanos* who were allowed to leave Cuba through the Mariel port in 1980, many of whom had been incarcerated for being openly gay. What do you think, Castel? You're probably wondering how the Cuban "thing" fits into all this craziness. Of course I'll have to provide culture-specific examples, local color. Must capture the humor, the *choteo* (wit, taunting) that would be innate to these characters, and which their situation would bring forth. The men are Cuban—or Cuban-American—because that's my thing, what I know best. Although the Miami scene might prove to be a stretch, since I'm definitely not versed in Sagüesera culture. I've considered setting the story in Los Angeles, but it'd be tough to pull off two Cubiches being in the same clinic, let alone sharing a room in this vast Southland! No. Miami it is.

What about my debt to Puig? It's obvious that this story line—two individuals from different walks of life, thrown into an isolated environment where they discover a major truth about themselves—sounds a lot like *Kiss of the Spider Woman*. As in that novel, the characters' dreams are passageways into their subconscious lives, that which Puig describes as the "secret realm of dark motivations." As silent observers, we invade the darkness that surrounds these people, listen in on their secrets, witness their fantasies and breakdowns. And once all the facts are revealed and the subconscious truths explored, the characters remain playful accomplices in a life-affirming game... Sound familiar?

Well, all I can do is thank Manuel for giving me a setting, a context as plausible or unlikely as the cell in his famous novel; thank him for being my guide. While it is true that I couldn't have come up with my story without *Kiss*, this book will be my own trip. Let us not call it stealing but a conscious borrowing. Or, as it used to be said in some of my lit courses, a case of intertextuality. Better yet, an homage. Whatever you call it, I'm sure Manuel would approve. My working title: *Love Insane*.

WONDERFUL LIES

I went on the road to promote *Love Insane*; did book-signings at Colby's in Berkeley and Barnes & Noble in San Francisco, with several pit stops at independent bookstores along the way. It went well, but I didn't sell enough books to make Sergio happy. And then, in need of a change of scenery and language, I booked a spring flight to Madrid to meet Luis Alejandro, the publisher of my new poetry collection. He was a Cuban exile in his thirties whose house, Presencia, was seeking material for a series featuring Cuban writers in the United States. Seemed promising. His editors wanted young yet well-regarded poets who wrote in Spanish, such as Lourdes Gil, Maya Islas, and the Marielito Osvaldo Barnet, all of whom I'd read and knew personally. So they contacted me, and I was thrilled but surprised—still considered young? Luis invited me to Madrid (at my expense, of course) and offered to set up a reading for me in some *centro cultural*. But I didn't see the point, since there was no book to promote and sell yet. (And that's the only reason to read your stuff to an audience, right, Dr. Milo?) Mostly Luis wanted us to meet in person, go over the details of the publication, and introduce me to some of the "local talent," the Cuban old-timers who'd made Madrid their home.

An old taxi driver almost whacked me when I observed that things must be better in Spain now that Franco was gone. He was livid as he struggled to explain that El Generalísimo was his country's savior, the only one who'd ever known what Spaniards really needed, which was order, discipline, decency, and solid, traditional values. And also (I wished to add but wouldn't dare), repression, stagnation, persecution, and death. The rabid *franquista* nearly had a wreck—he was that pissed off!—but finally dropped me off at my modest hostel by the Plaza Mayor, near Luis Alejandro's flat.

I walked to Luis's place after unpacking and grabbing some tapas at a bar. Luis was a burly, huggable bear. We had a *cortao* (espresso with milk) in the cramped second-story apartment or *piso* that doubled as his office. Then we did the exile rounds. We visited José Pedro first, a gifted poet who'd been imprisoned in Cuba for being openly gay. Sepe, as friends called him, was short and stout, an adorable queen. He'd founded the litmag *Recuento* in Havana in the mid-Fifties, then tried to publish it in Spain but couldn't afford to. Sepe lived in a dark attic den that was falling apart and which he planned to turn into a plush *buhardilla* some day. Hard to envision it.

The three of us called on Wilson Mauriat, a famous artist in his late forties whose height took me aback; he was the tallest Cuban I'd ever met. There was immediate chemistry between us. I felt drawn to that pallid, melancholy man; ached to run my fingers through his wild mane of curly gray hair. In Wilson's spacious studio on Calle Alcalá we talked about art, mainly about constructivism, a style he claimed to have invented. Wilson said he was interested in the medium, paint itself. He offered us cheap red wine, and surprisingly this *vino tinto* didn't make me opine about his monochromatic squares and circles, empty forms that seemed machine-made. The more Wilson drank, the more he turned zealously anti-Castro. "I won't go back to Cuba as long as that son of a bitch is there!" he bellowed. Luis Alejandro and José Pedro got into it too. "That motherfucker!" "That monster!" "That thief!" They all hated Fidel but loved to talk about him.

Two hours later we ended up in a gay-friendly joint with great tapas that Sepe recommended, on the Gran Vía, a happening street in the heart of Madrid. After a glass of sangría and a toast to freedom, Wilson gave me a clumsy kiss that he followed with a longer, more tender one. I let him kiss me because I was drunk and horny and Wilson liked me. "*Estás muy bueno,*" he said. "Thank you! And you're hot too, *viejo,*" I replied in all honesty. He invited me to sleep with him that night, and I chose not to react. I could tell Luis and Sepe were in on this; they were splitting. I confirmed my meeting with Luis Alejandro tomorrow, and we said good-bye. Now it was just Wilson and me.

"Will you go home with me?" he asked, stroking my thighs.

"I want to see what you look like," I said, "then I'll decide." What a tease!

"Not here," he objected. "In my studio..."

But this was my condition: "Let's go take a leak. If I like what I see, I'm yours."

He acceded, and what he showed me in the john was quite stunning, something I'd probably enjoy savoring. "*¿Te gusta?*" he asked, grinning. I peed, fondled myself. (If Tano could've seen me now!) Two other men came in, too much of a crowd for Wilson; he was leaving our Tea Room. "*Bueno, compatriota,*" I said, following him. "Now will you show me how you paint all those pretty circles?" He smiled, put his arm around me, "For a writer, you're sure lousy with words."

The next day, following a steamy session, Wilson told me he could get used to having me around. "I'd make changes," he said, "so we end up together." I asked him what he meant by "changes." Like, would he be willing to give up his fame in Spain and Europe to live with me in the States? "Yes, I would," he replied and burst out laughing, "because I'm in love with you, Camilo. Please marry me!" It was all a joke, I soon realized with a sigh of relief. Next he wanted unprotected fucking, "the real thing." But no way. I wasn't having anal sex with him, not the way he wanted it, with me on the bottom—he was just too big. But if I'd been amenable to the idea, it would've involved a super-duper condom, maybe double just in case. Party pooper! Wilson insisted. "As a poet, you must rejoice in risks. And welcome danger." It seemed I didn't live up to Mauriat's image of a writer; I wasn't eloquent and daring enough. "Trust me," he pleaded. "I don't have AIDS. I'm not a *sidópata*." Sad and telling, I thought, that in Spain an HIV-positive individual would be referred to as an *AIDSopath*.

"I'm glad you're not a *sidópata*," I reacted. "Make sure you stay that way."

My dalliance with Wilson didn't keep me from having several meetings with Luis Alejandro over sumptuous dinners of *paella, caldo gallego, cocido,* and too much wine. We tried and were able to come up with an attractive publication package for my collection. It would have an elegant font, glossy paper, and a beautiful three-color cover featuring a painting by Wilson (more pretty circles but it was a freebee—couldn't complain). The book was to include about thirty poems I'd written while immersed in my relationship with Susan, with English translations that I'd provide myself so the text could be read on my side of the globe. Upon considering several titles and running them by Luis, we settled on *Fantasías escritas con el cuerpo/ Fantasies Written on the Body*. There would be an inscription, *To Susan, more than a muse, my soulmate*. I could almost hear Tano's reaction, "You think you're a real man 'cause you wrote love poems to a woman?!" But I wasn't certain how Susan would react...

What Luis Alejandro had failed to tell me until now, when we were about to sign the contract, was that he needed me to cover some of the costs of the publication. *"Sufragar algunos gastos,"* he said. Hence I'd be doing exactly what I'd criticized in the Sagüesera old-timers. "Vanity press," I said to Luis. "No, Camilo," he retorted. "You'd be giving us a hand with a worthy venture, helping us produce something beautiful and important." Eloquently put, very flattering, but it still meant that I'd have to fork over eight hundred bucks to publish my own book, giving Presencia a hefty percentage of the royalties. Oh, but poetry didn't sell. The publisher was taking a big chance, doing this for the love of art and not for profit. It was all about bringing an outstanding oeuvre to light, making literary history, giving the writers a dignified venue, the limelight. Blah blah blah. In the end Luis and I made a toast to the future of *Fantasías escritas con el cuerpo*, the two of us now partners in a "worthy venture."

I said goodbye to everyone the day before my return to California. Wilson wanted to hang out with me till the last minute but I told him I couldn't. I wanted a few hours to myself on the eve of my departure. I read the *Guía del Ocio* and several other magazines at a Plaza Mayor café, hoping to soak up some pop culture but mainly looking for news or photos of my mother's idols, movie stars Carmen Sevilla and Joselito, icons of Spanish cinema. But I found nothing; they were just too old for the youth-oriented yellow press. I continued making my way up the Gran Vía, in search of a T-shirt announcing the historic "1992." Monumental events would be taking place that year, the Seville Fair, Expo, the Summer Olympics. It seemed that Spain, *La Madre Patria*, was finally dressing up to show the world its splendor, at long last dignified, proud of its Iberian destiny. If only she didn't seem so weary to me.

I sat on a bench at the Plaza de España, a filthy, dilapidated square where a young woman talked to an indifferent crowd about Jesus. She demanded that we save ourselves. *"¡Tenéis que salvaros en Jesucristo!"*

she cried out. *"¡Salvaros!"* That woman would be the final memory of my visit.

On my way home, immigration in Dallas. AGENT: What do you do, sir? CAMILO: (*Timidly.*) I write. AGENT: Pardon? CAMILO: (*Assertively.*) I'm a writer. AGENT: Do you work for Hollywood? CAMILO: No, I don't. AGENT: (*Flipping through Mr. Macías' passport.*) Tell you what. There's something I want you to do. Go over there so they can check your luggage...

Suddenly I was in Gilliam's *Brazil*, and vicious FBI agents were waiting to disappear me. They were after a medium-height, fair-skinned, black-haired, thirty-something Cuban male with a goatee and a black-stone earring, a Castro spy who would rot in a Texas dungeon. *Help!* The other agent inspected my suitcase and asked the usual questions. AGENT: What do you do for a living, sir? CAMILO: I used to be a professor, but now I make a living as a writer. AGENT: (*He smiles.*) A writer? Wow. CAMILO: Yes, wow. AGENT: Hey, writing should be better than teaching, right? CAMILO: Most of the time...

Still bitten by the traveling bug, I decided to attend a couple of conferences during the fall of that year, the first one in Santo Domingo. I snuck in with a paper on Puig, the usual excerpt from my dissertation. My reasoning: I needed a respite from writing, and performing as an independent scholar wouldn't be a stretch. Like most participants, I stayed at the SD Hilton, where the event was held. Breakfast was an extravagant buffet that included "exotic tropical fruit" like mamey. (Loved mamey when I was a kid!) Our luxurious accommodations, like much of what the Dominican Republic had to offer, were readily available for a handful of dollars. *¡Bienvenidos!* A sumptuous meal in that beautiful country cost three bucks, and a gorgeous whore ten. If it was a young man you wanted, Hotel Colón was the place; and for a girl, the Dominicano. But I wanted neither. I couldn't have lived with myself after taking advantage of those kids. Just the thought of it gave me a wet noodle. Plus I was afraid of the risk. Better to just settle for a leisurely swim at the beach and a visit to the Museo to see Taino stuff.

Had to play the part at the conference, show my face and my tag and read my paper—not a high price to pay for a ticket to the Caribbean. Went to a presentation by one Rodolfo Espinosa, a Dominican professor who taught English at the Coliseo. He was slated to present a paper on the Communicative Approach in the ESL classroom, which had piqued my interest, and I thought it was good though nothing new (same dog, different collar.) I introduced myself to Rodolfo, chatted with him a little. It pleased him to know I was sold on the Communicative Approach. Somehow it came up that I was Cuban-American but not from Miami, and that I wasn't a Castro-bashing maggot. Rodolfo seemed encouraged by that info, told me he was a Marxist who believed in class struggle, and he tried to impress me with his leftist mumbo-jumbo. We went out for a beer, and then he invited me to his house; an invitation I happily accepted. Rodolfo lived by himself in a beachfront apartment, not a place he could afford on his teaching salary alone. Did he hustle? He could have—handsome enough. He was possibly the son of wealth, a "Niño Bien" who wanted to *épater les bourgeois* by siding with the proletariat. A maid came in every morning at 8:30 to fix Señorito a hearty breakfast and to clean his house. He told me I was to leave before she showed up; she was a gossip. No, his family didn't know...

We listened to songs—poetic, melodic—by a young Dominican singer-songwriter, Juan Luis Guerra. Our hot bed overflowed with badly quoted Marx, with dreams of a revolution for DR. I was aroused by his *caribeño* manners: "Is this good? You like it? What else do you like?" But I was also put off by the travesty he lived. Hey, who was I to judge? Cast the first stone, Dr. Milo...

I called him the next day. "How did you get my number?" he asked, sounding put off. I reminded him he'd given it to me. Rodolfo was busy and would be dining with his fiancée that night. I was not to phone again. "Whatever happened last night didn't happen," he said. "*¿Tú me entiendes?*"

Oh, yes, I understand. Entiendo muy bien, I thought. No tang of your sweat in my mouth, no lard melting on your thighs. Your humid voice, your silent touch, I imagined it all. I pulled our love, your lips, my tongue, your throbbing heart out of a magic hat. Our walk on the beach at Boca Chica, the peddlers who jolted us out of our liberation dreams, the warmth of my skin soaked in your breath, none of it was mine to keep. We never said goodbye. We didn't even meet. Entiendo...

My next escapade was to Germany, a symposium on Latino literature held in Heidelberg. Was invited to read and talk about my work. Easy enough: Dr. Milo would face the crowds for me. But first a stop in Paris on my way to Deutschland, a quick fix of the most beautiful city in the world. But Paris was one huge disappointment. *C'est dommage!*

The Eiffel Tower had been shut down, a circus had been installed on the Champs Elysées, and the billboards hovering over the city advertised a Travolta movie with the face of a talking baby, *Allo Mama, Ici Bebé*. In a café along the Seine, a crabby waiter told me I should sit properly in the chair and not like an *ivrogne*, a drunkard. Otherwise he wouldn't wait on me, wouldn't even serve me a stale *croque monsieur*. I told him in crisp Cuban Spanish what he should do with his good manners, "*¡Métete los modales por el culo, comemierda!*" And then I repeated this suggestion in not-so-colorful French. There was a Warhol Retrospective at the Pompidou, but I wasn't in the mood to consume Andy's assembly-line art, not even to get an air-conditioned respite from the blistering heat. As I walked on, I thought of the bohemian, fantasy-drunk Paris of Julio Cortázar. That city I was exploring wasn't it. No, my Paris was a boiling cauldron where my soul sank.

Deutschland welcomed me with a downpour and a view of the Mainz in Frankfurt. The rain always makes me feel peaceful, but the feeling didn't last—too brief of a storm. At the touristy Strasse, a band of poncho-clad Sudacas were playing the lambada while a cluster of strapping Germans watched in awe. In Heidelberg, the taxi I hailed was driven by an old Sicilian who reminded me of Tano—sans the gay flair. He offered me a spectacular vista of the Necker River and talked about the city's famous castle in Italian at my request, since I didn't speak German. Although my junior-college *italiano* was rusty and his accent thick, I managed to gather from his story that the Heidelberger Schloss had been destroyed and rebuilt three times. The amicable driver then related several tales about the *schloss* in colorful detail, about a king who died of obesity, about an ugly queen who thought she was the loveliest woman in the world. But his most interesting story had to do with a midget called Perkeo (his name derived from a comment he usually made when asked to try something new: *Per che no?* Why not?) who was used to drinking only wine and fell to his death upon having his first glass of water.

At a modest, busy restaurant on the Hauptstrasse in old town, a young waiter struggled to tell me about one of today's specials. "We have chicken fried," he said, as he placed his right hand on the left side of his chest. "From here," he told me. I asked him in jest but amicably, "From the heart? The chicken is lovingly cooked, you mean?" He blushed. "No, no," he clarified, laughing. "The dish is chicken part from here!" I laughed, "Ah, chicken breast. Yes! I'll have that. *Danke!*"

The conference was mostly about Chicano literature, Cisneros, Castillo, Anaya, Hinojosa. As usual, that's what they meant by *Latino*. But there was one German prof (gay, my gaydar told me) who specialized in Cuban-American literature. At one of the receptions he briefly gave me his take on my work. "A postmodern master narrative for the Cuban-American canon," said the prof, "with the island as the absent signifier," and I was certain he was pulling my leg. Since I didn't ask him to elaborate, he proceeded to compare my oeuvre to that of Francisco M. Rodríguez, pointing out that we both had "Abuela" characters! And now he wanted to talk about Foucault, who had been his *guter Freund.* It was what he really wanted to discuss, his friendship with the late, great French intellectual. "Oh, Michelle," he divulged in a fake tone of secrecy. "Such a promiscuous gal! And a Leather Queen too! This is no rumor, you know. You're hearing it from the horse's mouth. Michel Foucault embodied his ideas. 'She' had the balls—and ass and everything in between, we must add—to parody virility and die for it. Not many of us are brilliant and daring enough to do that. Definitely *pas moi!*" Or *moi*, that's for sure.

I spent the remaining part of that year and most of the next homebound, writing. One smoggy day the following summer I got some terrible news. Manuel Puig had died in Cuernavaca, Mexico, at the age of fifty-seven. After reading about his death in the *Times*, I fell asleep on the futon as I tended to do when life seemed intolerable. Hours later I woke up crying, hoping I'd just had a nightmare about losing a dear friend. A friend? Could I make that claim about Manuel? Still groggy, I took a walk on the beach in Laguna, needing the repetition and solace of its surf. I sat on a rock near a cliff but was soon accosted by the waves, the tide coming at me. Then I saw Manuel's handsome face as a comforting mirage: the photo on the back cover of all his Seix Barral editions, Puig regaling us with a sexy smile; the wind blowing his hair; the ocean as backdrop with a gentle, foamy wave caressing the shore. See? He's an indelible image—I told myself—so he'll never really die. But this was no consolation.

The official story stated that Puig had suffered a heart attack while undergoing gall bladder surgery. I would eventually hear several variations of that report, but the details of his death didn't matter, not to me.

Fact was, the flesh and blood Manuel was gone, and I'd never hugged him nor told him in person how much I loved his work. I should've flown to Rio or Mexico or wherever he happened to be living to hang out with him. Instead I wrote him long letters, quoting key passages from my thesis and asking for his feedback. The latter usually amounted to a few words or sentences: *interesting; illuminating; not what I had in mind but it works; precisely what I was after, although I wasn't as aware of it as you are!* Then I sent him the complete dissertation, which he encouraged me to publish, and I never did. He was unpretentious and courteous in his handwritten replies (edgy yet graceful calligraphy) that I could now revisit, the only thing Manuel ever wrote that was truly mine...

Dear friend, I just received the latest chapter of your thesis, a huge and marvelous surprise! What I glimpsed so far pleased me a great deal, although, as you know, reading about my writing makes me nervous... I haven't communicated in a while because I've gone through some difficult times; Mamá's health was flagging. Fortunately she has recovered, and all that remains now is the scare she gave us... I just published novel No. 8, Cae la noche tropical. *Have you read it? I'd love to know what you think. The Spanish critics have generally liked it, even though they take every opportunity to reiterate their rejection of my recent work for reasons I don't quite understand. It has to do with how different* Pubis angelical *and* Maldición eterna a quien lea estas páginas *are from my previous novels. But that is not a valid criticism, is it, Camilo? Why can't one compose sonatas one day and symphonies the next? I hope we meet some day. I wish you the best with your writing... A big hug, Manuel.*

That day at the beach, I was heartened by Puig's smile, which didn't dissolve like the surf as I said to him, Sorry, *che.* Sorry for my refusal to carry on as a scholar of your work. There were plenty of other people willing to take over that job, academics who were thrilled to dismantle your exquisite texts in order to "understand" and "teach" them. The initial passion I felt for your novels is still with me, Manuel, but somewhere along the way I lost the drive to explicate you. I wanted to write symphonies and sonatas just like you, or at least tuneful ditties, not bleak discourses that purported to extract the truth out of your wonderful lies. Yes, of course I loved your last three books, two of them written entirely in dialogue form—quite a feat! But my love for your fiction has taken me to a place that critics and scholars aren't prone to visit, where I feel closer to you. Thank you for showing me the way.

I wonder if you saw the Spider Woman as you took your last breath. If you did, I hope that La Mujer Araña granted you one last wish, my friend. I hope she turned you into a gorgeous Hollywood heroine, the kind you so adored, the star of a dazzling film noir with a dapper leading man by your side. And I hope you'll find your utopia, *mi querido* Manuel, wherever you go from here. *Ciao...*

IV
The Way of Love

LOVE INSANE

W as it fate? I suppose it could be said that *Love Insane* led me to my first gay lover. It all started at a conference on gender politics at Harvard University. I was invited to participate in a discussion of my novel as part of a presentation by Cuban-born critic Aurelio Pérez Román, who had chosen to focus on my characters' "faux bisexual identity." According to Aurelio, the mask of bisexuality kept us *all* from facing the truth about our(gay)selves. It was an extremist stance that could be understood when one considered Pérez Román's history. He had suffered hostility and ridicule in his Ivy League department for a transparent reason: homophobia. Having been denied tenure unjustifiably, Aurelio engaged in a nasty legal battle to get it. He was seldom invited to Latino symposia. There was obvious trepidation in the people who ran the show, he said—be they Chicanos, Cubiches, or Gringos—when it came to "certain topics." As Aurelio eloquently put it, the gay academic closet was bursting at the seams like those in the *Three Stooges* movies, which spat out the contents of an entire house when the door was opened. Yet when a Latino scholar delved into a book like *Cuba in Silence* or *Love Insane*, he or she tended to do so from a heteronormative position, defining the characters as non-historical intrusions, as anti-Cuban. The same critics would lavish praise on Francisco's and Rafael's books, where the "normal" gender tenets of Cuban culture weren't called into question, where all was dandy in the family.

I admired Aurelio, what he did, what he fought for. But I also thought that he saw gayness everywhere and proclaimed it as "the definitive meaning" even when the texts he read didn't support his ideology. In his reading of *Love Insane*, for instance, the two main characters had been repressing their "true" gay identities all their lives, prior to their mental crises and hospitalization. In fact, this repression may well have been the cause of the mental collapse in both cases! Aurelio took issue with some of the dialogue, passages which—he claimed—derided and denigrated gayness; as when the janitor declared, "I won't be turning into a fucking *maricón* just because I'm nuts." To which the architect replied, "But letting me touch you like this wouldn't mean you're a *maricón*." Aurelio's interpretation of this comment verged on hysterical. "But what else could it mean?!" he asked. "We know that all that touching will lead to sex. Gay sex!" In his opinion, the characters' homosexuality should've been at the forefront in the novel, more than their mental illnesses. In other, simpler words, they had been faggots all along and didn't know it. Thus Pérez Román questioned their authenticity as well as my own.

I didn't want to antagonize my colleague, but he knew what my reaction would be. I had expressed my concerns about his thesis in my correspondence with him and had reiterated my position again when we met for lunch before our panel. I found his analysis of my novel reductive and misconstrued. "How can you be so sure," I asked him during the Q&A, "that gayness isn't also a 'guise' among others?" He didn't respond. "Which, by the way, wouldn't make it inauthentic." No reaction. "I believe that bisexuality," I went on, "is indeed an authentic experience, if by that we mean true to human nature." A handful of people in the audience started clapping, to my surprise. And it was surprising as well that Pérez Román didn't pursue the discussion. He split shortly after my comments, giving me a hurried kiss and saying, "This could've gone a lot better, Papito. *Ciao!*"

Several attendees came up to me then, one of them a young Latino who introduced himself warmly as Leon Barragan. He told me he had an essay in the anthology of testimonials *Bi Its True Name*, recently published by Lissom Press, and he thanked me for writing a novel about "his experience." I asked him if he was the one leading the applause. Leon nodded, laughing, then mentioned that he was a member of BABI (Bay Area Bisexuals). He talked briefly about his lover, Tony Anderson, with whom he shared a Mission District home in San Francisco. We exchanged phone numbers. "Please drop by when you're in the city," he said eagerly. "You can stay with us."

Three days later I got a call from Tony. In a playful voice he told me he'd read *Love Insane* and enjoyed it, and would I be interested in doing a reading from it at Mission Pages, the bookstore in the Mission District where he worked. I said I'd be delighted. We talked about possible dates and finally settled on one at the end of January, five weeks away. "In the meantime," he offered, sounding sincere, "you should come visit for a while. Leon and I would love that. *¡Mi casa es su casa!*" I immediately knew I'd take him up on his offer, that I'd start hanging out with Tony and Leon in the city.

Tony Anderson was four years older than me. Once upon a time he'd worked as a female impersonator; said he could still do a convincing Cher but wouldn't perform for me. "My head just isn't there anymore," he explained. Nowadays he preferred to sell books and do some freelance journalism on the side. Tony and Leon lived in a quaint Victorian row house on Valencia Street, around the corner from Mission Pages. Their home overflowed with tapestries, pottery, and indigenous art that Tony had collected on his travels. There was something calming about that place: the subtle way light moved through it, the view from the curtainless window in the living room—a forest of ivy. I got high on killer weed in that room whenever I visited, feasting with my hosts on Chinese takeout and listening on their portable CD player to Tony's favorite pop divas, Cher, Liza, Donna, Diana, Dionne, and Olivia among them. Some of the songs he loved were ones I dug too, "Dark Lady," "The Way of Love," "I Honestly Love You," "Maybe This Time," "I Feel Love," "I'll Never Love This Way Again."

Tony was a voracious reader and liked a great number of writers, Gore Vidal being at the top of his list. He'd read most of Vidal's novels but didn't care for his political essays. "Too bitchy and pessimistic," he explained. "She does tell it like it is, the truth about our imperialist nation. But I'd rather feel good about my country, and she's such a downer!" When I admitted to Tony that I didn't know Vidal's work, he was appalled: "And you call yourself a doctor of literature?!"

"Give me a break!" I said in my defense, "I've been busy reading Manuel Puig."

The next time I found myself browsing the shelves at Mission Books, Tony handed me an autographed copy of *Myra Breckenridge*, saying, "Here, this is Vidal's best, in my humble opinion. It's on loan! And don't ask me what I had to do to get it signed by the diva herself..."

I read *Myra* in one sitting and loved it. The novel was right up the Spider Woman's alley; it referenced Hollywood classics in a gender-bending story but with a comic twist missing in Puig. What a blast, the first of several Gore Vidal books (*The City and the Pillar*, *Myron*, *Julian*, *Creation*, *The Second American Revolution*) I've since devoured. Unlike Tony, however, I've come to consider Vidal a much stronger political thinker and historian than novelist.

Tony tried to get it on with me, paying occasional visits to his comfy couch, where I slept when I stayed over. "I don't go for married men," I told him, which was only some of the truth. He said I wasn't to worry about Leon; they had an arrangement. "He sleeps with a woman now and then, and I have my sporadic flings." But I wasn't budging: "Sorry, dude, but I'll stick to my rule." And eventually he gave up, or at least stopped trying. There was nothing specific about Tony that failed to arouse me. He was attractive enough—average height and weight, fair complexion, olive-green eyes, a medium-length mane of light brown hair with bangs, a roguish smile. He favored snug blue jeans and cotton shirts in bright pastels, all of them oversize. Tony might've done a number on my head had he been willing to perform as one of his divas for me. Or maybe not. Maybe not even that illusion would've drawn me sexually to him. It could be that he wasn't masculine at all. Femininity in and of itself has never been my thing, unless it is extreme and delivered in the guise of transvestism, performed as an act. Nelly men seldom attract me. Not that Tony was overtly effeminate, but there was something soft-mannered about him, something fragile. It was the same way with Castel, whom I loved dearly yet didn't desire.

I wondered what brought, what *kept* Tony and Leon together. They seemed worlds apart. Leon worked as a lab tech at a clinic, drawing blood. He bragged about having a gentle, well-aimed hand; he'd never missed a vein! This nine-to-five paid enough for Leon to make ends meet. He was meticulous; his tidy bedroom with minimalist decor didn't belong in that house. Leon wasn't into books. He talked almost exclusively about his kindred souls, the BABI's, who knew his "true name." Leon was a Chicano who didn't speak Spanish and had no interest in his roots. He considered it an insult when people assumed he was a Mexican immigrant, or when they "mispronounced" his name by stressing the last syllable, Barragán. Tony, on the other hand, spoke a basic yet acceptable Spanish, was captivated by Latin culture and had traveled through Mexico and Central and South America. He'd tried to instill in Leon some pride in his cultural heritage, to no avail. Leon, who looked like a Zapotec Indian, was bent on erasing his ancestry, on freeing himself from what he saw as an identity imposed on him by others. I suspected he secretly longed to be white, or, rather, a bisexual white man.

But Leon and Tony loved each other despite their differences, or so it seemed to me. Their arrangement worked for them, said Tony, yet he was constantly annoyed by his partner's alleged need to have female lovers. He sniggered whenever he talked about Leon's "hetero infidelities." "I don't believe him for a split second!" he'd intone. I told him once that I could relate to Leon's "need," and Tony laughed. "Don't fool yourself, hon," he said. "For us, that's not 'the way of love'..."

How could both Tony and Pérez Román be so sure of who they were, of the essence that determined their actions? I envied their ability to engage the world in full drag as characters they believed in, as people who reflected *exactly* who they thought they were meant to be. Such comfort! Such freedom! No rift between your inner voice and its output, no gap separating the secret utterance from the public one. I wondered if I'd ever know that certainty, if there would come a day when I felt the way I was supposed to; when I could don a single mask, the *true* identity, and embody it for good.

It seemed that Pueblo Press was about to have a hand in my search for that mask. Sergio had hired a savvy L.A. publicist to promote *Love Insane* with other PP titles from that season, and she marketed my book primarily as a gay work. She conjured up some reviews in mainstream venues. Two of these, in the *Los Angeles Times* and the *San Francisco Chronicle*, were for the most part laudatory. But not the *New York Times* piece. "The lack of a strong plot and in-depth characterizations," they said, "leaves one wanting something more substantial. We keep wondering who those two men really are." I'd written that book in a trance that lasted two months and hadn't let it age, obviously. But I consoled myself in thinking that perhaps my feverish rush had given *Love Insane* its strength, maybe its soul.

Tony's article in the *Mission Voice* was the most personal, as was to be expected. He got me to open up and make a statement that he quoted partially: "I don't feel like I fit in any group, not with my compatriots or with gays or bisexuals. I won't be a spokesman for the Cuban diaspora nor the gay community, either. Sorry. Can't. I don't believe art should serve any cause, no matter how worthy." Aside from sounding full of myself, I was honest only up to a point, since I was actually enjoying my newly found niche in the gay canon, being part of a community. Maybe this is it, I thought. *I am a Little Mary.* But how could I claim this identity if I'd never had a lasting relationship with a man? My homosexual experiences had been solely about sex. And my affair with Danny didn't count; there had been little emotional investment on my part. The only man I loved, Castel, didn't arouse me physically. So I had some convincing to do. And some homework. It was high time I lived up to my sudden fame...

I had just signed a handful of books at Mission Pages, after my reading, when I saw Tony pushing his way through the small crowd, bringing a tall blond man with him. "Camilo, this is Evan Dessler," he said. "You two should have a lot to talk about. Start comparing notes, girls!" The tall blond shook my hand forcefully and clarified, "Tony means compare notes about McAdam&Soulek. I rep for them and I push some of your stuff. Your readers. Which are selling well, by the way." Great news! Evan said he hadn't read my books because his Spanish was "pitiful." He'd learned only enough about the series—the minimum, he confessed—to promote it. He couldn't discuss any of the texts in depth, but he did have a lot to say about McAdam&Soulek. He described the company as a cutthroat bunch of slave drivers and corporate shysters. I didn't doubt he told the truth but couldn't share my own version of M&S's faults and abuses. I felt lucky to be one of their authors; had always been treated courteously, professionally by its editors and didn't think I was being terribly exploited.

Evan turned me on instantly. He was sexy, more of a SoCal dude than an M&S suit, what Castel would've called a *gabacho*, an Anglo boy. But he was also smart, self-assured, and he exuded good health. He seduced me that very night. I was flying high already when we got to my hotel room. Seconds after walking in, he stood naked before me flaunting his erection, a large penis the color of hot sand that moved impatiently and called me. By the time I had him in my mouth he'd ripped my clothes off, his arms had locked me in and seized me. I'd had no time to act insecure, to say no or later or let's take it slow. Somehow Evan knew it had to be this way; he seemed to know me...

Soon I learned that Evan had been born and raised in San Jose, with an Irish mother and a German father; that he'd spent the last ten years in San Francisco working for McAdam&Soulek. Out of the closet since age ten, he'd done a lot of psychotherapy, which had been helpful, he said. I wondered why he was so reluctant to talk about his parents—wouldn't answer my questions about them. Had he been abused, kicked out, disowned? The only topics Evan expanded on were his sex history (a vast catalogue of positions, places, and partners of varied ages and types) and his work in "our community." He was active in several organizations such as ACT UP and in fact had met Tony when they were both volunteering at the OutWrite Conference the year before. The therapy Evan had done was the Freudian kind with lots of egos and ids and superegos, lots of childhood-trauma psychobabble. He believed that psychoanalysis had prepared him to seize what he wanted in life, and what he sought was success. He made a great salesman but was meant for something bigger, maybe head of Higher Education at M&S.

Time seemed unending and porous during my first two months with Evan. We would spend most weekends together, commuting between his studio apartment in the Mission and my Colina condo. But he wanted more time with me and more sex, an act that must be performed once a day at least, he said, keeping us healthy and content. *Evan boasts about his prowess*—I wrote early on in my diary. *And yes, he can make it happen. When I'm with him I surrender, going where he takes me. I savor him for as long as he wants me to, longer than my lips and my tongue and my throat can endure. Then I'm his to take, a body that knows danger and power. A body that hurts so good.*

I had much to learn about myself, said Evan. "If we ever break up," he'd tell me, "you'll owe me for all the free therapy I'm giving you." He'd probe and define my complexes, those that apparently affected my interaction with the world: "You smile too much. You're afraid of people. You're still in the closet. You're indecisive, unmanly." There was some truth to his claims, I suppose. I could be malleable, unsure of things, but not a basket case and not in need of Evan's "free therapy." Okay, so manliness should be my goal, right? Then why did he expect me to perform as a total femme in bed? If I tried to initiate our lovemaking or attempt to penetrate him, he'd ridicule me: "You ain't got what it takes, so stop." *He likes me to tell him about my sex life*—I wrote. *He wants to know about my ex-lovers' bodies, what they did to me, in de-*

tail. The childhood memories I shouldn't have kept alive turn him on, those where I'm a boy in peril, molested at the age of seven by a man of twenty-five. Evan wants to know how I felt, what I imagined seeing while in the throes of these acts, and so I tell him I imagined being ripped apart and then devoured by a vicious sea creature. He wants to hear about the size and shape of the molester's cock, his dirty house and unmade cot, the pungent sweat smell of his pants. About the fear—and guilt and pain and scant pleasure—I experienced with that man...

Evan knew I was into Manuel Puig. He hadn't read *Kiss of the Spider Woman* and didn't plan to, but he'd seen the film version (a Brazilian production directed by the Argentine Hector Babenco) and hated it. I didn't think it was a great movie, definitely not one that did justice to the book, but nevertheless I loved it. And because I did, Evan took every opportunity to deride it. He once described his reaction to Babenco's film to some drunk we met at a bar, while I eavesdropped in disbelief...

"To begin with, the title is misleading," he said. "It makes you think of action and adventure, like the comics. I'm ready for some spider-woman action and what do I see? William Hurt in drag, his hair dyed red. Hurt pretending to be a queen named Molina pretending to be a glamorous leading lady in some Hollywood B movie. He's in jail for corrupting kids—big deal!—and talks about old films all the time. He tells the story of this French singer who suddenly appears singing off key and looking stupid and kissing her Nazi lover. Anyhow, there's also Raúl Julia, slim and hot; his character's name is Valentín and he's in this prison cell with Molina. They talk bull about his political ideals and Molina's homosexuality. Valentín says he's given his life to the Cause, whatever that is. And now here comes the singer again fluttering her fake eyelashes and saying *Soggy mon amour*. She ends up shot by some French insurgents for being a traitor, though the real reason is that she's such a bad singer! At the end she sails away with Valentín and they live happily ever after, though it's all a dream 'cause Valentín is tortured to death and Molina gets shot right smack in the middle of his feminine heart. Is there a message in that whole farrago? Yeah, I guess it's that society has done a number on our heads, that Molina had no other way of loving a man than as a woman because he'd been made to think that homosexuals were a defective version of females. And you know what I say to that? Bullshit! I'm gay and no one's gonna tell me how to fucking think, and I for sure don't wanna be a woman!"

Eight months into our thing, Evan made a decision: "We need to get a place together." But he didn't want us to live in Colina, a suburban town with no gay infrastructure. No, we were destined for San Francisco, a real city. Evan had had enough of his small apartment; he wanted "a nice pad" but couldn't afford one, so he was looking for a roommate, a partner of sorts. And I could play the part well for him, pay half the rent and utilities, clean house, buy groceries, cook, and have sex at his command. "Are we getting a place or what?" he kept insisting. I told him I'd think about it. "Okay, but think fast," he warned me, "or I'll call the whole thing off." Then I wrote up a wish list, my four conditions for our thing to make it. Evan must 1) stop fucking other men—he still "saw" several in the city; 2) stop making decisions for me—where to eat, how to screw, when to smile; 3) accept my feminine soul, embrace his inner woman, and be the bottom-man sometimes; 4) stop analyzing me!

Evan reacted to each point when I showed him the list: "Why should I stop fucking other people? You don't seem committed to our relationship the way you'd have to be. But maybe if we lived together, I'd consider monogamy... I have to make all the decisions 'cause you're a pitiful indecisive woman about everything. And no, I'll never accept your femininity or let you fuck my ass. And you should be grateful I'm willing to analyze your messed-up mind for free." So much for my four wishes!

I'm not good at his game—I wrote. *The rules are unfair; he's always in charge, I must play submissive. Things are fine as long as I do what he wants. But if I question his ideas or express any doubts, he gets angry, oppressive, at times violent. He complains that I'm not committed, too immature for the next step, which is living together in the city. But why would I want to make such a big change in my life for him? Just to get more of his power trip and his huge dick? Thanks but no thanks.*

Alina never met Evan because I didn't introduce them, afraid as I was that she'd see right through him and burst my bubble irremediably. Just a couple of words from her—*No good*, for instance—would've been enough to spoil my "fun," and I wasn't ready for the end just yet. But I did arrange for Castel and Evan to meet, while Castel was back from Mexico to visit his mother. The three of us spent an afternoon in Laguna Beach, had dinner at a funky seaside bistro, and wound up the day at the Big Bang. Evan was charming, as usual, and Castel seemed smitten with my lover. "He's totally hot," he told me the next day on the phone.

"But there's something about his smile I don't trust." I asked him what he meant; he wasn't sure. "Let me give it some thought," he said. "But don't worry about it, okay?" I needed Castel to tell me the truth I was certain he knew, that Evan was bent on crushing me, on destroying my self-esteem so he could remain on top; that I should run away from him before it was too late. Instead Castel was giving me this song-and-dance about the man's smile! In any case, I wouldn't have followed his advice, just as I didn't listen to Tony's. I was still blinded by the fantasy, willing to betray myself in order to believe Evan's fictions about me.

Tony's reaction to my "thing" with Evan was a kiss and a warning. "A sexy couple," he said. "Just don't go too fast, sweetie. It's safer that way." I asked him if he had any dirt on the man, and Tony was unusually evasive... "I've heard he likes to push people around and thinks he's above everyone, but I'm sure you'll be able to put him in his place if that's all true. Like I said, go slow, my love. And run for your life at the first show of the Dark Lady's fangs." Of course I didn't tell him that I'd glimpsed my lover's fangs already. Evan hated Tony, called him "a hysterical queen with self-serving politics." One day he decided I was spending too much time with him, which wasn't the case at all. I hardly ever saw Tony anymore when I was in San Francisco. Even so, Evan insisted that I drop him. "You don't need to hang out with that pathetic faggot," he said, "or anyone else. You've got me now."

Jokingly, I told him he had nothing to worry about, "Tony's not my type."

"Too fem for you, huh?"

"Yeah, maybe that's it."

Evan grabbed me by the throat, shouting, "But you're just as much of a woman as he is!"

I fought back. "You know I'm not a woman. You've had my hard cock in your mouth. And there's nothing wrong with being a woman, anyway. Or a queen!"

He shoved me against the wall. "Everything's wrong with being weak like a female!"

"No. I'll tell you what's really wrong," I said, containing my urge to beat the crap out of him. "What's wrong is being a fucking bully."

"A bully?" He was laughing. "What, we're in high school or something?"

"You know what I mean. An abusive motherfucker."

"Is that what you think I am?"

"Sometimes, yes."

"But you like it, right? You like to be treated like shit by your man."

"No, I don't!"

"We'll see about that the next time we fuck."

"Don't hold your breath."

"Let's do it now."

"Not now," I said, feeling repelled by him all of a sudden.

He clasped the back of my neck, said, "Come here."

I shoved him away. He hit the floor, banged his head against the wall. "Go beat off!" I said as I rushed out the door, not giving him a chance to come after me. I knew now that Evan and I were headed somewhere dark and vicious, not a place I wanted to be. Yet I kept hoping for...what exactly?

That scene should've signaled the end of our relationship, but it didn't. Thanks to Tony, my lover would still have a chance to show his fangs at their sharpest—and for the very last time.

Tony was enthused by the Bay Area sales of *Love Insane* that summer, and he asked me to do another reading at Mission Pages. He promised an ad in the *Chronicle* and a full house for sure. We set the date and time: September 18, a Saturday, at 7:00 p.m. "Will you be mentioning the recent developments in your love life?" he joked. "Your audience deserves to know!" My reaction was immediate. "No way," I said. "Mum's the word." But I was actually tempted to disclose my "credentials." Whether or not I belonged in the gay canon, at least now I felt legit, no longer the impostor. I was living up to my fame in the city; had turned into a full-fledged Little Mary with a hunky lover to prove it. So what if he was messing with my mind? Par for the course!

I had planned to spend the afternoon of the eighteenth at Tony's house, while he was at work. A few hours alone in that place would do me good, I thought. I knew that Leon wouldn't be there—never saw much of him, in fact. It was as if he'd decided I was Tony's friend, not his. We'd had some good discussions about bisexuality, united by this "bizarre tendency" of ours—as he called it—to feel at home with both men and women. "Most people don't get us," Leon kept saying. But his initial hospitality tapered off once he realized I wasn't joining his group, or writing an essay for the next edition of *Bi Its True Name*, or publicly defending his identity. Tony, always the drama queen, blamed the BA-

BI's for his lover's absences. "They're filling his head with hetero delusions. That boy breaks my heart!"

I was enjoying the silence at Tony's place that afternoon. Until Evan started calling... *I'll be late, a business meeting.* On a weekend? Yeah, right. *Or maybe I won't go at all. I've heard you read before, and, frankly...* Okay, fine. *Maybe I'll just catch up with you later tonight.* Good, whatever!

I hoped he wouldn't show up. I knew that my reading—none of my work, really—would ever meet with Evan's praise. He'd given me his take on my "mediocre" writing more than once... "Your novels get published because you're Hispanic, but only with a small press 'cause you're not good enough for the big houses. You don't even have an agent!" He would sneer at my McAdam&Soulek books, big-press titles that offered original fiction. "Those books don't count," he'd allege. They're all written in classroom Spanish. That's not real literature!" Then there he was at the door, an hour before my presentation. "For moral support," he said. He kissed me, caressed me, took his time to seduce me. And I let myself enjoy it all, even though I knew that Evan was turning a great performance as the caring lover. He thought he'd won; I had agreed to move in with him. His passion, so sudden and complete, was meant to be my reward, a preview of the life that awaited me with him.

It was 6:40 by now. I needed time alone! I offered him a practiced smile and suggested that he go on ahead. Evan agreed reluctantly. "I'll save you a seat," he said. But my solitude was short-lived; ten minutes later he was back, announcing, "There's hardly anybody there, just Tony and a couple of people. I thought you'd want to know."

"You're kidding, right? Not funny." I felt frozen.

"Nope. An empty house."

I'd had my share of empty venues, but this time it was different. This time there would be Evan watching me and waiting to prove his point. *You're not good enough!* It didn't cross my mind that he might be lying. When I finally showed up at Mission Pages it was 7:15, and I found the place packed. "A lot of people arrived early," said Tony, mildly reproachful. "Some have been here since 6:30. And the Cuban diva had to make them wait!" A full house, that's what Evan should've told me, the real news, not a wicked lie he'd fabricated to undermine my confidence, to weaken me so I'd fail.

There was energy in that room. I got excited. And somehow I managed not to see Evan, even though he was standing by the door in full view; there, grading me, taking mental notes in order to tell me later that my reading had had too much histrionics and no substance, that my act was over the top. It dawned on me then, as I read from *Love Insane* to my audience, that through all of Evan's "free therapy" I'd forgotten how lucky I was. Camilo had it made.

I knew now that our relationship was over for good, but it made no sense to bring up the lie he'd fed me; he would've denied flat out that he was trying to hurt me. I had come up with a better idea. Instead of confronting him, I'd let things coast along for a few days, waiting for the perfect moment. Evan decided we should go house hunting, so we did. There was a two-bedroom near Tony's house, on Valencia, that he liked. The rent was steep, but he thought we could afford it. He wanted to sign a one-year lease. When I said I wasn't sure, he accused me of being indecisive like a pathetic queen. But I kept my cool. "That's not true at all," I said. "In fact, I know exactly what I'm going to do."

"That's more like it," he stated, eager for my final surrender.

"I've decided..." I paused, which drove him nuts. "I've decided I'm not moving in with you."

"What?! Are you serious?"

"Totally serious. There will be no move. Not ever."

"Forget it, then! Forget about me!"

"I'll try to."

"Think about what you're saying, Camilo, what this means."

"I know what it means. It means I won't have to suck your ugly white dick ever again!"

"Go to hell!" he shouted.

"No need to," I said, walking away. "Been there already thanks to you."

The next day I flew back to Colina. He called a lot for about two weeks, left surprisingly warm messages on my machine at first, sounding apologetic. But as the days passed without me giving signs of life, Evan started leaving insults and threats... *You can't live without my rock-hard boner! No one's ever gonna fuck you like I did! You'll come back, crawling like a woman! Pick up the goddamn phone, you pitiful Cuban faggot!* I didn't answer any of his calls, and eventually he stopped harassing me.

I went to the beach almost every day for a month after our breakup, mainly to write and do some reading. There I read *Myra Breckenridge* (my own copy now) a second time. "A delicious sex joke," Tony had called the book, and thanks to that joke I was laughing again. But I was also feeling haunted by Tano's curse... *May you fall in love with a ruthless macho and suffer!*

Was I in love with Evan? I could've been, I suppose, if he hadn't been plagued by such dangerous contradictions. He bragged about his commitment to the gay cause, yet he was a parody of patriarchy, a fucking oppressor. I indulged him for too long, immersing myself in his madness yet knowing that his was a wicked madness. I was transfixed by the experience, high on the fantasy, but also scarred by the abuse. No, I didn't want to try again with another man, wasn't willing to take what I'd learned and make it work next time. I didn't see the point. By then I just wanted to be alone.

A MINOR MOVEMENT

The culinary trend in Miami that year was *nouvelle cuisine cubaine*, delicacies such as porgy in tamale cream, mamey flan, and sweet potato pudding with blueberry sauce; none of it great competition for the real Cuban food like *congrí* and *pernil* that one could still find at Versailles and other restaurants. Strolling down SW 8th Street, you'd hear émigrés lauding the imagined candidacy of the next president of Cuba, an anti-Castro lobbyist named Jorge Más Canosa who was destined to reclaim our beloved country: yet another pipe dream for the community. The hot news item in town was the Raft People, *los balseros*; they had displaced the Marielitos as the most recent chapter in our diaspora. It seemed that in Miami there was always someone who had just escaped the confines of communist Hell, and someone offering messianic hopes of saving the island from communism.

In November of that year, while Cuba was going through the most desperate economic crisis of its history, the Miami Book Fair (housed at Miami Dade College) was at full throttle. I had been invited to be part of a panel at the Fair with fellow Cuban-American writers Dina Pérez, Francisco M. Rodríguez, and Rafael Valdés Alfaro, all of us usually referred to as "the Guayaba Pack," though I wasn't part of their group initially. Amazing that, as distant as we were geographically (they were all Miami-grown but nesting now in NYC, CO and PA respectively) and, to some extent, artistically, we could still assemble as a troupe, a sort of minor "movement." The fact that we'd seen our names strung together in several academic articles and book reviews helped, plus the presence of Cuba in our lives.

Dina, Francisco, and Rafael shared another bond. Their work had appeared in *The Guayaba Pack*, the first and thus far only anthology of Cuban-American literature in existence. There were seven other writers included in this *Pack*, then-unknowns and still-unknowns. Surely the exiles who'd edited the project must've known about my work but decided to keep me out. Some of those editors were organizers of the readings and panels at the Fair. One of them, an older Cuban prof, called me at home to follow up on my official invitation. I asked him which of the anthologized writers were attending the Fair. He mentioned Dina, Rafael, and Francisco, in that order precisely and tellingly—Dina being the one with a big name and major deals, Rafael the academic wizard who had theorized about the Cuban-American canon, and Francisco last and certainly least, since he didn't have any mainstream allure yet. While it was true that we'd all shown up on the literary scene at about the same time, none of my fellow Cubiches dwelled in the murky waters and "wild side" of the Cubiche experience like I did, hence my prior exclusion from *The Guayaba Pack* anthology. I expected an apology from the Cuban prof about this faux pas, but it wasn't forthcoming. Too much to ask?

The Fair was putting us up at the South Beach Inn, musty yet quaint with its 1937 Art Deco interior design. I met up with Francisco at the hotel bar. Overdressed as always, he was impeccably clad in a light-gray linen summer suit with a blue silk necktie. The contrast between us was sharp; I was wearing blue jeans and a white T-shirt. Francisco was short, barrel-chested; he had light brown skin, a friendly smile, expressive eyes. Over Cuba Libres, we engaged in the usual discussion and mutual exaltation of our work. He liked it that way. Francisco couldn't handle *choteo*, even though it was the unifying element in his fiction, an explosion of jokes and translated puns that kept his readers—definitely if they spoke *cubanglés*—cracking up. His writing wasn't one of deep philosophical layers but it was fun and culturally relevant. Ironically, in his personal dealings, he preferred to have a gentle mood of camaraderie with no sarcastic turns. Hence we toasted to being part of Pueblo Press' Cuban-American legacy, to his flair for wordplay and his parody of Miami life; and to my work, described by him as lyrical and daring. *Cheers!* After this mutual pat on the back, Francisco told me I should find myself a sexy boyfriend and settle down with him. He didn't see me with a woman. "I doubt anyone would after reading your books," he said. "Thanks for your feedback and your suggestion," I told him, "but, as you well know, books can never tell the whole story..."

Dina joined us briefly for a drink, typically guarded, aloof, and unwilling to discuss her current projects. She wouldn't have dinner with us because her non-writer Anglo husband would feel out of place, she said. But also—we were sure—because she liked to play the mainstream diva, the unreachable celebrity of this and other events. She had, after all, a Pulitzer; and she was the most written about and academically enthroned of our bunch, our own Cubiche star. According to some machista critics, she also had the extra edge of being a foxy broad who looked and carried herself like a tall Gloria Estefan. Her best-known novel—youthful, poetic, linguistically exuberant—dealt with the travails of a Miami teenager born to wealthy exiles as she tries to plan a visit to Cuba against her parents' wishes and consent; an eloquent, stirring character who'd been compared to Salinger's Holden Caulfield.

We were having a late lunch at Versailles, hall of mirrors, echo chamber of gossip and politics and the quintessential Cuban meal in Miami. As expected, Rafael appeared with an entourage of three local profs, his "fans." Eight years my senior, Rafael saw himself as our wise older brother. He was tall, thin, verging on gaunt, and his face showed traces of adolescent acne. Handsome despite his blemishes, Sr. Valdés Alfaro proudly displayed his aquiline visage and his opinions. The "midpoint" was his big symbol, the one he put forth in much of his poetry and academic writing. It was the site where many of us Cubiches supposedly thrived, navigating between two cultures and two nationalities. He also talked about "fruitful ambivalence" ("fruity," if he tried to be funny) when defining the strength of our cultural character. And he referred to our group as the Limbo Generation, people who'd arrived in the United States as children and couldn't claim to be fully Cuban nor totally assimilated Americans. Not a particularly attractive or original place, in my opinion, though Dante did make room in Limbo for the great thinkers and artists of his time. Stimulating company, no doubt, yet if given a choice I would've been an eternal spirit in Lust, the Second Circle of Hell. Yeah! Of course I got what Rafael meant: that unsettling yet potentially productive neither-here-nor-there condition we all shared, whether we wanted to or not. I could relate, yes, I could see his limbo through the experience and discourse of sexuality. And wasn't there a midpoint in gender identity as well? Got it, Raffy!

Rafael observed and was envious of the fact that my English was more colloquial than his, because I said things like *veg out, dig, cool, dude,* and *for real.* He boasted about being our precursor, the first of us to have published a book in English with a notable house. Mischievous me, I pointed out that the book he referred to was a scholarly work with a limited readership and no mainstream press attention. Hence it didn't count! I also mentioned that, even though his oeuvre had become increasingly popular, he was still being published by a university press—not, by a long shot, a "notable house." And, anyway, there were Cubans writing in this country long before he and I and all the other Guayaberos came into the picture. We'd only been the most visible, thanks in part to the 1959 Revolution. Bursting his bubble even more, I indicated that José Yglesias was the one who truly deserved the title of Trailblazing Cubiche, since he had published his first novel, *A Wake in Ybor City* (a widely read book about Cuban immigrants in Florida) in 1963. Rafael stated that Yglesias was only Cuban on his mother's side, thus he was a *cubano manqué* who considered himself one-hundred-percent American. "Regardless of how Yglesias saw himself," I said, "the fact remains that he's our true precursor, the father of the Guayabitos, and the only one entitled to first place. So there! *¡Pa' que no jodas más!*"

Rafael dropped the subject, unable or unwilling to provide more counter-arguments. Evidently famished, he dug into his *pernil* with abandon. But now he was hung up on the word *guayabitos,* which I'd just used to refer to Cuban-American writers of our generation. "How dare you call us 'baby mice'?!" he said to me. Then he proceeded to complain that there was an excess of exile angst and old-school poetry about our "lost, suffering island" at the Fair. And I agreed but told him, poking fun at his terminology, that there was also too much of his "halfway house" and his "Limbo Rock" and his "ambivalent fruitiness." He retaliated by saying that I had it all wrong. "If there's a surplus of anything," he asserted, "it's your deviant contribution to our pack, the malcontent, suicidal faggots in your writings, an excess of pedophiles and dark widows and oneiric monsters. And too many nutcases!" I came back with, "Happy to oblige, *compatriota.*" As always, good old *choteo* was our way of getting to the truth without beating each other up for real. We laughed to try to bridge the chasm between us, though maybe we'd crossed the line this time. Maybe Rafael Valdés Alfaro had already placed me on his blacklist, along with a horde of left-leaning academics whom he had publicly denounced as his enemies. Still, we made a toast with a mojito to a bountiful guava harvest. *¡Salud!*

In the Miami Dade audience, the following night, we would find the scholarly version of ourselves, a handful of Cuban-American critics who "got" us, or who at least shared some of our cultural and historical concerns; among them Aurelio Pérez Román, who had delved passionately—yet without success, in my opinion—into *Love Insane*.

After lunch I took time to roam Little Havana alone, receptive to Miami's sweet yet deceitful caress. This other Havana was comforting like an image of home (a home I'd never lived in), yet I knew that its comfort and beauty had been forged from the ruins of a past that wasn't great for everyone. Miami's perception of itself was founded on the vision of an idyllic island, the lost paradise. Except that many Cubans didn't lose paradise but an inferno of poverty and racism. Official Miami reality fed from and defined itself in opposition to Cuba's ideological life. But Little Havana/La Sagüesera hadn't much to do with the Cuban people's struggle for survival, with their hunger. La Sagüesera strove to be a profoundly patriotic extension of the island but was only its photographic negative, a simulacrum.

Part of me wanted to feel at home in that city, but I didn't share its obsessions, the fierce homogeneity of its values. Miami imposed its *tema*, and silence on this topic wasn't an option there. Those *cubanos* who didn't scream out their anti-communist passions were considered suspect, untrustworthy. I was one of those. In spite of the familial older women who served *congrí* and *picadillo* at Versailles, and who won me over with their Cuban endearments; despite Gloria Estefan's "Conga" and Willy Chirino's music, which made me get down, I didn't belong there.

But what about the janitor and the architect in my second novel? Could they claim that Cuba-infused community as their own? Not according to the only review that had appeared locally, which criticized the book for its lack of authenticity, its failure of verisimilitude. The reviewer—a *Herald* reporter in the guise of literary critic—furiously stated that the Miami in *Love Insane* wasn't believable, that it had no substance and could be anywhere; that it had nothing to do with his beautiful, thriving city in Florida. A similar attack had been unleashed by a scholar with a Marxist agenda and a grudge against that metropolis of hard-core Republicans. What a missed opportunity—the critic

declared in an academic article—to portray the *real* Miami, to expose
the pernicious politics and superiority complex of Miami Cubans! Thus
both sides of the ideological divide saw the absence of specific historical references as a failure on my part. True: cultural markers such as
street names, typical dishes, and idiomatic expressions (all of which I
included to some degree in *Love Insane*) don't necessarily embody the
realness of a place. But when I wrote *Love Insane* I wasn't really interested in Miami's *anticastrista* fixations or its delusions of a pre-Castro
utopia. Rather I was focused on the world that was born within the
room of a mental clinic. I knew that, for the characters to seem believable, they had to express the right amount of idiosyncrasies (attitudes,
mores, tastes); and they did sound Cuban to me in that respect, or at
least like the types I was familiar with. Still, I kept waiting for someone
to commend the book precisely for its universality, its adherence to far-
reaching archetypes instead of local technicolor.

I checked in at the conference after my stroll and met a woman
named Iliana at the Miami Dade registration table; she was one of several Cuban-Americans doing volunteer work for the fair. We hit it off.
After providing me with a packet and a name tag, she described herself as an event gofer who did whatever was needed, from picking up
writers at the airport to serving refreshments and handing out tags. Iliana was hot, stylish, thirty-something, and divorced. She told me that
she worked in real estate, that she was a Democrat but not a Marxist.
"Many of us younger *cubanos*," she said, to my surprise, "don't buy into
the old-school party line. But *cuidado*, careful what you say! There's
Sagüesera fever all around us..." Iliana didn't know my work but wanted to "discover" me. She might attend my reading tomorrow evening
but it depended on how crazy things got at the fair. Done volunteering for today, she suggested we have coffee and maybe a *pastelito* at a
café near the college. Sounded good to me. I couldn't help wonder if
she might've been the emissary I was needing for *Love Insane*, someone
with access to some of Miami's deep truths. But it was too late for that
now. Maybe she could provide material for future projects, though I
doubted I'd ever want to revisit Miami in my fiction.

After the *cafecito*, Iliana invited me to her place for the obligatory
Cuba Libre. She drove us in her Honda Civic to her swanky remodeled house on Bayshore Drive. I saw minimalist furnishings, floors of
gray and white tiles, the kitchen in black and shiny silver; all of it a

reaction to the plastic, dime-store Baroque of the early Sixties refugee generation. How could she afford all that? A rich ex-husband? Outside there was a pool and a garden of amazing grafts, *caimito* with *mamoncillo*, *anón* with *guanábana*, plantains with Hawaiian bananas. The music from hidden speakers was mellow, jazzy. Suddenly Chirino came on. Iliana swayed, hips and shoulders ablaze with Willy's "Oxígeno."

"I've never made love to a *cubana*," I confessed, lacing her waist with my arms.

She laughed. "What makes you think you ever will?"

My reply, in character as Ricky: "The time has come, Lucy! Dun't try to splain it!"

I enjoyed our banter, our good-old *choteo*. And our kisses. Soon we were off to her bedroom and her waterbed. I dug her body as much as her words, all that mushy Cuban stuff like *Papito rico* and *Te estoy gozando* and *¡Ay virgencita, qué es esto!* I dug her code-switching, "*Sí, sí, chúpame los* nipples. *Ay*, what a *lengua*! *Coño, tú*, don't stop!" I dug it all.

Later she was in the mood for a promenade through the Deco District. We walked into a crowded boîte called Le Beat, a chic hangout for the Cuban-American crème de la crème. Iliana said we'd gone there to dance salsa, which played deafeningly, not to sit and get smashed. A jam session exploded, a hot *descarga* à la Cachao. She screamed, "*¡Manteca!*" and dragged me to the floor, moving freely, madly to the rhythm. Iliana was a beautiful image of energy and lust, of sensuality, of grace. But was she also a stereotype? If so, I willingly surrendered to it, embraced it. I felt awkward but tried to follow her. There wasn't nostalgia in our dance but a presence—born in the past, preserved in time yet alive. Instead of immigrant memories and patriotic reveries, a tangible, festive present.

She drove me to the hotel, having turned down my invitation to spend the night with me, maybe order room service. There was no talk of future visits, no plans for a bicoastal affair. All she wanted was a signed copy of one my books, preferably the poems. Iliana said she loved poetry.

"Any chance you might write a poem about me?" she asked with a gleam in her eyes, with a roguish smile that drew me to her lips. "I think you'd better, Señor Poeta."

And of course I said, "Yes, I'll write about you, but I can't tell you when. Could be as soon as tonight or it could take months. This sort of thing is unpredictable." My way of getting off the hook, in case the promised verses never came. "For now," I reassured her, "you'll get an entry in my diary. I'll even give it a title, *Iliana, a sexy Democrat but not a Marxist.*"

"Just don't call me the Event Gofer, please," she said, laughing.

"Got it!"

We said *Ciao* with a kiss and the promise of staying in touch, but I knew that neither one of us would make the effort. This was perfect, I told myself, exciting yet ephemeral. Like Miami. Even though I'd enjoyed myself thoroughly with Iliana (and vice versa, it seemed), it was the body of another woman I now craved, a woman who didn't cry out mushy Cuban stuff when she had sex but instead spoke a language of silence I understood. A woman who was in my thoughts while I flew home.

QUEER MARRIAGE

He told her that she'd saved him, that she'd given him a center, a role he could fully embody at last. It was a heart-felt confession, hyperbolic as were some of Camilo's pronouncements but also deeply truthful. He seemed unfinished to her, like a puzzle whose image you know yet whose pattern eludes you. There was a certain innocence in him, as if he hadn't quite learned the way he was supposed to act in certain situations, or the person he was meant to be. And in that respect he came across as a child, impulsive, sincere, and easily hurt when the world turned against him.

There was a spirit in Susan that he envied, a strength he hadn't seen in anyone. Ironic, she thought, since her life seemed bland compared to his, and sheltered. She had demons of her own—who didn't?—yet next to him she felt ordinary. Susan wanted to *become* Dr. Macías, and for a while she actually did. But this was more than just the admiration of a devoted pupil. It was an obsession, an urge to live in his mind, to be lost in his nightmares, in his exile, to be damaged like him. And damaged she began to feel eventually. Too many days their home was the extension of a classroom where Camilo lectured and she listened, where she tried to absorb his teachings without feeling inferior to him, overshadowed. An irrational fear began to assail her, that they'd be trapped in these roles if they stayed together. Would he always wield such power over her? No way to tell, and not a chance Susan wanted take. She loved him, still needed his guidance but at a distance, far enough away so she could think her own thoughts. This is not the end, she kept telling herself. But Susan knew it was over.

The reality of their breakup hit her soon, and hard. Camilo wouldn't be there anymore to listen to her dreams each morning, reflecting her nightly images back at her as if through a looking glass. She'd never lose herself in his arms again, or savor his lips or be turned to fire by his tongue. Adrift, that's how she felt after their separation. Moving back with her folks was out of the question—not the best place for her at the time. But she could always count on Jennifer, who offered to let her crash at her place for as long as she needed to. They both welcomed the late-night chats, the sharing, the sex. Jenn made love to Susan because she knew that Susan needed that love. They were old pals who knew how to comfort and excite each other. But pals they were meant to remain, affectionate, trusting yet fully aware that this, their love-making, was essentially a bridge to pleasure and intimacy, their own definition of friendship. Not a definition most people could grasp, let alone accept; surely not the folks in the Thompsons' social circle or even some of Susan's friends. But Camilo got it; he knew this type of bond was as natural as desire itself. Susan wondered at times if her thing with Jennifer, however one defined it, would ever turn into something stable, some sort of marriage. She hinted at it during her stay, and her friend was frank in her reaction. "I love you more than I've ever loved anyone, man or woman," she confessed. "But the core of me wants a husband and a bunch of babies." A confession that didn't come as news to Susan, though it still surprised her. The image Jenn projected was that of a professional, self-made woman. Yet under her liberated, cosmopolitan varnish—such a believable performance!—Jennifer was waiting to embrace the true role of her life, that of wife and mother.

Susan's "core" didn't long for marital bliss, certainly not for "a bunch of babies"! But there were mornings when she'd awaken feeling lonely and wonder if a family of her own would mitigate her existential pain, if children wouldn't be the soothing antidote to the angst that burdened her heart in moments of silence. Averse to tradition, reluctant to give in to her parents' and society's expectations, Susan might be denying herself a chance for happiness—if happiness was to be found in domestic stability—because she thought she was meant for something greater, a fate more fulfilling than a family.

The teaching job she took at Bethel College in Newton came as a gift at this point, a full-time load of first-year Spanish courses to keep her busy. But Camilo lingered in her thoughts. Now it was the teacher in him that she kept seeing, hearing, missing. He had a spark that turned students on, and Susan wanted that spark in her own classes. She'd practice her gestures and facial expressions in front of the mirror, impersonating Camilo, telling his jokes and input-rich stories as she prepared to face her students. In time she developed her own style, a classroom persona that didn't depend on her mentor to be funny and successful. And still somehow he was always there, guiding her.

She thought she might finally stop thinking of Camilo when she hooked up with Paul. Tall, blond, athletic, Paul blended in. It was easy to be with someone who looked like her. They met at a fundraising event on the Bethel College campus, and Susan was drawn to him for the same reason she enjoyed working at Bethel: the way those Mennonites saw the world, as a community where everyone helped and respected each other. She admired Paul's Mennonite faith but soon began to see a dark irony in his beliefs. He'd work pro bono for the underdogs, yet he couldn't bring his passion for justice and equality to his relationship with Susan. Machista and old-school, Paul alleged that she was too obsessed with her career, always clamoring for attention. And he figured she'd change once they got married. In the future Paul envisioned, Susan would quit working, since she'd have her hands full with their kids. "But don't worry," he'd say, "I'll provide." Paul had no burning questions and no painful memories. He was completely sure of his masculinity, untroubled by gender ambiguities, so different from Camilo and some of the boyfriends she'd had, all sensitive, complicated men. Those relationships were doomed from the outset—too complex. Susan thought she wanted something simpler for a change, with fewer layers. And she let herself be dragged into a farce, this role of a lawfully-wedded Bethel wife; into a life of daily fights and dreadful silences, of infrequent sex that left her feeling empty.

She had already decided to call off the engagement, severing all ties to Paul, when she received a letter from Camilo... *Go on learning, growing, my beloved Susan*—he told her. *Continue being strong. Be truly yourself.* And thus he helped her realize she was settling for stagnation, not growth, not freedom. Camilo wouldn't accept the end of their relationship yet he'd set her free. He loved her unconditionally, whereas Paul's feelings for Susan were contingent upon her willingness to settle down, to be the self-effacing spouse behind the great man, a part she could never play.

Alone again, Susan applied for graduate studies at several schools with Alton University as her first choice, and Alton came through. She got accepted into their doctoral program in twentieth-century Latin American literature. Meanwhile, Camilo had quit his job in Kansas—she'd been told—and was living in Colina, a short drive from Alton. She phoned him one day and said, "Here I am, following in your footsteps." He laughed and asked her, "What took you so long?" She knew he was adamant about a reunion. "I don't think we can be mere friends, Susan," she heard him admit, and she was honest with him too. "You're more than a friend to me," she told him. "I'll always think of you as my soulmate, the one who encouraged me to seek my own answers." And she made him laugh again when she reproached him, "You got me into this whole academic mess, Dr. Macías. Now help me get through it!"

Shoptalk, mainly news of the AU department, was the needed ice breaker in those early days of reunion. The Latin American literature program at Alton University still relied on the same core list of writers, chiefly Borges, García Márquez, Rulfo, Fuentes, Roa Bastos, Donoso, Vargas Llosa, Cortázar, and the more recent Isabel Allende, whose photo now graced the department's central office, tellingly placed between the portraits of Cervantes and García Márquez. But lately, emulating their colleagues in English, some of the professors—with Sofía taking the lead—had been applying new terminologies. They didn't discuss Lukács and Goldmann much anymore, nor did they talk about problematic heroes and intertextuality. Instead they fed on Homi Bhabha and pondered the signs of postmodernity. The profs now sought to "deconstruct" novels rather than analyze them, and they were prone to define many characters as postcolonial subjects. "Same dog with a different collar," joked Camilo, although he did see these changes as a sign of much-needed growth in that department.

Susan knew that the greatest Latin American novels had been written in the 1960s and given the bizarre label of "Boom fiction" in academic circles, supposedly because many of them had "exploded" onto the literary scene like a sonic blast, appealing to a mass audience. For once, it was claimed, there was a market for literature in the Spanish-speaking world. Most of those Boom novels were fascinating, but so much had been written about them! Susan couldn't bear the thought of having to come up with a new take on the "magical realist" elements in *One Hundred Years of Solitude*, on the multiple narrative voices and the

Revolution theme in *The Death of Artemio Cruz*, on the "homo ludens" in *Rayuela*. How could she make a fresh contribution? After hearing Susan's concern, Sofía suggested that she look into U.S. Latino literature—Rivera, Cisneros, Anaya, Rechy, Yglesias, Laviera. And Susan found her niche thanks to her mentor, this growing field that Camilo had been the first to show her through his own work. He, too, should be included in Susan's reading list, said Sofía.

Professor Varela was now a Latino specialist. This development in her career made sense, thought Camilo; she was always dreaming up great projects. But her proposal for a Latino track in her department's PhD program had met with resistance. She'd been in a similar situation once before, when she tried to include women writers in the curriculum and was derided by her colleagues. Now those same men were alleging that Latino literature didn't belong in a Spanish department because most of it was written in English. "But that's not the real reason," said Sofía to Susan, warning her. "Those old snobs just don't take Latino authors seriously." Then Dr. Oropeza made some compromising remarks at a faculty meeting. "Ours is a department of Spanish," he affirmed, "not the depository of misguided immigrant or so-called ethnic attempts at literary creation in the English language."

His pronouncement appeared subsequently in the minutes of the meeting, and from there it leaked to the department's newsletter, which was fortuitously overseen by Sofía. The issue was brought to light, provoking a flurry of letters to the editor in the university paper and a formal complaint by the campus chapter of MEChA. The AU president intervened, calling Oropeza's comment injurious and unprofessional. The only consequence the prof suffered, however, was having a letter of reprimand placed in his file. But he was punished enough, since the Latino track was ultimately approved, and Dr. Varela got to work. She would be joined by Elena Medina, a graduate student of the department who would eventually transfer to UC San Diego to attain a doctorate in Ethnic Studies. A brilliant scholar, Elena was given the unprecedented task of teaching the lower-division courses offered in the new track, all of which were supervised by Dr. Varela. Not surprisingly, Elena and Susan became good friends.

As one of the department's first grad students in Latino fiction and egged on by Professor Medina, Susan coined the phrase "ethnic performance," basing her coinage on gender theorist Judith Butler's famous "gender performance" paradigm. Camilo heard from Susan about a group of Latino writers who expressed "an array of performances of 'Latinoness' in the United States," authors he knew personally. He was part of a mixed bag of Chicano/Portorro/Cubiche literary texts that Susan now devoured, cranking out papers, organizing and leading panel discussions in collaboration with Elena. As expected, the ideas she was advancing didn't go over well with some Chicano scholars, the "essentialist Aztlán bunch," Elena called them. But for Camilo, Susan's fundamental concepts—that there's no ethnic essence, only performances of ethnicity, of its themes, archetypes, and stereotypes—fit his writing perfectly, since he'd always felt like a performer of Cubanity, not its embodiment.

"So now you're the 'top man' in our relationship," Camilo said to Susan, jokingly. He couldn't have imagined back in Kansas that one day she'd devote one chapter of her dissertation to his novels. Nepotism, a handful of critics called this inclusion. But there was nothing nepotistic about it. Of course Susan discussed things with Camilo. He was the first Latino writer she'd ever read; his work had gotten her thinking about the elusive nature of identity, an idea that would prove central to her thesis. Yet when she delved into his books, she was the one in charge. She was the critic, not the disciple.

The process of writing a dissertation was so exciting! Susan was amazed to learn there were several university houses interested in publishing her project. But she hadn't yet applied for a real job, having taught only upper-division courses at AU and done guest lectures at neighboring universities. She wasn't prepared for the realities of the Latino field, for the rejection she felt by several Chicano scholars because she wasn't Latina herself. How could she know what it was like to be "ethnic"? *How dare you write about us?!* It was assumed that, in order to be a specialist in Chicano/Latino fiction, one had to be a member of that community. According to this essentialist argument, only Spaniards could study Spanish literature, and only gay scholars could specialize in homosexual writers. There was no logic to it, but those were the cards Susan was dealt. One case in particular threw her for a loop, a job at a university in Riverside that seemed designed for her: PhD in hand, strong research record, teaching experience. And she didn't even make it to the first round of interviews! When Susan talked to a Chicana colleague she knew in that department, and who was part of their search committee, the professor didn't mince words. "Those kids need a role model," the woman alleged, "someone they can identify with and look up to. Not literary theory." Susan's reaction was ingenuous: "But an Anglo woman can be a good role model." To which the Chicana replied, "No, she can't. And she shouldn't."

Elena was incensed by the situation, calling it ridiculous and retrograde. Upon hearing about this exchange, she fired off a letter of inquiry to the search committee, questioning their decision not to interview Susan, a highly qualified student she'd recommended. And she got back the standard line about there being many highly qualified candidates, a tough decision to be made, etc. Ironically, the person who landed the job was a Mexican national who hadn't yet finished his dissertation and who specialized in La Onda writers José Agustín and Gustavo Sainz. Oh, but he looked right for the job, could "perform" as a Chicano and as the "right" role model. It was all about performance, after all.

"Don't let them stop you," Camilo told her. "Show them instead how good you are." The ideal job was waiting for her, he said, though she might have to be strategic, maybe look for it on the East Coast, a place where the politics of ethnicity might not work against her. But by now Susan knew she wouldn't want to relocate without Camilo; she'd only move if he was willing to follow. No longer needing to cleanse herself of his angst and his memories, she'd come to realize that his past was now a part of her. Susan couldn't leave any of it behind; didn't wish to, because that meant leaving Camilo.

One night they found themselves making a toast to the short life they'd forged as lovers. "*Te quiero*, Camilo," she confessed. "And I love you," he told her, "forever, beyond this life." That night he presented her with a gift. It was his latest book of poetry, containing poems that were an homage to the thoughts and fantasies they'd shared. A book dedicated to Susan, *more than my muse, my soulmate*. And she was profoundly touched, unable to speak but propelled to kiss him, hold him, make love to him. *I still see you in my dreams*, he read. *I still crave you like a benign addiction...*

They started spending weekends in New Mexico, a land Susan had explored with Jennifer. Like Susan, Camilo was taken with that state, with its grand skies, its Sangre de Cristo mountains; and with the town of Las Cumbres, which was small and cradled in the thick of the Jémez forest, a place where they imagined living some day. They wrote their wedding vows there, envisioning a ceremony that would reflect the spirit of their commitment to each other, with words they could live up to.

She moved in with him, this time for good—they were both sure. And rumors didn't take long to reach them, mockery from gay friends and colleagues who couldn't understand nor accept what Camilo was doing. "What did you expect?" she asked him, "cheerful acceptance?" After all, his work had been promoted as Gay Latino Fiction. In interviews, he had spoken candidly about his abusive homophobic father, about his hot male lover. Then, seemingly all of a sudden, he was marrying a woman!

But Camilo hadn't been dishonest in performing as a gay man; Susan knew he hadn't. There was just more to the truth of his identity than simply "coming out of the closet." He had felt encouraged by Manuel Puig's message in *Kiss of the Spider Woman*, the Argentine writer's vision of a society where people were sexually fluid, capable of love beyond prescribed cultural and social obligations. Camilo wanted to belong in that ideal community. Unfortunately, Puig's novel offered only a utopian dream, not an acceptable reality for many homosexual men. It was subversive, liberating for Valentín to set free the woman in him, but not for Molina to perform as a "man," or for "gay" Camilo to love and desire a woman. The latter was seen as a farce, a crime against nature. Against gayness.

Camilo thought they should tell people that their marriage was queer—he and Susan did have a gay sensibility. This was a definition his skeptical friends might be willing to handle. It was all right for him to marry a woman so long as she was gay. That sounded novel, courageous, *acceptable*: a faggot and a dyke "joining forces" as husband and wife in order to experience the "opposite" sex. Yet that wasn't quite their case. Susan agreed there was something "queer" about their union, yes, but not in the way Camilo meant it. She'd had the occasional fling—some of the sex actually exciting—with women. She knew homosexual desire; it was there whenever a certain type of woman appeared before her, hard-bodied, spirited, smart. There would be an adrenaline rush, a tug, the onset of moisture, of wetness and excessive salivation. But she felt the same way, sometimes more so, when the object of desire was a man. Was she bisexual, then? Perhaps, but this was just a label, and labels were shackles—limiting, deceptive. Why would you want to define yourself on the basis of your bisexuality, when all of humanity had a bisexual nature? She and Camilo seemed to be in tune with that nature more than a lot of people, and aware of the prevailing opinion that deemed bisexuality hedonistic and decadent, or that saw it as a deceitful mask that hid our "true" gay selves. Yet, having fallen in love with each other, they saw their love as the only identity they were willing to fight for, the one whose performance felt real and honest and rewarding. It was that simple: They belonged together. He completed her in ways she hadn't yet begun to fathom, and she shared with him the kind of vitality that moved one to enjoy life.

There were days when he pulled away, when her body wouldn't arouse him. And then he'd be as passionate as ever. Until his next flight. Susan knew what happened to him during those times. His writing, his desire for a man, his dreams, his memories; it all conspired to drive him away, though never for long. Nothing and no one could ever alienate her from Camilo. He lived within her.

TRACES

———————————————————————

The news of our plans brought a Cuban expletive out of my mother, "*Coño*, Lito, I'm so happy for you!" But we had problems with Susan's parents, unavoidably. "Mom" wanted us to have a church ceremony in the Thompsons' Presbyterian church with a minister, a wedding party, flower girls, and then a reception at a swanky hotel. She offered to take care of the invitations, to rent the reception hall and book our guests at the ritzy Kansas City Plaza. She even suggested the place for us to buy our rings and the boutique where Susan *must get her dress*. It was all going to be fabulous!

Liz was dismayed when Susan told her that there would be a dozen guests at most and no minister, and that we'd be married at a national park in New Mexico, not in a church. Oh, and we didn't need rings since this part of the ritual felt superfluous to us. "But that's not the way we do things," Mrs. Thompson protested, pleading with us to reconsider. "It's all *so* different. No religious ceremony? I can't get all dressed up just to stand in the sun at some Indian ruins in New Mexico! And what am I going to tell my friends, that they can't come to my daughter's wedding because they're not invited?"

We agreed to a compromise, concerned that "Mom" might decide not to attend at all. We could send out invitations, yes, and we would have a reception at a four-star bed and breakfast in Santa Fe (the Thompsons' wedding present). But everything else would be as Susan and I had planned it. Liz would just have to put up with the New Mexico sun and ruins!

Yet "Mom" was relatively easy to deal with compared to "Dad." He disapproved of our marriage and made things very unpleasant for Susan. "That Cuban commie has clouded your thinking," Dave told his daughter. "He's turned you against your country and your family." He also blamed me for getting Susan involved in such a "ludicrous" field of study. Latino fiction. Bah! What the hell was that? Learning Spanish was practical, but why make a career out of it? There were many other, better ways to make a living. Besides, those immigrant writers Susan was studying were unknowns, hence they had no value in the market-place. What a waste of her time and her intelligence! Susan told her father that he was mistaken. "Camilo didn't cloud my thinking," she said, "he enlightened me. And how can you speak about writers you haven't read, Dad? What do you know about literary worth, anyway?" His reaction was silence, as usual. But he did let his daughter know that he wouldn't give her his blessing or attend the ceremony. "I'm sorry you feel that way," she said. "I'll miss you at my wedding."

Susan and I realized now that we had a fundamental experience in common: We were both starved for paternal love; fatherless, in a way, and in a way patricidal, for we believed that much of the world our fathers had built was ill-conceived and deserved to be banished.

The only relative of Susan's who supported us wholeheartedly was Euphemia, her Canadian aunt, a.k.a. Auntie Effie, an affectionate woman and amateur photographer. She couldn't make it to our ceremony, unfortunately, but we talked to her on the phone. Effie sent us one of her beautiful photos, a picture of a yellow-billed loon in flight—a bird that thrived on Salt Spring Island, where she lived. *That's what wings are for!* she wrote on the back. We promised her we'd go visit her in Canada.

We took care of the "contract" at the Santa Ana courthouse in Orange County, with Alina and Castel in tow as witnesses. Later we all enjoyed a meal of gourmet Mexican food at Boca Rosa in downtown Santa Ana. There was a touch of comic relief, thanks to Alina. She decided to use her own pen to sign the marriage license—both witnesses had to. She'd already scribbled her unintelligible signature on it when we all realized her pen had red ink. "Sorry about my red smear," Alina apologized, seeming mildly upset, "on your perfectly beautiful and white and clean license!" I teased her about it, "What could that color symbolize, Cicada?" And she immediately replied, laughing, "Passion, communism, or blood. Take your pick!" On the subject of blood: it was in Santa Ana, too, where Susan and I had our obligatory HIV test. My second time, her first. The wait was nerve-wracking, especially for me. (Susan claimed to have no concern about it.) But luckily it came back negative for both.

Our wedding was celebrated one sunny morning at Bandelier National Monument, among pine trees and aspens, surrounded by kivas and caves in the rocky mesas that were once home to the Anasazi Indians. The music: Andean songs, Native American flute, Chopin's *Valse in A Minor*. There was poetry; Alina read a poem she wrote for us... *We hadn't planned to return to this sacred place, to hear its silence, to ask the wind about our future. Yet here we are, in love again.*

We emerged from the greenness, a sudden presence on a hill, Susan clad in a knee-length white cotton dress with subtle embroidery of Anasazi symbols (a crescent moon, a star) and I wearing a white guayabera with beige-toned needlepoint on its four pockets. Then we made our way to greet everyone: Jennifer, who'd shown up with one of her power-suited "lawyer girlfriends" from work; Laura with her current boyfriend, a nondescript math teacher; two of Susan's grad school pals, one a bubbly L.A. woman who specialized in Medieval Spanish literature (the poor thing!), the other her now close friend Elena Medina; (Sofía was profusely apologetic for not being able to attend; she'd committed to a summer-long teaching job in Buenos Aires); Mrs. Thompson, dowdily attired and bearing a frozen smile; Alina with Bill and Leah (I was happy Leah decided to join us); Castel, who'd chosen to be a single guy for this event because, as he put it, "I don't want to be distracted"; and my gorgeous mother looking like Carmen Sevilla, one of the Spanish movie stars she so admired. They all witnessed our oath... *I promise you, through the challenges and joys of life, to be honest, to stand by you and support you. Because you're my home, my anchor, my strength...*

Would Papi have attended my wedding, just like he'd attended my college graduation, to spoil it with his sullen face and his silence? I did want to see him there, or I wouldn't have worn a guayabera (not just an elegant linen shirt we'd ordered from a store in Miami, hoping for a Cuban touch, but also my way of having Elio present.) He wouldn't have chatted with any of the guests, especially Liz Thompson; not the way Mami did, cheerfully, unfazed by her accented English, displaying her sincerest smile. No. Papi would've let it be known that none of it—the place, the people, the ceremony—felt right to him. None of it felt "Cuban." And he would've drilled into me the fact that Mr. Thompson's absence was an affront. *How dare he not show up, the fucking Gringo! Who does he think he is?*

Or maybe Papi would've been on good behavior to please my bride, grateful to her for bringing order and decency to his son's life. Elio fell in love with Susan the first and only time he saw her. This was obvious in the courteous way he talked to her, in the hungry looks he gave her. Yes, perhaps Elio Macías would've overcome his hatred of social events to be there—thrilled, utterly realized in his role as paterfamilias, telling me, "*Coño, chico,* you finally got yourself a Gringa with a big ass!"

The wedding was followed by an early dinner at the Adobe Inn in Santa Fe, where our guests were being lodged courtesy of my in-laws (part of their wedding present). It was sunny, warm. Susan and I sat with Mechy, Liz, Castel, Alina, Bill, and Leah, all of us stuffing ourselves with honey-filled sopaipillas and green chili soup, before we were to dig into our main courses of chicken and cheese enchiladas, chiles rellenos, and fajitas of carne adobada.

"What a beautiful ceremony," said Mami. "I didn't even mind that there was no priest."

"A hummingbird whirled around the two of you when you kissed," offered Castel, and I couldn't tell whether he was being genuinely romantic or sarcastic. Probably both.

"When you appeared all of a sudden on the hill," added Alina, winking to let us know she was about to wax poetic. "Garments white as clouds, and you made your way down prancing like children and waving, it seemed to me as though the sky had sent you."

"The sky?!" I laughed, needing some levity. "You mean we looked like angels?!"

"No, *hermanito,* not like angels." She was laughing too.

"Like lightning, then," Leah chimed in, cracking up.

"A thunderstorm!" exclaimed Bill.

"No and no," replied my friend. "They appeared to me like a wonderful memory."

"Yes, that's right," said Mami. "A new memory, something you never want to forget."

"I looked up and around us," said Castel then, seeming pensive. "I saw the clear blue sky, the caves, traces of people from long ago, and I thought, Now there's a new trace here..."

"The only thing missing," remarked my mother with a laugh, "was the rice!"

"Instead of rice," Leah observed, "we got a warm little rain as you two were leaving."

"Actually," said Liz, much too seriously, unable or reluctant to join in our festive mood. "There were many things missing, in my opinion. To begin with, a minister."

"Well," said Mechy to my mother-in-law, smiling politely. "It was the kind of wedding that Susan and Camilo wanted, and that's what matters, doesn't it, Liz? I for one thought it was lovely."

"You're right, Mercedes," Liz assented in her usual tone of rehearsed cordiality. "What's important is that this event was exactly what your son and my daughter wished for."

Mrs. Thompson was on her way back to Kansas early the next morning, eager to leave our "ruins" behind. Susan offered to drive her to the airport in Albuquerque, but Liz chose to take a shuttle. Minutes before she parted, I hugged her and thanked her for the generous wedding present. She gave us both a hurried kiss and said, "Congratulations. And thank you for everything. I wish you both the best."

Liz's presence wasn't the only dissonant note of the event for me. There was an incident having to do with Alina's husband, inconsequential but nevertheless an exchange that gnawed at me for some time. (Obviously it still does.) Bill shook my hand after our celebratory dinner and, pulling me aside, admitted he'd been pleasantly surprised. "I didn't think you had it in you, buddy," he said, and I asked him what he meant. "This, your wedding, your marriage, all of it," he explained. "I'm proud of what you're building with Susan, and sorry for the way I felt about you...all this time."

"You're sorry," I said. "About what, exactly?"

"Well, I thought you were... I didn't think you'd ever be one of us."

"You mean one of you married people?"

"Yes, no, actually, I was referring to..." He seemed nervous now.

"I understand. You mean one of you 'real' men."

"No, but..."

"Men who dig women and who'd rather die than fuck other men, isn't that it?"

"What?!"

"Wow, Bill, so all this time you thought I was just another pathetic faggot, huh? Not a man like yourself. How could you stand to be around me?"

"You've got it all wrong, Camilo."

"Really? I don't think so."

"Listen, buddy, I just..."

"You should know I'm marrying Susan because I love her, not because I've had some kind of conversion to the Church of Machismo or seen the light or joined the hetero club. But, hey, thanks for coming clean about your feelings. I know it's hard for you straight men to open up this way. Maybe there's a feminine side to you after all!"

Not my best moment. Bill seemed genuinely happy for me, but I just couldn't believe his view of human nature was *that* simplistic. He didn't speak to me again until he, Alina, and Leah were parting, and he thanked me for inviting him. I doubt he ever told his wife about the incident, or she would've brought it up with me. I meant to tell her about it but ultimately decided there was no point.

The most memorable wedding present came from Castel, of course: the complete Jerry Herman collection on cassette, plus a book of Herman's songs arranged for piano. (A gift that was really meant for me, though Susan did like playing Jerry's music.) Castel and I had a little outing in Santa Fe the day before he left. We'd be saying goodbye soon, *adiós* to each other and to New Mexico, a land he called the Forest of Echoes. We were listening to Lansbury in *Dear World* while I drove our rented minivan back to Las Cumbres, after lunch at Tomasita's. A song called "And I Was Beautiful" was playing when Castel said, "I love this place, especially at night. The stars, the moonlight on the hills, the echo of some distant howling. And being with you. I'd like to make it all last, Camilo."

"Me too. But we'll come back," I reassured him.

"I hate it when things come to an end. Good things..."

"Hey, but this is only the beginning, Castelín."

"You're right, it is... in some ways."

"Listen, *príncipe*, Susan and I are moving to Las Cumbres as soon as we can. We haven't told anyone yet, but that's our plan. And you'll visit us a lot, won't you, Castel? You and I will have our own secret spot somewhere in the forest of echoes."

"Yes, we will," he said, smiling, and he hummed Angela's song...

One of the other wedding presents was a hoot, I thought, and it came from Michael Levine: the definitive coffee-table tome on the uses and misuses of cannabis; a nationwide bestseller and yet another gift to me, since Susan didn't like the stuff. How fitting, this present from my pothead buddy, a frequent visitor to my bachelor pad, later self-exiled from it when Susan moved in. I wasn't going to kick her out just so Michael could get stoned in secret, like he wanted.

The stories I could tell about that guy, about his megalomania and paranoia, his late discovery and then frequent consumption of weed, his self-loathing pot trips. And, oh, his disdain for reading! Levine got a flat fee for his preface to the Reader Series, but I thought—and told him—he should've received royalties. (His stamp alone had gotten adoptions at some major universities, and he also promoted the series at his talks.) When we discussed this possibility, Michael said okay but he didn't want a big cut, maybe just two percent. "That's all?" I teased him. "What kind of Jew are you?!" He knew me well enough to have replied, "As much of a Jew as you are a Cuban!" Touché.

It was Susan's idea to have our honeymoon in Veracruz, Mexico. "For a taste of *caribeño* culture," she said. A suggestion I welcomed. Veracruz was charming in its Caribbean exuberance. We stayed at the Hotel Melao, a shadow of its former beauty but still one hell of a place. Built in 1935, it had three swimming pools, several fountains, lush flower gardens, blue-tile benches and marbled stairs, palm trees, and a breathtaking view of the ocean. I couldn't help thinking we were in some sort of virtual realm, a movie set that was all image, all façade yet felt completely real...

At the zócalo, we were enjoying a glass of *aguas frescas* one morning while we listened to lively harp music played by a smiling *mulata*. Sewer stench permeated the air as it merged with the cloying aroma of freshly baked *pan dulce*. Before long we were surrounded by peddlers who offered us a variety of knick-knacks, and I began to feel like prey, a sitting duck under the *portales*. Suddenly, an old woman appeared out of nowhere, feeble, wrinkled, with long braids. She dangled a trinket in front of our faces, hoping we'd buy it. It was a necklace, beads of thick brown glass like stale candy. I meant to say to her, *Sí, señora*, I'll buy your necklace of hardened tears but you get to keep it. In exchange for my pesos I want something else. A perfect honeymoon, perhaps? You see, I don't want to feel guilty as a tourist in your country. I'd like my mind to be light and clear and empty of concern, of remorse. Better to feel carefree and entitled, right? No heavy thoughts about how unfair it is that a few pesos, an amount insignificant to me, could feed a peddler like yourself for a month; that I be allowed to sublimate my guilt with words. Do we have a deal, *señora*? Thanks for your trinket. *¡Muchas gracias!*

I recalled then a comment Castel made in one of his first letters from Mexico City... *I am a foreigner in this country*—he said. *I know I don't belong in Mexico and yet I am here. It is a pleasant feeling not to be at odds with your environment...to understand and accept your position even if that position is outside...* But of course Castel and I went to the great Tenochtitlán from different places. I felt at odds in the Aztec capital as much as I did in the States. He at least had been born in California and, albeit reluctantly, was entitled to claim the United States as his home. I couldn't claim any land as mine (surely not Cuba), even if only for the sake of rejecting it and wanting to leave it behind.

The TV was on while we dressed for dinner one evening. It was a show on Televisa, the story of a boy who'd died in a car accident, and the retina of his eyes had been donated to his blind mother. The operation had been performed in Mexico City, where the family resided. They showed a school photo of the boy, named Roberto, alias Betito, smiling. The bandaged mother was interviewed; she said she'd never imagined this could happen. "It's both a tragedy and a miracle. If I get my eyesight back," she declared, her voice breaking, "Betito will remain alive for as long as I live. And I'll show him wonderful things through these eyes. That's a promise I have made to my little boy."

My immediate reaction: great idea for the next Reader Series book. But the story should be set in Veracruz, where I'd heard it, and the main character had to be professionally successful so the students could relate. She was a brilliant woman who didn't believe in mystery or magic, until the day she was faced with a miracle. But no, that story deserved an intimate, literary work, not a bestselling textbook. And no, I didn't have the right to turn someone's tragedy into one of my profitable little books. What did I know of a mother's pain? I couldn't live in the heart of a woman who'd lost her son, yet I felt moved to tears by this image of a dead boy's eyes bringing light to his mother's night, and I wanted Betito to be remembered. The idea would simmer on a back burner during our remaining days in Mexico, haunting me until I jotted it down— one more seed that might or might not grow...

The honeymoon over, I was on the road again, curious to test the professional waters now as a married man. The news of my marriage had spread, not like wildfire (my small-time fame didn't provide much underbrush) but fast enough to burn me. Comments kept getting back to me, sometimes spoken in my presence... *For real? Is he serious?; People get married for all kinds of strange reasons; What is he trying to prove?; What the fuck does he think he's doing?; So he's a breeder now?; But that's impossible. I've read his books!* Two encounters from those days stand out in my memory, one at a conference on Cuban literature at the University of Michigan, the other at the San Antonio Book Fair.

In Michigan I was part of a panel entitled "The Other Cuba: Writing Beyond the Island" with Francisco M. Rodríguez and the Mariel poet Osvaldo Barnet, who happened to be gay and very out. Rafael Valdés Alfaro would be leading the discussion with his same old *"fruity* limbo" stuff. Minutes before the panel started, Osvaldo turned to me and asked in a whisper, *"Oye,* is it true you married a woman? Some of us are wondering if you've gone nuts!" I reacted noncommittally, "People like to gossip." He came back with, *"Sí, chico,* especially when they've got something juicy to talk about, like you going from *loca* to *loco!"* I told him that Susan and I were proud to have the first queer marriage in Cuban-American history, and Osvaldo liked the idea. Maybe my wife was a lesbian. Maybe I was just being subversive and forging a different kind of family. "That sounds interesting," he said. "I'd like to hear more about it." Of course he would have. But I knew I was going to avoid him like the plague once the thing was over. Not in the mood to justify my actions and decisions, fed up with having to explain myself. Osvaldo would never understand. Neither would Tano and Tony and... Forget it.

My publisher Sergio was sponsoring a poetry reading at the Book Fair in San Antonio, featuring my work and that of two Pueblo Press up-and-coming Chicano poets. Sergio had been suspiciously silent on the subject of my marriage. Our professional relationship hadn't changed; he was supportive and encouraging as always. But, knowing the way he thought, I presumed he was concerned that I'd lose my edge now that

I'd gotten hitched. Too happy or settled? Too straight? There was a good turnout thanks to Sergio; he had lots of friends and business contacts. I might've brought a few people in too. In fact, I could see one of my "fans" in the audience, seated in the front row: his boyish grin, his bangs, his black leather jacket. That fan would stick around after my reading, I was certain. We might take a walk along the river, sit somewhere under one of the colorful waterfront umbrellas and have a beer and catch up while we watched the boats; maybe join one of the boat tours and scream for a split second, holding hands, when we went under a bridge, much to the shock and disgust of our fellow tourists. For sure I'd be spending the afternoon with that man, not because he winked and smiled warmly at me but because I knew him. He had opened his home to me once upon a time and made me feel welcome...

Sure enough, Anthony Anderson waited patiently till everyone was gone and it was just the two of us. He greeted me with a wet kiss, told me I'd sounded "delicious" and mentioned briefly some of the poems he'd liked. Then he informed me he was there to present an anthology of fiction he'd co-edited.

"I know. *Gay by the Bay*," I told him. "I saw you in the program. Congratulations!"

"Thanks, hon."

"It's been too long, hasn't it?"

"Yes, shame on you!"

"There's been no call from your end either, Tony."

"Well, anyway, what's this joke I've heard about you marrying a woman? What gives?"

"It's not a joke. I did marry a woman. Her name is Susan."

"You're not fooling anyone, Camilo."

"I'm not trying to."

"To tell you the truth, I was pissed when I heard about your wedding through the gay grapevine. I thought, the bitch didn't invite me! How dare *she*! But if you had, I would've felt obligated to go and put on a cheery face and pretend I was one of your straight pals. Or I might've ignored your invitation and not shown up at all and instead sent you an expensive present and..."

"I didn't think you'd want to be there, Tony."

"And you were right. You know I'm not into hetero fantasies."

"Got it."

"So you've decided to become a breeder."

"No, Tony. I found the love of my life. Just be happy for me."

"Ah, you're delusional. Just like Leon."

"How is he doing?"

"Fine. Still indulging his bisexual thing. He has a story in *Gay by the Bay*."

"I'll have to read it. I look forward to digging into the whole anthology, in fact."

"Are you sure? It's mostly about faggots, you know. Not your kind of people."

"You're being a bitch, my friend." I stroked his face. "It becomes you."

"Truth is, I've missed you, darling."

"I'll call you. And we'll get together in the city, I promise."

"You can stay at my house."

"Thanks. Just like the good old days."

"But sans the wife, please!"

"Really? I think you and Susan would hit it off..."

"Okay, I'm willing to have dinner with both of you but that's it. After that you're all mine."

"Agreed."

"I promise you I won't invite any of your old friends. Definitely not one Mr. Dessler."

"Who? I don't know anyone by that name."

"Sorry, hon. Salt in the proverbial wound, I know."

"Why didn't you ever tell me Evan was nuts?"

"I was sure you could handle him. And you seemed so in love."

"Water under the bridge, anyway..."

"You really will come visit me?"

"Yes, we'll get high and listen to your divas. Maybe you'll finally do Cher for me?"

"You bet," he said and kissed me. "But only if I get to sing 'Dark Lady'."

"I'd love that."

"And only if you have lunch with me today."

"My pleasure."

"There's a place down the river that serves the best smoked salmon I've ever had—small portions on a corn tortilla, as hors d'oeuvres. Doesn't that sound exquisite?"

"It does. I'm starving."

"Me too. *¡Vamos a comer!*"

He took my hand and led me out of the room, already intoning Cher's hit, singing of a fortune queen and her strange perfume, of the card that foretold her deathly fate...

THE OTHER FACE OF EDEN

We were crossing from Vancouver on a ferry that October morning, en route to Salt Spring Island to spend a week with Susan's aunt Euphemia. Gradually the island appeared—hills, houses, the quaint little harbor—while I listened to Susan's conversation with an attractive blonde woman. I'd soon find out that her name was Patricia and that she was a nurse in her forties, a second-generation Ukrainian-Canadian who'd grown up in Vancouver and had relatives she visited frequently on the island. Patricia was eager to share her views of Canada with us. She loved her country but deplored its public healthcare system, which she considered ill-conceived and inefficient. She also lamented Canada's divided soul. "There are really two nations here," she said, "and sometimes it's hard to navigate between them."

That image of a divided nation intrigued me. I knew there had been much strife between Francophone Canada, proudly represented by the province of Québec, and its Anglophone neighbors in the rest of the country. The French had fought for cultural and linguistic autonomy, sometimes going to extremes in order to prevent the English-speaking Canadians from swallowing them up. The French, after all, had arrived in Canada first. And their sense of superiority over the Anglophones could be understood in light of the many historical, cultural, and political accomplishments France could take credit for, such as their encyclopedic contribution to the Enlightenment and a revolution that greatly impacted modern history. I had no right nor sufficient knowledge of Canadian history to take sides, yet I couldn't help admiring the Québécois for standing up to the British empire, for rejecting the world's most dominant language and fighting not with weapons but with laws against English assimilation.

The prospect of our predominantly Spanish-speaking states in the U.S. doing the same was exciting if totally unrealizable. At most we'd attained bilingual recognition in a few communities after some hard-fought battles. Yet this ongoing struggle shouldn't have been warranted at all, considering that Spanish was spoken in the United States before English. Unfortunately, bilingualism continued to be perceived by many U.S. citizens as an aberration, at best a dangerous concession made to all of us undesirable immigrants, not the true reflection of a country and its people.

Just as I was about to voice these thoughts, Patricia turned to me and asked, "Where are you from originally?" The word *originally* cued me in. Based on my features and the accent she noticed when I made a comment, she had assumed I was from somewhere other than "America."

"I'm Cuban," I told her, "though I've lived in the U.S. for almost twenty-five years."

"That's practically a lifetime," she reacted. "So you're a bona fide American, then."

"I'm a U.S. citizen, if that's what you mean. Been one for some time now..."

Susan laughed. "You've paid your dues, Camilo. You're legit."

She was right: I could call myself American based on my naturalization papers and my personal history in the United States. Yet I'd just presented myself as *Cuban*. How could I allege to be from a place I hadn't seen since childhood? I tried to come up with a reason, so I imagined myself telling Patricia, No, there's nothing "bona fide American" about me. I am one hundred percent Cuban because I was born in Las Tinajas, province of Camagüey, and I have an island-shaped scar on my face to prove it. Look, touch it. This mark of my origin is real; it's a symbol of flesh that brands me as *cubano*.

Patricia smiled, turned to me again, said, "My grandmother was a little girl when she left the Ukraine, but she still has vivid memories of her childhood, of her friends and the games she played and the food she ate in her hometown... Do you, Camilo? Do you have memories of Cuba?"

"A few," I replied, smiling back and withholding the truth: *too many.*

Susan and Patricia exchanged phone numbers and e-mail addresses. Chances were we'd never see her again, but such are the gestures we enact for the kind strangers we meet along the way, in airplanes and trains and ferries: Let's honor this encounter by pretending we'll be friends.

Euphemia Crowther, a.k.a. Auntie Effie, was waiting for us with a hug and a kiss on the Salt Spring dock. She was in her late seventies, had piercing eyes and abundant, disheveled gray hair. Auntie Effie planned to house us in her log cabin, a lived-in home "too full of mementos and scrapbooks," she warned us. Our hostess was the daughter of Scottish immigrants, the widow of a military man; also a gifted photographer. Her diminishing eyesight wouldn't deter her from spending hours in search of inspiring landscapes on her beloved island. She preferred hills and trees against the backdrop of a deep-blue sky, and pictures of snow, although winters were getting hard to bear. "After all these years," she said, "I can still find new images to capture and then give away."

She'd had one of her photos matted and framed for us. It was a spectacular shot of the lake from her deck, a view she knew we'd love. "Put it up in your favorite room," she suggested, "or the room where you spend most of your time. And think of it as a window."

"A window open to this place and to you," I told her and thanked her with a kiss.

Mrs. Crowther said she felt lucky to belong in that lake. She wanted to have her ashes spread over its waters—not for a while yet!—and be one with the soul of Salt Spring. Hard to believe that Effie was the sister of Elizabeth, not judgmental, not ethnocentric but accepting and down-to-earth. Was it because she had an artist's heart? Like my mother, Euphemia chuckled when I talked about the beauty of her photos, though she wasn't self-mocking like Mami. "I like some of my pictures," she admitted, "but only because I find their subjects beautiful. It's the places I love, not my rendition of them." Even so, I suspected there was a dream folded away somewhere. Effie confirmed this suspicion when I asked her if she'd ever considered a career as a photographer. "I sure did—for about five minutes!" she replied, laughing. "I attended UBC for a while but then got married." Marriage was a priority, an obligation that young Euphemia was expected to fulfill and which left no room for a career or even a hobby. She took up photography as a pastime after her three boys were grown and out of the house. "They're all married and awfully busy nowadays," said Auntie Effie about them, "concerned with their children and their demanding lives. But I get to see them and my grandkids often enough. They love to visit."

I told her about my mother's love of photography, promising to send her some of Mami's work. "How nice," she noted. "And what a lovely coincidence!" She talked about her favorite photographers, Ansel Adams and William Henry Jackson, of course, but also and primarily Yousuf Karsh, the Armenian-Canadian portraitist. "Taking pictures of people is not a passion of mine," she said, "but I do love a good portrait." Effie guided us to her bedroom where she proudly displayed some of Karsh's best-known photographs. "I have a weakness for royalty," she confessed, pointing to an 8x10 print of then-Princess Elizabeth and one of Clark Gable, "the handsome Hollywood kind included!"

She loved the wedding album we brought to show her. "Sorry I wasn't there," she apologized. "I'm not much into traveling these days." Our hostess wasn't much into cooking either. "It makes no sense to go to all that trouble when you eat alone," said Effie. Her only weakness was scones, which she got by the bagful in Victoria once a week. So feeding our aunt would be a worthy project while staying with her. We'd fill her up with creamy pastas and spicy soups, with chicken casseroles and quiche and picadillo, feasts she'd consume with gusto. In exchange for these meals, she'd give us an ephemeral haven, the tranquility and beauty of an ice-cold lake where one could kayak from dusk till dawn; where we were awakened each morning by bird songs and loon cries, amused by fish that somersaulted, by seagulls plunging into the blue-green water. The dense October foliage gave us powerful reds and oranges, mellow yellows; and the sunlight didn't have to forge its path through clusters of smog. At night the midget frogs greeted us with booming voices, croaking their way into our dreamless sleep.

Susan went swimming in the lake daily. She was great at it; had taken her high school swim team to many a victory. Compared to her I looked like a paddling dog when I swam. "You're either joking or out of your mind," I told her when she first announced her decision to plunge in.

"Neither," she stated. "I need the exercise."

Auntie Effie humored her. "I envy you," she said. "I can only swim in the summer."

"That water is freezing!" I wailed, but nothing I said would stop Susan. All I could do was to sit on the deck with my eyes peeled, searching the vastness of the lake for a glimpse of my wife. Saw her. Didn't. And there she was again! Caught sight of her arms, her head, then she was gone.

"Relax," Effie reassured me. "Your wife knows what she's doing. She's half Canadian!"

When Susan approached our pier, finally, I dashed to greet her, relieved, enticed by the sight of her firm thighs, her hair soon turning golden in the sun, the water glimmering on her skin.

"You're next, Camilo," joked Effie. "The water is cold, yes, but your body adjusts."

"Either that or you drown!" said Susan, laughing.

"No way!" I reacted. "I'm not going in. My Cuban bones couldn't take it!"

Back in the cabin, we'd always sip hot cider by a fire, one of the best moments of the day for me. There we heard family stories from Effie while the burning logs did their crackling thing. She asked us once if we were going to have kids and when. We pondered the question, neither one rushing to respond. "In a few years," Susan replied. "We'd like to enjoy each other for a while," I added.

"You're wise to do that," said Effie. "Life changes once you have children; it absolutely did for me. Don't get me wrong; I loved being a mom. My three darlings were generally good kids. But bringing them up was no easy task, mainly because I was the one doing all, and I mean *all* the child rearing. Of course those were different times. Men are more involved these days..."

"When we do become parents," announced Susan, "I hope we'll have two kids. An only child is a lonely child, in my opinion. I wish I'd had a sister or a brother."

"There's nothing good about being an only child," I admitted.

"I take it you don't have any siblings either," Effie told me.

"No, I don't. My mother hoped for more children, but my dad felt that kids were too costly."

"So you'd better have at least two, then," observed Auntie Effie.

"That sounds about right," Susan offered, seemingly done with the topic.

"What was it like for you, having a sibling?" I asked Euphemia.

"Sometimes fun, sometimes not so much," she acknowledged, frankly. "Lizzie is two years older than me and tended to act like she was my mother, bossing me around and telling me how to act and think. Not directly, mind you, because she's always tried to be nice and proper, like a lady. Yet she had a way of making me feel inept and even dumb with her comments and insinuations. It's obvious to me now that she wanted me to be a replica of herself." She turned to Susan, took her hand. "Sorry, dear, if my words about your mum upset you. But you know I'm not one for keeping things in."

"Don't worry," said Susan. "I know what it's like to live with my mother."

"You get what I'm saying, then."

"I do. Please go on."

"We grew up in Winnipeg, an awfully cold place. You think this is cold, Camilo? Try twenty degrees below zero on a 'warm' day! Lizzie and I spent a lot of time indoors. Oh, the inclement weather didn't stop us from frolicking outdoors and having fun like children everywhere. But we did tend to gravitate toward the room we shared, and that's where things usually went from bad to worse. I mean, Lizzie and I were good to each other, typical sisters, you know, playing together and keeping secrets from our parents. But we were different in some essential ways. I wanted to go with the flow, as they say in the States, while she was bent on going by the book. One must obey the rules!"

"So you were the rebel," I put in.

"Well, as much as a young woman could be in those days, certainly more than Liz."

"Did the two of you stay in touch," I asked her, "once Liz moved to Kansas?"

"Yes, but we didn't see each other much."

"How come?"

"You see, her husband and mine didn't get along that well. Two alpha males...always a brawl waiting to happen. Dave didn't care much for me, either. I think it bothered him that I didn't sing the praises of his beloved country. He made fun of our "royal complex," as he called it, and he talked about our queen in rather lewd terms. Lizzie came to visit a couple of times by herself and brought you once," she said to Susan, "when you were little. I bet you don't remember that visit, do you, dear?"

"No, I'm afraid not. But I've seen the pictures."

"Lizzie had a conniption the first time she saw my house," Euphemia related, laughing. "She couldn't cope with the mess, the lack of structure, the absence of a schedule. She said, 'Effie, you haven't changed a bit! This place brings back memories, and not pleasant ones.' And then she got progressively more offensive... 'What do you mean you eat when you get hungry, regardless of the hour? That's preposterous. So uncivilized and so like you!' But I was used to her snide remarks."

"I don't think your house is messy," I told her in all honesty. "It's homey and inviting."

"Thank you, dear. Your mother-in-law would beg to differ."

"I assume the two of you don't see eye to eye politically, either..."

"Oh, no, not whatsoever! I've liked most of your Democratic presidents, especially Jimmy in spite of all his blunders. Whereas Liz has turned into a clone of her Republican hubby."

"I can't believe how different the two of you are."

"Like day and night, dear. Like day and night."

"I know who you like better," said Susan jokingly.

"Really? How did you guess?"

"That's the end of this conversation," Effie announced. "More cider, anyone?"

As I sipped more of the sweet, steaming beverage, I gave myself over to further comparing the two sisters. It wasn't just their homemaking styles and political views that set them apart. There was something else about Elizabeth that Euphemia didn't have, and that was the older sister's voice, a pesky, drilling pitch that dominated her every utterance and which, were it to be constant, could drive someone to the brink of madness. Lucky for Susan, she'd been genetically spared her mother's "gift." What I didn't understand was how she'd endured listening to Liz without climbing the walls or punching her so she'd shut up. And how did Mr. Thompson bear it? Maybe he didn't! In any case, it was Euphemia's good fortune not to have such a voice. Apparently it wasn't a family thing, I hoped. But what if it was? What if that piercing sound got passed on? My poor children!

Two kids, said Susan. I wished I could be that sure. There was something holding me back, away from the idea of that miracle, and it was the island that lived in my nights. I felt prepared to protect my children, if I ever had them, from any criminal anywhere in the world. But how did I protect them from the rapists of my memory? How would I manage to distance them, save them from a past that still haunted me? Maybe by reinventing my childhood for them. Could it be done? Should it?

Auntie Effie assured me, on the eve of our departure, that she would have read my first book by the time we came back to see her. "I'm excited," she said, "to have a nephew who's a writer! But please don't tell me anything about the novel and spoil all the fun. I want to be surprised."

"Oh, you can count on being surprised," I reacted.

"It'll be a welcome break from my romance novels, all those pretty damsels and valiant heroes."

"Nothing wrong with a little romance," Susan observed.

"It's all hogwash, dear," Effie pronounced. "But I don't have the energy to digest very complex and lengthy works of literature anymore. It's bad enough that I've had to learn French."

"I had no idea you spoke it, Auntie Effie," I told her.

"Neither did I," said Susan.

"It's been a recent development, dear," Effie explained.

"So we could've been speaking French all this time?" I asked, looking forward to a little practice. "I guess it's never too late, *n'est-ce pas, ma chère tante?*"

"Don't you dare!" Euphemia exclaimed. "I get plenty of practice as it is already. You see, Charles, my eldest, is married to a woman from Montreal; their children are bilingual but prefer to speak French. And of course my daughter-in-law refuses to speak English, even though I know for a fact that she's fluent in it. Oh, those Montrealers can be such a pain in the derrière! I'm all in favor of their linguistic independence, and I admire them for the pride they have in their culture. It takes courage to do what they've done. But I'm too old to have to speak another language!"

"I'm sure it's keeping your brain cells nicely lubricated," Susan told her.

"Probably so, and God knows we can all use some help at this stage of the game. But you can surely understand why I go for the romantic lightweight when it comes to reading material. It's easy and fun and so much better than television! They can offer such delight late at night, those little books, when solitude and darkness seem too heavy for an old widow to bear."

Susan and I could relate. We knew the comfort reading could bring, the company it offered. But I also knew that *Cuba in Silence* was not the "light-reading" kind of book our dear aunt liked to indulge in. "You don't have to read any of my stuff, Auntie Effie," I said. "We're cool."

"But what if she wants to?" asked Susan.

"Well, then..."

"If anyone can appreciate good writing, that's my aunt."

"Thank you, dear. I did put myself through Joyce and Proust and Faulkner in my youth. And I've read our home-grown celebrities, Munro, Atwood, Ondaatje..."

"I'm sure," added Susan, "there's nothing in Camilo's novel you can't handle, Auntie Effie."

"And if I do," said Euphemia with a naughty smile, "then that's my problem, is it not?"

"Fine," I caved. "I'll mail you a signed copy of *Cuba in Silence* as soon as I get home. But don't go feeling sorry for me because you think it's my story, okay?"

"And why would I assume it's your story? I thought you said it was fiction, didn't you say that? Well, then, of course it's not an autobiography!"

Yet it was, in many ways. I did write about myself in *Cuba in Silence*. There was too much invention in it to be autobiographical, details I filled in when memory failed me, or when the story needed them. But there was also a wealth of personal experiences that I gave my child character. I didn't want Effie to feel sad for me when she read the novel, the way Susan still did. I didn't want her to know me *that well*. Better for her to think of me as the light-hearted man who'd married her niece, a jovial lad who cracked jokes about his Cuban bones and his aversion to swimming in cold lakes. That *cubano* wasn't tormented by his distant past. He never wrote about the fear that drove him as a child to hide in a make-believe world, a secret place where no one could hurt him; a realm devoid of violent, abusive people where life could be lived, not just survived, and which eventually became contaminated too.

My books, according to Susan, derived their strength from the cruel realities I had dared to fictionalize. "In *Cuba in Silence*," she stated in one of her articles, "the main character's life becomes a constant flight from love because love brings no protection." And *Love Insane*, she said elsewhere, "imagines an ethnic/sexual space where homophobia and ethnocentrism have been expelled…"

Susan contended that my texts were harsh, blunt "counternarratives" that thrived on their marginality, presenting a necessary vision of the island, the other face of Eden, an image of Cuba that had been concealed, denied. Or so went Susan's interpretation of my work, and maybe what she said was true. But having accomplished all of that hadn't helped me significantly—or changed anything. There was still a sad, silent widow lurking in the dark, haunting me. Susan believed that only by returning to Cuba would I be able to banish that creature from my nights. Which implied an actual voyage to the narrow dirt street where my childhood home once stood and accepting that I'd lived there once upon a time, that I did have roots. My wife used to insist that I go back for a visit, before she realized that the journey couldn't be forced, that it had to seem endurable to me or it'd never happen.

It was on Salt Spring Island where Susan dug the deepest into the reasons I had for not returning to my native country. And it was there where the truths of my life and my fiction finally merged for her. The conversation we had while hiking was one we'd been owing each other. I told her I hadn't felt ill at ease on Salt Spring Island because nothing there reminded me of Cuba. But of course I'd have to assume form if I stayed for good, be stamped, identified. I'd have no choice but to admit that I came from a Caribbean city that might be called Camagüey, Jatibonico, or Ciego de Ávila, but which became Las Tinajas as the substance of my creative work, a composite but also none of those places. I knew that my nightmares would resurface (all that oneiric stuff about ominous caverns and a flying merman and a place called El Kiosko), and I'd still be trying—illusively, ingenuously—to erase myself from all maps, to break all those mirrors that reflected back an image of my childhood.

"Your nightmares won't go away until you return to Cuba and face them," said Susan.

"I can't do that," I told her. "I'd never want to relive the pain I left behind."

"But you haven't left it behind, Camilo," she insisted.

"Las Tinajas isn't even real, Susan. It doesn't exist. I made it up!"

"Don't fool yourself, Camilo. You gave it a different name, that's all. Like you tend to do in your writing. The city in Kansas I call home, for instance. Yes, it could use a moniker as classy as 'Overland City,' or as mythical as the 'Emerald City' of *The Wizard of Oz*. But call it what you might, it is what it is. Some places are real, Camilo, and you must accept their existence."

"Accept it, maybe. Embrace it, never."

"Your hometown is still there."

"Yes, I've seen the pictures. And it all looks the same. Hell never changes."

"But it does. It has to."

"You get only one small glimpse of that Hell in *Cuba in Silence*. I could write ten more novels and still not manage to convey the stuff that went on... The words I heard everywhere, every day when I was a kid, all alluding to sex. *Pinga, tolete, cojones, bollo, culo, tetas*. I still remember men boasting about their virility, ordering the world to bow before their balls. Women parading their flesh, proudly announcing their submission to the macho's *tolete*. And danger always awaiting children. The many times I barely escaped the claws of an adult, someone I was supposed to trust; the times I didn't..."

"I wonder what was happening in your country during those years."

"A fucking revolution!"

"Yes, and maybe the excessive performance of sex was a reaction to communist repression."

"Could be. As you know, Reinaldo Arenas points to the late sixties in his autobiography, specifically 1968 as the year when things started to get crazy in Cuba. It was a moment, he says, when there was great sexual freedom on the island, when everybody wanted desperately to fornicate. Not that he minded, of course not; he was very much a part of that 'movement.' But I think he's wrong; I believe it all started long before. Maybe this is simply who we are, Susan, and we should just face it. Maybe this is our essence: Sex permeates all Cuban social spheres, every thought, every gesture and action."

"You know what I think about essence..."

"But it wasn't just the sex. There was also verbal and physical abuse in many homes. Arguing, screaming. Papi would boss Mami around, deride and humiliate her, and he'd give me a thrashing at least once a week because I was too "delicate." That's the precise word he used to describe me, *delicado*. Elio, the Cuban paterfamilias, wouldn't tolerate gentle manners and artistic reveries in a male child, for he knew that if

I didn't flaunt and impose my *cojones*, I'd end up with a broken asshole. Those were the only choices, *hombre* or *maricón*. Macho or Little Mary. I'm sure it's all still the same."

"You don't know that. Besides, you're depicting a country on the basis of one child's experiences. And that's not wise, Camilo."

"Wise?! You think this has anything to do with wisdom?"

"Obviously not for you."

"I know there are children all over the world, many of them, who've endured greater suffering than I did. Kids who are starving, enslaved. But I can only speak for my own pain."

"Cuba is more than anything you could say or remember."

"True. I wouldn't claim otherwise."

"Yet that's what you're doing, defining the island based on what happened to you."

"Like I said, I can only attest to what I know."

"Aren't you concerned that you might be confirming the prevailing view of Latinos in the U.S.? You know, the stereotype of Hispanics as savages and brutes and perverts?"

"Maybe we deserve that stereotype."

"No, you don't!"

"You're right. But *Cuba in Silence* has been around for a while; it's too late for me to start painting a rosy picture of 'my people.' The word is out."

"I'm not talking about that book, or anything you've written, Camilo."

"What, then?"

"You! I'm talking about *you*. The way you express yourself about Cuba, the things you've said to me and that you might say publicly to condemn those people, *all* of those people."

"I know. It's irresponsible, immature..."

"And unfair."

"I know, Susan."

"At least you didn't end up in some Midwest orphanage, like the Cuban children who were sent to the U.S. alone and never saw their families again. The Peter Pan kids."

"Yeah, I guess I was fortunate in some way. I escaped with my parents."

"And now it's time for you to retrace your lost steps."

"Let 'em remain lost."

"Let's go to Cuba, Camilo. We'll go together. Wouldn't you like to see your grandparents and your aunt and cousins? I'm sure they'd love to see you."

"I'm afraid, Susan. Afraid of returning."

"You need to work through your fear. Turn it into words..."

"I've tried. You've heard me describe my fear as both specific and abstract, indefinable. Fear of reliving our exodus. Fear of walking by El Kiosko, which is probably still there. Fear of..."

"I know you've tried, my love, and yet..."

"I can't go back," I repeated, on the verge of tears.

Susan kissed me and said she understood. "I know that somewhere in your heart you're a boy who feels alone, forsaken, and who won't forgive his parents for not protecting him."

"They should've done something!"

"They couldn't. What was happening to you was unthinkable."

"Yet it *did* happen. And not just to me; there were other kids..."

"Friends of yours?"

"Boys I knew. Some of us played 'the grown-up game' with each other, though we didn't really know what we were doing. And *that* I can understand. It's natural for children to be curious about their bodies and their physical changes. But adults abusing children sexually, that's something else. That's a hideous crime. Nothing can justify it. Nothing good can come of it."

"Your parents had no clue. They were young. And trusting."

"Ironic, isn't it? I couldn't trust anyone and least of all my father. My valiant Papi, so proud of his role as provider, as guard..."

"And he couldn't save you from a rapist who haunts you to this day."

"Eduardo threatened me. 'If you don't let me fuck you,' he'd say, 'I'll tell your father that this was your idea, that you started it, that you kept coming back and asking me for more.' And I thought Papi would kill me if he found out. So I went back."

"Because you wanted to live."

"Sex with that man hurt. Sometimes I'd bleed. I'd bite my lips, my tongue, try not to scream. But my pain didn't stop him. There were times when I didn't think I'd be able to bear it."

"Was there any pleasure at all?"

"Yes, a dense and confusing kind of pleasure. Like the thrill of mischief or a dangerous adventure; also the excitement of feeling special, being desired by a man who resembled my father. And keeping this amazing secret from Papi was also part of the thrill... What a trip, no?"

"A trip that led you to writing."

"Lucky me."

"I wouldn't call it luck, but..."

"Truth is, I'd give up the wicked pleasure of my childhood memories; all my books, too. I'd gladly trade in 'the strength of my fictions' for the memory of a normal childhood."

"No one has a 'normal' childhood, Camilo. How do you define normality?"

"Okay, just more typical then. You know what I mean."

"I do. And I also know that you can't cut that kind of deal. You'll never be a boy again. You're stuck with the past, my love. Don't let it poison your future."

"Too late for that, Susan."

"It's never too late."

"I'm sure, at a rational level, that I wouldn't be at risk if I returned to Cuba. But there's the realm of irrational truths, a worst-case scenario where I see myself trapped on the island, uprooted once again and unable to share my life with you. And that's what I fear the most."

"Nothing will ever keep us apart, Camilo."

"I want to believe you, but I heard a similar statement from my grandmother once. 'Nothing will ever separate us, Milo,' she told me, and you know how that story turned out..."

The eve of our departure came upon us too quickly. That day we had a brunch of fruit salad, goat cheese, and scones on the deck, enjoying the view and the sun, which was unusually bright. One last time I took note of a golden lake that welcomed me through Auntie Effie's "window." I would miss our hikes, our kayaking, the trees, the thoughts and feelings I had there, the freedom I felt; the hope for healing, thanks to Susan; and my fantasy of reinvention. But most of all I'd miss our hostess, Mrs. Euphemia Crowther, my very own Auntie Mame. She had been joking about not letting us go, about starving to death without our feasts. We made several meals to be put in the freezer for her gradual consumption, and she was overwhelmed with gratitude for this gesture. "When will you come back?" she asked, hoping for an encouraging soon. And that's what we told her, "Soon, we hope." I was saddened to leave Salt Spring but relieved to be going home with Susan, headed to that other island where returning was easy, where memories were kind and there dwelled no bona fide citizens.

CUBA IN SILENCE

That voice he hears, what is it telling him? *La luz estorba y la palabra humana.* It's just sounds now and cries and pleas, all entangled. Oh if he could only call for help, if he could bring his mother here, hold her hand through this darkness. Mami's warmth on his skin, her bosom a pillow comforting him, her love building a home for the two of them. Her gentle words would keep him safe, alive.

There's always fog, but it's lifting tonight. And as it lifts it unveils the porch of his house, where he's sitting alone, playing. He hears an unfamiliar song; it's lively, tropical, inviting. Lito wants to sing along but doesn't know the lyrics. *La luz estorba...*

Suddenly there's thunder, lightning! He's swept up by the storm, a monstrous force to be braved by little boys caught in its rage. *El universo habla...* The weak children will perish, the strong ones will triumph, but is Lito weak or strong? Hard to tell while the raindrops pelt his face like poisoned arrows, blinding him. Hard to know what to do. Is it valor that's needed or fear? Valor will help him face death, fear will give him the strength to run from it. But which will keep him from hurting?

Outside. Is this his backyard? Grayish light on the patio, a path on the side of the house, a red-tile roof, a long stretch of dry ground where he'll be out of harm's way. The sky is blue at last. Where is he? Alone but not in pain. There's that music again, beautiful sounds caressing him, not thunder but a melody entering his pores, moving all the way to his head. Are there words to this tune? Perhaps, but he doesn't understand them. *El universo habla...* The song rocks him to sleep.

Awake now, trapped in a small, empty room. No windows, no door, no escape. He must find a way out! Who cares if there's danger outside, thorny weeds all around. He'll run through them, cut them down with his hands. *Está vacío mi pecho, destrozado.* He'll withstand their acrid smell, their sting, so he can be free. *Vacío en donde estaba el corazón.* But where is freedom? Lito can't find it but he knows what it means. Freedom is a dream that won't tear out his heart.

Leafy trees, flowers. He's surprised to be wearing a red cape and no shoes. He notices the basket he carries, full of ham croquettes, fried plantain, and bread pudding. He's going to see Matilde, a loving woman he calls Abuela. She's sick and needs tending to. Don't stop along the way, said his mother, but Lito can't help it. He stops to throw rocks in the stream and skip stones. He picks up a flower, breathes in its scent, leans against a ceiba tree thinking good thoughts. And then he falls asleep.

He hears Abuela's voice. Wake up, Milo! He opens his eyes and sees a chimney and Matilde's house but not Abuela. He walks to the door, gets distracted by the candy covering the house—chocolate kisses, melcocha, lollipops, raspadura bars. Lito peeks through the bedroom window and sees a neatly made bed, embroidered quilt pillow cases with pink lace, old pictures on the dresser. Abuela isn't there, maybe she's in the kitchen making chicken soup, good for sick people. She'll be happy to see him, excited like a little girl when she digs into her favorite treats that he brought her. He wants to go in and give her a hug but he's tempted by the yummy things falling on his lap. A feast! Lito eats candy till he's full, too full to move. He'll drag himself or crawl if he has to so he can knock on Matilde's door, or better yet he'll take another nap for now, before he brings his bounty of goodies to his grandma.

It's snowing! How can there be snow in this evergreen forest? His hands and feet are freezing, the ground is made of ice, the ceiba trees are dead. There's no stream, only giant rocks dressed in frosty white. He trips, falls, cuts himself with a pine branch, grabs it, throws it far where it won't hurt any other children. And something strange happens then. He can't believe his eyes! The blood from his cut is giving life to the dead branch, and the dead branch is rooting itself deep. How fast it grows! So fast it soon turns into a tree, and from its trunk the resin flows like a river, and the river casts a shadow on the mantle of whiteness. The tree is now a beast, with branches like paws. A monster has awakened!

He snaps his fingers and the pine monster disappears. But so does Abuela's candy-covered house. Lito's parents are gone too. Were they ever here? No, they don't exist in this place, in this secret life he's living. He's afraid but curious. He hears a voice deep inside, an echo in his guts. *La llama roja de la vela flamea...* Somewhere in the maze of his mind there's a person Lito recognizes as himself. But then that person leaves, and he's a blank page needing words, meaning, feelings. Needing to breathe.

He thinks of fireflies. Lito has light in his eyes like a *cucuyo* and can see far away. There's a calm sea with foamy waves, and he'd like to dive in but is afraid he'll drown. Wait, there's a boy in the water! *¡Oye, chico!* he calls out to him. He knows him, it's his friend Roli! But now Roli's going in too deep, where the mermaids dwell. Roli must turn back! *Ya es hora de empezar.* A creature rises from the depths, a ravenous being that's headed for the boy. *Ya es hora de empezar a morir.*

Lito cries out, Rolando! But Roli can't hear him. Lito wants to save him and share his lunch with him. He'll buy Roli a car, a green and silver Chevy so he can drive around the park. He'll bring Rolando to his house to meet a fat pig named Fili, and Mami will make yummy things to eat, like a bowl of chocolate pudding that won't taste like dirt. And on Sunday they'll go to the Hunters Club and walk through the gardens and swim in the pool and hold hands all they want. Roli's father will appear wearing a peasant hat, smiling among the palm trees. The man has changed, he's a good father now. And when the evil teacher with rotten breath shows up, Roli's Papi will punch her and make her say she's sorry for poisoning Snow White and stealing her kingdom. The teacher will scream and ask to be forgiven but there can be no mercy for her. She'll soon turn into smoke.

Roli, please come out of the water! Lito pleads. Soon it'll be too late to tell him stories or make plans. I promise you Roli, he says, if you come out I won't let anyone call you Little Mary again or pull your hair or say that you have duck shit on your head. I'll kick their butts and fist-slap them, who cares if I end up with a donkey hat on my head. I'll defend you and tell you it's my duty 'cause I'm your hero and I love you and we'll get married some day. It doesn't matter that you're a boy and so am I. We'll break the rules! We'll make it normal for boys to be married, to be husband and husband living happily ever after. What do you say? You like the idea? It's what you wanted, isn't it? So please come out...

Rolando can't hear him, and the hungry creature is staying on course. Roli swims fast toward the shore. He's almost there, soon to be greeted with a hug and lots of kisses. But it's too late. Roli is doomed, there's nothing Lito can do. Goodbye, my friend. *¡Adiós!*

Where to go now? Lito is afraid, what if he gets eaten too? The pain Roli must've suffered! He runs, but his legs can't propel him, his feet are sore. He stands on a cliff overlooking the waves and sees a strange shape in the distance. It's an island, a moving island! It wiggles its tail like a lizard and has the mouth of a cayman, and it's trying to flap its tiny wings to fly. The island is going up to Heaven to fight the forces of Good. But is Good strong enough to defeat a giant cayman? It'd better be, for if Good is vanquished there will be no salvation for him. He'll be left alone in this nightmare, in this river of blood where monsters abound, where Lito drowns and hurts and cries. Alone with the island.

There's hope. The angels are here all around him, three of them hovering. One has golden hair that flows like clouds, one is a woman with a beautiful boy's face, one has tiny curls that resemble seashells. They're the most powerful beings in Heaven. They can make water rise and plants grow, but their most important mission is finding lost children. He asks them if they're here to rescue him, and they say, Yes, little one, but we've been deceived. Sorry. You must understand, angels are too credulous, we can be easily fooled by sirens when sirens appear as cenzontle birds. So evil wasn't banished from the world. Goodness won't win after all, it is too weak. We're sorry, Lito.

Fight this dream, he urges himself, and forge a happy ending. No more vanquished angels and shape-shifting islands in the night. He's going home at long last—on a train! But wait, there are no other passengers in this car. And where will the train take him? Where are his parents?! A man's voice tells him to relax, to enjoy the ride, so Lito looks out the window. *Las ventanas abro, ya estrecho en mí.*

There are houses in the distance, a castle, tall towers. But he's not riding the train anymore, he got off somehow and is heading toward the castle. A bridge appears before him, over the moat where hungry mermaids hope for his misstep. Lito sees their gray, scaly faces. He can do it, yes, he will cross without falling. A vaulted door cracks open like a shell, and he's shoved inside. It's dark and moist, this chamber, full of rancid air. He's pulled by a callused hand, its fingers feel like dry branches. Who are you?! he asks but no one answers. Only the silence speaks. *Ya es hora de empezar.*

He's naked and cold, begging for mercy. Help! Please, whoever you are, don't hurt me, don't cut me, don't eat me! Icy air that now turns red hot, scalding. Flames below, and hands crawling up, digging into his flesh like knives. *Mis pedazos palpo: ya no soy vivo.* Then darkness gives way to light but not the light of freedom, it's a merciless sun that burns his eyes, that burns all of him.

Lito knows at last whom the strange words belong to. *La luz estorba y la palabra humana.* He recognizes the voice he's been hearing, can understand the lyrics of a song he couldn't sing before. He knows, he finally knows! Oh, but knowledge won't save him. Knowledge has come too late.

V

Islands and Forests

HAVANA ICE CREAM

H e wasn't very famous when I first wrote to him back in grad school. Yovani López was only a young novelist I thought I had "discovered." But by the time we met, my pen pal had become a celebrity. He arrived in Southern California from Havana one summer day to promote *Helado habanero* (*Havana Ice Cream*), a trailblazing film for which he'd written the screenplay, based on his award-winning novel and directed by Osvaldo Quiñones, a protégé of the great Cuban director Gutiérrez Alea. The writer's ten-day tour was organized by Alina Sotovélez. Surprisingly, her college footed the bill for his airfare and expenses, in return for an exclusive showing of the movie at Alton City College.

Yovani's book and film both told the story of Álvaro Echevarría, chief editor of Cuba's major publishing house, Casa de las Américas. Comrade Echevarría favored stories of social realism with an approving view of the Revolution, thus influencing his country's literary history. Married with three children, Álvaro led an exemplary life but guarded a dangerous secret. At his home in the Marianao district, before a mirror tucked away in a loft, the editor became Rosita Fornés, the Cuban singer and television star when she was in her prime, circa 1967—blonde, voluptuous, modern. This was the woman Álvaro dreamed of incarnating, the recurring image—vivid in close-ups—of his reveries, and a fantasy the editor couldn't keep hidden for long. He would come out as La Fornés during Carnaval and party incognito in seedy Vedado apartments along the sea wall, driven by a liberating promiscuity. But then Rosita began to take over his life. And so one day, while enjoying a cup of *helado* at

Copelia, the popular ice cream parlor, Álvaro's fate came rushing in. In a fit of anger, his current boyfriend unmasked the transvestite (a daring drag queen, out in bright daylight!), making wig and rubber boobs fly off. Accused of perversion, ridiculed, Álvaro was found guilty by a People's Tribunal and declared an enemy of the Revolution, and he was banished from Cuba in shame with his family.

Echevarría's sentence was no doubt a symbolic gesture. Thus Yovani's story depicted exile as the only fitting punishment, the ultimate prison, not a space of freedom. And the message was twofold, depending on who manipulated it: There was no place for degenerates in Cuba; these undesirable elements were corrupt and belonged elsewhere. Echevarría deserved the same fate as the *gusanos* who had fled the country, a life of uprootedness and disgrace. Or: The Revolution condemned those who didn't conform to its homophobic, patriarchal ideology. Álvaro shouldn't have been penalized at all.

I wondered, when I first read the novel and later, after seeing the film, if López had written about his own predicament in *Helado habanero*, if the story cut to the core of his identity. Perhaps his dream was to come out and fight for his right to be both gay and revolutionary. If Álvaro was indeed his alter ego, then Yovani had sublimated his desire ingeniously. And if *Helado* wasn't his personal trip at all, then he was a sensitive interpreter of someone else's desire. Most likely the truth was obscure, indefinable even for the work's creator. Ultimately it didn't matter whether Yovani was gay, straight, or whatever, nor that I was a bisexual expatriate and he a communist. Our "true" identities became inconsequential once I met the Cuban writer in Colina and spent some time with him. For years to come I'd miss his laughter, and I'd feel comforted by a fleeting illusion: that I belonged in Cuba, with him.

Alina brought him to my condo. "This is your time, *muchachos*," she said upon seeing us embrace. "Make the best of it!" When she left a little later, I guided Yovani upstairs to the loft where I did most of my writing. There he noted a handful of books on a shelf, Kundera's *The Unbearable Lightness of Being*, Atwood's *Handmaid's Tale*, Puig's *Kiss of the Spider Woman*, Amy Tan's *The Joy Luck Club*, Cortázar's *Hopscotch*, Lezama's *Paradiso*, Arenas' *Before Night Falls*, Didion's *The White Album*, Cisneros's *Woman Hollering Creek*... He also took notice of the portrait hanging on the wall behind my desk, above the sound system. "She looks very Cuban!" he observed. "Is that your wife?"

"No, it's my mother," I replied, laughing. "A painting I did when I was in high school. Not very good, I know, but it's like having Mami here with me. I love that woman."

"There's a certain Impressionist thing about it, I think, especially in the eyes and the hands."

"Thanks, but..."

"Visual art isn't my thing, but I enjoy it. Do you have any more recent work?"

"Oh, no, no. Art didn't turn out to be my thing either."

He walked to the window, took in the whitewashed beauty of my faux Mediterranean complex, its palms and manicured lawns. "What a great place to work," he said.

"It really is, most of the time."

"Right, when you're not napping!"

There was no obvious resemblance between us, but something about him reminded me of my relatives on the island; his dense black hair and crinkly eyes, perhaps. His Spanish was colorful and soft and slightly *guajiro*, as befitted the son of a peasant Cabaiguán family; nothing like mine, which had been infused with myriad accents. My *cubañol* had gradually become an amalgam that couldn't be placed in any country yet passed for real. I could speak Cuban with my mother, but even hers was a language that had stopped evolving in 1969, fossilizing colloquialisms of the past. I sounded standard, bookish, sometimes Mexican and sometimes Southern Cone but mostly pan-Caribbean. But, hey, I could still drop my esses and spice up my speech with Cuban terms like *asere*, *tonga*, *pa' los fósforo*, *le zumba el mango*, *le ronca el merequetén*. And it seemed to work; Yovani was perceiving me as *cubano*.

I seized the moment to talk about *El rey del campo*, his first novel. "When I read that book," I told him, "I had a warm yet unsettling feeling, as though you were telling the story of my childhood, or at least some of its key passages. It was like seeing my reflection in someone's eyes."

Yovani knew. He remembered the first letter I wrote to him, one of the few he'd ever kept, in which I expressed my reaction to his novel and shared a fantasy with him: Had I stayed in Cuba, I might've lived the life he'd lived. Thus in a strange, Cortázar sort of way, Yovani was filling the void I'd left in my country. "An intriguing literary fantasy," he'd said at the time. "After reading that letter," he told me now, "I imagined this moment, today..."

The *doppelgänger* illusion enveloped us like a warm mist. Yovani shared the story of how, unbeknownst to me, he'd met me already. Or so he'd thought then, when he was traveling by train from Madrid to Rome some years ago, and seated not far from him was a man who looked Cuban. Yovani had a realization: that man was Camilo Macías, and there was a sad, lost air about him. Unfortunately, the passenger got off the train before Yovani could talk to him. His exit was sudden, hurried. Staring at me now, López remarked, laughing, "You look just like he did. Are you sure you weren't on that train?"

"If you saw me sitting near you," I replied, "then I was!"

He smiled, seemingly amused by my response. We had coffee out on the terrace, under a eucalyptus tree. It was strong French roast, and Yovani took it black. "Coffee is my only vice," he said. The stuff untied his tongue, propelled him. He said he'd read and enjoyed some of the poetry I'd written in Spanish, especially the poems in *Fantasías*. He hadn't tackled my fiction because his "Inglich" wasn't up to it. But he was studying hard, and the practice he was getting during his visits to the U.S. would help. Good, I told him, since there was no plan for a Spanish translation of my novels any time soon, and I definitely wanted his feedback on the original.

"The filming of my script," he related, moving his hands excitedly, "is the most fantastic thing that's ever happened to me. I'm hooked on filmmaking!" He spoke of the mind-blowing experience of seeing one's words come alive, of reaching so many people. And he talked about the actors who auditioned for the starring role in *Helado habanero*, some of them talented, others just handsome. He mentioned the drag queen, "*aquella loca*" who sparked in him the idea for his story. "It was my lucky day," he said, "when a transvestite sat across from me at Copelia." Yovani was at the ice cream parlor one afternoon, alone, when a beautiful blonde woman asked if she could join him. Since he didn't object, she daintily proceeded to eat a cup of chocolate ice cream at his table. She propositioned Yovani minutes later and informed him that "she" was actually a "he." The drag queen would do it for free because she liked him. Yovani declined, feeling flattered. Instead of indulging the queen, he went home and spent the next two days writing, describing a world he'd been observing for some time. And in his gifted hands that world became *Helado habanero*.

We headed to Trudy's Diner in Laguna Beach for lunch.

"Let's get the best this country has to offer," I joked. "Shake, burger, and fries."

"Why do you drive a Japanese car?" he asked, tapping on the dashboard of my Datsun as if rewarding an obedient dog. "Why not a Ford or a Chevrolet?"

"Because Japanese cars are made to last," I said, eager to praise my faithful blue friend. "I've had this old clunker since before I started college; it was secondhand when I bought it, and it's only broken down a couple of times since then. It just needs gas and some oil to be happy."

"So it's true, then," he reacted, "not everything made in USA is better."

I offered him the spare sunglasses I kept in the car; he put them on with flair.

"The sunlight can be blinding here," I told him.

"Obviously," he said, laughing, "you don't remember what the sun is like in Cuba!"

We sat next to a jukebox, below the retro poster of a rosy-cheeked girl sipping Coke from a classic bottle. Here Yovani talked about his wife, Nancy, a filmmaker who made documentaries about the subjects that impassioned her, such as Cuba's emerging biotechnology industry. They had a good marriage but no plans for children. Nancy was a fierce political worker, very active in the Party, and she kept herself busy. She had no time for motherhood.

After a stroll on the beach, it was time to go. Yovani had a dinner engagement with Alina and her colleagues. His movie would be showing at Alton City College tomorrow night, and they wanted to thrash out the details. The plan was for Professor Sotovélez to talk briefly about López's work, introduce him, and then present his extraordinary Cuban film. And of course she'd invite everyone to stay for the Q&A session. This wouldn't be the first showing of *Helado* attended by Yovani in the States, and it wouldn't be the last. He knew what to expect. He was sure there would be an assortment of professors, students, people from neighboring towns, and a small contingent of gay fans. "The students are always surprised by the critical tone of the movie," he recalled, and Yovani had a response ready for them: "Contrary to popular opinion, the Revolution is open to constructive criticism." At this point there would be accusations from some of the Cuban exiles in the audience... *No, the Revolution isn't open at all! How can you live there? How can you support a dictator who has caused so much suffering?!* None of those people would praise the writer for having had the *cojones* to expose and criticize the Cuban government's homophobia. And, as usual, Yovani would ask if they could please return to discussing the film. Not always possible.

On our way to his hotel in Alton, I casually mentioned Fidel, and Yovani said he'd met him at a Casa de las Américas event. He spoke of Castro as though the Comandante were a brilliant and obdurate grandfather, an incorrigible dreamer. He admired the Máximo Líder for many of the things he'd done for the Cuban people, for his "extraordinary vision." But Yovani wasn't interested in politics. "I'm not militant," he insisted. He was more inclined to talk about his sudden fame. "In Havana people stop me on the street, or they whisper when I pass by." He hadn't expected the effusive welcome they gave him in Spain, his words transmitted by every major radio station in Madrid. It was the same in San Juan, Santo Domingo, Caracas. Yovani felt overwhelmed by this popularity that had secured him tours, travels, and a powerful literary agent from Spain—though not wealth. He'd been paid a measly three thousand dollars for the *Helado habanero* script, and, because of the blockade, he might not be remunerated for distribution of the movie in the U.S. "Well," he mused, "it's a good thing I don't write to make money!"

Our second day we had an early supper at the Il Nostro Ristorante, one of several four-star eateries in the Alton Business Center. Through my spare shades Yovani glimpsed the heart of town, a manmade world of recently grown palm trees and tinted-glass towers, right across from Ambassador Suites, where he was staying. Going up the stairs from the underground garage, he stopped suddenly. "*Chico,*" he blurted out, "why am I walking like I never wore shoes before? I'm a hick but also a famous writer, *coño!*" He turned playfully haughty, "*¡Echa pa'alante, guajiro!*"

In the restaurant the atmosphere was pleasant if perhaps too swanky for my taste. We sat in the Rotunda, sipping connoisseur's wine, eating freshly-made bread, the finest pasta, the booziest tiramisù. And Yovani was now describing his *compañeros* in Havana, three women and five

men, all about his age, all into writing and filmmaking. He believed I'd
fit in just fine among them.

"You should come back to Cuba," he urged me, as he devoured his
meaty lasagna. "Come live and work among your people for a while.
You'd feel welcome in my group, and rooted."

"Maybe," I reacted, "though I'm not much for putting down roots."

"But you have them, don't you?"

"Yes, but my roots are not in Cuban soil. Not anymore."

"You'll never know for sure until you go back."

"It's a tempting offer, *chico*."

"I'll meet you at the airport," he said, and I was sure he meant it.

I thought Yovani was seeing me as that other Camilo he'd almost
met on a train, uprooted and lonely in his exile. Ironically, true freedom awaited me in my country, according to him. I was surprised he
couldn't see the vastness between his island and mine. If it was true
that Yovani had lived the life I might've lived in Cuba, it was also true
that he'd done a much better job at it than I would have. The Revolution
had made it possible for Yovani and his family to become literate. Party
leaders encouraged him to develop his writing, offered him a scholar-
ship to study at the University of Havana. And there were many other
opportunities, the most fruitful of them being the publication of his
work by Casa de las Américas. Hence, Yovani owed his career to the
Revolution; he was indebted to it. But did he ever question the abuses
of Cuba's political leaders? In *Helado habanero* he famously came out
against homophobia, and that was brave. But before that, somewhere
along the way, did Yovani ever repudiate Fidel Castro for his megalomania and his messiah complex? He must have, for no good writer is ever
blind to the misuse of power; silent, perhaps, but not blind.

I might have had the same opportunities as Yovani in Cuba, but the
Revolution would've been an intolerable challenge for me, a stifling
home where I'd have to be at the mercy of my father's whims, submit-
ting to his orders and delusions. I wonder if I would've remained silent,
fearful of Castro like I used to be of my father, accepting the most atro-
cious lies—like that of a revolution by and for the people—in order to
stay alive. I might've contested Fidel, denouncing things that can't be
justified in any way, like censorship, no matter how grand the ideals.
Would my criticism have been woven into a literary work or publicly,
dangerously spoken? Would I have suffered the same fate as that of

countless dissidents on the island, imprisonment, possibly death? I do know that I wouldn't have thrived in Cuba. Not because of my dangerous opinions (I'm not *that* brave) but because I would've gone off the deep end, keeping my distrust of military power, my disdain for nationalism, my hatred of machismo and personality cults locked inside. Until that toxin held within me would poison my soul and kill me.

Yet I'd never be able to grow roots among many of my compatriots on this side either. Our island gave birth to a power-drunk *caudillo*, a genuinely Cuban type—judging from our long array of despots—that shouldn't have surprised us. But it has also orchestrated a sinister chorus beyond its shores, people who define themselves through their anti-communist obsessions; who insist on fueling their vendettas, on recovering their alleged wealth and their lost paradise. At whatever the cost. Theirs is a self-serving agenda that ignores—denies—the plight of *guajiro* families like that of Yovani's before the Revolution; an agenda that embraces terrorism as a necessity for freedom. Not my kind of people. No, I would never hoist our flag, on or off the island, not if I have only those two choices...

Back in my loft after dinner, we listened to Gloria Estefan and Willy Chirino, Cuban-American artists that Yovani couldn't openly enjoy in his country. He liked two songs in particular, Gloria's "Mi tierra" and Willy's "Yo soy un tipo típico"—two of my favorites as well. Over rum&Cokes we got personal. Yovani wanted to know about Susan, so I told him about this woman I loved passionately.

"I wish I could've met her," he said.

"Me too. But there was this conference she had to attend. By the way, Susan loves your work, Yovani. She says you're a literary phenomenon. *¡Un fenómeno!*"

He laughed. "*Bueno, chico,* I take that as a compliment. It sounds a lot better than some of the other things I've been called... like Señorito Copelia, El heladero, El guajirito..."

"That's what you get for being famous."

I played some of the Cuban pop music that was in vogue when we were children, LPs I'd been collecting and guarding for years. Yovani couldn't believe I had those memories to regale him with. Yes, he remembered Luisa María Güell, Los Memes, Wilfredo Mendi, Marta Estrada...

He asked how I'd happened to find such treasures, amazed at the sheer number of LPs I owned. I told him I used to be compulsive about collecting record albums, even when I couldn't afford them or had to go out of my way to find them—in Mexican stores in downtown L.A. and garage sales and a dinky Cuban-owned minimart in the city of Gardena. Why the effort? Because of the pleasure records promised and provided, of course, including the fancy graphics on some covers. But I also collected them because I thought they placed me historically, thus consuming their offerings was like taking a journey through time. Bottom line was, I wouldn't have been able to throw the best parties in Alton without my LPs. So here was the main reason I had so many: I secretly longed to be a DJ!

"You know," mused Yovani after a third drink, "some people will always see you as that other person you were in Alton...before you got married."

"What do you mean?"

"They'll see you as a man...who shouldn't be with a woman."

"I know. Most of us need clear-cut definitions."

"We have a mutual friend who sees you that way."

"Must be Pérez Román..."

"It is. I talked to him not long ago, mostly about a possible visit to his university. He's a fine scholar, I think. And he likes your books, Camilo. He's published articles about them, right?"

"Yes. He's also compared your work with mine. And you've fared a lot better than me!"

"Pérez Román says he doesn't understand what you're doing, this 'farce' of yours..."

"He calls my marriage a farce?"

"He sees it as a betrayal of who you are, of your true identity."

"The 'true identity,' that's Román's thing."

"It is hard for most of us to handle ambiguity."

"Is it hard for you?"

"No, not for the writer in me."

"But what about your friends in Cuba, your *compañeros*?"

"You'd feel welcome among them. Believe me."

"Sure. As long as I kept my mouth shut about the gay men in my life, about the bisexual and gay characters in the books I've written..."

"Things have changed in Cuba, Camilo."

"I know, and your *Helado habanero* attests to the changes."

"Besides, you're married now. And you seem happy."

"I am happy with Susan. But I have no intention of denying who I am."

"So you're not living a double life like Echevarría?"

"We all live double, even multiple inner lives, Yovani. If we're lucky, one of them will be more fulfilling than the rest, and we'll stick with it and make it work."

"Álvaro couldn't make it work."

"True, and we both know the reasons why."

The Havana audiences would reject Álvaro at first—Yovani told me—but would gradually start to identify with him. The character's "coming out" was both subversive and cathartic.

"That's quite a victory for the Gay Cause," I said, "a homophobic audience voicing its frustrations and doubts through a homosexual man."

"I'm glad it worked out that way. But I didn't write *Helado habanero* to help any cause, except maybe that of the writer's freedom to write."

The gay community worldwide had claimed Yovani as one of its ambassadors, but he wouldn't attend conferences devoted to gay literature exclusively. "It wouldn't be honest," he acknowledged. He was quick to point out that he wasn't a bona fide member of that community. No, he was only a novelist who'd depicted a certain reality as a witness, an observer. And, so, here was the answer I'd been seeking, or at least the truth Yovani wanted me to believe: *Helado habanero* didn't tell *his* story.

I brought up the topic of AIDS, curious to hear his take on the Cuban clinics where HIV-positive and AIDS-infected citizens were being secluded, *excluded* from society.

"The contaminated individuals must be isolated," he alleged, "so they can be treated."

"Oh, yes, and it's the Revolution's duty to protect the 'normal' and 'healthy' citizens."

"You're right. It is."

"So you think it's fair to take people away from their families, to disappear them?"

"They're not taken away or disappeared, Camilo. They receive the best care in those clinics."

"It seems you and I have different definitions of 'best care.'"

Our first impasse.

"Have you lost anyone close to you?" he asked after an awkward pause.

"No. Not yet."

"Me either." He reflected. "Except for Reinaldo..."

The subject of Reinaldo Arenas' suicide turned him somber. Yovani hadn't known the brilliant writer personally, but the author of *Celestino antes del alba*, *El mundo alucinante*, and *Antes que anochezca* was the Cuban novelist Yovani most admired, the one he wanted to emulate.

"Reinaldo died alone in New York, taking his life...and when I heard the news I cried," he confessed. "I felt like I'd lost a close friend."

"I know how you felt," I admitted, thinking of Puig. "But Reinaldo wasn't alone. There were friends who looked after him and got him the medical care he needed."

"He lived a miserable life in exile, Camilo."

"We don't know that for sure. But if he did, it was surely because he had AIDS and got sick. At least he wasn't persecuted and belittled and imprisoned like he was in Cuba."

"He was very critical of the Revolution..."

"Yes, and of course he deserved to be treated like a criminal for that, right?"

"No, he didn't, Camilo. Big mistakes were made by some of our leaders."

"Yes. Irreparable mistakes."

"It saddens me to think of the way Reinaldo's case was handled."

"He was so fucking brave! In Cuba he risked everything—his career, his freedom, his life. And then what he did in exile took guts. Reinaldo didn't want to suffer a slow and painful death; that's why he put an end to it all. I'm not sure I'd have the balls..."

"Neither am I, to be honest. You know, he'd always thought of himself as a coward and yet he was one of the first young men to join Fidel's guerrillas in the Sierra Maestra. And in the end he was fearless. He became his own Celestino, a little boy now all grown up and..."

"Grown up and turned valiant, maybe even heroic."

"He's a tough act to follow."

"That's true, Yovani, but you can certainly try."

"No one could do that, my friend. And I'm not in his league, anyway. *¡Qué va!*"

Maybe not. But his credentials were impressive enough for the job. Yovani had brought his provincial candor and poetic prose to the Cuban literary scene. While his *El rey del campo* was heavily influenced by Arenas' *Celestino antes del alba*, in his next book he fictionalized a reality that had never before been openly, publicly named—let alone turned into literature—in his country. Not even the daring author of *Before Night Falls* could've made such a claim. Indeed, Yovani had uttered compromising truths. He believed that the Revolution merited a hard, constructive analysis. And, inexplicably, he'd been allowed to do some of his own analyzing without any repercussions.

"Today in Cuba," he declared, "a man like Reinaldo wouldn't suffer like he did."

"What about Álvaro?"

"Álvaro wouldn't have to leave the country in shame."

"Would he continue to be trusted by the government?"

"I think so."

"I doubt it, my friend."

Always the skeptic, I chose to drop the subject. I knew that the greatest stories were told from within repression, and thus they transformed the world, making it less inhospitable. And *Helado habanero* was one such story. Yovani had paved the way; he'd earned the right to be idealistic, to believe that age-old prejudices could be stamped out by one great novel-turned-film.

We talked briefly about his current project, a novel that further developed the main character in *El rey del campo*. "In my fiction," he explained, "I always try to explore aspects of some previous work. Because everything is related in the universe one creates. It's all part of the same story."

"Any chance you'll write a sequel to *Helado habanero*?" I asked him.

He pondered the possibility and said, "Maybe. But only if Álvaro returned to Cuba. I wouldn't want to deal with his life in exile. I know so little about it."

"I could help you with that part."

"I'm sure you could. Maybe we should write the book together. In Cuba."

"That would be a first."

"A perfect excuse for you to spend some time in your country."

"You keep trying to tempt me, Yovani."

"Is it working?"

"Maybe..."

And we left it at that, a possibility. I could fantasize about us collaborating on a book, yes, or perhaps coauthoring a story that reflected on the deeper knowledge we now had of each other. The dreamer in me wanted to think that Yovani would never again see exile—mine, at least—as a death sentence. That dreamer hoped he would now regard Camilo as his *compañero*, but I knew I wouldn't be very convincing in that role. I wouldn't want to be anyone's *doppelgänger*, either. No, that fantasy had run its course, being supplanted by this other tale of parallel lives, worlds apart that somehow converged, seeking some sort of union. I'd never grasp Yovani's allegiance to a communist state, to the suffocating truths of Nationalism. Just like he'd never understand my willful uprootedness and lack of patriotism. Could we bridge that distance between us somehow? Our collaborative project still awaits...

During our drive to Alton City College for the showing of his movie, Yovani told me he was ready for the event but also anxious to get back to Cuba. It was his duty to be there during his country's Special Period, to live and work in a nation cut off from its life source (the former Soviet Union) and facing the biggest economic crisis of its revolutionary project. Many such phases awaited my friend, a history he would continue witnessing, portraying, imagining. The place he came from was real; it survived in a present of daily struggles and unlikely triumphs. Whereas mine was made of memories: an elusive past. Yet for a moment, when we embraced and said *adiós* after the show, I felt tempted by the comfort of belonging, by the warmth of Yovani's Cuban arms.

FOREST OF ECHOES

The prince towered over me, tall, tender, and his words were a gift. Passionately Castel told me about Mexico City, about its beauty, its corruption and failures. Ciudad de México, *el D.F.*, was terribly polluted but alive and powerful and welcoming. He liked the people he hung out with, *telenovela* actors, models, a couple of UNAM professors; and surprisingly a female impersonator, "Angelique," who did a convincing take on Mexico's pop diva Angélica María. Most of them were a far cry from the dwellers of Gertrude's Rue de Fleurus but, hey, *c'est la vie*. Castel made a living translating American gay pulp into Chilango Spanish, which paid enough to keep him in ritzy Coyoacán, in a city where he turned real and believed in who he was. Thus the circle closed, this ancestral voyage for a Chicano who wrote like a Modernist poet, an English speaker to the bone, making his nest in Tenochtitlán...

I am a foreigner in this country—he told me in one of his letters. *I know I don't belong in Mexico and yet I am here. It is a pleasant feeling not to be at odds with your environment the way I've always been in the United States, to understand and accept your position even if that position is outside. I am an outsider in Mexico and this is deservedly so. I am not part of this world. Though I speak Spanish, I do not speak their language— their language is yet foreign to me. These people speak through a very different historical experience, through their own set of cultural norms and prejudices and values. But there is a peace in knowing your position well and understanding it.*

The feelings I have about the United States are quite different. I was born and raised in California and yet I am as much (if not more) a stranger to California as I am to Mexico. I do not belong there either and do not fully understand why I have always felt marginal and out of touch with my own milieu. My uneasiness with the States comes from feeling out of place in a world of which I should be an integral part yet cannot be; from a desire to speak a "language" that I haven't been allowed to master. Even though I am U.S.-born, I have remained a stranger in that country my whole life. A stranger to those who cannot or will not see me as an American.

In my reply I told him that, after having lived in Kansas, I could relate. That experience in the Midwest, more than any other, confirmed my outsider's position in this country. Never before had I felt so culturally out of step with my environment, so singled out as a foreigner as I did in Overland City. But exile was a way of life for me, whether I found myself in Los Angeles, Alton, Overland City, Colina, or Las Cumbres. I seemed to have no choice about it; exile was where I lived, regardless of the geographical context. Yet I would never know what it was like to feel alien in the place where one was born. Perhaps if I'd stayed in Cuba, I would've had a better grasp of Castel's predicament.

And while on the subject of language and strangers—he went on—*and on a lighter, if perhaps no less interesting note, I would like to tell you about the work I am doing these days. As you know, I have been translating bestselling novels from Lissom Press (the San Francisco publishing house) into Spanish for the Mexican market. Thus far my job has proven to be quite a challenge, as I'm sure you can imagine, although I find myself encouraged by the fact that the demand for such "literature" is huge in this country and hence my income—substantial for this part of the world—is guaranteed. But there are several problems that I've had to face as I set out to turn gay American porn into Chilango Spanish. For one, I don't feel confident enough in my knowledge of the latter to do justice to the material. I have equipped myself with some excellent dictionaries, one of which purports to offer the latest colloquialisms and idiomatic expressions of D.F. Spanish. Each entry is given a thorough definition and abundant examples for correct usage. And of course I consult with my Mexican friends here on the finer linguistic points, asking them for clarification and further explanation.*

Fortunately there are numerous sources I can tap, since not all the people I have befriended in Mexico are entertainers. I also know several intellectuals and a couple of fairly successful writers. One of my close friends in fact is a lawyer. (He's the older gentleman I told you about, someone I respect and who reminds me of you, and not because of his age! I should rephrase: my relationship with him is not so different from the one you and I have. Although of course the love you and I feel toward each other cannot be reprised nor replaced.) But even with all of that help, many times I find myself in way over my head. Take, for example, the colloquial words for penis in English, as used in the following passage from a book entitled The Bottom Acrobat: *"Long before I ever saw another man's dick, I knew I wanted to have one up my ass. I longed for a cock inside me, a gargantuan boner breaking through the virginal tissue of my butt hole and filling me up completely." The problem here is that the only word I have access to in colloquial Mexican Spanish for dick and cock and boner is "verga." But there's obviously an intention by this writer to provide three different words for the male organ, and American English is more prolific than Spanish with regards to genitalia, it seems. Of course I could be wrong about this particular case. But I wanted to illustrate one of the problems I am encountering.*

That problem is not as grave as my lack of enthusiasm for the books I am translating. I keep telling myself that I will be handsomely remunerated for my effort, that I should simply regard this work as a job, not a project, not a literary venture. I must confess that I felt aroused by the material at first, as I worked on the first two books, sometimes to the point of my having to pleasure myself before I could proceed. But eventually the "literature" turned me off entirely, or, rather, it stopped eliciting any sort of reaction in me, other than repugnance and tedium. I became weary of the crudeness of the language, its repetitiveness, its utter lack of artistry; bored with each narrative's reliance on an established set of fantasies, stereotypes, desires, performances, behaviors, drag disguises, and sexual positions. It all started to blend together, each book and main character becoming part of one single lifeless text. Frankly, and all modesty aside, I can do and have done better than the men in these stories. Sex can be raw and devoid of love, yes, but not devoid of imagination. And that's where this material fails, in its utter disregard for our creative spirit.

Still, I must plow along, reminding myself that this is only the first step, the dues I must pay in order to undertake more meaningful projects in the future. For I do love translating. I love the power it grants us to recast a given world into a different linguistic and cultural universe. The power to recreate, to infuse a text with new life: such is the magic of translation, isn't it, Camilo? Maybe I'll tackle Manuel Puig some day. Or Gertrude. What

*great fun that would be! I'm sure Gertie has been translated into Spanish
already (I'll have to look into this), but there is always room for the "definitive" translation by Yours Truly. "Una rosa es una rosa es una rosa..."*

Pallid yet handsome, Castel smiled. I offered him a beverage that he
accepted, as long as it was non-alcoholic. He had quit booze months
ago—a challenge when he went out to the bars and the parties, hence
Castel was also cutting down on his social outings to avoid having to
explain that mixing alcohol with his meds (a treatment for depression,
he said) could be lethal. He could use a snack, yes, but nothing elaborate, please; he just hadn't been very excited about eating lately. Or
about sex. What?! Yes, I'd heard right: Sex was sporadic and who cared.
His grandest pleasure these days was writing...

*Not very diligently, but at least I am trying—he said in another letter.
I no longer feel paralyzed by a numbness that restricts my every move, my
every thought. I feel and I think and I write. Finally! Not because I need
to or because it has to be done but simply because—I just do. Yes, there
are things that must be said and denounced, that must be changed in our
world. But that is not why I write.*

*I have recently realized that I begin to sound like the text I'm reading,
if it is one I love. Thus the shadow of Gertie is now cast between my mind
and the light from my lamp. As you know, I admire Stein a great deal. I feel
very much the way she does about many things. I love her interminable
sentences that seem to resound from the page. She has an innate sense of
rhythm, yet I have read that she wasn't fond of music. I suppose it shouldn't
surprise me. Writing is its own music—music apart or distinct from that
which is audible, yet with rhythm and color and, yes, also musicality.*

*This mimetic tendency of mine is natural, it seems, and one that most
writers share. In fact, now that I am familiar with Puig's work and, having
read your two novels, I can surely hear an echo of his voice in those books,
a certain directness in a style that is no less poetic for being direct. But of
course you've always been very honest about your artistic objectives, admitting your debt to Puig and other writers. As for own my inclination to
copy (or "borrow from," "pay homage to") the masters, it hasn't been—not
yet—a conscious process like yours. I hope it will all work itself out in the
end, as I seek my own voice and style. But I am not sure I'll ever manage to
do away with those long sentences...*

There he was again in his wicker throne (a chair I'd bought just for
him), under the skylight, beautiful as ever. He was reading Gertrude

Stein's *The Making of Americans*—a passage about a little boy who collected butterflies—while he listened to *Mame*. My gifted friend, submerged in Stein's seminal Modernist work and at the same time indulging in happy Broadway ditties.

But now I must force myself to take a break from Gertie to read Borges. "A mind-blowing trip," you called his stories in your usual jester-like manner, which I understand to be your way of bringing down to earth the stars of our literary firmament, humanizing them so people like me can approach them and maybe enjoy them, or at least learn from them. Oh but I find Borges much too complicated, too dense with references to his amazing readings. I am simply not as well read and foster little hope of ever becoming so. Something that astounds me is how dissimilar two writers from the same country can be, as I dare compare Borges to Puig. Two different trips, you would probably say. There are some elements that they share, mainly the context of the pampas and Argentine Spanish. But Manuel is more accessible without being less complex and thought-provoking. Do you agree with this assessment?

I am not giving up on Borges yet, though, the way I gave up on García Márquez after making my tortuous way through One Hundred Years of Solitude. *I plan to finish this book,* El Aleph, *and the other ones you recommended. By the way, thank you again for leading me to Puig's wonderful novel, which has in turn led me to the works he mentions as references in the footnotes, such as* Eros and Civilization *by Herbert Marcuse. And of course I want to read all of Puig's oeuvre. He is now one of my favorite novelists. And Julio Cortázar is next after Borges, along with Arenas and Lezama Lima and Juan Rulfo. The list is long, so, before I start feeling overwhelmed, I'll stick with Manuel for now.*

And speaking of Puig, one last comment, if I may. His novel has gotten me thinking about how complacent I have become, how oblivious to the things that used to mortify me. What fills me with a sense of shame is the fact that I am happy with my life at this point, for a change. I am working long hours and reading with a hunger I have never had; sometimes—I confess—taking time off from the books you put on my list to revisit the Modernists I love. I am occupied with work but also with thoughts about literature. And this is what bothers me: It is not a bad life for those who repress and comply, is it? Yet I should not feel ashamed of my happiness, no matter how much a byproduct of compliance and repression it might be, should I?

I told him there was no shame in being happy. Enjoy your work, your voracious reading—I said to him. Conjure up the fantasy of a musical while you delve into the best Latin American fiction. And if that literature doesn't evoke the right mood and thoughts for you, then forget Borges and Cortázar for now and indulge yourself, *querido amigo*. We all could use a little pampering now and then. So cuddle up with your good old friends Gertie, Joyce, Conrad, Faulkner, Fitzgerald, and Woolf. I know they're the writers you love, the ones who help you see your own reflection...

It seems that I am constantly resisting myself, Camilo. Fighting myself. Not to do any harm but because I have to be certain about the things I am thinking of. Particularly because I am dull-minded. That is not to say that I am stupid, just not as sharp as I would like to be. It takes me so long to react to things, to understand things—not in an abstract way but from deep inside my body and deep inside my head. I think that ultimately I do feel and understand things, but only after I have thought about them for a while. I talked to you about this issue when we last got together in Colina. It had to do with some song that was playing on the radio and that you immediately identified as "fusion," and how I marveled at how quickly you felt things and understood them and explained them. That is what I am getting at: You interpret things immediately. You are more tuned-in than I am.

Although you and I are of one mind in many respects, sharing thoughts and feelings that are true and deep within our souls, we nevertheless have different ways of valuing those things we see and feel. And as much as I admire that quality of immediacy and directness in you, I have realized that my sensibility is unlike your own. You have always been the one to make me think, though sometimes you torment me. But I see that this is the only way with people like myself. We are so impervious to feelings we are unfamiliar with, that we must necessarily have those feelings beaten into us in order for us to really experience them. But that is okay; the bruises eventually go away...

How could he think of himself as dull-minded? He, who happened to be one of the most brilliant people I'd ever known! Castel didn't do well with compliments but took my criticisms to heart. And I'd been harsh, insensitive with him at times, too impressed with my own opinions to realize I was hurting him. "You need to focus," I'd told him, as I'd told Ricci more than once. "You seem averse to following up on your projects. Desultory is the way I'd describe your approach to life, Castel. You must shed some of your baggage. All your issues with your mother, for instance. It's time you faced your feelings. Condemn or forgive your mamá and then get on with your life!" He was too kind and respectful to fight back; afraid, perhaps, of my reaction, or unsure as to the future of our friendship if he contested me. Yet how much stronger our bond would've been if he'd dared to confront me. *Thanks for your feedback on my messed up life*—I imagined him saying. *It's desultory, yes, I get that. But please cut the professor shit, drop the psychoanalytical crap. You, of all people, criticizing my baggage! Let's see, where should you start dealing with yours? Childhood abuse, fear of emotional intimacy, patricidal fantasies, an inability to trust anyone with your heart because it was savagely broken when you were a boy. Hah! You, criticizing me! You, whose middle name might as well be Sisyphus!*

If Castel had learned from me, I was also, in significant ways, a disciple of his. I was no quicker and no deeper than him in assessing and reacting to the things that truly mattered. Sure, I had access to a lengthy reading list, to the teachings of some scholars and the insights of some learned people, but "more" in this case wasn't necessarily more. And knowledge didn't always open a door to your soul.

Please forgive me for having stayed away, my sweet friend—he wrote. *But you require a great deal of energy, and it seems I've been running on empty of late. You require me to look within myself, an act that I prefer to avoid. Nevertheless, here I am, looking into my soul while Judy cries out about a man that got away. Her song speaks for me. It shows me stars without glitter, images written on walls, and thanks to La Garland I hear a languid melody that creates this moment...*

Only now did I realize that I had been dreaming, that Castel wasn't really sitting in his wicker throne but hovering over me like a ghost, a benign spirit who talked and sounded just like my friend, the specter my subconscious had created to help me deal with his absence. Once again I sought solace in his words, in his meandering thoughts and Gertie-like long sentences, in his charming repetitions. I found contentment in knowing that, when Castel wrote to me, he felt free...

Dear Camilo, it seems I should write my own name in beginning this missive. It does feel as though I am writing to myself. Sometimes I really am. But you understand all of that nonsense. I must admit that my thoughts have been fragmented lately; I wander and roam constantly. Forgive me if I ramble in this letter. It is so good to write to you! You know your way out of my labyrinths. You can make sense of my funk. What freedom I find in our friendship!

Yet that sense of freedom didn't prompt him to share with me the most life-threatening thing that ever befell him. Why didn't he tell me he was deathly ill? Did he think I'd judge him or be angry? Was Castel ashamed of his illness, of himself? *No, none of that, my love. I just assumed you knew.* Maybe he broke the news to me in his own way, and I didn't listen. Maybe I stupidly thought Castel was just being poetic, using his angst to fuel his creative impulse...

I have been thinking of you, my dear Camilo, needing to know that you are there. Somewhere. This has been a terrible month for me. No concrete reasons why. I just fell into a well of depression that I had not seen in quite a long time. I stumbled into it unwittingly. I am not quite sure what it is, not precisely. I only know that I spent the last week in bed, paralyzed with this despair that at times has me sobbing for no apparent reason. Only a couple of hours ago was I able to pull myself from the depths into which I had fallen. I bathed, fixed my hair and put on a pair of white linen pajamas that I had pressed rather nicely. The act of pressing them was relaxing, reassuring...

Here is something I wrote back in Hollywood that describes how I've felt the past few weeks... "Driving home last night after visiting a friend, I saw the moon through thick cloud cover. Its light was so muted. Other nights the moon is clear, brilliant. One feels its life and energy, an iridescent glow that holds you still, demanding, proudly, that you gaze at it. But this time it was hidden behind a death-like vapor, its life diffused. Now only a dull glimmer remained." And this is how I feel, diffused, suppressed, all my life force bottled-up and capped. Darkness insists on enveloping me, on suffocating me...

What I must do is to exorcise the demons that live within me. This was a suggestion of yours. Such sage advice! "Don't let your pain define you. Turn it into words instead." That is no easy task, particularly for me. I am too ordinary a person, too slow a mind to ever see the sunflowers that grow inside the dark caverns of a writer's mind. I know that very little grows in darkness and certainly not a flower. If I am pressed I might see how the ceiling of the cavern has eroded over millions of years, and how that erosion has produced an opening. I might see rain pouring through there and becoming a well, a pond, a lake, as life emerges from its depths. But I might see all of that only if I am pressed...

There is a silver lining to this process, Camilo, and it is the promise of catharsis that it brings, the prospect of expelling those obdurate demons. I live for the fulfillment of that promise, yet I know that my demons still lurk somewhere closely, waiting like a thorn that breaks the skin and multiplies, roots like myriad knives that cut and tear; like a virus, a cunning parasite that builds its house deep within you. I wouldn't feel this profound wistfulness, this melancholy if I had destroyed them. But I'll try to be better now. Dare I promise you I will be better? It is so difficult at times... The endless summer hurts, dwells in my eyes the way it always has, blinding me. I have resigned myself to living outside life.

I looked for Castel in my wedding album. There he was among all those friendly faces, tenuously emerging from the dark, through the verdant branches of a pine tree. Mischievous eyes in chiaroscuro, looking right at me, glowing. But it was an image that ultimately faded, leaving a void, a painful absence. His smile sank into the night. Castel was dying already when this photo was taken...

I revisited his poems as I listened to Judy, Billie, Edith, and Angela. Their sorcery brought him back momentarily, but there was no way out of the truth: Castel Romero had died in Mexico City the previous week. His sister Ana called with the news. She sounded broken, could barely speak or describe the cause of her brother's death. Castel had been sick with a virus lately, she said, and there were infections, complications, something to do with his immune system. He was in agony for the last month. His last wish: cremation, and the ashes to be guarded by his mother. A hard wish for a Catholic Mexican family, but it was what Castel wanted. Ana meant to call me sooner but couldn't. Sorry. The funeral was only for family. Sorry. It was Mamá's decision. *Lo siento mucho...*

I felt cold suddenly, freezing cold. I heard Castel's voice trying to break through the noise in my head, all that damn sobbing, so we could be together one last time. Yes, there was a semblance of my friend rising before me. He looked sad, or disappointed. Hard to tell what his expression conveyed. *Don't you believe my sister,* he said. *She lies. Ana will tell you I'm dead but I am not. Part of me is still here, mi amor. Still alive.* How was I to know you were going to Mexico to die? *I didn't know it myself.* I would've been there with you! *And you were. I felt you there.* Thank you for telling me that. *You will be glad to know that my mother never left my side.* You must've been grateful for her care. *I was, yes, and also sad for the suffering I caused her. But she denied me my friends! "Mala compañía," she called them. Bad company. Unwilling to accept my gay soul, she blamed you all for my illness.* She was the target of your ire, wasn't she? She became the archetypal Madre Tierra at your deathbed yet for too long she was the Terrible Mother. Still, I wonder if, in the end, you granted her a moment of reconciliation, if not forgiveness. *Don't worry, Camilo. I made sure she heard what she needed to hear; among other loving things, that I was grateful to her for teaching me Spanish. And for having kept me with her after I was born and for telling me she loved me. She could have given me up but she didn't. I was never tossed aside, never treated like an unwanted thing, a mistake. I said to her, "Te quiero, Mamá," right before we said goodbye. It was the first and last time I would say those words to her...*

The truth. How could I accept it? How could I face the fact that I'd never see Castel again? *No need for tears, Camilo. Here, touch my heart. See? It isn't made of glass. You should go now, my friend. I must refuse this vision. Fine. But I have a question for you.* What is it, Castelín? *Have you managed to develop a taste for my beloved Gertrude?* No, I'm still getting lost in the repetition, looking for the story, resisting the spell. I'm sorry. *Oh, that's all right. I believe we are even, Señor Gabosopher. I love you, Castel. And I love you, but let us not be sad. You know where you can always find me.*

He placed a ring on my finger. It was a jade stone encased in massive golden roots. The trunk of a tree formed the hoop, which caressed the skin. Then Príncipe Romero brought his warm lips to my face. He kissed me softly and whispered... *See you in the forest.*

THE IMAGINARY ISLAND

The condo got too small for us. We couldn't fit our married life into it. Colina had offered me the niche I needed after Kansas, but it was time to leave. Susan had seriously considered only one of several job offers, a tenure-track position at Forbes University in Pittsburgh. She would be teaching Latino fiction with lots of support for research. The profs there had no problem with a Gringa from Kansas discussing the politics and performances of ethnicity. But neither one of us was excited about living on the East Coast, and Susan didn't want to join the rat race just yet. Her profs in Alton were urging her to take the job and become the academic star she was meant to be. If she waited too long to enter the field, they warned, she ran the risk of not being marketable when she decided to go to work. But we knew that a research-oriented post would devour Susan's time and energy and keep her away from the baby (or babies!) we hoped to have. She didn't want to feel torn, exhausted. So to hell with academia, she said, but just for now. And in the meantime, we could count on my Reader Series to keep us afloat.

We started thinking of northern New Mexico, dreaming of a modest adobe house surrounded by leafy trees and mountains; ideally, a home in Las Cumbres, a town cradled in the Jémez Mountains, forty-four miles north of Santa Fe. The town was peopled mostly by commuters who worked in neighboring cities. Fairly small (pop. 11,500), Las Cumbres offered all the charm of Santa Fe but none of its tourism. It had a plaza with a fountain, circled by a lush row of aspens, and the usual amenities: a grocery store, a movie theater, a couple of down-home restaurants that served some of the best green chili in northern New

Mexico, a clinic, a pre-school, a primary school, and two parks with playground equipment. A handful of artists lived in Las Cumbres, those fleeing the overcrowded Taos art scene, but also teachers and doctors and other professionals. Living in the Southwest and away from the ocean would be a stretch for me, the beach-bound islander, the Califusa near-native, but I had found a certain peace in those quiet forests. There was a welcoming presence there, a feeling of home. The ocean called to me but not always for the right reasons or at the best of times. The sea enveloped me yet stripped me. The mountains enveloped me too, but I felt free under their mantle. And happy. And alive.

Before long we found a house on a paved street named Ponderosa, all adobe and spacious enough for us. It had a large living area on the first floor with magnificent picture windows, and two bedrooms up- stairs. In the backyard there was a small forest of pine trees and scat- tered aspens, a gazebo, and the canyon, San Ildefonso Canyon, not far beyond. We rented with the option of buying eventually. There were several families with children on our street; the moms and the kids (very seldom the dads) hung out most mornings at Pinocchio Park, a playground with safe equipment for toddlers. They also liked Estanque Park in the central part of town, which had a pond with friendly ducks that the little ones loved to feed crackers to. We enjoyed imagining our children playing in those parks some day...

We hiked the Las Conchas trails on occasion, and I combined that with some jogging too. We loved the silence, the greenness all around us, the perfume of pine. During one of those hikes, Susan told me there was a certain image that had been recurring in her dreams, that of a pulsating clot. "That's what I feel inside," she said, "a speck containing life." She smiled, hugged me, and thus she broke the news to me: We were pregnant! Nothing as basic, no bigger mystery, this tiny heart that was beating within her, the blueprint of a person in search of a home; someone who'd call us Mommy and Papá.

We decided to find out the baby's gender (we were having a girl!) so we could pick a name and start getting used to it. Our short list includ- ed Nadya, Maya, and Karina. Our initial idea was naming the baby after my mother, but Mami was dead set against it. "One Mercedes in the family is plenty," she said. "Besides, your daughter deserves a prettier name." And the prettiest one was *Nadya*.

I was there when Nadya came into the world; saw her curly black hair first, then her eyes looking up at me just minutes after delivery. We thought she had Papá's face (poor baby) and Mommy's long legs (I hoped). Susan didn't endure a drawn-out labor; it was all over in forty-five minutes. She did great, "like a sturdy Kansas breeder," she bragged, feeling exhausted but thrilled, and so fortunate. We had a great new truth, our beautiful daughter! I was drawn to Nadya's skin, soft, un-blemished, a dark shade of rose; to her smell and the sounds she made. I loved having her sleep in my arms as I sang to her. I used to read in the morning, but mornings were suddenly nonexistent. Time became amorphous, evenings blending into dawn, our only guide being the in-tensity or absence of light. It was liberating.

There were changes in Nadya's features that we noticed daily. Her nose was nubby like mine at first, but then it began to look pointy like Susan's. She had a powerful little mouth that seemed to be getting stronger and more demanding by the minute. Mommy was having a hard time feeding Nadya; it hurt when the baby latched on. So we de-cided to alternate bottle (Susan's milk) with breast. This way Mommy got a break, and Papá got in on the nurturing action. I loved it.

Mechy spent two weeks with us right after Nadya was born. A big help. (Liz, on the other hand, had to be told that she *needed* to come see her granddaughter before she made plans to visit.) Mami was happy for us but also upset about our decision to settle in New Mexico. She couldn't believe we weren't closer to her in California. She wanted to be part of Nadya's life, and I did want Nadya to have her *abuela* around as she grew up. But I also wished to do my child-rearing thing with Susan, our way, far from malls and freeways and *telenovelas*; far from the Land of Oz too, from its bigotry and its flatness; and with the Ivory Tower nowhere in sight, for if Susan had been employed as a prof then, she would've been sequestered by her tenure committee and denied access to her offspring.

We spoke to Nadya normally, no baby talk, having agreed that Mom-my would be the English speaker of the family, and I'd be in charge of *español*. I'd pretend I didn't speak English, so, by the time Nadya fig-ured out the truth, Spanish would feel natural to her, and it'd be Papá's language (or "voice," what she'd end up calling my native tongue.) This process was to take persistence and discipline. Everywhere the domi-nant culture would endeavor to snatch Nadya from me. *You're in Amer-*

ica! Speak English! I had to be strong, never cave. Spanish was my gift to Nadya—the best one I could give her.

I had no tormenting dreams for about a year after our daughter was born. Had the sleep of parental exhaustion killed my demons? I'd expected nights filled with images of my child, with her sounds, her crying, her games, with fantastic stories that would assuage my fear of losing Nadya. But there was nothing. For the first time ever I was enjoying restful nights. I faced this fear during my waking hours instead, coping with my anxiety by telling myself, No, nothing bad will ever happen to our daughter. She's safe with us. And she'll always be a part of my life...

Some of our friends visited us frequently during the time we lived in New Mexico, Jenn and Alina more than anyone else. Alina loved our skies, our honey-drenched sopaipillas, the silly guffaws we still indulged in, and most of all playing with Nadya. I got a kick out of seeing her running with the baby all over the house and the backyard, pretending to be a bunny, a piggy, a mermaid. She and Susan seemed at ease with each other, like good friends. Which they were, or would be eventually.

Susan connected with other mothers of small children in Las Cumbres. They got together once in a while and shared concerns, anecdotes, discoveries about their kids. Susan was lucky to be part of that group. I envied her. The first time she was invited to a Mom-and-baby brunch, she asked the woman who was hosting the gathering if I could attend. "Well," the hostess hemmed and hawed and then said, "I don't think he'd fit in." Susan didn't insist; she knew that the other moms wouldn't feel relaxed having me around. In their view, men didn't bond that way. And they weren't supposed to.

Most of the families we knew were very traditional with regard to child rearing. They were progressive folks for the most part, except in the Baby Department; that's where all liberal thinking stopped. The recurring scene had Mom looking after the kids while Dad earned a living, and it was Mom who was expected to give up her career to be a caretaker. Before Nadya was born, I envisioned a tight-knit community of both women and men who loved being nurturing parents. But such a village didn't exist, not for the men. How uneasy they seemed when I brought up Nadya's colds, teeth, first words! They looked at me condescendingly or tried to change the subject to something more dignified, such as politics, work, cars, or humor. Politics: *What does getting a blowjob have to do with a president's ability to run a country?!* Work: *My job isn't ideal, but I feel I'm making an important contribution.* Sports: *You don't watch the Super Bowl?!* Cars: *Have you heard of the Prius? It's the first hybrid car for the general public.* Humor: *The president lost weight; now he can see his intern!* Some of those dudes actually boasted about never having changed a diaper. And there was that engineer who said to me, "I can't relate to what you're saying, man. You should talk to my wife!"

If the families in that town were representative of society at large, then we were stuck with all those pictures of Mommy with Baby in parenting magazines. Apparently, those publications depicted reality. We stay-at-home dads didn't get our picture taken because, according to Mother Nature, we didn't exist. In most situations having to do with our daughter, if both Susan and I were present, people would only address her. So I ended up feeling erased. The looks of surprise Nadya's doctor and nurses gave me! Because I was there for every appointment, asking questions and involving myself in my daughter's health and well-being. It took time and resolve on my part to get our pediatrician to accept me. I don't think she ever did completely.

We felt like we'd joined a Stepford society, a world strictly divided into fathers and mothers, breadwinners and housewives. There had to be great comfort in those roles, or people wouldn't be falling that easily into them. Susan and I questioned such models, laughed at them, took pride in each of us being both mother and father to our child. But even within the liberal circles we frequented, our gender-bending approach to parenting was seen as an aberration, at best an intellectual project that was bound to fail because it had nothing to do with the Truth of Nature. And this truth was clearly evident in the way children behaved when they played. We'd observed that most of the girls who were Nadya's pre-school and neighbor *amiguitas* built lavish scenarios, homes, families, and lush gardens. They weren't driven by conquest and bloodshed. The older ones were gifted storytellers, readily able to enjoy flights of imagination. They weren't as motivated by competition as the boys nor were they interested in gadgets and machines. Some of their games were based on fairy tales, with the usual set of archetypes (gallant princes, lovely maidens, ogres), but those games didn't depend on weaponry to be played.

Boys, on the other hand, were prone to impose their authority by force and dominate their environment. They lacked patience to observe the world, wanting to rule it instead. The youngest boys we knew were barely one, but there were five year olds among this group of neighbor kids, and many of them felt drawn to action heroes, to weapons and fighting. *You're dead! I killed you!* Their ludic space was infested with explosives, with warriors and lethal enemies that had to be crushed. *No way, I killed you first! Die now!* It was easy to see those male children as men-in-training, preparing to embody the qualities that society celebrated in their gender: competitiveness, aggression, self-centeredness, a fascination with machines, total disdain for domestic chores and child rearing, and a tendency to belittle the "weaker" members of society. Considering that our world had been ruled forever by the male principle those boys embodied, Susan and I wondered how the species had managed to still be around. No doubt we owed our survival to the female principle.

There were exceptions, of course. Among the girls, the "tomboy," and among the boys, the "sissy." Children who, unbeknownst to them, were rebelling. Children who didn't fit into any mold. And there were those who showed traits of both genders, who related to the world as both "male" and "female." Ambiguous creatures. Too few of them, it seemed, to spawn a genetic mutant, a welcome anomaly that would point to a third sex. Maybe some distant day, we thought.

Where did Nadya fit in? What were the inclinations we could already detect in her character? She was of a curious nature, assertive, a tad bossy. She tended to demand realism from the world she was discovering but was fond of fairy tales and fantasy as well. Nadya could roughhouse like boys yet loved princesses, pretty dresses, and uberfeminine mermaids. And she wanted to know about machines. How did they work? What made them go? How could a heavy object fly? We had to be watchful not to overanalyze our daughter's behavior and turn her into a case study, in hopes that she'd grow up to become the person we dreamed of creating, the person we both wished we could be. Yes, Nadya was a precocious little girl, but she was also and primarily a two-year-old child.

Before I became a parent, I used to believe that gender roles stemmed solely from social conditioning, how we trained children from an early age, what we expected from them, the actions and attitudes we rewarded, and those we punished. Then I came to accept the biological truth that seemed to determine our conduct to some extent: hormones, genes, and the brain of our cave-dwelling ancestors. We were cursed by that brain, which evidently propelled the male of our species toward warfare and violence, and the female toward domesticity. Faced with this reality, Susan and I clung to the exceptions, aware of the fact that human society tended to discourage ambivalent bodies *and* identities, that it wanted things cut-and-dried. Any signs of crossover were nipped at birth or punished by law. Hybrid first-borns had to be turned into "normal" boys and girls because they were a danger to humanity. Yet our planet overflew with gender-bending creatures! I pictured Mother Nature laughing at us, these foolish humans who thought they could bend her will; our grande dame wreaking havoc on our best intentions. The hell with her! We would keep trying to subvert it, or at least distract it, catch it off guard. Nothing could be done about the past, but we were eager to imagine for Nadya a world without gender or race distinctions, without bigotry and wars. No more warriors and killing machines. No more bloodshed. We wanted Nadya's life to tell a nonviolent story, to be safe from the future.

Ah, yes, the future. The temptation to think ahead is too great for a parent to resist. But I wasn't ready to go there yet, not keen on the idea of a time when I'd no longer be Nadya's source of comfort, when she stopped seeking my answers, my stories, my knowledge. Couldn't envision the landscapes of her life as inaccessible to me, when Papá was the past, when he was dead. I kept telling myself that I had a huge job to do for now, one that made me immensely happy; telling myself I'd be wise to cherish it, because every moment I was spending with Nadya was all I could count on.

The age gap between us was wide but no obstacle to our friendship. We played hide-and-seek and other games we invented. I fed her frequently, or sat with her when she ate, overseeing her attempts at feeding herself. In her room, she offered me exquisite dishes: macaroni sandwiches, black bean soup like the one her Abuela made, but poured over tofu pancakes; peanut butter ice cream; and *café cubano* that she brewed in a yellow plastic pot (she hated the real stuff; to her it smelled dark and sour) and served me in a fancy porcelain demitasse—another one of her grandmother's many presents. Coffee made me happy and giggly, and Nadya loved to see me act that way.

We had a daily repertoire of music, songs that she'd inspired me to write and that I sang to her every night. She favored those with the word "baby" in them and songs with catchy, tropical melodies and fun refrains that included the word *Cuba*: the part where she usually joined in. And most of all Nadya loved the stories I told her. The tales used to feature her dolls and toys, and characters from her favorite books. There were teddy bears, cotton-candy clouds, flying carpets, genies, fairies, and singing mermaids. Then, unexpected creatures started showing up, and I found myself weaving entirely new tales with Nadya's help. In some versions she'd be the main character, a heroine whose escapades took her to the skies like a *sinsonte*, up the highest trees like a monkey, or deep into the chipmunks' dwellings. But she preferred the stories where she had a partner in her adventures, a boy named Lito who lived on a beautiful island called Cuba. He was a child with the mind of a grown-up who knew what Nadya wanted to see and hear. And she felt safe with him.

Lito and Nadya liked to go to the park, which was right smack in the middle of his backyard. The park had nicely trimmed grass and a playground and a shallow pool covered in ivy. They loved that pool. They made ripples in the water and looked at the many-colored fish. The fish were friendly; Nadya and Lito liked to hold them, but only for a very short time because the fish could only breathe in the water. Lito had a pig named Fili, chickens, some crazy lizards, and lots of pigeons in his backyard. The pigeons lived in a large birdhouse on the patio; it was fun to peek in through the round doors of the house to see their nests and tiny eggs. The birds emitted a sweet sound, *zunzunzun*, and Lito and Nadya knew the pigeons were saying *¡Buenos días!* in their language. How nice it was to wake up to that *zunzunzun* in the morning! A cheery whisper to start the day. And there were other sounds they enjoyed, like the peddlers' shouts, "Fresh sugar cane!" "Ice for sale!" "I buy bottles!," and the voice of the woman who ran the *bodega* on the corner. Lito liked her because she gave them *raspadura* candy. Nadya liked her because she spoke with the pretty words of songs and reminded her of Mercedes, her grandma. And they both loved the woman's voice because it made them feel welcome.

The beach, called Varadero, was just a short walk from Lito's house, so they went there every day. Nadya always noticed the water's light blue-green color and the starfish at the bottom. The waves were gentle sometimes and sometimes like angry giants. The two friends enjoyed swimming, but they didn't spend all their time in the water. They also went exploring, looking for crabs under rocks, and they visited the cavern in the cliffs at the end of the shore. Nadya and Lito would never go in too far; they stayed by the mouth of the cave, watching the water turn from a deep blue to an incandescent gold. They pretended that the cavern was someone's secret home, and that those shapes carved into the walls were chairs, tables, a bed, all made by nature for that person. Once they saw a human face on a cavern wall! It was a boy's face with big sad eyes, a tiny mouth, curls, and he was staring at them! To Nadya and Lito he looked like the spitting image of themselves, combined into one. A fantastic discovery, this boy who lived inside the rock, his whole little body made of stone. They wondered how he'd gotten there. Was he the victim of an evil spell? Oh how they wished they could help him, pulling him out of the rock and back to life! But the boy wouldn't speak; he just kept looking at them, staring and staring...

Lito and Nadya decided to come back now and then and keep the boy company for a little while each visit. Maybe this place was his home, and he couldn't leave it because he was stuck in the wall. But he could have friends over, couldn't he? So that was their decision: they would be the boy's friend. And then he wouldn't be lonely and maybe would be happier. They might throw a party for him and invite all their animal friends, and the animals would teach the boy to laugh.

Oh, Nadya's sweet words! A daily discovery Susan and I treasured, a language that was always reborn. I remembered the stories Alina used to tell me about Leah. Sometimes I'd wonder if she was spicing them up, adding her own magic. But now I knew she wasn't. I knew better thanks to Nadya...

She had just turned three when she cried out one evening, excited, looking up at the sky, "So many lights, Papá!" I told her that those specks of light were stars, and that they were actually made of fire. Nadya couldn't believe it. "Fire, Papá?!" she asked. I said, "Yes, like the sun." And she was surprised to learn that the sun was a star, too. "The sun gives us light and warmth," I told her, and Nadya was worried now: "So the stars can burn you, Papá?" I tried to reassure her, "Yes, but only if you go near them." She smiled and said, "Then we'll just watch them from here, okay?" A brilliant idea!

She complained to her Mommy that her eyes didn't get any rest. "They look and look all the time," she said. Susan told her that her eyes got to rest when she slept. To which Nadya reacted, "No, Mommy. They see more things when I sleep." Then Susan explained that those things Nadya saw in her sleep were called dreams, "When you sleep, you dream. We all do." But Nadya was still concerned, "Oh, Mommy, my poor little eyes. They work all the time!"

We were enjoying a warm, sunny morning on our backyard one day when, suddenly, Nadya turned to me and asked, "Papá, is our home this house?"

"Not just this house," I replied. "Home is also that other place we visit sometimes. Our island, remember? Where there's a forest of palm trees and a beach..."

"Yes, yes, Papá, it's the Cuba island. But that place is pretend."

"It's both pretend and real. If you can see it when you close your eyes, then it's real for you."

"I like our island, Papá... It has birds, trees, and a cute little monkey!"

"What else? Are there butterflies?"

"Yes, and chipmunks and a pig that smiles at me."

"What else?"

"A beach with little crabs under the rocks. Oh and there's a mermaid and she's like the princess of this island and she kind of looks like me, kind of, maybe a little."

"Maybe she's your sister."

"Can I swim with her?"

"You bet. But don't go in too deep!"

"I won't, Papá."

"*Gracias, mi niña.*"

Mermaids populated Nadya's world. She loved to be told about them, draw them, impersonate them. The print version of Disney's *Little Mermaid* was our nightly story; Susan and I started reading it to her when she was only weeks old. Nadya's little arms would flail excitedly while her eyes feasted on the bright carmine of Ariel's hair, on her turquoise tail. Eventually our daughter began to request her favorite scenes. "The good part, Mommy, please!" she'd say, and Susan would read about Ariel saving prince Erik. "Ursula, please, Papá!" and I'd sing the octopus' song about poor souls.

Through all the storytelling about mermaids I had to repress my own vision of those creatures, careful not to ruin Nadya's fantasy by telling her how I imagined them: with slithery skin, fangs, nails as sharp as scalpels; and gills protruding from their bulky, creased necks. My mermaids were beasts who survived by eating each other and who'd eat us all if they had the chance. They were more like the ones in *Peter Pan*, nothing like the humanoid characters in Hans Christian Andersen's tragic tale, even less did they resemble the romantic Ariel. Mermaids, I thought, were beings we willed into existence, like fairies and ghosts and time travelers. For some reason we needed to believe in them. Carnal yet angelic, they held the mystery of life, which began in the sea. They lulled us with their tempting voices, summoned us, deceived us. And yet we kept hoping to hear them.

Nadya would never know of the childhood nightmare I turned into fiction: the Merman of the Depths, a winged demon who flapped its wings like a crazed crow; who demanded abnegation, coveting our souls. The archetype had gotten passed on, although in Nadya's universe it had become benign and tender and lovely. With a little help from Mr. Disney, she had succeeded in transforming my monster—a wicked merman who'd imprisoned a little boy for eternity—into a marine angel. Good for her! Good that she could believe in Ariel's beauty and kindness and pure voice. Some day she might have issues with the character's plight, might question why Ariel had to give up her world to be with the man she loved. Or possibly she'd see in Ariel an empowered young woman like herself. After all, it was the mermaid who saved the man of her story from a shipwreck. As it was meant to be!

EYES INSIDE

That morning we found the perfect spot by the stream and under a pine tree at Las Conchas, one of our favorite campgrounds. Nadya was excited about our picnic, as usual. She wanted to taste it all, chew it all. Forget her own food! She'd rather savor our baked corn chips, our Caesar-salad wraps, the grass and flowers and leaves around us, the tree bark, the ants making their way to our basket. The tasty stuff. I watched her play and explore, and I thought about Castel... He was supposed to come back to those hills, his forest of echoes, but he never did. I suspect he thought that our quality time together wouldn't be possible anymore, not with my family in the picture. And then he just...ran out of time.

Susan knew I loved Castel, and she respected that love. She understood he was like a brother to me. And Castel admired Susan, maybe even liked her. But he also resented my wife, for she had access to a part of me that he'd never know. This is no ego trip (not about this), but a truth I've had to accept: In an ideal world, Castel and I would've progressed to something bigger that included friendship but also sex and a home and commitment and...? He wanted it so. *We could be very happy together,* he said to me once. I wish things could've turned out that way. Maybe he would still be here...

I needed to get off that train of thought, recapture my fatherly mood so I could enjoy our picnic. As always, Nadya was doing her best to bring me back to her neck of the woods, the magical forest she'd been inhabiting for the last twenty minutes. Susan had already finished off her wrap, and I was almost done with mine when I saw a woman approaching. She had obviously been hiking and now moved briskly toward the campground and the parking lot. The sight of my family distracted her; she greeted us, smiling. She had a wrinkled face yet seemed almost young in tight-fitting blue jeans, a leather belt as worn as her forehead, and a canvas bag hanging from her shoulder. She took off the baseball cap she wore, freeing a mane of graying hair, and told us that her name was Margaret. I introduced myself and my family. "What an adorable baby girl," she noted. "And she has such a beautiful name! Nadya. I like that. I have three girls myself, all married." Margaret paused. "I'm a writer," she said then. "And it sure was hard to work when my children were that young."

I told her I could relate. "I write for a living."

Her face beamed. "Wow," she exclaimed, "this is what I'd call a fortuitous encounter!"

"No kidding," I said, though it wasn't really. New Mexico is chock full of writers and artists.

She sat by me in sudden camaraderie. "There's something I know about you," she announced.

I played along, "You do?"

"Yes, I know that you'd rather spend time with your daughter than write, true?"

"True. But I also know that I must work."

"We certainly must. That's our predicament as parents."

Excitedly, Margaret handed me a bookmark of pressed flowers. "I make lots of them," she informed me. "It's a hobby of mine." I thanked her and said it was beautiful. She gave one to Susan, who was too busy looking after Nadya to be sociable. "And this here," she went on, searching her bag, "this is my latest." She placed a battered manuscript in my hands. "A murder mystery set in Taos. Based on a true story, but of course I changed a few things. Worked on it for two years."

I did a flip read, enough to see that it was well-crafted writing, and returned the copy to her. "Congratulations," I said. "It's exciting to finish a project, isn't it?" And now I heard myself offering too much personal info: where I was from, what I wrote about. Out of character but not surprising because I, too, knew something about Margaret. I knew about one of her passions. Her career, I'd soon find out, consisted of three unpublished novels (one under her arm) and two self-published books about the flora of northern New Mexico. She was known in small circles but dreamed of a mass audience.

"I've heard of a novelist whose name escapes me," she said, laughing. "He published his first bestseller at the age of eighty. So I figure if I'm that lucky, I've got fifteen years to go!"

A storm was brewing, too real to be just a symbolic backdrop. The aspens would soon cease to be our sanctuary. Why hadn't we checked the forecast?! We needed to go but Margaret wouldn't let us; she couldn't hear my daughter's cries, my wife's plea. She couldn't detect my tedium as I heard, again, the same old words on the writing life. It was about the sacrifices and the joy of it all. Margaret had a story to tell, a bone to pick, and I was to be the mediator between the storm and her dreams. But I wouldn't listen anymore. I had to beat the storm and get us home! She followed me, tried to help me load the car. Behind the wheel at last, I described Margaret to myself in uninspired poetry...as longing incarnate, windswept roads, the meaning of a certain hunger. Her manuscript fell on my lap. "I'd love your feedback if you could make the time," she said. "My number's on the title page." I thanked her again, "Sure, I'll call you when I read it." And now I could focus on bringing my family to safety—a valid reason to flee the writer's dream, wrinkled and spent yet alive, much too familiar.

My own version of that dream started long before *Cuba in Silence* but came into its own with that novel. The young man who wrote it was too ingenuous, obsessed with intellectual games and intertextual puzzles and subversive discourses on sexuality. What else could be expected from a literature student overdosing on Cortázar's mind trips, on García Márquez's palimpsests and Puig's pop-culture bricolages? Yet those writers, too, had their own revered predecessors. There wouldn't be a Cortázar without a Borges, and Márquez wouldn't have written his magnum opus without William Faulkner. Puig admitted his debt to film director Jacques Tourneur. And even Shakespeare felt burdened by the literary weight of Christopher Marlowe! We are living proof of Harold Bloom's theory; we all suffer from anxiety of influence. Call it what you will—cribbing, borrowing—or define it with a fancy term like intertextuality, you can't escape it. In order to create, a writer must first resign himself to not being original, then learn to live with the truth: Ain't nothing absolutely new.

I suspect that deep within *Cuba in Silence* there's the seed of a more profound book. Is it good literature? Some academic critics thought so, but the majority of them—in journals like *Revista Iberoamericana* and *Chasqui*—had a hard time finding the right box for my work. Was it American, Latin American, Cuban or Cuban-American literature? Should it be part of the ethnic or the exile canon? The reviewers rambled on about this issue, seemingly unable to assess the artistic and historical value of the book. Yet perhaps my novel's value lies precisely in its resistance to be categorized!

Should I never have published *Cuba in Silence*? Don't know. That book had one main reason for existing, and it was fully realized. It saved me. But what did it save me from, exactly? A meltdown, ennui, depression, or perhaps the terror of being "outed" as the impostor of a scholar—all those questions I couldn't answer in Sofía's classes, making a total ass of myself while Alina shone in all her discursive brilliance. Intellectual insecurity, that's it, my novel saved me from death by insecurity.

No, let's be poetic and say it was my demons, even though demons can't be exorcised through writing. That's the task of a fool, like hoping to be pardoned in confession. Say twenty Hail Marys and you're forgiven. Easy enough, right? I used to tell my friends who were in crisis, "Write about it." Why couldn't I see that written words would be like salt in the proverbial wound? I should've listened to those friends, should've offered them my empathy—my heart!—instead of some hollow advice. Writing, after all, doesn't kill demons; it only tames them. Patient and persistent, many of them will end up as memories, in spite of the crowds in your head. They'll wait a lifetime if that's what it takes for you to listen, for you to acknowledge their right to have a home. Demons or angels, your mind can't tell them apart. Your beggar heart can't be a chooser. You'll take whatever guise they wear, friend or foe, and seek the perfect turn of phrase to infuse them with life. You and they are bound together, for better or worse, all linked by fortuitous experiences: the day you saw a familiar face or felt possessed by an image or a memory. When you hated yourself for being selfish, cruel, blind to the suffering of others. When you recalled the love betrayed, the friends forgotten, the words that used your voice as a weapon.

Writing never heals in the present, anyway. It takes years. Time is a better cure, the only one that delivers. Time is the true god, the only maker of a poem. Pass the so-called test of time and you're a survivor.

Fail the test and give up access to history, insight into the myth of who you are, a glimpse of immortality. Fail the test and you might as well never have existed.

Sometimes I wish I'd failed the test. Damn the characters (demons *and* angels) who live within me, these parasites! The carcasses of time, decrepit runners. Which ones shall find refuge in my words? Who deserves more than a passing mention? I'm not a fool. I know I'll never exorcise them. All I can do is try to keep track of the casualties (though they might be too many); among them a boy in grade school whom I didn't defend from a pack of wolves, an old man in a clinic whom I didn't save from a fall, the street musicians in a Mexican zócalo who begged me for a smile, not just a handful of pesos; the crippled woman, a peddler of rhymes who dragged herself in my direction, and whose eyes I didn't meet. And last but certainly not least, my father's frail and dying body, which terrified me.

Papi again and always, inevitably. When did he and I become enemies? The first time I refused to play a ball game with him, perhaps, or long before he and I were born. Did I embrace the tenets of Marxism to spite him? Elio witnessed, in sheer horror, my transformations. I turned into a Castro apologist, a U.S.-bashing liberal fond of spouting truths that were in vogue in academic circles (some of them unquestionable truths, I admit); a left-leaning professor who sided with the underdogs, those who, according to Elio, were inferior minorities. And Papi kept holding onto his resentment, some of which was justified, yes, for the abuse he suffered at the hands of his compatriots could never be forgotten, let alone forgiven. But what about the abuse Mami endured because of him? I escaped his dictatorship, but she didn't. There must've been something she found worth protecting (her status? a home for her child?) and for which she was willing to remain submissive whenever he stepped on her. She loved him, I'm sure, but she had to pay too high a price for that love. Why did she? Do I dare ask her?

Elio taught me that the world was clear-cut. There were the evil, soulless communists, and there were the humane, superior Americans. On one side the normal folks, all decent, clean, law-abiding heterosexuals; and on the other the deviants, *maricones*, *tortilleras*, hippies. There were the blacks, *los negros de mierda*, and above them the whites, again, all superior. But my father's lessons didn't prepare me for the world I was to discover. None of it humanized my heart. I wish there was something in his life, his actions, in his beliefs that I'd be willing to share with my daughter. Something to pass on.

How about this: Manolo was true to himself. I suppose there's a lesson there, one Papi wanted to teach me. Never waver. Never abdicate. You hold the truth, and the rest of the world is just confused, nonsensical. But how do you get to be that sure of your credo? Are some people born with such self-confidence? It's obviously a trait I didn't inherit, and not what I'm seeking, anyway. There has to be a more notable legacy, a single belief that could make my father admirable in the eyes of his descendants. Perhaps it's his conviction that you must do the right thing by your loved ones, *lo correcto*, whatever sacrifice that takes. I admit I've wanted to be like him in that respect, not always succeeding at it.

Still, I'm pressed to find a bigger truth in Papi, his most valuable gift to me, and I think I can name it at last: Elio believed in freedom. Too big of a word, *libertad*, so let's say instead that he wanted his son to live in a world where he had choices, where ideology wasn't a mandate and dogma didn't curtail his chances for success and growth. For happiness. Yes, that's what my daughter needs to hear.

Elio would've hated Alina, had he known her for real and not just as an *hembra guitarra*; had he known that she spoke to me of class struggle, of the evils of socioeconomic inequality; that she helped me understand the plight of *los de abajo*, the underdogs for whom a revolution is sometimes the only hope for change. Why did Alina pursue my friendship? Did she see in me the person I could potentially become? In those days I was an anti-Castro *gusano* and she a Marxist, a pro-independence Puerto Rican who admired the Cuban Revolution. I didn't like her at first, and not just for political reasons. Alina embodied the archetypical Caribbean female. I couldn't fathom that there was no split between the outer self and the essence of Alina. She was both brilliant and beautiful, a whole person.

It was Sofía Varela who gave me the tools (a framework, she called it) to apply Marxist thought: *Dialectical materialism is the road to truth.* But it was Alina who made it all seem true by describing the abuses she'd witnessed in her colonized country; the case of her nephew, drafted by the U.S. army along with thousands of other young Puerto Rican men and killed in Vietnam. Or the fact, now painfully evident to me, that my maternal grandparents saw the Cuban Revolution as the light at the end of the tunnel after a lifetime of hard, poorly paid peasant work and hunger and humiliation. They would no longer be exploited by the middle class and the filthy rich elite. Matilde and Mariano, people whom my father detested, had found in Castro's ideals a source of meaning and community. An identity.

I wonder how much of the change I underwent in Alton had to do with my rejection of Papi, to what extent my "conversion" in the hands of Alina Sotovélez and Sofía Varela was simply, arguably, my path to separation from my father. That rejection was part of it, no doubt. But there was also a genuine quest in me. I knew that Alina and Sofía had an enlightened view on many issues, and I wanted to see the world through their intelligent, empathetic eyes. Ideology became incarnate in Alina's voice. Through her I discovered Fidel's infamous "Words to the Intellectuals," a speech from 1961 whose key message can be summarized in one phrase: *Within the Revolution, everything. Outside the Revolution, nothing.* Thus Alina and I explored the role of the artist within a socialist process; rather ingenuously, we both can see now, for you can't tell an artist—anyone!—what to think and feel and dream.

"There's a critical period," had said Alina, "that will eventually abate. During that period, the role of the artist will be clear and prescribed by the State. But a time will come with a larger scope for artistic expression, when there won't be a pressing need to change the attitudes of workers, peasants, intellectuals. The revolutionary process moves toward a transformation of society that will result in the elimination of all class systems, and that process is the Revolution's crowning achievement. Once that goal is realized, the artist will enjoy more freedom. She or he will be less obligated to work at the political and collective levels. Her contribution won't be 'forced,' if indeed it was forced before..."

Together we dreamed of a better world. We lauded Cuba's achievements and wished the same for Puerto Rico. And, years later, we suffered the pain of disillusionment when the *Revolución cubana* turned into dogma, when it was gradually unveiled as a dangerous invention, the project of a young lawyer named Fidel Castro Ruz. The Revolution of 1959, like all such events, had been led by men, and men will inevitably succumb to their hunger for power. Cuba, in Fidel's hands, became the farce of an epic world that allowed no private quests, where national tenets couldn't be challenged and hegemonic truths would never be subverted. In that world, all basic human needs were met, and most questions were answered with promises. And dissidence was a crime.

One day, lounging with me by the pool of my condo complex in Colina (of all places!), Alina told me that she finally understood what Marx was about. "He was the prophet of doom," she said. "Marx couldn't foresee the breakdown of his ideas as interpreted by Lenin, Stalin, Mao, and Fidel. He couldn't have imagined that Stalin would become an executioner; that communism, as embodied by Castro, would turn into the personality cult of *fidelismo*. Marx's dream is dead," Alina lamented, painting a dystopia that had no semblance of the perfect society she'd once envisioned. "Socialism—that is, the human potential for creating an egalitarian world—wasn't meant to be. Obviously human beings aren't meant to be socialist, or they wouldn't have invented the world we live in, run by transnational companies, by cutthroat corporations that determine the course of history. A world of mergers, unemployment, rampant technology. An economy of warfare..."

"Perhaps the reason for Marxism's failure is intrinsic to the philosophy itself," I ventured. "That's what one of Puig's characters claims in his novel, *Eternal Curse*."

"And what reason is that?"

"Well, the character says that, because Marxism makes such a strong critique of society and has such a grand mission, it tends to displace other problems that need tending to. Specifically, Marxism ends up negating the need for a deeper exploration of one's psyche."

"Puig might be right," said Alina after some thought. "Marx's philosophy no doubt concerns itself with the collective well-being at the expense of the individual. And that's one of its flaws, because you can't have a healthy collectivity—no matter how egalitarian and just—without healthy individuals."

"Okay, so there are flaws in the Marxist method. He still had a worthy dream for humanity."

"He sure did, *hermanito*. And now it's up to us to forge a new one."

"As bourgeois as you and I are, Cicada, we could never help forge any big, collective dreams. Life is too cozy for us; we've turned complacent. Why make waves? If it ain't broke..."

"But life *is* 'broke' for many people."

"As it has always been and shall be."

"I'm not giving up, Camilo. I'll never stop believing in change."

"I know, and your optimism is tempting, admirable, but not realistic. Look at us, Alina! We're not as bad as Cortázar's pathetic bunch of Paris dilettantes but getting there."

"You're talking nonsense. We'll never be like those fools in *Hopscotch*."

"We're a lot happier, more settled and dull than they were, I'll grant you that."

"There's no harm in being happy, content with the place you inhabit, with the world you've created for yourself. Bourgeois and all, we can still..."

"We can still hang out by the pool sipping Cuba Libres."

"You're turning into a bitter old man, *hermanito*. And it's too soon for that."

"I was born a bitter old man."

"Then you must be ancient and immensely wise by now. I bow before you, Methuselah!"

"Happiness can't start a revolution, Cicada."

"You're right. But the changes I'm talking about aren't as big as that. They're small and personal, those we can make in the people we love, in my students and your readers and..."

"Right. Our grain of sand."

"Or, rather, our drop of water. So we can make a stream some day, if not a river or an ocean."

"How about just a cool pool for now?" I said, plunging in against the rule. *No diving!*

My dear Alina still resembles the young woman I met in Alton, gorgeous, serene, given to easy laughter. She's till the Cicada I named, singing her song in a river of light. I've tried to emulate her kindness, her compassion. "*Hermanito*," she said to me one day back in Alton, "please talk to me. Tell me about the pain you've kept hidden in your heart since you were a child..."

Such a mighty witch! How did she know?! Alina could look straight and deep into my soul. That day I opened up to her, and for the first time in my life I felt understood. And I felt real.

She used to tell me that the best stories were out there, roaming the world, and it was my task as a writer to find them. A simple, basic truth I learned thanks to Alina. She was right, and, as it turned out, I just wanted to tell a good yarn. Alina knew how torn I felt sometimes, cooped up in my bedroom-cum-office and hearing my daughter's voice out there in the world she was discovering, creating, transforming. "Just write a little each day," she'd advise, "maybe when she naps. You know you must."

True: I must. And there was a contract and a pressing obligation this time. I wasn't just indulging one of my "creative moods" while Nadya clamored for my attention. Still I struggled not to become a stereotype: that of certain men I knew about, the famous ones who'd been ruthless, abusive, as they'd set about producing whatever they thought they were meant to give us—paintings, novels, poems, films. Men who lived for their visions, to nourish their egos and fulfill their creative or intellectual needs, convinced that their work was more important than friendship, love, parenthood. Why should one have to embrace this self-serving credo, this romantic definition of the writing life as all-consuming? Why should a great novel or a visionary work of art be the justification for neglecting your humanity, for abandoning the people who love you and exploiting a long array of lovers? Forget your novel or your painting! We don't need it. Not if you think it grants you the right to be a monster. No, I didn't want to be one of those men, though I knew I was never too far from becoming like them.

I tried to heed Alina's advice, write whenever I could. Thus I managed to keep working on the third book of the Reader Series. Its plot was loosely based on a story I'd heard in the news while in Mexico. A boy dies in a car accident, and his eyes are donated to his blind mother, who regains her eyesight thanks to him. In my retelling of the story, however, it wasn't her son's eyes that the woman carried, but the soul of a child who died after conception yet lived on in spirit form. As this baby begins to mature, it reaches out. *I can see with your eyes, feel with your heart*—it tells its mother. The woman believes she's going mad but soon settles into a loving relationship with her disembodied offspring...

The McAdam&Soulek editors didn't go for this story at first. They felt that the premise was esoteric, that it sounded too much like a real novel. Would the MTV generation want to read about a "spiritual" baby? Where was the hook, the suspense, the fun? They agreed that my choice of Mexico was the right one for the setting, after having explored the Caribbean previously. But how was I proposing to teach history and culture through this uneasy fantasy? The editors found it necessary to remind me of the template I myself had come up with for the series. Of course I knew I was supposed to deliver a pleasurable text with an extensive glossary, specs for a photo gallery, and comprehension questions, not a work to be analyzed in literature courses. There were to be no narrative complexities, no thick metaphorical layers. My two previous books—the editors argued—were successful because they relied on formulaic plot lines, with adventure and romance but no sex, and with an uplifting message.

I agreed that those stories were more accessible than the one I was now pitching. Even so, a glimmer of literary art could be found in them, for no story can be effective, regardless of its target audience and pedagogical goals, without evoking some semblance of beauty through its telling. And, inevitably, there was a personal subtext in everything I'd written for the series. Encoded in the time-traveling journeys and amorous entanglements, in the thinly-disguised history lessons, one could read my passions and desires, my obsessions. It had to be that way, and the editors knew it.

What about teaching culture with this third book? No problem: As the mother unveils the world to her unborn child, the reader discovers *el mundo mexicano*. She sets out on a journey for this being who inhabits her soul, and her voyage takes her from Veracruz, where she lives, to Taxco and Oaxaca and Guanajuato, to Teotihuacán and Guadalajara and to every corner of her great, diverse nation. She only stops at a place long enough to witness its splendor, learn its history, and share it all with her baby—and the reader. Ultimately, the child as a symbol prevails, the future, hope, *la esperanza*; that which, in line with the idealistic thrust of the series, would bring together the cultures and peoples of Mexico.

All this having been discussed, the editors gave my third story the go-ahead, and I got to work. The process would prove to be more intense than before. There was an urgency this time, a certain purpose, for this was a tale I felt I was meant to write. Its title would be *Ojos adentro* (*Eyes Inside*), and I would dedicate the book to my dear friend Castel Romero, *from his forest of echoes*. The epigraph was to cite one of his favorite poems: *For you in the glass heart...the world is a faraway dream.*

THE MOST BEAUTIFUL THING

We had to leave Las Cumbres one Monday in May, fleeing the Cuesta Fire, not knowing when we'd be able to return. Our county's worst catastrophe had begun the previous Thursday as a controlled burn in the Santa Fe National Forest. Only three hundred acres were earmarked, but drought conditions and high winds gusting up to fifty-five mph caused the blaze to spread out of control, having already devoured 3,700 acres. By now, there were hundreds of firefighters in our town from all over the state; they had brought tankers, airplanes, bulldozers to do a heroic job for which they'd have our heartfelt gratitude. The governor said this shouldn't have happened. The people in charge weren't adequately informed. They made a costly mistake that had now become a monster with a name and a deadly mission.

We decided to wait for news in Santa Fe; should've left earlier but didn't think it would get that bad. And there was also my book, the deadline. Just the night before I was still doing one last tedious round of editing. I tried not to think—fixate, according to Susan—about the shitty way I'd handled things. But there were thoughts I couldn't shut out, and there was remorse. Because I sat at my computer until the very last, dangerous minute, unable to break through the wall of a writer's obsession. I was at work on *Ojos adentro*. After devoting a year to this project, I wasn't about to let a controlled burn stop me, not so close to the end. A couple more hours, I kept telling myself, then I'll let it go.

The air was laden with smoke when I finally stopped. We had to hurry. Susan collected some of our daughter's toys, among them Winnie the Pooh, Ariel the mermaid, and Nadya's beloved stuffed kitten;

also some books, *Brown Bear, La cucaracha Martina, Angelina Ballerina, Olivia, Pepita Talks Twice*; most importantly *The Little Mermaid* and its Disney film version on VHS, Nadya's favorite movie. I packed snacks, the cell phone, a photo album devoted to our daughter and another one of old pictures, a hard copy of *Ojos adentro*; and two floppies with files containing my diary, many of my letters, and some of my unpublished work. "In case everything else is lost," I said as we walked out the door that morning. "No reason to be thinking of losses," Susan reacted. "I know our home will be here when we return." But the refugee dwelling in my heart couldn't believe in Susan's good karma; he'd learned long ago that nothing lasted. Even so, I'd try to have faith. "You're right," I told my wife. "The canyon will protect the houses on Ponderosa. We'll be spared." I imagined San Ildefonso Canyon the way our daughter might, as a moat housing a water-bound dragon that would protect our castle.

We spent part of the morning at the Santa Fe Children's Museum, this time focusing on face-painting (butterflies on Nadya's forehead, tiny daisies on her cheeks) and marveling at the soap bubbles that could grow as big as our child before they burst. Then I stopped by the post office, bent on meeting my deadline. At the Internet Café I printed most of my unpublished writings and e-mailed my editors: *Third reader manuscript shipped today for overnight delivery. It'll need some tweaking in copy-edit and a vocab check. Enjoy!* And now it was Via Linda Mall for a late lunch. As always, Nadya was excited about pizza. Our tradition called for a stroll through the mall, then a ride on the merry-go-round with Papá while Mommy waved at us. We were laughing. This was just another fun outing to the city. Nothing was going on back home, except for the usual visits from squirrels and deer.

The ride ended. Where to now? While I strapped Nadya into her car seat, Susan called the hotline. Her expression, blank at first, was a portrait of despair. "The flames jumped our canyon!" she cried out. We decided to dash back to Las Cumbres. What exactly we were hoping to accomplish, I wasn't sure; maybe just to see our home one last time, salvage some trinket or memento, sit in Nadya's room for a few minutes, grab some of her clothes—all those dresses my mother had made for her, worthy of a princess, and which Nadya liked to put on to play the "castle game." If indeed the fire had jumped San Ildefonso, there was no way they'd let us in. Too close to the flames. But forth we went. The forty-minute drive took us thirty. Our minivan got through the first road block, but at the second an officer stopped us and announced, bluntly, "The town is being evacuated. You must turn around."

"We just need to grab a few things," I said to him.

"We left our home this morning just to spend the day away," Susan put in. "We didn't know we wouldn't be able to come back. There are things we need, clothes for our daughter mostly."

"Please turn around," said the officer again, annoyed by our insistence. And we did.

We knew the government had set up shelters throughout the county, and a couple of hotels in Santa Fe were offering low rates to the victims. We could stay in a hotel for now, one near the mall, on Cerrillos. So we headed to Don Diego's Inn, cramped old quarters but clean, and with a kitchenette. Our immediate needs: clothes and food. Once Nadya was asleep, we fell into bed exhausted, though there was scant relief in rest. Weather forecasts called for more wind...

Tuesday. The governor declared a state of emergency in Las Cumbres County. Only now?! We had agreed to keep the news from Nadya. When she napped, we watched in awe the terrifying footage on TV, walls crumbling, ceiling beams falling like bested giants. Those were the only images they showed, wreckage and collapse like a time loop, eternity in Hell. The reporters flew over our town in helicopters, bursting with excitement. *The fire writhes like a snake. We can hear its roar!* They had descended on us like vultures, eager for a boost to their ratings, unmoved by our misfortune. *Homes and vehicles blazing, consumed!* And they hadn't even done their homework. In their flawed reporting, Estanque Park at the center of town had become Ashley Pond, which was in Los Alamos; and our high school had exchanged names with the recreation center. Oh, but how they loved the name of the catastrophe; you could tell they'd practiced it in front of a mirror. *The Cooooesta Fire.* Sounded exotic, kind of cool, and not too hard to pronounce. Out! I wanted those people out of Las Cumbres!

Why do we christen our catastrophes? Hurricanes, blizzards, fires, they all go down in history with proper monikers because naming is knowing, and knowing is possessing. We knew and reined in our natural phenomenon in Las Cumbres by calling it the Cuesta Fire. But it was a delusion, this christening. The Cuesta Fire didn't know it existed, and if it had been sentient it would've been laughing at us, at this anthropomorphic impulse to change the world into an image of ourselves. *The monster is coming!* I imagined myself facing the fiend, trying to defeat it by taking away its name. *You can't hurt me now!* Then, seconds later, I saw myself running from it, crouching in a pond, seeking shelter among a bed of rocks, but it was no use. Woodland fires can't be outrun. I was engulfed. I would be one with this enemy whose name I'd robbed but still couldn't vanquish. Burn baby burn.

Wednesday. On the phone with family and friends. My mother tried to be strong, supportive; she held back the tears. Susan's parents urged us to take refuge in Kansas. We were touched by gestures of compassion from people everywhere. Easy to spot, we were the Cuesta Fire victims. Must've been our body language, the way we talked to our daughter, to each other; or the tears we couldn't hold back.

Thursday. To pass the time, we all sat and looked at our photos. There was a soothing repetition in doing this; it was a path we could trace together, parenthood memories. We also indulged in my mother's snapshots, the few we'd snuck out of Cuba and some of the ones Mechy had taken in Bay City, all of which she'd put into an album for me. I loved the captions she included in her ornate script... *Our family at Bella Mar. Elio ready for work. Lito with his watercolors.* Nadya found these images "funny" and marveled, in her childish way, at the outmoded clothes and coifs, the awkward poses. But she was also intrigued by the fact that Papá had been a child once upon a time, just like her. "That's Lito!" she exclaimed, finally putting a face to the boy who'd been guiding her through many adventures. Again I described the island to her, painting a place not unlike the one we visited in our make-believe escapades, not entirely fictional but certainly idealized. I would offer her a more realistic picture some day, when she was older—leaving out the grim details, of course. And if Nadya ever visited my *patria*, I hoped she'd be able to speak *cubano* and not reject the heat, the blinding sunlight, the overpowering yet loving voices and gestures. For the time being, I'd let her see the island's contour on my scar, have her touch the country I bore, which was real too. She'd noticed it before, and now I reminded her that it had the same shape as Cuba. "There it is!" Nadya called out. "I can see Cuba on your face, Papá!"

Yes, my love—I thought. That's my own secret homeland that I bestow upon you as a family treasure, a land where you'll never be a stranger, where you'll always feel at home.

Friday. Our summit of verdant hills and forests of aspen and pine, most of it had perished. Yet there was hope for us; the houses on Ponderosa were still standing. Our governor said he'd do everything in his power to "make us whole again." But what did that mean? Can wholeness be attained by rebuilding a house? How many parts of a life can be replaced? Life is made up of shifting boundaries, but it is fixed in time. My parents, like so many adult Cuban immigrants, lost everything when they left their country, hence they were never "whole" again. But returning to Cuba years later wouldn't have "completed" them. They could never be placed back within a story that had been interrupted, left unfinished. That past was gone. And so, it seemed, was our present.

Saturday. Residents wouldn't be allowed into town for another week. Seven endless days. We were sick of our hotel room. "This vacation isn't fun," Nadya complained. "I want to draw with chalk!" Her daily activity—drawing characters from her favorite stories on the sidewalk—couldn't be done there, and the coloring books we'd bought didn't do the trick. She wanted to sit on cement, have lots of space to sprawl and cover with likenesses of friendly bears, of dancing mice and baby mermaids and regally attired lady cockroaches. So we drove to Albuquerque in search of some fun, the Zoo and the Aquarium. And then it was the parents' turn. We headed to First Page, our favorite bookstore, while Nadya napped in her car seat. This time I'd stay with Sleeping Beauty while Susan browsed the shelves and gathered the books she'd special-ordered, going down a list of titles on culture and gender studies that she would read to stay abreast of the research in her field—but also for pleasure! My list was short by comparison: the latest Kundera, García Márquez, Atwood, Vidal, and whatever jumped out at me.

Sunday. The fire continued to rage, but there was a silver lining: 1154 Ponderosa hadn't shown up on the List of Destroyed Properties. And we had no chores, no bills to pay, no deadlines. We were thinking of driving to L.A. and staying with my mother, or maybe moving in with Susan's parents for a while. Or both. Still not sure I could handle living with the Thompsons, though I would have for Nadya's sake. After all, Susan's father had changed. He'd been calling, asking us to please take good care of his granddaughter. "Make sure she's safe," David pleaded. All his bigotry had vanished the day we put our baby in his arms. I was no longer the red Cuban demon who'd corrupted his daughter but the man who helped her make this miracle happen. You could read his transformation in his gestures, in the fatherly way he held Nadya and touched her little hands; also in the warm embrace he gave Susan and me. I'd been guarded but pleased that Nadya would know and learn to love one of her grandfathers.

Nights brought no relief. I spent sleepless hours skimming the files I'd printed from my floppies. Musings I'd forgotten; notes about my graduate school days and my academic years in Kansas, about friends and lovers and inspiring teachers. And there were diary entries I'd transcribed. Poems. Letters. Stories. Life turned into words, existence as a source of *material*. Obviously I believed there was something in Camilo's biography that deserved to be documented. The sexual abuse? A cautionary tale, let this be a lesson! Nah, that story had been told already. My gender trouble? Possibly. My immigrant struggles, then: Refugee triumphs against all odds. Not entirely true nor very original. Perhaps there was a simple reason for those writings: Without them there would be no big picture. No picture at all.

Did I have the energy, the excitement to bring it all together in a book? Should it be labeled fiction, memoir, both? Would it be yet another autobiographical novel? I could already see the one-sentence blurb for promotion and cataloguing: *Professor-turned-writer explores his bisexual nature, confronts a painful truth about his past, and finds happiness in parenthood.* There I was again, damn it, having just put my family at risk and already dreaming up a project. But what the hell. No one had to know that this new venture was keeping me going, that today I needed an anchor, a reason to stay sane.

Monday. One week since we were cast off, the Week from Hell. On Tuesday, May 16, we learned that the fire had been contained; the town would open up soon. But our celebration was short-lived. Hope ended on Wednesday, when our address appeared on the List. We held each other and held Nadya, trying not to cry or scream. It was over. Our light-filled abode could house us no more. Nadya's toys and drawings, Susan's research files, our books and videos and LPs, my portrait of Mami, our computer, my high school trophy, the bed where Nadya was conceived, her crib, the apple tree outside her window. All gone. Grief was all we had left, our claim to consciousness, to sanity. Leaving Cuba used to be the most crucial event of my life, the one that changed things forever.

But the Cuesta Fire had now claimed that privilege, stripping me of all meaningful icons, uprooting me once again.

Temporary shelter was set up by FEMA for the victims, prefab houses on the outskirts of town. The homes were free and ours for as long as we needed them. While we decided. While we rebuilt. The least they could do, since it was the government's fault. Surprisingly, our insurance company had been forthcoming—minimal paperwork, a check, a letter expressing their support.

E-mail from Susan to friends and relatives: *We're in relatively good spirits, but this has been a very difficult time for us. We are grateful to you all for your concern, your thoughts and prayers, and we're touched by gestures of compassion from strangers wherever we go. During the days when all the news was bad, we found strength in our love for each other. We felt fortunate that our daughter was safe with us and were convinced that none of our possessions mattered. We thought of rebuilding our home in Las Cumbres, but that is no longer an option. There are too many reminders of loss...*

It was time to tell our daughter. My attempt: "We don't have a house anymore, *mi niña*."

She thought I was relating a once-upon-a-time: "Ursula took it from us, Papá, like she took Ariel's voice? She's mean! Bad Ursula! Mean Ursula!"

Susan was firm, "No, sweetie, this is not a story."

Nadya, confused, asked, "Why not, Mommy?"

"Because we're telling you the truth. A fire burned our house to the ground. We can't go back to live in Las Cumbres. Not for a long time."

"It's the fire monster," said Nadya, weeping. "He's more mean than Ursula!" And she named the things she'd never see again, her pillow, her magical ruby slippers, the portable toilet she called *pipupú*, her Winnie the Pooh blanket, the dolls in Triton's castle. "I can get a new one?" she asked about everything. We reassured her, "Yes, we'll get you a new one."

Nadya needed the comfort of certainty; she needed to believe that her world would come back to her intact. Yet nothing would feel the same. The new objects would be missing details, traces of her body on them. Wrong color, wrong fit, wrong smell. At least there was no exodus awaiting Nadya. She wouldn't be thrown into exile because of the Las Cumbres catastrophe. She was loved and protected, safe from experiences that lurked in bright daylight when I was a boy, waiting to become memories of hell. Nadya wouldn't live her childhood in fear, an abused prisoner in her father's home. She was now temporarily a refugee, yes, but not like the one her friend Lito had been...

The victims were bussed to Las Cumbres on Friday. Time to assess the damage, to confront the loss. Susan suggested I be the first to walk through the ashes; she'd go later. And so I rode the bus with Nuevomexicanos, Anglos, Native Americans: New Mexico's diversity as represented in Las Cumbres. I thought there was some consolation in the fact that we were primarily a town of commuters (many of whom worked in Santa Fe, at the Lab in Los Alamos, or in Albuquerque), so a good number of the victims who'd lost their homes wouldn't be losing their jobs as well. But this was a small consolation, as I considered our teachers, librarians, restaurant employees who were left without both an abode and a means of subsistence. I knew several of those people riding with me, friends and neighbors whose children used to play at our house. I should've talked to them but couldn't. I felt mute, invisible.

There were murmurs as we passed the pueblos, Camel Rock, Pojoaque. Then silence set in: We were about to cross the threshold. The air was dense; it stank. The blue skies seemed oblivious to the darkness below. High above us, a pleasant spring day. All around us, blackened chimneys rising from the ruins like mute survivors. Surprisingly, the downtown had been spared, as was Mesa Lodge, our historical treasure. But the school and the Montaña recreation center had vanished. The Cuesta Fire was capricious; it picked houses at random. Vehicles were left unscathed a few feet away from dwellings burned to the ground. And it had rare moments of compassion. Pinocchio Park, our favorite playground was still there on Alamo Street, untouched, while all the buildings that surrounded it were gone.

As we turned at the intersection of Camino Real and Ponderosa, the nightmare began. I imagined bony hands breaking through the scarred landscape and stabbing me, binding me forever to those ashes. I saw a black, vacant lot where my home used to stand, then a half-melted computer monitor with a shattered screen. But where was Nadya's room? Upstairs! I had to find a way to fly up somehow, find the mobile and watch its little bears do their dance, sit in the chair where I sang to my daughter, *Duérmete mi niña, duérmete mi amor, duérmete pedazo de mi corazón...*

Suddenly, on the sidewalk, I was greeted by a wondrous creature. I stood there, admiring her beauty, unaware of time. Part of her tail erased, she had flowing strands of crimson hair and was wearing a necklace of sea shells. There were tiny marine flowers in her hands. She was Nadya's creation, powerful enough to save a prince from a shipwreck and to vanquish a mean fire monster. The most beautiful thing I'd ever seen.

A MERMAID'S HAIR

We decided to head west, settling in a small California coastal town, in a modest fixer-upper where Nadya grows, thrives and has quickly learned to love the beach. Ocean-bound again, expelled from the mountain, I hear the sea calling me for the right reasons this time, or so I want to believe as I listen to its surf. I thought I had made my peace with the icy winters of New Mexico, but it was wishful thinking. The cold wasn't for me, not for the Cuban boy who wanted to run around barefoot. I did learn to appreciate the beauty of snow, its cleansing power in Las Cumbres. Loved gazing at it when it fell and enveloped our mountain. I'd think of whiteness as remembrance, the very act of rescuing the past, a blank page I'd turn into a mess of mud and melting ice and slippery roads. Into a reality. It was tempting to keep things clear and simple, to be seduced by the whiteness and invent what wasn't, what should've been; to skip over the gruesome stuff and paint a perfect picture. But no, I found no perfection in the bitter cold. The summer rainstorm would have to prevail, the thunder of an island in my guts. I needed the ocean, the truth, the warmth. There was no need to invent anything, only to let it all unfreeze.

We've rented a piano. Susan serenades us now and then, in the evenings, with Mozart, Brahms, Vivaldi, Chopin, Schubert, Debussy. Once in a while she indulges my craving for Chopin's *Valse in A Minor*, and for a Jerry Herman tune. And she's teaching Nadya to play.

This other future has given us a respite from loss, the illusion of safety. My mother spends a great deal of time with us, content to have a hand in Nadya's upbringing. Watching them together moves my heart.

I want to capture the scene in writing but can't seem to do it justice. The tale I've imagined about Mechy and Nadya would be worthy of our Cubiche canon and quite a departure from the grim no-happy-ending stuff I've been prone to write. It involves a back-to-roots journey, a voyage of return I can now envision at last. Until that story unravels (as I'm sure it will), I've decided to let Mami's camera do the work for me. Our home is awash with Mechy's photos. Her gift, which keeps on giving.

Susan got a lecturer job at a local college, content to have time and energy for our daughter. I treat myself to a five-mile run at the beach every other day, working up to a daily routine of exercise that would eventually include a brief swim—if my Cuban bones can handle it. And I write occasionally, not enough yet and with no contractual obligations. The third reader isn't doing well compared to the previous ones, hence my editors have let it be known, boastfully, that they were right: The premise of the story was abstruse, the book too much like a real novel. As a result, McAdam&Soulek won't be bringing out any more Reader Series titles for the time being, unless *Ojos adentro* picks up substantial adoptions before too long (an unlikely prospect.) If it's any consolation, my editors add, the low sales are also a sign of the times. This new generation of university students just isn't into reading.

In a bout of paranoia, I've pictured Evan Dessler sabotaging the sale of my books. *Ay*, the wrath of a lover scorned! But I know he's not that powerful within the company, not yet anyway. Word did get back to me from my editors, all about the nasty rumors he'd been spreading about me. The editors wouldn't elaborate but assured me that nothing he said could affect my good standing as an M&S author. Mr. Dessler's gossiping only reflected on his character, they said, and not well. However, because Evan was such a successful rep, there wouldn't be any action taken against him, they informed me. But it did behoove me to have a good talk with Mr. Dessler and resolve whatever issues we had.

Thanks but no thanks. I'd just wait it out. I knew that Evan would forget about me soon enough and stop the badmouthing. (What the hell was he saying?!) Hearing about him was shocking, I admit, not because of his actions, which didn't surprise me, but because he had ceased to exist for me. Oh, but what a joke all his extreme masculinity turned out to be! How easily he fell into the stereotype of the gossipy, scornful, backstabbing queen. How readily he became the thing he hated most!

In conclusion, I'm free now to work on my own stuff. Not that I'm in any hurry, or bolstered by the commercial success of my novels. I'd scarcely be able to buy our monthly groceries with the money I make from *Cuba in Silence* and *Love Insane*. And let's not even mention the book of poetry. No, let's be brave: I've barely recovered my investment in *Fantasías escritas con el cuerpo*. The reviews have been laudatory for the most part, "a rich experience of quotidian life as lived through love," "the poetic voice is a confessing lover who woos us to listen," "Macías rejects traditional lyric forms in his search for an anti-poetry of desire." But one critic found my book chock full of "mundane metaphors," and another questioned my poems' "claim to Poetry," since I'm not sufficiently "poetic"! Good or bad, the critiques have guaranteed me a place in the canon but the canon doesn't pay the bills.

"We'll manage," says Susan, and once again I try to believe in her good karma. "Just keep writing," she exhorts me. And of course I will, as long as she's willing to read me.

The Cuesta Fire could be my next project, perhaps, the starting point for the chronicle of a relentless exile that would lead to this new chapter, giving a certain meaning to the life I've lived. But I'm not ready yet. Time needs to do its job first, which it seems to have started already. For I don't feel angered by fate anymore when I think about the fire, or robbed, the way I feel about my childhood. Because we survived the flames. And, like the flowing strands of a mermaid's hair, the embers have given me a map for finding hidden treasures, roads leading me to Susan and Nadya, leading me home.

ACKNOWLEDGMENTS

Because *Diary of Fire* had a long gestation, many people became part of its life along the way. My gratitude goes to those who planted the seed for this novel: Miguel Gallegos, Lucía Guerra, Tede Mathews, Eugenio Matibag, Zulema Mirkin, Teresa Rozo, Jorge Salessi, Lydia Vélez, Juan Villegas. To those who've patiently listened to me talk about this and other ongoing projects: Nick Bach, Tarik Benbrahim, Edith Dimo, Douglas Gary, Polly Hodge, John Miller. And to novelist Alejandro Morales, for the suggestion he made regarding my "next novel" during a reading tour we did together, arranged by Arte Público Press, our publisher. I am deeply grateful to all those remarkable, creative people —for sharing ideas, dreams, stories that would become the stuff of my fiction, for embarking on some wild rides with me, for encouraging me to write, and, in some cases, for having stuck with me (not an easy undertaking) as my closest friends.

To my compatriots and fellow caribeños who've supported my writing, be it with their reviews, articles, books, panels, courses, anthologies, publishing houses, or by good old word of mouth: Vitalina Alfonso, Odette Alonso, Isabel Álvarez-Borland, Ruth Behar, Jesús Barquet, Emilio Bejel, Uva Clavijo, Jorge Febles, Francisco Feito, Roberto G. Fernández, Carolina Hospital, Ylce Irizarry, Nicolás Kanellos, Felipe Lázaro, Mercedes Limón, Lillian Manzor, Fabio Murrieta, Achy Obejas, Andrea O'Reilly Herrera, Senel Paz, Gustavo Pérez Firmat, Antonio Prieto, Marisel Reyes, Eliana Rivero, Virgil Suárez, Marina Tristán, Isabel Valiela, and Alan West-Durán.

To the people directly involved in the recent history of *Diary of Fire*: Lázaro Lima and Felice Picano, who published a chapter from the novel in their trailblazing *Ambientes*. To editor Peter Dubé, who found his way to that piece and included it in *Best Gay Stories 2012*. To Steve Berman, the indefatigable publisher of Lethe Press, who gave my novel a resounding yes; and to his amazing team: Alex Jeffers and Matthew Bright of Inkspiral.

This book could never have been written without the unflagging support, editorial advice, patience, and love of my soulmate, Karen Christian.

Thank you all for helping me bring this story to light.

Elías Miguel Muñoz is a Cuban-born writer whose fiction deals with friendships that empower, sexuality, and new definitions of family. His critically celebrated novels include *The Greatest Performance* (1991), *Brand New Memory* (1998), and *Vida mía* (2006). Muñoz's stories and poems have appeared in numerous anthologies, including *Best Gay Stories 2012*; *Ambientes: New Queer Latino Writing* (2011); *Herencia: The Anthology of Hispanic Literature of the United States* (2002); *The Encyclopedia of American Literature* (1999); and W.W. Norton's *New Worlds of Literature* (1994). Muñoz resides in California and welcomes visitors at eliasmiguelmunoz.com.

CPSIA information can be obtained
at www.ICGtesting.com
Printed in the USA
FSOW02n1739260916
25419FS